A BULLET IN T

When he looked back, the Hunsackers were clearly within range. He moved his rifle sights around ever so gently, so that he was focused on the broad chest of Jim Stock. Now he could see the man clearly. He was wearing the brocade vest that he was known to wear. His rifle was still in the boot, but Longarm had no doubt that this was a man who would cause him trouble. He leaned down over his sights, calculating the wind, calculating the distance, calculating the drop of the bullet. Then, very gently, he pulled the trigger, and the sharp crack of the shot rang harshly off the rocks . . .

DANCE OF DESIRE

Cairo pulled away from him, but only slightly. "I didn't think you liked me very much," she said.

He laughed aloud. "It seems you've begun to grow on me, little minx."

"And I . . . I like you better than I thought I did. I mean . . ."

"Do you, Cai?" He trailed his forefinger over her cheeks. "Do you really?"

Her arms slid over his shoulders, drawing his lips back to hers. "I do, Lawton," she whispered against his mouth. "I never dreamed it could be like this . . . with you . . ."

His hand curled beneath her chin. "I have this wild, compelling need . . ." But her lips stopped his with another kiss.

One kiss—no, two—and he wanted her like hell on fire. One caress and he blazed like a human torch. Another corner of his heart crumbled when her lips sought to memorize his by taste and touch. Determined to keep the upper hand, he pulled gently away and gazed into her eyes. "You still have a lot to learn about men," he told her, his voice still ragged with the aftereffects of her wild kiss.

"Indeed I do," she whispered. "And there is no better time to learn than now . . ."

OTHER BOOKS BY CAROL FINCH

Rapture's Dream
Endless Passion
Dawn's Desire
Passion's Vixen
Midnight Fires
Ecstasy's Embrace
Wildfire
Satin Surrender
Texas Angel
Captive Bride
Beloved Betrayal
Lone Star Surrender
Stormfire
Thunder's Tender Touch
Love's Hidden Treasure
Montana Moonfire
Wild Mountain Honey
Moonlight Enchantress

CAROL FINCH

PROMISE ME MOONLIGHT

ZEBRA BOOKS
KENSINGTON PUBLISHING CORP.

ZEBRA BOOKS

are published by

Kensington Publishing Corp.
475 Park Avenue South
New York, NY 10016

First Printing: February, 1993

Printed in the United States of America

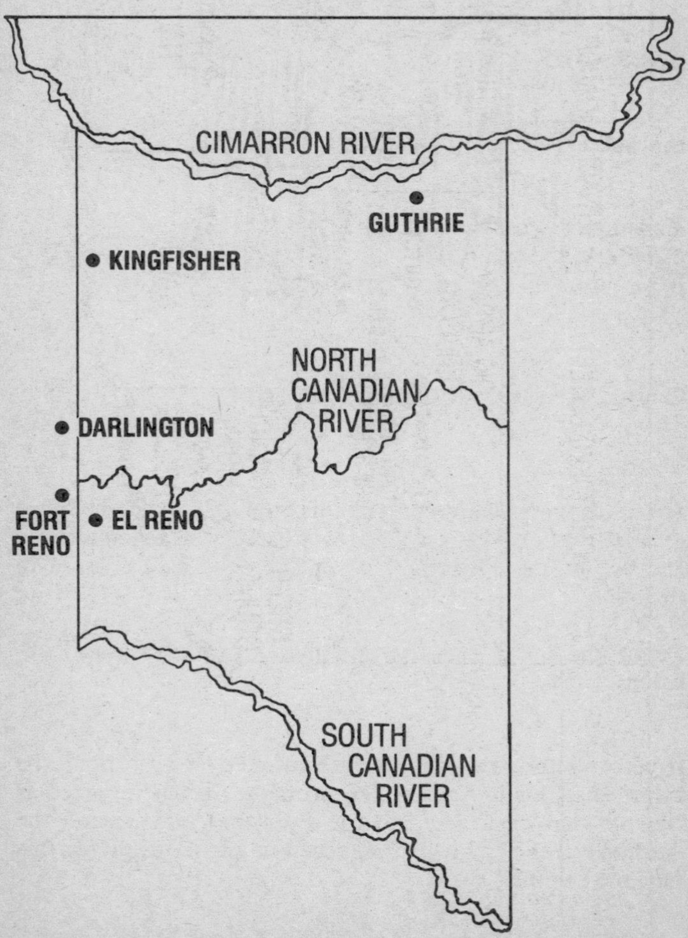
CIMARRON RIVER
GUTHRIE
KINGFISHER
NORTH CANADIAN RIVER
DARLINGTON
FORT RENO
EL RENO
SOUTH CANADIAN RIVER

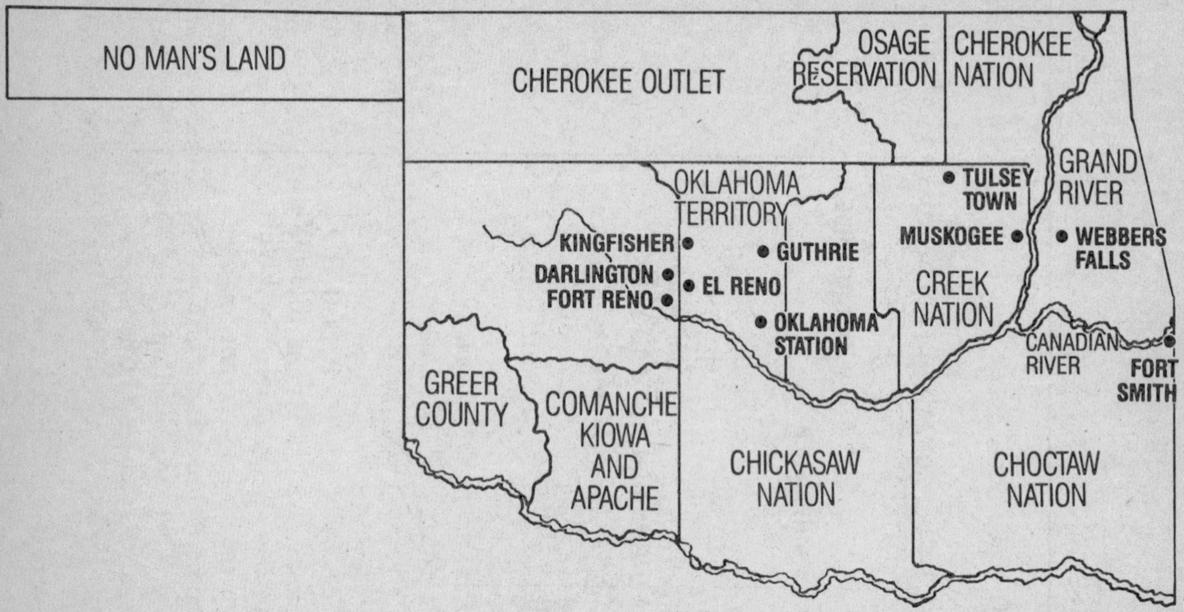
NO MAN'S LAND
CHEROKEE OUTLET
OSAGE RESERVATION
CHEROKEE NATION
GRAND RIVER
OKLAHOMA TERRITORY
TULSEY TOWN
MUSKOGEE
WEBBERS FALLS
KINGFISHER
GUTHRIE
DARLINGTON
EL RENO
FORT RENO
OKLAHOMA STATION
CREEK NATION
CANADIAN RIVER
FORT SMITH
GREER COUNTY
COMANCHE KIOWA AND APACHE
CHICKASAW NATION
CHOCTAW NATION

Chapter One

Cherokee Nation,
Indian Territory
October 1889

Just as dawn spilled over the peaceful countryside that lay on the banks of the Grand River, an unexpected shout of alarm resounded like a booming cannon.

Lawton Stone scowled, snapping his Winchester rifle against his muscular shoulder.

"I'll watch the back door," Tucker McGuire volunteered before he scuttled through the canopy of trees.

"The side window is mine," Woodward Hall announced as he clutched his rifle and pistol in hand and then circled north.

In the still of the morning, Lawton could hear the vehement curses and scuffling of the notorious outlaw gang. They had holed up in the crude cottage that belonged to a half-breed Cherokee who had been given the name George Tinsley. The Gardiner gang had seized

George's home in their attempt to escape the U.S. marshals who had been tracking them for three days.

Lawton didn't have to speculate on what had become of the old Indian. His steel-gray eyes focused on the crumpled form of the man who lay sprawled facedown in the grass, fifty feet from his front door. Lawton wondered if George Tinsley even knew what hit him.

There was no time to give the victim a second thought as a volley of bullets hissed through the partially opened door of the cabin. The shattering of the windowpanes exposed the long barrels of Winchesters that blasted away at Woodward Hall and Tucker McGuire. Lawton darted his companions hasty glances, assuring himself that they were unscathed by the barrage of bullets that danced in the dirt.

Rifle lead zinged past Lawton to ricochet off the tree a few inches above his head, and he dived to the ground, gritting his teeth as he crawled toward his horse. Casting his Winchester aside, he reached into the saddlebag to retrieve a stick of dynamite. He and his partners had hoped to take the Gardiners by surprise and without a bloody showdown, but that was not to be. The light of dawn and the nicker of their steeds had betrayed their approach.

After striking a match against the bark of a nearby tree, Lawton lit the fuse. Taking careful aim, he hurled the dynamite at the roof of the cottage. Retrieving his Winchester and clutching it, Lawton waited for the blast to produce results.

Pandemonium broke loose as shingles and boards were launched into the sky and fire crackled along the roof.

Another flood of curses echoed in the air. Lawton levered up on his elbows. His narrowed gaze was intently focused on his rifle sight. Like a coiled rattlesnake, he waited for the most opportune moment to strike.

Rifle lead kicked at the fallen leaves around Lawton, causing the horses to rear and strain against their ropes. Lawton rolled away before his black stallion brought his hooves down on his skull. Piercing whinnies mingled with the whine of buckshot as the horses broke loose and bolted away from danger.

Lawton slithered through the crackling leaves and braced himself on his forearms. Smoke rolled from the shack and rifle blasts roared from both doors and windows of the cottage as the renegades prepared to make their escape.

Poised and ready, Lawton stared at the door. When he spied the first desperado emerging from the shack, he squeezed the trigger. The blond pistolero, who was making a dash for freedom, darted sideways at the bark of the rifle. Because the outlaw zigged instead of zagged, as Lawton anticipated, the bullet caught the young bandit in the chest instead of the shoulder. Lawton muttered under his breath. He had meant to wound, not kill, the escaping desperado.

A sneer puckered the fugitive's face as he clutched his chest with his left hand and aimed at Lawton with his pistol. But before Billy Gardiner could fire, a blank stare glazed his eyes and his weapon tumbled from his fingertips. As his knees buckled, he collapsed in the dirt.

A muted curse bubbled in Lawton's throat when two more blond-haired bandits emerged through the door, protected by shields of fallen timber. Their pistols blazed as they scurried toward their pen of horses.

Lawton ducked away when buckshot danced in the leaves beside his shoulder. Every muscle in his body tensed when he heard Woody Hall's howl of pain. Lawton jerked his head up in time to see Woody spin like a top and then drop into the tall grass.

"Damned fool. Always trying to be the hero," Lawton muttered.

His cold gray eyes swung toward the clump of bushes where a puff of smoke rose above Tucker McGuire's blasting pistol. The weeds rustled as Tucker flattened himself on the ground to dodge the barrage of bullets that came his way.

Two more bandits whizzed around the corner of the house, keeping Tucker pinned down in the brush. In the batting of an eyelash, Lawton vaulted to his feet and charged toward another clump of trees.

"Tucker? You okay?" Lawton yelled over the crackling fire and barking pistols.

No answer.

Lawton's booming voice drew the fire of the fleeing renegades who had swung onto their horses. Lawton stepped from behind the tree and wheeled to fire at the desperadoes who were pumping rounds of buckshot at him.

Imagining the worst had happened to his two best friends, Lawton cursed, then fired his Winchester at the fleeing bandits.

A pained growl erupted from Nate Gardiner's lips when Lawton's bullet embedded itself in his thigh. Blazing blue eyes riveted on the giant hulk of a man who was now partially shielded by the trees.

"I'll get you for this, you son-of-a-bitch!" Nate sneered as he kicked his steed into a faster clip with his good leg. "I'll see you die a slow, agonizing death for killing our kid brother!"

Lawton paid no heed to Nate Gardiner. He gathered his composure and fired at the scraggly-haired buscadero who was leading the gang away from the burning cottage. The bullet went astray, much to Lawton's dismay.

With the rolling smoke as camouflage, the desperadoes tried to make their getaway. Squinting at the images in the fog of smoke, Lawton fired again. This time the bullet caught Vance Gardiner in the side, causing him to double over on the saddle.

Lawton watched the Gardiners and their bloodthirsty accomplices thunder toward the skirting of trees that lined the river. The splash of water indicated the outlaws were utilizing the narrow channel to conceal their tracks.

"Curse your soul, Lawton Stone!" Vance Gardiner's mutinous voice rumbled through the distant trees. "You'll pay for this. I'll see you fry in hell!"

And then there was silence, broken only by the occasional crackle of the fire that had engulfed the cottage.

A cough, snort, and muffled curse rolled toward Lawton from the clump of bushes where Tucker McGuire had been pinned down several minutes earlier. The faint aroma of skunk mingled with the smell of smoke. The odor became more pungent as Lawton strode toward the clump of reeds.

Tucker wheezed and staggered to his feet. Tears rolled down his freckled cheeks as he peeled off his shirt and shook it, as if that would rid the garment of the offensive smell. "Wouldn't you know I'd leap into a bush where a dad-blamed skunk was digging himself a hole."

The tense expression on Lawton's craggy face evaporated after he ran an inspecting eye over his friend. Tucker hadn't been maimed by outlaw bullets, but he stunk to high heaven.

"How many of 'em did you get, Law?" Tucker inquired as he propelled himself toward the river to wash away the smell that saturated him to his skin.

"Just the kid," Lawton murmured, falling into step. "I wounded Vance and Nate. It will slow them down, but it won't stop them."

"I figured you got Billy when I heard his brothers shouting their death threats at you." One thick red brow raised when he spied the trail of blood on the ground. "You must have winged the Gardiners pretty good, from the look of things."

Tucker scanned his surroundings. "What happened to Lover Boy?" he asked before he plunged into the river to wash himself. "If Woody isn't all right, half the female population in Fort Smith will be garbed in black."

"Lover Boy," as Tucker and Lawton insisted on calling their friend of long standing, appeared on the riverbank—alive but wounded in the left arm.

"I'm here, Tuck," Woody growled. "At least I can say I was shot in the line of duty." The handsome marshal looked down his nose at his wiry-haired friend who was in the process of rubbing mud all over himself. "You were a lot of help when the going got tough. Law and I were being pelleted with buckshot and you were nestled in the bushes like a damned coward. Serves you right for getting sprayed by a skunk."

"I'm no coward," Tucker protested. At the moment he looked like an Egyptian mummy embalmed with layers of mud. All that was visible of him was his wild bush of red hair and the white circles around his blue eyes.

While Tucker and Woody argued over who had been the least amount of help in the gun battle, Lawton ambled back to the smoldering cottage. He was left with the unpleasant task of burying the dead. He paused beside the limp form of Billy Gardiner. The kid looked to be in his early twenties. Unfortunately, Billy had come under his two older brothers' influence and it had led him into disaster.

Lawton sighed. In the two years the Gardiners had been terrorizing Indian Territory, Kansas, Arkansas, and Texas, they had left a trail of terror and destruction behind them. Young Billy Gardiner and his brothers each carried five-thousand-dollar rewards on their heads. Thanks to his brothers, Billy's life had ended in a gun battle, and the money he'd made robbing banks, trains, and army pay wagons would now be divided up between his family and the other members of the gang.

Lawton's somber gaze swung to George Tinsley's crumpled remains. Another wasted life. When he noticed the knife protruding from George's back, he frowned. No doubt this was the work of Idaho Joe, as he had come to be called. Joe rode with the Gardiners and he had a morbid fascination with knives, a sadistic taste for cold-blooded murder. Lawton had seen Idaho Joe's gruesome deeds more times than he cared to count. Since Lawton had become one of the two hundred marshals who policed Indian Territory and the newly formed Oklahoma Territory, he had trailed Idaho Joe. The man seemed to enjoy maiming and murdering his victims. Lawton thought the Gardiners were too high-class to accept Idaho Joe as one of their members, but violence bred violence, and the Gardiners had become more deadly and vicious as time wore on.

Vance Gardiner was a shrewd, calculating outlaw—one of the cleverest in the country. Until the past few months, Vance and his family had been involved only in the theft of money and livestock. No doubt the arrival of Idaho Joe accounted for the rash of senseless killings, Lawton speculated. The Gardiners had limited their activities to well-organized train robberies and bank holdups. Idaho Joe and another ruthless ruffian by the name of Panhandle Dick, who hailed from No Man's Land, had spoiled the reputation of the Gardiners in a hurry . . .

Lawton's thoughts trailed off when a vision from the past leaped to mind. Absently, he went to retrieve a shovel and began his grim task. The Snowbird hadn't been with the Gardiners this time. That was the name Lawton had given to the mysterious and very elusive female bandit whom he had linked to this gang.

Lawton had seen her once the previous year when the gang had fled from the three marshals who had been tracking them. Lawton and his partners had picked up the trail south of Cherokee Nation, but the renegades had posted a guard and they fled in the night. In the moonlight Lawton had seen a mane of silver-blond hair that appeared white as snow, undulating in the breeze like a flag.

Since then, Lawton had posed questions and described the woman when he investigated the scenes of robberies. Some of the townsfolk recalled seeing a fetching young woman who was either passing through town on the stage or train or who posed as a prospective schoolteacher or a young female seeking respectable employment.

From what Lawton had ascertained, the woman was an informant and spy for the notorious gang of outlaws. Lawton didn't know what her relationship was to the gang—sister, whore, or a starry-eyed chit who had been enticed by one of the desperadoes. But one thing was certain, Snowbird was reported to be a beauty—unlike Belle Starr, Cattle Kate, and some of the other female desperadoes Lawton had heard about. The mysterious female, Lawton decided, was part of the reason why the Gardiners had been so successful in eluding posses and U.S. marshals. From what Lawton surmised, the Snowbird scouted the area before a strike was made. If she suspected danger, she warned the gang away. But wherever Snowbird was, she had managed to remain on the loose and had escaped this recent disaster without exposing her identity.

While Lawton tended his unpleasant task, he asked himself why he'd become so intrigued by the elusive beauty who was somehow connected with the Gardiner gang. It wasn't as if Lawton had ever seen the Snowbird face-to-face. He had only heard reports of her striking good looks. And yet, he kept finding himself speculating on why such a bewitching female would involve herself with a pack of renegades.

"I patched Lover Boy up," Tucker announced,

dragging Lawton from his silent reverie. "It was only a scratch, but it will probably hamper his amorous pursuits for a couple of weeks."

"Damn it, Tuck, if you call me Lover Boy again, I'll—" Woody stalked forward, his left arm cradled in an improvised sling. He broke off in mid-sentence when he saw Lawton pluck up a late-blooming wildflower to place on George Tinsley's grave.

The teasing camaraderie gave way to reverent silence. This was the part of the job the three U.S. marshals hated the worst—reading the last words over innocent victims. There were times when Lawton thought he'd become callous and insensitive—a hazard of a job that had to be done for the protection of the citizens of the Twin Territories. But it always got to him when he was forced to send another poor departed soul to a higher sphere.

Lawton didn't know where the young renegade Billy Gardiner would end up—heaven or hell—but he decided not to spend too much time grappling with that thought. He'd leave the grieving and speculations to Vance and Nate Gardiner. They had put the death threat on Lawton's head, but they were really the ones who had brought their young brother to this tragic end. They had sent death and destruction crashing down on themselves when they chose their lives of crime. Now they had to suffer the loss of their own flesh and blood. Billy's death would be on *their* consciences, not Lawton's.

Judge Isaac Parker had ordered the Gardiners to be brought in dead or alive, and Parker always stressed that his marshals were his foremost concern in the heat of battle. They laid their lives on the line to protect the innocent and Parker mourned each lawman who fell beneath an outlaw's blazing pistol.

"I wonder where the Snowbird is," Tucker mused aloud as he ambled toward the horses he and Woody had rounded up.

"Probably waiting somewhere to nurse the Gardiners back to health," Lawton said.

"I'd give a month's wages to have a good look at her," Woody remarked, hurrying to catch up with Lawton's long strides. "I'm tired of hearing how pretty she is. I'd like to see her for myself."

"You've got enough women drooling over you the way it is, Lover Boy," Tucker said as he swung into the saddle. "The Snowbird would probably be the death of you, because you never met a female you didn't love at first sight. Whether she's a lady or outlaw, young, old, fat, or—"

"I happen to be a man of discriminating tastes!" Woody insisted.

Tucker shrugged and glanced at the muscled giant who rode silently beside him. "Now, Law here is another matter entirely. Since he doesn't have much use for women, he wouldn't let himself be lured by the Snowbird's feminine charms."

"You might be surprised," Woody snickered, casting his taciturn companion a taunting smile. "The Snowbird might even crack Lawton Stone's heart of rock."

"Not likely," Tucker replied. "There isn't a female on the planet who could best Lawton Stone."

"We'll just see whether the Snowbird turns Law's head if we ever catch up with her," Woody contended. "I'd bet twenty dollars that even Lawton would have misgivings about turning that pretty renegade over to

Judge Parker for trial."

"For trial?" Tucker hooted. "Hell, there isn't even a warrant out for her arrest and she's never been accused of doing anything illegal. All we have is speculation. But I'll still take that bet. If we apprehend the Snowbird, I'll wager—"

"Tuck! Woody!" Lawton's voice snapped like a whip.

"Yeah?"

"Clam up. It's a helluva long ride to Muskogee to retrieve our jail wagon and prisoners. And it's even farther to Fort Smith."

"My, aren't you touchy," Tucker razzed their somber companion. "It's not like this is the first time some desperado called the wrath of the devil down on you."

"He's just sour because he's got his own weird fascination for the Snowbird and he can't ever get close enough to catch her," Woody ribbed him. "Law is just like the two of us. He's wondering if even he could resist the strange spell the Snowbird holds over every man she meets. Why, it wouldn't surprise me to learn she's the mastermind behind the Gardiner gang's success. She's probably plotted every holdup in the territory."

Lawton rolled his eyes heavenward. He was immensely fond of Tuck McGuire and Woody Hall, but there were times when he wished he was policing Indian Territory alone. These two babbling magpies could talk a man's leg off!

To overshadow his partners' constant chatter, Lawton broke into a chorus of "Skip to My Lou," just as he always did when he was riding from one place to another. He couldn't wait to return to Fort Smith, and

Woody's wound was the perfect excuse. The three marshals had been on this tour of duty far too long and they could all do with some rest, relaxation, and diversion.

Unfortunately, the "Men Who Rode for Parker" were forced to track outlaws and renegades for as long as three months at a time before they returned with their prisoners in tow. And when law and order was restored in the newly formed Oklahoma Territory and its counterpart, Indian Territory, Lawton was going to seriously consider settling onto an obscure farm to raise livestock. It had been a dream of his since he had been forced to leave his stepfather's farm in Texas. Someday he would have a home to call his own again. Someday he would enjoy a quiet, peaceful life . . . if an outlaw's bullet didn't permanently plant him in one place first.

Chapter Two

Fort Smith, Arkansas
Late October 1889

After endless days of traveling through the wooded hills, creeks, and rolling prairies, the three U.S. marshals paused to gaze down on the Arkansas River that glittered in the sunshine. The prison caravan, comprised of a jail wagon, supply wagon, and extra horses, rolled to a halt. For weeks, they had camped under the stars, eating with their Winchesters draped across their laps. The lawmen had done battle with the Gardiners, posted a summons here and made an arrest there. They had scoured the countryside, where outlaws and thieves knew every trail and hideout. They had tested their skills as trackers and gunmen to the very limit time and time again.

"Fort Smith sure looks good from here," Tucker remarked with a relieved sigh. He forked a morsel of beans into his mouth, munched on them, and smiled when he noticed the crowd gathering on the east side of the river. "It seems the news of our arrival reached town before we did."

"The only thing good about reachin' the Hangin' Judge's jail is that we don't have to listen to no more of Marshal Stone's gawd-awful singin'," one of the prisoners groused before wolfing down his meal. "If I'd've had to listen to that croonin' another day, I'd have hung myself before Parker could get a noose around me."

"I don't know which is worse," one of the other criminals grumbled, "His off-key singin' or his lectures on the evils of crime."

Lawton strode over to jerk the tin plates from the two prisoners' shackled hands. "You know the rules, boys," he snapped. "You complain and you don't eat. Now which is it going to be?"

Both prisoners stared hungrily at their plates and then into Lawton's stormy gray eyes.

"I love yer singin'."

"And I regret the sins I committed," the other man smirked, his tone indicating he regretted nothing of the kind.

A smile hovered on Lawton's lips as he regarded the cocky outlaws. He dropped their plates at their feet, catapulting the beans onto their shirts. "And I regret having to haul you to Judge Parker," he mocked. "I can't tell you how many nights' sleep I'm going to lose, wondering whether the judge plans to lock you in prison for the next hundred years or send you marching to the gallows."

The comment took the starch out of the two men. In all honesty, they didn't know which was worse, confronting this man who was carved from rock or the judge in Fort Smith.

While the prisoners were herded back into the jail wagon, Lawton glanced at the huge congregation of people that had gathered on the docks beside Poteau Bluffs to watch the marshals ferry their wagonload of criminals across the river. The townsfolk were always curious to learn which notorious outlaws had been brought to justice.

Just as Tucker predicted, news of Lawton's showdown with a member of the infamous Gardiner gang had preceded him to town. As the prison wagon rolled down the street toward the newly constructed jailhouse, the crowd closed in around the huge man on horseback.

Lawton nodded in response to the accolades that were heaped on him. One would have thought he was the reigning king returning to court, the way the citizens of Fort Smith were carrying on. Though he was hailed a hero for taking the life of the young desperado, the incident had left a sour taste in Lawton's mouth. He didn't want praise for doing a job he'd have preferred not to do. He would have relished dragging Idaho Joe to court for murdering George Tinsley. Young Billy Gardiner was the last person Lawton wanted to kill, but the inexperienced kid had leaped in the wrong direction, taking a fatal bullet that had only been meant to slow him down. Damn . . .

"My Lord! There's fifteen prisoners wedged in that wagon," the guard exclaimed in disbelief. "You must have had a busy three and a half months, from the looks of things."

Lawton shrugged and left the explanations to Tucker McGuire, who had already talked both

Lawton's legs off during the return trip.

After collecting his monthly wages and the substantial rewards, Lawton saw to the time-consuming business of identifying and incarcerating the string of prisoners whom his partners were shepherding into the cells.

At least the jail conditions had greatly improved, Lawton mused as he glanced around him. The three-story brick jail had replaced the two-story building which had served as both the court, jury rooms, and jail. The damp, foul-smelling basement had housed prisoners for too many years and the conditions had become intolerable. Now the jail boasted fifty-two cells, each five-by-eight feet in size and each equipped with two iron cots. The lower floor was designated as Murderers Row, the second story reserved for criminals charged with burglary, robbery, and assault, and the top floor held prisoners charged with selling whiskey in Indian Territory.

Lawton glanced down at the roll of bills that were rolled in his fist. With the latest reward money and the savings he had stashed in the bank, because he never had time to spend it, he could walk away from his dangerous profession. He could settle down on his own place—a thousand miles away from humanity.

"Now that you're a hero, are you too good to celebrate with your lowly friends?" Tucker teased as he watched Lawton stash the money in his vest pocket.

The hint of a smile bordered Lawton's full lips. He was in the mood to pour himself a tall drink and forget the gunfight on Grand River. "You get the whiskey, Tuck, and we'll celebrate until the liquor runs out."

Tucker nodded. "I'll meet you in the cabin in an

hour." His gaze swung over his shoulder to the lanky, good-looking marshal who stood behind him. "You coming, Lover Boy? Or have you got too many women standing in line to welcome you home and fuss over your arm?"

"Have I ever missed celebrating our return with the two of you?" Woody snorted. "Of course I'm coming. I delight in watching Law get liquored up. It's the only time *he* talks *our* legs off!"

It was true. For the most part, Lawton Stone kept to himself, quietly and efficiently going about his business of tracking wanted men. He rarely expressed his emotions and sentiments, and when he did, he was brief and concise. Only when he had several drinks under his belt did his mask slip and his tongue run away with itself. And the only time Lawton let his guard down and guzzled excessive amounts of whiskey was when the three marshals returned from their long forays in the Twin Territories.

It had become their custom to deliver their prisoners, collect their two-hundred-fifty-dollar monthly wages and rewards, and then adjourn to the cottage on the edge of town. There the three lawmen, in the privacy of the cabin, proceeded to get riproaring drunk and unwind from their harrowing experiences. These binges lasted two or three days before the men spruced themselves up and reappeared in public.

The marshals led their horses and wagons to the blacksmith barn for repairs, then went their separate ways. An hour later, they congregated at the whitewashed cottage that belonged to Tucker and Lawton. While the marshals were on their tours of duty, the shapely Widow Herman, who had set her cap for

Lawton Stone, came once a week to tidy up the cottage. As always, it was polished to a shine. Clean sheets awaited them, and even vases of flowers were placed on the table, along with three sparkling crystal goblets.

Lawton surveyed the freshly mopped parlor and dustless furniture. He would have to remember to compliment Molly Herman. She had outdone herself this time. The house was spotless.

"I'd say Molly is knocking herself out to claim the position as your wife," Tucker snickered as he flung his Stetson aside, plunked down at the dining-room table, and popped the cork of the whiskey bottle. "You gonna marry the widow one of these days or just keep stringing her along like you've been doing for the past three years?"

"Law? Married?" Woody chuckled as he straddled a chair. He extended his glass, waiting for Tucker to pour it level full. "He hates women, remember? He has only one use for them, and you damned well know it."

"My love life isn't open for discussion," Lawton grunted before he dropped into his chair. He eyed the goblet of liquor with anticipation. He could use a drink . . . or six. It had been a long three and a half months. "You're the one who volunteers all the juicy details after you're spread yourself around town like hot butter on loaves of bread, Lover Boy."

Woody grinned in that boyish way of his that had stolen the hearts of many young ladies. "Can I help it if women like me? And the only reason I tell all is to keep you two up to date on the pleasures of love."

Lawton took a long slow sip of his whiskey. "Females are nothing but trouble. The less a man has to do with them, the better off he is."

"Drink up, cynic," Tucker encouraged his friend. "Then maybe you'll let us in on this mysterious secret about why you think women are the lowest form of life."

Lawton would never get so inebriated as to reveal the reason he held all women in contempt. It was a deeply embedded, long-harbored bitterness that had been with him for most of his thirty-one years. Concerning the topic of women, Lawton Stone would now and forevermore keep his own counsel. It was, after all, nobody's business but his own.

"As for me, I like women well enough," Tucker was saying. "But with this ugly mug of mine, I don't attract them as readily as you and Lover Boy." His pale-blue eyes focused on Lawton. "Now you, on the other hand, draw females like flies. But you're too standoffish. If you'd practice some of Woody's techniques, you'd have to beat off your female admirers with a stick."

"I have no complaints about the way things are," Lawton mumbled before downing half a glass of whiskey in one swallow.

"Of course not, you never complain about much of anything because you don't talk much," Tucker pointed out. "That's why Woody and I are always speculating on which mean, fickle woman broke your heart along the way. Who was she?"

Lawton wasn't about to confess the secrets of his soul, even if Woody and Tucker were sitting on the edge of their seats, displaying enough curiosity to kill a cat. "Pour me another drink," Lawton demanded, shoving the glass toward Tucker.

The redheaded lawman complied. "Well, I personally don't see the harm in socializing with females every chance I get," he said. "After three months of chasing the worst scoundrels on the continent, a man needs a diversion."

"*Obsession* is nearer the mark," Lawton corrected.

Woody shrugged, undaunted.

Lawton regarded the handsome marshal who was only a year younger than himself. Woody naturally gravitated toward women and vice versa. He lived with his younger sister and her husband and children when the three marshals weren't tracking renegades. Well, Lawton corrected himself, Woody didn't actually *live* on his sister's farm. He headquartered there and took a few meals with the family. Where he spent his nights was anybody's guess. He made his rounds like a postman, calling upon a passel of women and then wandering back to the farm when the spirit moved him.

Lawton swore he'd never become so dependent on any woman that she preoccupied his time and his thoughts. He didn't want a wife, a mistress, or a harem. He bedded a woman when his male urges demanded satisfaction, but even then, he limited himself to brief, infrequent encounters with the Widow Herman and two other women who greeted him with open arms.

While Woody and Tucker speculated on what kind of husband Lawton would make for the Widow Herman, the sinewy giant simply guzzled his liquor. Lawton had only one objective in mind—to get rip-roaring drunk.

The borders along Indian and Oklahoma territories had rightfully earned the name of Hell's Fringe, Lawton thought as he poured another whiskey down his throat. There were throngs of bandits, gamblers, bootleggers, thieves, and raiders terrorizing the twin territories. A man couldn't swing a dead cat without hitting one of them. Just as soon as Lawton and his partners hauled in a jail wagon heaped with offenders and caught their breath, Judge Parker slapped another two dozen bench warrants in their hands and sent them out again. Two hundred men weren't nearly enough to police the seventy-four thousand square miles of countryside where outlaws were as thick as swarms of mosquitos.

Lawton didn't want to think about the job he'd already done and the tremendous one that was left to do in weeding out the undesirables in the twin territories. He just wanted to drink until he couldn't think. When he sobered up in a few days, he'd scrub himself clean, shave the beard and mustache off his face, and start all over again.

After all, Lawton mused, life was hard. A man just had to accept it. When he got too old to sleep on the damp ground and square off against cocksure gunslingers and desperate murderers, he'd hand in his badge and start his ranch. He would sit back and reflect on his years as a U.S. marshal. There wasn't any glory in his task; he was doing his civic duty to protect those who couldn't defend themselves.

This was as good as life got. This was what living was all about, Lawton thought. A man went through his paces, doing what he could to make the world a better place. There were no beds of roses or mystical rainbows. Life was cold and hard, cut and dried. There were those who broke the laws and those who upheld them. A man lived and then he went to meet his Creator. In the hereafter, a man answered for his unpardonable sins. When he reached the pearly gates, Lawton mused as he took a swig of his fifth drink, he was going to ask his Maker if perhaps He hadn't made one tiny mistake Himself when he created woman.

Cairo Calhoun sailed out of the hotel and marched purposefully toward the newly constructed courthouse. She paid no heed to the way men's heads turned as she walked past. She wasn't vain about her looks. The Lord had created her and bestowed talents on her. She had nothing to do with it, she thought. Cairo was neither flattered nor dismayed because men found her attractive. She simply ignored their interest and went about her business.

Since her arrival at Ford Smith, Cairo had learned that Judge Isaac Parker resided over his court from eight-thirty in the morning until dark, six days a week. He tried an astonishing number of cases in his attempt to clear the area of riffraff. When his task each day was done, the judge would walk the mile between his home and the courthouse, returning the following morning to begin the procedure all over again. Cairo intended to stop the renowned judge the instant he emerged from the courthouse and beg his assistance in a matter that was of vital importance to her.

Somehow or another, she would enlist Judge Parker's help, even if he was incredibly busy with his cases. She had no time or inclination to flounder through the customary channels of legality. It was her contention that if one wanted something done, one went immediately to the highest-ranking official, and Judge Isaac Parker was the symbol of authority west of Fort Smith.

From the descriptions she had obtained from the hotel clerk, she knew she had found Isaac Parker the instant he stepped out the door. He was a broad, intimidating figure of a man with his mustache, goatee, and a shock of gray hair that made him appear older than his fifty-one years. Parker was dressed in his Prince Albert coat and breeches. He stood over six feet tall and weighed at least two hundred fifty pounds. He was the symbol of hope to the law-abiding citizens in the West and the flapping scarecrow of doom to the outlaws who inhabited his domain.

When Isaac Parker glanced down at Cairo with his piercing blue eyes, she squared her shoulders and strode determinedly toward him. "Judge Parker . . . sir . . . I am in dire need of assistance. You, and only you, can help me. I'm sorry to be so inconsiderate as to detain you after a long day on the bench, but I have an important request and I pray you will hear me out."

Isaac's eyes twinkled behind his spectacles while he assessed the strikingly beautiful blonde. She was a petite young lady who couldn't have weighed more than a hundred pounds dripping wet and probably stood barely five feet two. But small though she was in stature, she had charged toward Isaac like a cavalry and had dived right into the heart of the matter that concerned her. Cairo was primly dressed in a green silk gown that couldn't begin to match the lively color of her emerald-green eyes. Although she looked fragile and dainty, determination and vitality radiated from her and her very stance indicated she wouldn't be pushed aside until she said her piece.

Judge Parker offered the young lady his arm. "Is this

matter so serious that it cannot be discussed while we sip a drink to refresh ourselves?" he inquired. "It has indeed been a long, harrowing day. Perhaps you would care to explain your dilemma over a glass of sarsaparilla."

Cairo relaxed and broke into a smile. While Isaac escorted Cairo down the street to his favorite restaurant, she unfolded her tale in a concise narrative, emphasizing her concerns and her need for immediate assistance.

"So you see, Judge Parker," Cairo summed up. "Time is of the essence in this matter. And without your help, I will be forced to brave the dangers of cross-country travel and repeat my story to every marshal in Oklahoma Territory. By that time, it may be too late and this matter of life and death might resolve itself . . . for the worst! To say I'm frantic and desperate is an understatement."

Cairo inhaled a quick breath and plunged on while she still had Isaac's undivided attention. "I will not detain your best marshal any longer than necessary. The instant law and order is restored in Canadian Station, I will gladly pay him for his time and effort and he can be on his way."

Judge Parker assisted Cairo into her chair in the restaurant and sat across from her. A pensive frown puckered his brow. What Cairo was saying was a mite irregular but hardly unheard of. Essentially, what she wanted was to hire one of the marshals who headquartered at Fort Smith—the best man on the staff, to be specific—as a guide, detective, and an authority of justice.

Her claim that due process of the law in the newly

formed territory of Oklahoma was infuriatingly slow and inefficient was certainly justified. The area was struggling to construct its foundations, and lawlessness was the rule rather than the exception. Courts and judges in Oklahoma were even more swamped than Isaac's, but he needed each of his marshals to patrol Indian Territory.

The judge would have voiced that particular point to the young lady. *Would have,* if not for one very disconcerting tidbit of information that had come to his attention that morning. He had been informed that his most competent marshal, Lawton Stone, was now followed by a deadly curse of vengeance. The Gardiners wanted Lawton's head because he had killed their youngest brother two weeks earlier.

Lawton Stone had been plagued with death threats before. But when the Gardiners raided a train in the Creek Nation, they had left a message to be sent to Lawton. They were goading him to take to their trail to settle their feud.

Isaac Parker had no intention of sending Lawton back into the area where the Gardiners were last sighted until things simmered down. The plea of this distracting female was just the excuse Isaac needed to keep Lawton a safe distance from his vengeful enemies. Lawton would probably protest, but he was going to take this assignment. And that was that.

"Sir, will you spare me one of your talented marshals?" Cairo asked impatiently, dragging Isaac from his deliberations. "I took it upon myself to inquire around town about the men who ride for you. I have been told that one by the name of Lawton Stone is considered the best to be had. He comes highly praised by the citizens of Fort Smith."

Judge Parker grinned to himself. The lady had wasted no time in selecting the most outstanding man on the staff—the very one who needed to make himself scarce in Indian Territory for the next few weeks.

"Lawton Stone is just the man I would have recommended to you," he declared. "We will try to muddle through without his expertise for a month or two."

Cairo sank back in her chair, looking quite pleased with herself. She had anticipated an argument and she had mentally listed the points she wanted to make in case they wound up in debate. Thankfully, Judge Parker had not voiced a protest.

"And where can I find this Lawton Stone?" she quizzed the judge. "I am most anxious to approach him on this matter and make immediate preparations for our journey."

Judge Parker chuckled. "I will introduce you to him, my dear . . . if I have your permission to finish my sarsaparilla."

Cairo's face heightened with color. No doubt the judge perceived her to be a very impatient and pushy woman. Well, maybe she was, she mused as she squirmed in her chair. But when Cairo Calhoun made up her mind to see something done, she wanted it done yesterday. Patience, she was sorry to report, was not one of her endearing virtues.

"Do finish your drink," Cairo insisted, and then broke into an impish smile that very nearly melted the man's heart. "I can, if I must, wait another two minutes."

Two minutes? Isaac Parker threw back his head and

laughed out loud. Cairo was so full of fire and undaunted spirit. The lady wanted to see heaven and earth moved to resolve her problems and she was hell-bent on ensuring that her purpose was served. Just wait until this bewitching ball of fire confronted the Rock of Gibraltar!

Lawton Stone was a man who played by his own rules and sometimes made them up as he went along. He wasn't going to take kindly to having this fiercely determined female relentlessly prodding him in the direction she wanted him to go. But this was just the distraction Lawton needed to make him forget Judge Parker was shuffling him out of the way—for his own safety, of course.

What amazed Isaac was that this saucy female and Lawton Stone were very much alike. Both of them were dynamic, determined, and self-confident. On the other hand, Cairo Calhoun looked like a well-groomed sophisticate and Lawton Stone was a rough-and-tumble, no-frills sort of man. What traveling companions they would make!

Before the judge could gather his feet beneath him, Cairo vaulted from her chair and scurried out the door. Yes indeed, Isaac thought with a wry smile, the invincible Lawton Stone was about to meet a very shapely but unstoppable force. Sparks were about to fly.

Chapter Three

Feeling very pleased with herself, Cairo strolled alongside Judge Parker. Although he had been called the "Hanging Judge," "Butcher Parker," "Bloody Parker," and several other disrespectful names by the renegades he'd tried and sentenced, Cairo liked him. He was kind, companionable, and obviously civic-minded. With great pride, Isaac spoke of the progressive changes in Fort Smith. He boasted of the sidewalks, street cars, and string of lights that had transformed the backward frontier hamlet into a respectable town. The Queen City of the Southwest, he'd called it.

The judge also informed Cairo that the town operated the largest cottonseed oil mill in the world and maintained three efficient cotton gins, two grist mills, and three saw mills. To their credit, the citizens had also founded furniture factories, wagon factories, and even an ice factory.

"Yes, indeed," the judge said with a proud smile. "This town has come an incredibly long way since my wife Mary and I stepped from the riverboat onto the muddy docks more than a decade ago." He gestured toward an impressive building to the left. "We have a fifty-thousand-dollar opera house to promote cultural interests, and a twenty-five-thousand-dollar canning factory has just been completed. We are now raising funds to construct an expansion bridge across the Arkansas River so we can dispense with ferries."

"And what of your educational programs?" Cairo questioned. "Having been a teacher in Missouri, I am always curious about the progressiveness of schools, not only for the men in our future, but also the women."

Isaac smiled. "I advocate a better educational system," he assured her. "In fact, I prepared a bill for which Congress donated the old military reservation to our schools. The fund of more than a half-million dollars has been dedicated solely to education."

Cairo was impressed. "When I take a teaching position in Oklahoma Territory, I will be sure to inform my students of our meeting and boast of all your accomplishments. You are a very remarkable man, sir."

Judge Parker chuckled heartily. "Perhaps then, my dear, you can dispel the ugly rumors that are buzzing through the Twin Territories that I am Satan himself, come to hurl my wrath upon mortal man."

Cairo tilted her delicate chin and met his sparkling blue eyes. "I daresay, sir, that those who consider you to be the devil incarnate are the very ones who tread the path of evil. I for one applaud your attempt to bring law and order into those territories where thievery runs rampant!"

Judge Parker chortled again. "If ever I find myself in need of a character reference, Miss Calhoun, I will seek you out." He paused to indicate a quaint cottage. "Here we are, my dear. I expect you are most anxious to make Lawton Stone's acquaintance."

"Indeed I am." Cairo squared her shoulders. "It will be an honor to meet two living legends in the same day."

Cairo had already sketched a mental picture of what the famous U.S. marshal looked like after hearing his praises sung all over Fort Smith. The famous Mr. Stone would be the personification of law enforcement. He would be dressed in fashionable garments like Judge Parker and he would be poised with an air of authority. He would be as conscientious about his appearance as he was about his duty of preserving order. Cairo knew Mr. Stone was a giant of a man, even taller than Isaac, and she was certain he would carry himself with pride and dignity.

She was all set to be impressed and then plead her cause. Mr. Stone would readily accept her request and they would become good friends. Ah, thought Cairo with a contented sigh, things were working out splendidly.

"Damn it, Tuck, if you call me Lover Boy one more time, I'm going to punch you right in the mouth," Woody slurred.

Tucker McGuire broke into a toothy grin as he peered at the blurred image of Woodward Hall. "Lover Boy . . ."

The challenge was offered and quickly accepted. The

brawl that broke out in the dining room of the cabin was as much a part of the ritual as consuming huge amounts of whiskey was. It didn't matter what started the fisticuffs. One reason was as good as any other, and there had been scads of excuses over the years. If the three men couldn't find a reason to fight, they invented one.

As had become their custom, each man took his turn at throwing the first punch. Tonight it was Woody's turn. He swung sluggishly at the fuzzy redhead across the table, but drunk as he was, his aim was off its mark. His right arm swung in an exaggerated arc that caught Lawton upside the head before the doubled fist landed straight on Tucker's lopsided grin.

Lawton, who had glanced at Tucker in anticipation, found his head snapped backward by the unseen blow. His chair reared up on its hind legs and the drink in his left hand slopped in his face as he toppled backward. When the chair and its oversize occupant crashed to the floor, the toe of Lawton's scuffed boot hooked around the leg of the table, lifting it as he went down.

The lantern slid sideways and Tucker snatched it up. Though he managed to set it on the bureau, he could not latch onto the whiskey bottles and glasses before they clattered to the floor. In less than ten seconds, the dining room that Widow Herman had scrubbed and dusted was in pathetic shambles.

While Tucker was rescuing the lantern, Woody climbed upon his chair to make a spectacular dive over the upended table. He leaped on the unsuspecting Tucker, forcing the older man to the floor to deliver another punch in the jaw.

Anxious to let off steam himself, Lawton floundered

like a gigantic overturned beetle and finally rolled off his broken chair. Doubling his fist, he swung wildly at Woody who had given Tucker a sound blow. Woody landed atop Tucker who grunted in pain. With a growl, Tucker smashed his fist into Woody's handsome face a couple of times, only to find the younger man reciprocating.

Lawton pounced on both of them, squishing them flat. And there the three musketeers lay—their arms, legs, and bodies entangled, like a pile of squabbling schoolboys. These three grown men, who guarded each other's backs in the face of danger and who had often risked their own lives to ensure the safety of a dear friend, were beating each other to a pulp!

Strange though it might seem, the men had no qualms about what they were doing and why. They needed this rough and rowdy display to vent their bottled emotions and to counter the hazards of their jobs. This drunken brawl was well earned.

It was into this scene of tangled bodies and broken furniture that Judge Parker and Cairo Calhoun walked. Receiving no response to his rap at the door, Isaac invited himself inside. Having heard the racket, he suspected his marshals were blowing off steam. He never begrudged them their rituals since they were private affairs and they always restored order after they enjoyed their rowdy celebrations. The judge believed his marshals deserved to humor themselves and unwind. However, he hadn't realized the extent of these drunken bashes because he'd never viewed one firsthand until now.

Isaac found himself immediately uncomfortable when he imagined what the prim and proper schoolmarm thought. But it was too late to explain what this harmless brawl was all about.

The look on Cairo's face was one of stupefied disbelief. Her visions of a knight in shining armor, come to assist in her noble crusade, shattered in a zillion pieces. She stood frozen in the doorway between the parlor and the dining room. Her mouth gaped and she stared goggle-eyed at the scene before her.

These drunken galloots were the symbol of law and order west of Fort Smith? That was a laugh, thought Cairo. They, who should have been preserving peace and tranquility, were the very ones who were disturbing it! In all her twenty-one years, Cairo had never seen a more repulsive or childish display. This was a disgrace, that's what it was!

Unaware that an audience was watching from the doorway, Lawton staggered to his feet and jerked Tucker up beside him, but Tucker was delighting in the rowdy brawl far too much to cease throwing punches. He wheeled as he cocked his arm and delivered a right cross to Lawton's jaw, even though his friend had kindly assisted him to his feet.

Lawton stumbled over the legs of an upended chair and flapped his arms like a duck preparing for flight. But gravity got the better of him. Swaying like a felled redwood, he teetered backward, slamming into the young woman behind him.

A shocked squeal erupted from Cairo's lips when the huge hulk of masculinity toppled on her. She was on the floor before her paralyzed reflexes could respond to imminent disaster, and Lawton was sprawled, faceup, on top of her. The air surged from her in a whoosh. Although Lawton's fall had been cushioned by shapely feminine flesh, leaving him staring up at the ceiling, Cairo was left to glare furiously at the back of his raven head.

Jaw gaping, Judge Parker stared down at all that could be seen of the vivacious blonde. Lawton's bulky body covered hers, crushing her into the floor.

"Gentlemen!" His voice boomed like a gavel pounding out a sentence of doom. "Is this any way to greet guests? Now look what you've done!"

At the sound of his voice, Tucker and Woody untangled themselves and rolled to their knees. Both men plopped down cross-legged on the floor to peer bleary-eyed at the judge. They did a double take when they noticed the green silk skirt and petticoats that protruded from beneath Lawton.

Lawton squirmed, bumfuzzled by the feel of a womanly body beneath his. He twisted, accidentally jabbing Cairo with his knees and elbows. When he had turned over, he stared down at the elegant features of the lady who was pinned beneath him. His brows jackknifed when he peered into Cairo's green eyes and assessed her bewitching features—puckered in a mutinous frown though they were at the moment.

"Get off me, you wooly gorilla!" she cried. The man's knee had wedged itself between her legs and Cairo was outraged by the suggestiveness of their position.

Stumbling drunk this man looked faintly dangerous to Cairo. She wondered how intimidating he would be when he was stone-cold sober. It was for certain that Cairo would never want to be this close to this unruly-haired, unshaven baboon ever again! She was sure she would suffer nightmares after having this miserable excuse of a U.S. marshal sprawled on top of her as if they were the most intimate of lovers.

"I said get off!" Cairo shoved the heels of her hands into Lawton's massive shoulders, knocking him off balance and sending him rolling beside her.

"Are you all right, my dear?" Judge Parker questioned, his voice registering his concern for the trampled beauty.

Isaac assisted Cairo to her feet and slipped his arm around her to lend additional support. When he was certain Cairo had emerged from near disaster with only her dignity crushed, he glanced at the bruised and battered faces of his famed marshals.

"Gentlemen—and I use the term loosely—I would like to introduce you to Miss Cairo Calhoun, up from Missouri way, I believe she said."

Cairo wasted no time in acquainting the marshals with her look of marked disgust—especially the big ape who had squished her flat. She had prayed for a saint to assist her in her mission. Instead, she confronted three unruly devils.

Squelching her outrage, Cairo surveyed the three men who reeked of whiskey. All of them were long overdue for a shave and haircut, that was for sure! Their clothes, twisted about them and devoid of buttons, looked as if they had been slept in for days on end. Their shaggy manes of hair drooped over their foreheads and drops of whiskey clung to their mustaches and beards. What a pathetic and deplorable lot they were!

"This is Woodward J. Hall." Judge Parker broke the brittle silence with his introduction and stifled an amused grin.

He knew what the dignified lady must be thinking,

not that he blamed her. The marshals had made quite an impression on her, but hardly a good one. The judge made a mental note to explain what these shenanigans were all about—later.

Cairo surveyed the chestnut-haired man who was absently massaging his arm. He was thirty or thereabouts and, despite the unkempt mop of hair and thick beard, possessed refined features and was rather pleasing to the eye. When his chocolate-brown eyes flooded over her in roguish appreciation, Cairo tilted her chin and nodded a cool greeting to Woody.

"This is Tucker McGuire," the judge announced.

Cairo assessed the bushy red hair that capped Tucker's broad head. The wiry carrot-colored mop jutted out in all directions from his square head. A generous smattering of freckles covered the bridge of his wide nose and cheeks. Her gaze landed on the trickle of blood that dripped off the corner of his mouth to dam up in his scraggly beard and she frowned before nodding a curt greeting to the man who looked to be in his mid-forties.

"And this"—Judge Parker focused his attention on the muscular giant who sat Indian-style on the floor, studying Cairo with an indecipherable expression—"this man who accidentally fell on top of you, the one you have selected to assist you, is Lawton Stone—our hero." His eyes twinkled with amusement as he watched Cairo and Lawton size each other up and dress each other down.

Snapping green eyes riveted on Lawton's tousled raven hair and thick beard. Cairo's expression registered blatant distaste as her gaze slid over his gaping flannel shirt which revealed the curly matting of hair and padded whipcord muscles on his chest. He had shoulders like a buffalo, the hairy face of a gorilla, and long legs that bulged with steel-honed flesh. And didn't she know it! She had felt the imprint of this mass of masculinity mashing into her in a most indecent manner!

Both Woody and Tucker looked apologetic about being caught rolling and tumbling around on the floor, but Lawton Stone did not. He simply sat there, staring at her with those piercing silver-gray eyes that seemed to look right through her to pluck out the hidden secrets in her soul. In a matter of seconds his eyes had turned from glistening mercury to shimmering silver and then to smoky gray.

His scrutiny was so unnerving that Cairo shifted awkwardly from one foot to the other. For the life of her, she couldn't imagine why she should feel embarrassed or ashamed. After all, she had done nothing wrong. It was Lawton Stone and his uncivilized friends who were making a mockery of the law. Why the devil was that man looking at her as if she were on trial for some hideous crime?

An involuntary shudder slithered down Cairo's spine when those granite-gray eyes raked over her again, not missing even the smallest detail. She knew men found her reasonably appealing because their glances said as much, but there was nothing about the way Lawton was peering at her that suggested compliments or apologies. If anything, he was silently consigning her to hell. What could he possibly have against her when they had only met? She was the one who deserved to hold a grudge, not he!

Judge Parker cleared his throat to break the strained

silence. "Lawton, I'm fully aware that you have just returned from a most difficult foray through the Cherokee Nation, but Miss Calhoun has requested my assistance and yours as well. Yours in particular," he clarified. "After she explained her dilemma to me, I consented to spare you from your duties so you can accompany her to Oklahoma Territory."

Lawton said nothing. His thoughts and his emotions were locked behind his well-schooled mask of indifference. Again, he silently and thoroughly appraised the voluptuous blonde whose trim-fitting gown accentuated her alluring assets. And she did, he begrudgingly admitted, have assets that could tempt and bedevil a man. He ought to know since he had been lying on top of her, feeling those delicious curves against his body.

Under the plumed hat that sat at a jaunty angle on Cairo's head was a fashionably twisted mass of hair that was so blond it almost appeared white. The Lord had generously bestowed this angelic-looking creature with the delicately carved features of a mythical goddess. And Lawton, who was known for his incredible powers of observation, noticed every dazzling detail about Cairo Calhoun—the refined bone structure, cupid's-bow lips, intelligent green eyes that danced with living fire, and the statuesque figure. All her curves were in the right places and her very presence demanded a man's rapt attention.

Lawton had met very few women who sparkled with a rare natural beauty. Cairo Calhoun—if that was her real name, and he doubted it was, since it sounded hokey to him—was exceptional. She was the devil's own temptation.

He gave himself a mental slap after he'd looked

Cairo up and down for the umpteenth time. "And what, may I ask, is the nature of this trip for which I've been volunteered to accompany Cleopatra to Oklahoma?" Lawton questioned in a mocking voice.

Cairo's head snapped up and she glared at the insolent marshal. "The name is Cairo, not Cleopatra," she informed him tartly.

She didn't like Lawton Stone one iota. No, sir, she did not! Every glance directed at her was a silent criticism and a taunting insult. Cairo sorely resented the way those mercury eyes flooded over her, picking her apart as if she were a cadaver. She could endure Tucker and Woody's roguish stares far better than she could tolerate Lawton's probing glances and intimidating words.

Lawton shrugged off her attempt to correct him and glanced at Isaac. "So what's the deal, judge?" His voice reflected extreme boredom.

An angry blush stained Cairo's cheeks and she gnashed her teeth until she swore she would grind off the enamel. Cairo detested his arrogance and his ridiculing attitude. First he had given her the once-over, as if she were a piece of horseflesh he had considered purchasing. Then he refused to pay her the courtesy of speaking directly to her. It was as if, being a woman, she didn't have the intelligence to answer his questions without a translator. His total lack of consideration and respect galled Cairo. She would have grabbed him by his thick neck and shaken him if she thought she could have gotten away with it.

Judge Parker smothered a snicker. Cairo and Lawton's personalities had already clashed and sparks were indeed flying. These two feisty individuals had taken one look at each other and had seen their own reflections. In her own way, Cairo was as tough and resilient as Lawton.

Yes, Lawton was a man among men. Judge Parker had studied Lawton's impressive credentials before he called him to service from the ranks of the Texas Rangers. Lawton was courageous to a fault. He possessed a gambler's daring and an uncanny intuition about danger. He was vividly imaginative and remarkably resourceful in his pursuit of elusive renegades.

Isaac glanced back at Cairo. This woman clearly considered herself a man's equal. It hadn't taken Isaac long to figure that out and it required even less time for Lawton to come to the same conclusion. Cairo looked a man straight in the eye and spoke her mind. She was willful, persistent, and intelligent. She would put a lesser man off with her bold confrontation, Isaac speculated. She, like Lawton, was a dominant force to be reckoned with. At present they were staring at each other like two combatants, pondering strategies for battle.

"Well?" Lawton prompted the judge who had been distracted by his wandering thoughts.

"I think I will allow the lady to explain her motives at a more appropriate moment," Isaac remarked, clamping down on his lips before a sly smile surfaced. He pivoted on his heels and offered Cairo his arm. "Miss Calhoun can contact you after you have had the opportunity to make yourself presentable. Obviously, we came at a bad time."

Before Cairo exited, she flashed Lawton a scornful glance. Then, with a toss of her silver-blond head, she swept regally out of the room on Isaac's arm. How was she going to tolerate that gorilla for the duration of her journey? It was going to be an exercise in patience and self-control, that was for sure. The moment he opened his mouth to fling one of his rude remarks, she would launch herself at him and the fight would be on!

When the front door creaked shut, Lawton glanced over his shoulder. Tucker and Woody were still lost to the bewitching image and the lingering feminine scent of the goddess who had graced their humble cottage with her divine presence.

"Do you think it's *her?*" Lawton's gruff voice shattered the silence.

Tucker blinked like a disturbed owl. *"Her* who?"

"It's *her* all right," Woody sighed whimsically. "That was the light and love of my life . . ."

Lawton scowled at the moonstruck expression on Woody's and Tucker's puffy faces. Tucker was too old to be bedeviled by a woman, thought Lawton. And Woody, God save his soul, had always been blinded by a pretty face and bedazzled by a fetching figure. Both men were so caught up in lustful fantasies that they had been sidetracked from Lawton's train of thought.

"The Snowbird!" Lawton snorted, his voice shattering the spell Cairo had cast on her witless victims.

Both men gaped at him when the light of recognition dawned on them.

"Good Lord!" Tucker croaked. "She *could* be the Snowbird, judging by the descriptions we've received. But why would the Snowbird waltz right into Fort Smith, bewitch the judge, and request that you accompany her cross-country . . . ?" As the words tumbled off his tongue and the thought soaked into his spongy brain, Tucker realized why the daring beauty would do such a thing. "Good Lord . . ." he repeated incredulously.

Woody was still all eyes and sagging jaw. "You think she's setting a trap for you, Law?" he chirped.

Lawton nodded grimly. "The death trap," he murmured as he grabbed the overturned whiskey bottle and guzzled the last drop. "Who better to deliver it than the Snowbird? The Gardiners probably don't think we know about her connection with them."

"They plan to lure you out to some isolated spot and ambush you!" Tucker hooted before he crawled on his hands and knees to fetch an unopened bottle of liquor. "We've got to warn the judge and have that witch arrested."

Lawton stared at Tucker's hunkered form. "Have her arrested for what?" he scoffed. "You said yourself she isn't wanted for anything. And who the hell would believe that vision of beauty is guilty of anything except causing a man to consider committing a crime of passion?"

Woody grinned rakishly. "I'm guilty," he declared unrepentantly. "Just looking at her made me go hot all over."

"Careful, Lover Boy," Lawton warned. "Your sap is rising."

"Quit calling me that!" Woody demanded.

"Then quit acting as if your brain is situated below your belt buckle," Lawton replied.

Tucker propped himself against the bureau and took a swig of whiskey, straight from the bottle. A thoughtful frown knitted his brow. "Judge Parker has heard about the death threat on your head. I mentioned it to him myself. I'd bet a king's ransom that he agreed to send you off with the Snowbird just to get you away from the Gardiners' stomping ground until this blows over."

Lawton grabbed the bottle from Tucker. "My thoughts exactly, Tuck." He took a gulp of whiskey. "And what a coincidence that Cairo Calhoun, or whoever she really is, claimed to be a schoolmarm. Twice, I've heard reports of a gorgeous blonde arriving in town looking for a teaching position just a few days before the Gardiners struck a bank or train."

"Good Lord, that's right," Tucker squawked. "It has to be her! She's sure enough trying to set you up for the kill."

Lawton stared at the lingering image of Cairo Calhoun and reflected on the night he'd caught a glimpse of the mysterious Snowbird as she sailed across the moonlit prairie beside the outlaw gang. "And I'm going to let Cleopatra think I took the bait," he announced decisively.

"The hell you are! I'm telling Parker first thing in the morning and he can reverse his decision to send you to your own funeral."

Lawton gave his ruffled raven head a contradictory shake. "I'm going with her, Woody. And that's that."

"You're loco!" Tucker howled.

A slow smile worked its way across Lawton's lips. "Look at it this way, Tuck. Which one of the Gardiner gang would dare to take a shot at me when they risked killing their precious little Snowbird? They will be the ones who walk into a trap and Snowbird will be *my* bait. They won't shoot through her to get to me, now will they?"

Woody raked his fingers through his chestnut hair and sighed. "I don't know about this, Law. It sounds a mite risky to me. The Gardiners may track you the minute you cross the river. There are too many places in the wooded hills and creekbeds to pick you off." He stared thoughtfully at Lawton. "Now if it were me, I'd try to worm my way into the Snowbird's heart and win her loyalty. She wouldn't let the Gardiners dispose of you if you became the object of her affection."

Tucker erupted in a horselaugh. "Lawton? Woo a woman? That'll be the day! He wouldn't use that ploy, not even to save his own hide. You seem to forget, Lover Boy, that Law hates women."

While Woody and Tucker leaped into spirited speculation on why Lawton had an aversion to women, he mulled over his encounter with Cairo Calhoun—the Snowbird. That sassy blonde was bold and daring, he'd give her that! But of course, any female who consorted with outlaws, spied and cased towns before robberies, was bound to be gutsy. Cairo was a cool one all right. She oozed self-assurance and confidence. The smug little chit probably thought she had pulled one over on Judge Parker and his marshals.

Lawton chuckled to himself. Isaac Parker, conscientious man that he was, thought he was removing Lawton from harm's way for his own protection. Well, the joke would be on Little Miss Cleopatra. That saucy little snip was going to learn, too late, that she had walked into a trap of her own making. She thought she was safe from any jurisdiction. Wouldn't she be surprised!

It had always annoyed Lawton that women were accorded special privileges. Western juries had never convicted them of crimes until just lately. Women in the West had been treated as if they were unique, prized creatures because of their scarcity. That had always rubbed Lawton the wrong way. Women committed crimes just like men did, but they usually got off scot-free and, on occasion, with murder—literally.

Lawton didn't believe in granting women special privileges or placing them on pedestals that put them above the law. And if Cleopatra Calhoun thought she was Lawton Stone's equal match, she had misjudged herself! No woman was going to get the best of Lawton, not now, not ever, not even that breathtaking beauty with eyes like polished emeralds and hair like moonbeams.

Lawton would have bet his life that Cairo Calhoun was the elusive Snowbird. He was absolutely convinced of it.

Chapter Four

Although Judge Parker had taken great pains to explain why his marshals needed to unwind after their long tours in Indian Territory, Cairo's opinion of Lawton Stone did not improve. She disliked him intensely. His every glance sought to cut her down several notches. His tone of voice and his remarks conveyed his disrespect.

But like Lawton or not, Cairo was bound and determined to elicit his help. She needed his seasoned expertise and by damned she would have it! She would tolerate his insolence if she must, but he would help her solve her father's dilemma and that was the beginning and end of it.

Resolved to those noble convictions, Cairo polished off her breakfast at the restaurant where Judge Parker had taken her the previous evening. Determined of purpose, Cairo aimed herself toward Lawton's cottage. Drawing herself up proudly, she knocked on the door. Receiving no answer, she let herself in.

Bold though Cairo had always been, she found

herself screeching to an abrupt halt when she rounded the corner and saw the bare-chested Lawton Stone. He had perched on the edge of the commode and was in the process of pouring water from the basin to wash his bearded face.

Cairo would have died before she let herself swoon over the sight of his magnificent physique. Yet, she couldn't help but admire the powerful width of his shoulders and the rippling muscles of his belly that flexed and relaxed when he moved. His flesh was bronzed from exposure to the sun and finely tuned from years of physical exertion. A crescent scar curved around his lower rib and a bullet hole marred his left shoulder. Other than that, he was masculine perfection, she reluctantly admitted.

Cairo was annoyed with herself for finding this swarthy baboon so appealing. Lawton hadn't shaved his mustache and beard yet, and his face was covered with three months' growth of whiskers. His silver eyes were streaked with red, giving him a most foreboding appearance. He was a walking contradiction of sensual appeal and danger, and Cairo was stung by a myriad of conflicting emotions while she studied him.

"Am I allowed the same privilege of visually undressing you, Cleopatra?" Lawton smirked, just to get her goat.

Cairo's chin jutted out to a defensive angle and she fought down the blush of being caught gawking at him. "I thought you did more than your rightful share of assessing me last night, Mr. Stone. Shall I strip naked or have your eyes seen enough indecently clad females to form your own conclusions as to what I look like in the altogether?"

Despite his hangover, Lawton broke into a grin. The Snowbird was all spunk and gumption. She gave as good as she got. He idly wondered how a woman who obviously had all the advantages in life had strayed from the straight and narrow path to cavort with the Gardiners.

"Don't bother undressing on my account," he drawled as he plucked up the razor. "If I've seen one woman I've seen them all. And beauty, so the adage goes, is only skin deep at best." He scraped a clean swath on his cheek, raised a dark brow, and shot forth a devilish smile. "You weren't born with an extra breast or anything that makes you special enough for me to bother looking at you naked, were you?" His critical gaze swept over her form-fitting gown. "If you possess more than the normal amount of feminine assets, I can't imagine where you're stashing them, since your dress reveals everything you've got."

Cairo was positively livid. A bright red hue spread all the way to the roots of her silver-blond hair. Her green eyes flashed sparks hot enough to ignite a forest fire. Lawton didn't care one whit that his crude remark had put her in a snit. He intended to rile her. Her discomfort and embarrassment was the least of his concern. After all, she was a woman and he didn't like her on general principles. And knowing she was a thief charading as a schoolmarm was another strike against her.

A lesser woman would have burst into humiliated tears and sprinted from the house, clutching her wounded dignity. But despite Lawton's menacing affront, Cairo struck like a coiled rattlesnake. She stormed up to him and whacked him soundly on the cheek. The razor went flying after it cut a chunk out of his chin.

Calmly, Lawton bent over to retrieve his razor and went back to his shaving. "What do you want, Cleopatra?" he demanded in a tone that implied he really couldn't care less why she was there.

The man was downright impossible! Oh, how she despised this rude, insulting cad! Must he mock everything about her, even her name? "I want to know what time we will be leaving," she bit off, her fingers itching to curl around his neck and shake the stuffing out of him. "I want to be sure I have gathered all the necessary supplies for our trip and that I will be prepared when you have readied yourself."

Lawton turned and gaped at her for a full minute. She was certainly in a great hurry to deliver him to his doom. Had young Billy Gardiner been her lover? Was that why she was so all-fired anxious to dispose of him?

"I'm not going anywhere today, lady," he assured her in no uncertain terms. "I was on a tour of duty for three and a half months and I just got home yesterday."

"Tomorrow then?" Cairo inquired without the slightest sympathy for his plight.

"Maybe in a week," he replied before starting to shave the left side of his face.

"A week?" Cairo railed in frustration. "Judge Parker said—"

"Judge Parker isn't the one who'll be traipsing off across the territory with a fluffy bag of wind," he ridiculed. "And I have yet to hear just where the hell it is we're supposed to be going and why."

He knew where and why, of course. He was only curious to hear what excuse this sassy vixen had dreamed up to lure him into a fatal ambush.

Again Cairo's fingers curled, yearning to place a stranglehold on his throat. Calling upon her willpower, she restrained herself from doing him bodily harm. "My father staked a claim during the land rush into Oklahoma this past April," she explained through gritted teeth. "He constructed a hotel in a small settlement called Canadian Station, which is situated on the southern and western border. A loathsome scoundrel—I'm sure you know the type, being one yourself—" she inserted nastily, "has gone to devious extremes to swindle my father out of his investment. Since the courts have so many claims filed for hearings, my father has found it impossible to resolve his problems."

Cairo inhaled a quick breath and plunged on. "This vile vermin hired women of . . ." Cairo floundered for a delicate description of the floozies who had invaded the respectable hotel to drive out decent clientele.

"Whores," Lawton supplied bluntly since the chit had stumbled in search of an accurate term. How sly of her, he thought. She was probably a whore herself, even though she was trying to pass herself off as a prim and proper lady.

Cairo turned all the colors of the rainbow. "Whores," she echoed.

What an actress she was, Lawton mused as he went back to his shaving. If he didn't know better he would have sworn she was as pure as driven snow, and that was exactly what she wanted him to think. But he wasn't fooled by her performance.

"Anyway, these ladies of the evening have been swarming around my father's hotel, spoiling his profits and his reputation," she rushed on. "My father's life has been threatened since he refused to leave the premises and sacrifice his claim so the building can be turned into a house of ill repute. Already he has been shot in the arm for his defiance. Naturally, he couldn't file charges because the incident happened in the dark of night and there was no law official in the newly established community."

Lawton threw back his head and burst out laughing. That was the most ridiculous story he'd ever heard. "You expect me to drop what I'm doing and race off to Oklahoma to prevent a bordello from seizing a hotel?"

"I most certainly do! My father is an honest law-abiding citizen who deserves protection from threats on his life and his investment."

"What the hell's all the shouting about?" Tucker mumbled as he staggered to the bedroom door. "Keep it down, Law. My head is splitting . . ."

His voice trailed off when he noticed the vision of loveliness in pink satin. "Oh, *her* again . . ."

"Cleopatra was just explaining why it's so important for me to escort her to Oklahoma," Lawton reported. "Terribly important, she says." His tone suggested it was nothing of the kind.

"It *is* important!" Cairo blustered, stamping her foot.

"Of course it is," Lawton mocked dryly.

Tucker surveyed the shapely beauty and frowned wearily. With a deep sigh, he wheeled around and closed the door to the room in which he and Woody had slept the last few hours of the night away.

When they were alone again, Lawton stared Cairo squarely in the eye, wondering why he'd been assaulted by the ridiculous urge to yank this feisty lady to him and kiss her blind. It was the oddest sensation he'd ever experienced. Why did she have to affect him so? Her magnetic appeal was dangerous. She was a lying little thief . . . and she had the most kissable mouth ever to be placed on a feminine face.

I've been too long without a woman, Lawton diagnosed. Like Lover Boy, his sap was rising . . .

"I'll thank you not to look at me like that," Cairo bit off, cheeks aflame. She had seen that hungry look on men's faces before. However, she had never expected to see it on this particular man's face. Lawton had made it clear the previous night that he was immune to feminine charm, that he had absolutely no use for her.

"Look at you like what, Cleopatra?" Lawton drawled, amused by the flush of color that stained her cheeks. Damn, what a skillful actress! She could portray the blushing virgin as if she *were* one.

"You know perfectly well how you were looking at me, and I don't appreciate it," Cairo flared. "You looked as if you were contemplating kissing me, or some such ludicrous nonsense." Hands on hips, she glared at him. "If you were the very last man on earth and I were the last woman, I assure you that I wouldn't allow you near me! All I want from you is your expertise to guide me cross-country."

It was more Woody's style to grab a woman and kiss the breath out of her on impulse, but it was Lawton who yielded to the unfamiliar urge, if only to shut Cairo up and teach her that he wouldn't be ordered about like one of her lovesick lackeys. Served this haughty sprite right, he thought. She and her arrogant denials!

Cairo's mouth was still hanging open after Lawton pounced on her like a panther. Her body slammed against his bare chest and powerful thighs. She felt the matting of dark hair brush against the exposed flesh above her neckline and his knee wedge intimately between her legs. Shock waves rippled through her when he bent her into his hard contours. His face—one side shaved clean, the other bristly with whiskers—moved deliberately toward hers. His silver eyes flashed devilishly as he took her lips under his. He proceeded to kiss every ounce of breath out of her.

Since Lawton had daringly initiated this kiss of death, as he chose to refer to it, he expected it to taste like poison. Wrong! Cairo tasted of biscuits and jam and smelled like roses. The feel of her curvaceous body molded intimately to his nearly buckled him at the knees.

Lawton had intended to prove his defiance and his domination over this mere wisp of a woman who was teeming with spirit. What he inadvertently proved, unfortunately, was that no matter who she was, she had the power to devastate him in a way no other woman had ever been able to do. She seemed to draw some forbidden emotion from the carefully concealed well deep inside him. Sensations of unexpected pleasure and compelling need came bubbling up, spilling through him like molten lava.

Cairo hadn't even kissed him back or encouraged him in the least and still he was on fire for her. She simply hung in his arms like a limp dishrag, gasping to inhale a breath, battling for enough self-control to resist his bold assault. And still, when she did nothing to entice him to continue the kiss, Lawton couldn't pry himself away from her pliant body. Holding her was like clinging to a fluffy cloud that somehow seemed to absorb his body and clog his senses with delicious scents and tantalizing sensations.

The Widow Herman always kissed him back, and quite enthusiastically, but even her eagerness didn't stir Lawton the way Cairo's soft, lush lips did, the way her womanly flesh did when they were almost as close as two people could get.

If Lawton was stunned by his reaction, Cairo was doubly dumbfounded by hers! She had experimented a time or two with kisses, just to see what the fuss over sex was all about, but her limited experiences had in no way prepared her for the electrical jolt that seared her lips and body to Lawton Stone.

Who would have thought an infuriatingly obnoxious man such as this one could awaken her slumbering passions. The sensations crackled and sizzled like fire! Cairo hadn't thought she could feel anything but intellectual stimulation from the male of the species. She never had before. Yet, she and Lawton were nowhere near any intellectual plane! They were floundering in a sensual dimension of time that caused her to lose sight of reason.

Lawton was so miffed by his spontaneous reaction to this sassy imp that he had already begun to kiss her for the second time before he realized what he was doing. His hands had slid down her spine to settle familiarly on her hips, pressing them against his loins, allowing her to feel the drastic changes that had overcome him. His breath came in shallow, irregular spurts and his body shook with needs that he had long denied. What was happening to him? He was supposed to be the man of stone!

Cairo was a witch who possessed an incredibly powerful spell, he decided as his tongue darted into her mouth to explore the honeyed recesses. She was dangerously exciting. Heaven forbid that he—a man who had religiously avoided women whenever possible —would be lured by her charms and drugged by the potion of a kiss that was far more intoxicating than all the whiskey he'd consumed the previous night. But God help him, this green-eyed beauty did stir and arouse him to the extreme! She had touched the corner of his heart and had crumbled its very foundations.

That startling thought prompted Lawton to release Cairo from his arms as if he were holding live coals. Unprepared, Cairo folded at the knees and plopped backward into an unceremonious heap. Wide green eyes that were surrounded with thick lashes peered up at him with a mixture of astonishment and humiliation.

It was bad enough that he had kissed her senseless and she hadn't resisted, but it was mortifying beyond words that she had actually collapsed at his feet! She might have gathered her shattered dignity and stormed out with a smidgen of pride if she hadn't tripped over her weighted feet. Now nothing could salvage her pride or her dignity. Lawton Stone knew perfectly well that his kiss had melted her knees and turned her body into the consistency of marmalade. Curse it!

A gloating smile pursed Lawton's lips as he extended a hand to hoist Cairo off the floor. At least he knew he wasn't the only one who had been devastated by their embrace.

"Well, I never . . . !" Cairo spewed in outrage, her

face flushing crimson red.

"Haven't you?" One black brow arched in mocking contradiction. "Somehow I doubt that, Cleopatra. But it wouldn't take us long to learn for certain." He inclined his head toward his sleeping quarters. "There's no one in my bed. Shall we go find out whether you *never* have?"

The degrading remark and lurid question shocked Cairo back to her senses. The man was a credit to his flaws. He was lousy with them—starting with arrogantly insolent and ending with obnoxiously rude!

Cairo struck out at him, intending to leave her handprint on the same cheek she had slapped earlier, but Lawton was lightning-quick. He caught her hand in midair and employed it as a rope to tow her rigid body back to his. Again he mashed her against him, reminding her of what had happened to her betraying body only moments before. Cairo didn't even want to think about that, much less repeat the incident! It was too demoralizing to know that the very man she despised could also arouse her as no one ever had. It was inconceivable!

"Let me—" Before she could say "go," Lawton did just that. Cairo stumbled back, tripping over the upended table that had yet to be uprighted after the brawl the previous night. She landed in an untidy heap. Her petticoats fluttered over her head, exposing her shapely legs to his gaze.

Cursing like a trooper, Cairo untangled her legs from the table and bounded to her feet. She snatched up an empty whiskey bottle, wishing it were a boulder, and hurled it at Lawton. Chuckling, he ducked, refuting her attempt to knock him silly. When Cairo grabbed another bottle, Lawton threw up a hand to forestall her.

"Do you want me to take you to Oklahoma or not? If you throw that, Cleopatra, the deal is off."

Cairo allowed the bottle to slip from her fingers and clank against the floor. A mischievous smile pursed her lips, causing Lawton to frown warily. This big oaf had warned her not to throw the bottle, but he hadn't said anything about throwing a chair at him. And so she did, catching him in the groin.

Lawton doubled over in pain. If her aim had been any better, he would have no need for a woman for the rest of his life!

Satisfied that she had landed at least one memorable blow, Cairo lurched around and stalked toward the door. "I'll be back tomorrow, Mr. Stone. You had damned well better be ready to leave. I will not be put off by the likes of you, no matter how disgusting and repulsive you are. I'm paying you two hundred dollars to act as my guide, and you are going to lead me to Canadian Station whether either of us likes it or not!"

Lawton stared at the petite blond terror in pink satin. After inhaling a deep breath, Lawton turned back to shave the other side of his face. Maybe she wasn't the Snowbird after all, he mused. He really didn't want her to be, not when she had such an incredible effect on him. *The only woman who has ever had any noticeable effect on me,* he begrudgingly amended. Perhaps he had leapt to the wrong conclusion simply because the Gardiners' death threat was so fresh on his mind. Maybe that spitfire simply looked like the mysterious Snowbird, he mused as he floundered in a sea of uncertainty.

But if she wasn't the Snowbird, why had she sought *him* out in particular? And there was that flimsy excuse about a father in Oklahoma. She probably didn't have one, he thought cynically. The green-eyed hellion had probably hatched from an egg.

No, Cairo Calhoun wasn't the Snowbird, Lawton told himself. *Oh yes, she was,* he then decided. He was only allowing his fierce physical reaction to her influence his logic. She was the Snowbird all right, come to lead him into the valley of doom.

"Aw, hell," Lawton muttered, slopping water on his freshly shaved face. "Whether she is or she isn't, she is still trouble. If you have a grain of sense, Stone, you won't let yourself forget that."

"Who are you talking to?" Woody croaked. His voice had rusted after pouring so much whiskey down his pipes.

"The wall," Lawton grumbled grouchily. "Go back to bed. You look like hell."

"That's good," Woody mumbled as he massaged his throbbing temples. "I'd hate to look better than I feel."

As the door squeaked shut, Lawton braced his hands on the commode and stared at his reflection in the mirror. But it wasn't long before a pair of glittering emerald eyes materialized before him. The faintest hint of a grin skitted across Lawton's lips. He mulled over his confrontation with the blond hellcat.

No, she couldn't be the Snowbird . . .

"Yes, she is . . ." Lawton mused aloud.

No, she's not, one side of his soggy brain argued.

Lawton didn't know which part of himself to believe. And so he decided not to think about it anymore. Already, he was sporting a headache that crashed through his skull to beat dents in his brain.

With a miserable sigh, Lawton aimed himself toward his bed. What he needed was a few more hours' sleep. And he wasn't going to spare Cairo Calhoun another thought for the rest of the day!

That was easier said than done, Lawton realized each time he awoke to find thoughts of the curvaceous pixie dancing in his mind.

Chapter Five

Cairo had been in Fort Smith long enough to pique the interest of several eligible bachelors, as well as quite a few married men. She had accepted the invitation of an up-and-coming young lawyer who was praised highly by Judge Parker. She agreed to the outing with Daniel Siler only to reassure herself that all men weren't as difficult to handle and as annoying as Lawton Stone.

Since the previous morning when Lawton had kissed her blind and stupid, Cairo had repeatedly analyzed her unexpected reactions. But no matter which way she turned the encounter over in her mind, she couldn't explain why a man who infuriated her so could also ignite such fiery sensations within her. Lawton Stone was an enigma. He behaved as if he disliked her as much as she detested him, but the kiss he bestowed on her indicated an internal fire and burning hunger that had thrown her completely off balance. What was infinitely worse was the flame that had flickered inside her. After only one kiss Lawton had left Cairo to deal with fiery sensations she had never before experienced.

"Isn't your meal to your liking?" Daniel inquired of his bewitching companion.

Cairo jerked her head up, suddenly aware that she had been so immersed in thought that she had been staring at her plate as if she had been served a three-day-old fish. "The meal is fine," she insisted, absently fiddling with her silverware. "It's just that I have a lot on my mind."

Daniel smiled compassionately. "I understand, my dear." His attentive gaze flooded over the dazzling lady in burgundy. "I'm sure you will be relieved when you arrive in Oklahoma." He reached across the table to pat her hand. "And if your father's case comes to court, you have only to send me a telegram and I will be there to speak in his behalf."

While Daniel was consoling Cairo, Lawton was squiriming in his chair in the corner. He wondered why the sight of that sassy minx and her lovestruck beau drew his constant attention and irritation.

Lawton had entered the establishment to take his meal while Cairo was pensively studying her plate. He had told himself he didn't care that she had already found some upstart lawyer to court her . . . until his dark suspicions about her identity surfaced again. He concluded that Cairo was laying the groundwork, just in case she was ever hauled back to Fort Smith, accused of conspiring to commit murder—Lawton's.

The Snowbird was a clever one. If she ever went on trial, her bedeviled admirers would rush to her defense. Cairo was making friends in all the right places before she carried out her murder attempt. First she had batted her big green eyes at Judge Parker to earn his allegiance. Now she was practicing her feminine wiles on Daniel Siler.

His wary thoughts trailed off when the hotel clerk scuttled into the restaurant to hand Cairo a message. Lawton frowned. It probably was a note from the Gardiners who wondered how long it would be before the Snowbird lured out her victim, Lawton decided.

When Cairo had come marching onto his doorstep this morning, Lawton had informed her bluntly that he wasn't going anywhere today and that she could try again tomorrow. Lawton hadn't dared to invite her inside, fearing he would be compelled to pull her into his arms and torment his mind and body all over again.

His thoughts scattered when Cairo excused herself and left Daniel to finish his meal alone. Lawton discreetly followed her down the street. He half expected to see some suspicious character draw Cairo into a darkened alley for some private words, but that didn't happen. Cairo scurried back to the hotel and disappeared inside without incident.

Being suspicious by nature and cautious by habit, Lawton trailed along like her shadow. He gave his head an incredulous shake when he realized just how suspicious he'd become. He was so wary of the shapely nymph that he pounced on her every move and every remark.

Hell, he was going to feel like an absolute idiot when he learned she wasn't really involved in some devious plot to kill him.

"She's innocent," Lawton assured himself as he strode through the hotel lobby. *No, she's guilty as original sin,* a cynical voice warned.

After questioning the clerk, Lawton took the steps

two at a time to reach Cairo's room. Just to be on the safe side, he was going to find out what was in that mysterious note that prompted Cairo to abandon her dinner companion. Hoping to catch her unaware, Lawton sailed into the room.

Cairo wheeled to see Lawton Stone filling her doorway. Clutching her bosom, she sagged back against the bed and struggled for composure.

"Curse it, Mr. Stone, you scared ten years off my life," she scolded him. "You could have been considerate enough to knock instead of frightening a body half to death!"

"Why should I bother knocking?" Lawton countered.

His keen gaze circled the modestly furnished room. What did he expect to find? The Gardiner gang stashed under her bed? A crate of loaded rifles under her pillow?

"It would have been the polite thing to do," Cairo snapped. "Obviously, though, politeness and courteous manners are things you know nothing about."

"You didn't bother waiting for an invitation when you barged into *my* house," he parried, his gray eyes fixed on the bouquet of flowers that graced the nightstand. "Who sent you those?"

Cairo's chin shot out and defiance flickered in her eyes. Why was it that the mere sight of this man caused a riptide of emotions to flood through her? And why was he bombarding her with questions? He had the infuriating knack of putting her on immediate defense. And yet, at the same time, she was stung by a total awareness of the man himself. That was downright scary!

Lawton was ruggedly handsome without his unkempt beard and mustache. Since she'd last seen him, he had clipped his shaggy mane of midnight hair and had donned a black frock coat, vest, and black breeches, all of which accentuated his lean, powerful physique. His very size and stature filled her room to overflowing and Cairo cursed the warm tingles that his mere presence created in her.

"Don't make me repeat myself, Cleopatra," Lawton smirked, watching her green eyes run the full length of him in an unguarded stare. "I don't usually give women credit for possessing much sense. You, however, are the exception." His gaze riveted on her. "Now I asked you who sent the flowers. Don't pretend you're so dim-witted that I have to speak slowly and pose my question thrice."

That snapped her out of her daze. Cairo glared daggers at him. With a flare of rebellion, she threw her head and shoulders back. "My flowers are none of your business," she spat at him. "Now kindly take your leave. Surely you can amuse yourself by finding someone to arrest or gun down in the street. That is, after all, what the legendary Lawton Stone does best, isn't it?"

Why had she referred to his ability to bring down hardened criminals? Her remark left his mind drowning in another pool of doubt. Was she speaking of Billy Gardiner's untimely end?

In long purposeful strides, Lawton crossed the room to pluck up the note that lay beside the vase. Realizing his intention, Cairo darted in front of him, snatched up the message, and ripped it to shreds, just to be contrary.

That made Lawton all the more suspicious of her.

She was the Snowbird and the message had been from her notorious friends. Now he was sure of it.

With an exasperated growl, Lawton clamped his hand around her forearm and yanked her full length against him to breathe down her neck. "Who sent you the flowers and the card?" he demanded to know that very second.

What a strange man he was, Cairo decided as she squirmed for freedom. He harbored the notion that everyone's business was his own. Why was he making such a fuss about her bouquet?

"Get out of my room before I call the—"

Effortlessly, he imprisoned her in his sinewy arms. "Call the law?" he finished for her. "You seem to forget, little spitfire, that I *am* the law."

"A distorted version of it, to be sure," Cairo retaliated.

The feel of his muscled body moving against hers set off a chain reaction of sensations. Cairo stopped, stock-still. Her wide eyes locked with the glittering pools of mercury. Suddenly her lips went bone-dry and her heart flip-flopped in her chest.

Lawton peered down into her captivating face, baffled by the compelling desire that pulsed through his veins. Here he was, wandering through the dark corridors of suspicion, thinking the worst about this firebrand. Yet, the instant he felt her delectable body molded to his, his male needs warped his logic.

Danger signals were flashing in his brain. Intuition warned him that this female had fatal charm—the kind that could get him killed. But despite the demons of doubt that leaped at him, he wanted her the way he had never wanted anyone in all his thirty-one years.

Suddenly, Lawton didn't care that the Gardiners had sent the Snowbird a message. All he knew was that the taste of this dangerous vixen's kiss still lingered on his lips. He had become addicted to her, addicted to the feel of her delicious body fitted familiarly to his.

"The hell with it," Lawton muttered when he felt the invisible attraction tugging on him like a magnet on metal. He ached for this nymph up to his eyebrows and kissing her was all that would make the gnawing hunger go away.

Cairo, who had never been prone to fainting spells, feared she was about to have one when his sensuous lips rolled possessively over hers. Sparks leaped from his masculine body to hers, setting instant flames in the core of her being. And this time, Cairo found herself kissing him back without understanding the ravenous need that consumed her. Her reeling senses took flight as his kiss deepened, stealing the last of her breath.

Cairo was stung by the urge to explore the rock-hard chest she had caressed up to now only with her eyes. Brazenly, her hand glided over his shirt to delve beneath the fabric. Her fingers curled into the springy hair that carpeted his chest. She felt the accelerated beat of his heart, which she had assumed was chiseled from granite, but to her surprise, it was beating as frantically as hers.

Her adventurous investigation prompted Lawton to take privileges of his own. His inquisitive hand traced the scooped neckline of her gown, marveling at the exquisite texture of her skin. She felt like expensive satin—soft and inviting—and he hungered for more.

Displaying more tenderness than he realized he possessed, Lawton caressed the taut peaks of her breasts and cupped his hand around the firm mounds. His lips followed, tasting her silky flesh and driving himself mad with desire.

Cairo's quick intake of breath confused him. It was as if she had never dared such intimacies before. Lawton was sure this minx had been far more intimate with other men—the entire Gardiner gang, he suspected. And yet, knowing she had lain in other men's arms didn't prevent him from wanting her in the worst way. She had cast her magic spell on him and he was hopelessly entranced.

Although Cairo swore the world had slid out from under her, she realized that only the floor had. Somehow, they wound up in a prone position on her bed and her legs were dangling in midair. Lawton's hands and lips were upon her quaking flesh, tracing a fiery path over her breasts and abdomen. She arched toward his greedy mouth, craving his kisses and caresses, wanting something she didn't quite comprehend.

Her fingertips mapped the padded muscles of his chest and shoulders before skiing down his lean belly. Lawton's groan of pleasure encouraged her to continue her sensuous exploration and her own wild needs ensured that she did. Boldly, her hand tracked along the band of his trousers before dipping down to measure the hard flesh of his hips.

Monstrous needs burgeoned inside Lawton, shattering logic, unleashing the ardent cravings that threatened to devour him. He resented the garments that separated them, resented the fierce, uncontrollable hunger that throbbed in his brain and in his loins. He could think of nothing except appeasing the white-hot ache.

While his lips suckled at the throbbing peaks of her breasts, his free hand flooded over her hip to delve beneath the hiked hem of her skirts. He groaned again when his fingertips made tantalizing contact with the silky flesh of her thighs.

Lord, this mysterious sorceress was exquisite—every perfectly formed inch of her. Touching her drove him over the edge. Making love to her would be the ultimate pleasure.

Cairo swore she had melted into a puddle. Her body was ablaze with so many fervent needs she couldn't begin to count them. The whisper of her conscience bade her to stop him from doing what he was doing, but recently awakened feminine needs begged for what he offered. She was so lost in the heady pleasure of his touch that she could think of nothing except exploring this new, tantalizing world of rapture.

"Lord, how you tempt me, Cairo," Lawton rasped. His body moved instinctively toward hers, settling exactly upon her, even though his breeches and her petticoats formed a barrier to separate them.

The sound of her own name on his lips was her undoing. He had never uttered her real name before. The caressing huskiness of his voice against her cheek was pleasure in itself, though not nearly enough to satisfy the needs that intensified with each passing second.

It was crazy, absolutely insane and totally illogical, she knew, but Cairo needed to investigate the mysterious dimensions of desire with this man. Why? Cairo was afraid to answer that puzzling question for fear of what she'd find. It was wicked and shameful, but she adored the feel of Lawton's arms around her, the possessive pressure of his sensuous lips on her skin . . .

The rap at the door splintered the silence like a rock shattering a windowpane. Lawton jerked away, automatically reaching for the snub-nosed pistol he concealed in the right pocket of his jacket.

Cairo blinked at Lawton's lightning-quick reflexes and the sudden appearance of the weapon which took deadly aim at the door. The man had been living on the edge for so long that it must be force of habit for him to draw and aim. His survival instinct was at work and he obviously carried enough weapons on him to equip an entire cavalry!

Cairo had felt the pistol in his pocket when he lay upon her. She had also touched the derringer that was strapped behind his left shoulder. She couldn't help but wonder where else he stashed weapons when he wasn't wearing his holsters that held the two ivory-handled Peacemakers.

"Cairo? Is everything all right?" Daniel Siler called from the hall.

No, everything wasn't all right! She had taken leave of her senses! What woman in her right mind would allow herself to be seduced by a man who obviously had no regard for women in general and her in particular? He had made his dislike for her perfectly clear each time he spoke to her. He saw her only as a physical temptation which stirred his male lusts. No doubt, Lawton Hard-Hearted Stone resented his attraction to her.

"I'm fine, Daniel," Cairo chirped, her voice one octave higher than normal.

"I was afraid that message you received had upset you." There was a slight pause. "May I come in?"

Someone had damned well better come in! thought Cairo as she vaulted to her feet to straighten her rumpled gown and tousled hair. Without some sort of interruption she was likely to wind up flat on her back again, doing the same shameful things she'd been doing before the knock at the door jolted her to her senses.

"Send him away," Lawton urged as he replaced his pistol.

"Come in," Cairo called, flagrantly ignoring Lawton's demand.

Daniel pulled up short when he realized Cairo wasn't alone. His wide-eyed gaze bounced off the bewitching blonde who was propped against the dresser and then landed on Lawton who lounged negligently on the bed.

"Mr. Stone came by to discuss the arrangements for our departure," Cairo hurriedly explained, refusing to spare Lawton a glance.

Daniel smiled at Lawton. "I'm glad you are the one who is escorting Cairo to Oklahoma," he commented. "I know she'll be in good hands."

Cairo grimaced at his choice of words. Obviously Daniel didn't know just how good Lawton was with his hands!

But will I *be in good hands? That's the question,* thought Lawton.

"I'll rest better knowing Cairo will be safe and sound," Daniel added. He was aware of Lawton's standoffish reputation with women; he was glad it wasn't Woodward Hall who was accompanying her west.

Safe? SAFE? Cairo nearly choked on her breath. She and Lawton had yet to leave town and she had come dangerously close to embarking on the most intimate, perilous journey possible. She shuddered at the thought of spending more time alone with him. She wasn't sure she could trust him or herself!

"If you and Lawton have finalized your arrangements, I would like to escort you to the theater," Daniel remarked, checking his timepiece. "The performance will begin in half an hour."

Cairo graced him with her most disarming smile. "I'll meet you in the lobby in five minutes."

When Daniel left, Cairo spun to face the man who was still sprawled on her bed as if he belonged there. "I have begun to have my doubts about our journey together," she said, awkwardly toying with the folds of her gown. "I don't think I can go through with this."

Lawton frowned in wary trepidation. *Through with what?* he wondered. His murder? "What's the matter, Cleopatra? Have you become so fond of me that you're regretting your plans?"

Cairo's face flushed furious red. "Fond of you? I'd like a rattlesnake better, Mr. Stone!"

Lawton sat there, telling himself she wasn't the Snowbird but only half believing it. Hell, he was so confused he didn't know *what* he believed. He swayed back and forth between her innocence and guilt like the pendulum on a clock. Muttering at his inability to decide, Lawton came agilely to his feet.

"I'll be ready to leave in the morning. If you still plan to go, be at my cottage at ten o'clock."

He shoved his Stetson down on his raven head and swaggered out the door. He didn't have the slightest idea where in the hell he was going. All he knew was that he needed to put some space between himself and this fascinating creature. He hated his unreasonable weakness for her.

When the door clanked shut, Cairo collapsed in relief. She was thoroughly ashamed of herself. She had behaved like a trollop, and worse, Lawton thought she felt something for him.

Well, I don't, Cairo told herself fiercely. She might have a phenomenal physical reaction to the man, but she wasn't going to permit it to become her downfall. She had her crusade to consider and that was far more important than her feelings for this midnight-haired devil with flashing silver eyes!

Cairo marched toward the door. She was going to enjoy the theatrical performance with Daniel Siler, even if it killed her. And she wasn't going to compare the amiable lawyer to Lawton Stone, either, not even once.

Her gaze strayed over her shoulder to the delicate bouquet of flowers on her nightstand. For the life of her she couldn't imagine why the flowers had piqued Lawton's curiosity to the point he had stooped to trying to read her messages without her permission.

An impish smile pursed her lips as she studied the flowers and contemplated an ornery thought. If those roses annoyed Lawton so much, she'd make sure he saw a great deal of them. Would serve him right, peculiar man that he was!

Chapter Six

At ten o'clock sharp, Lawton heard the nicker of a horse outside his cottage. He was in the process of sending the Widow Herman off after what could only be described as the most awkward situation of his life.

After breezing out of Cairo's room without a thought to where he was going, Lawton had landed on Molly Herman's doorstep. He'd thought sure her eagerness would cure what ailed him. What a disappointment it had been to realize the agreeable widow could only give him what he *needed,* not what he really *wanted!*

The entire time Lawton had been kissing Molly he had the feeling he had the wrong woman in his arms. He cursed himself a million times over when he found himself comparing his lukewarm reactions to the gentle widow to his explosive responses to the feisty Cairo.

How in the world could a sensible man yearn for the kisses of a woman who wished him dead? he wondered. He was accustomed to flirting with danger and courting disaster, Lawton reckoned. Being the daredevil he was, he had allowed himself to become intrigued by a woman whose motives he couldn't trust.

Molly Herman had been shocked when Lawton had pulled away and voiced an excuse that he couldn't stay the night because he was leaving town the following morning. He had stated that he needed his rest and he'd felt like a fool the moment he blurted out the words. Molly, of course, was heartbroken. It was written all over her face.

Molly had appeared on Lawton's stoop at nine-thirty this morning, wondering what she had done to lose the small grasp she'd had on the man she loved. Lawton, who was usually direct and to the point, had hem-hawed like a tongue-tied idiot. But he wasn't about to admit Cairo Calhoun had caught his fancy and that she stood like a wall between him and Molly. Nobody would have believed it. The whole community had Lawton pegged as a dedicated bachelor who wanted no complications with women.

Tearfully, Molly peered up at the muscular hunk of man who stared over her head and out the front door. "Lawton, I know you don't love me, but you know how I feel about you. Don't you find me physically attractive anymore? Did I do something to displease you? If I did, tell me what it was and I won't do it again."

Lawton winced. He wasn't accustomed to any kind of emotional scene with Molly. She understood him as well as any woman did and had accepted him for what he was. She was convenient for him—an outlet for physical pleasure with no ties to bind. Still, Lawton hadn't wanted to hurt Molly. She was a good woman.

Molly's hand folded around his, giving it an affectionate squeeze. "Can we start all over when you get back?"

If he got back, he silently corrected her. Fool that he

was, he was riding into the valley of death with the witch who'd lured him into her potent spell. And that witch was waiting outside his door. And the damnedest part of all was that he was actually anxious to see her. God have mercy on his soul!

"I'll see you . . . when I get back," Lawton mumbled as he grabbed his hat and strode toward the door.

Lawton stopped short when he spied Cairo garbed in breeches and a shirt that complemented all her alluring assets. Yet, what really baffled him was seeing her sitting atop a small-size pinto pony like a duck on a nest. Encircling the saddle and concealing it completely, was a menagerie of unnecessary supplies. The saddle weighed about fifty pounds, the lady one hundred, and her ridiculous pile of "necessaries" must have burdened down the pinto with another hundred pounds. Lawton couldn't fathom what kept the poor pony from collapsing beneath its excessive load.

"What the sweet loving hell is all that stuff?" he asked incredulously.

Cairo's greeting smile slid off her lips when she noticed the comely brunette peering around Lawton's broad shoulders. It only took an instant for Cairo to deduce what the woman was doing in Lawton's cottage. He, after all, had only one use for women. Curse his granite heart!

Casting the twinge of jealousy aside, Cairo patted the heaping stack of supplies surrounding her. "These are my necessities," she announced. "Even though I am traipsing across the frontier, I still intend to enjoy a few conveniences."

"A few?" Lawton hooted. "What the hell did you do? Disassemble the hotel and pack it on your pinto? You'll break his back with all that junk!"

Having Lawton scold her like a witless child in front of his paramour was more than Cairo could bear. Her chin jutted out and her emerald eyes flashed hot sparks. "If such a disaster occurs, Mr. Stone, then I will lug my supplies on my back," she snapped. "You are being paid to guide me to Oklahoma, not lecture me!"

Molly stared at the shapely young woman who dared to defy Lawton. Her gaze swung to Lawton, watching him watch the sassy beauty. What she and Lawton had shared was over, Molly realized. The way Lawton was looking at the pretty blonde told Molly all she needed to know.

When Molly cast her a rueful smile, nodded a silent greeting, and scurried down the street, Cairo stared after her. "It seems you found something else to do last night after you finished badgering me."

Nothing had happened between him and Molly, but Lawton wasn't about to let Cairo have the satisfaction of knowing that. "Jealous, Cleopatra?" he drawled as he walked off the porch.

Anger splotched her cheeks. "I'm thankful it was her instead of me," she countered haughtily. "You probably have all the sensitivity of a foul-tempered wolverine when it comes to bedding women."

His mouth quirked in sardonic amusement. "Wouldn't you like to know."

Another crimson blush stained her face. Cairo would have leaped off her steed and clobbered him if it hadn't been so difficult to untangle herself from the mound of supplies. Instead, she pelleted him with a barrage of rapid-fire insults. "I'm positively certain that when the Lord was passing out the milk of human kindness, Mr. Stone, you were standing in line with a teaspoon. And how you have prevented developing a backache from carrying around that stupendous male pride of yours I'll never know! If you think for one minute that I have any inclination of winding up in your bed, you have deceived yourself. I'd rather be whipped!"

What a temper this vixen had! And what a way she had with words. With her quick wit and rapier tongue, she could slash a lesser man to shreds. Luckily, Lawton's hide was thick, a result of deflecting the scores of curses directed at him by the criminals he'd apprehended.

The jingle of bridles and the clomp of hooves drew Lawton's attention. He swiveled his head around to see Tucker McGuire and Woodward Hall approaching, a few saddlebags and knapsacks loaded on their mounts.

Tucker tipped his hat to Cairo and then slid Lawton a glance. "Hope you don't mind if Woody and I accompany you part of the way," he began as he shifted in the saddle. "Marshal Hendrick was supposed to ride up to Tulsey Town to collect a couple of horse thieves who were arrested by the Indian police patrol. But since Hendrick's missus is expecting her first baby any day, we volunteered to take his place."

"A likely excuse," Lawton snorted.

He wasn't fooled for a minute. Woody and Tuck were afraid Lawton was riding into a trap and they had grabbed the first plausible reason to ride with him.

"It won't throw a wrench in your plans if we travel with Tuck and Woody, will it, Cleopatra?" Lawton inquired, trying to gauge her reaction to the news.

"I welcome the company," Cairo declared, miffed by Lawton's sarcastic question. "Why would I care if I have the protection of two extra marshals?"

"Why indeed," Lawton mumbled. Maybe she wasn't

the Snowbird. She certainly didn't seem disappointed by the change in plans.

Thoughts of Cairo's innocence quickly transformed into guilt when he spied the bouquet of flowers she had wrapped in wet rags to preserve them as long as possible.

"Taking those to somebody's funeral?" he scowled at her.

His reaction to the roses was small consolation, even though Cairo still didn't know why the bouquet upset him. But she was glad it did. He constantly upset *her*.

"They are for your funeral," she sassed. "At least they will be if you don't stop being so snide and sarcastic."

The remark earned her Woody and Tucker's suspicious glances, but Cairo didn't notice. She had already flung her nose in the air, presented Lawton with a cold shoulder, and ridden off.

"All I can say is that you're lucky we're going with you," Tucker muttered to Lawton. "I'm afraid you're right about that female."

Lawton was afraid he was right, too.

They hadn't even made it through town before Lawton called a halt in front of the livery stable. Despite Cairo's protests, she was dragged from the saddle. Without ado, Lawton swapped the pony for a taller, sturdier horse that could handle her load of supplies. His ulterior motive was to discard the colorful pinto, just in case it was to be a signal to the Gardiner gang that the Snowbird was on her way with her victim in tow.

Lawton became suspicious again when the hotel

clerk, with his coattails flapping behind him, came scurrying down the street waving his arms in exaggerated gestures.

"Miss Calhoun!" he shouted breathlessly. "This note arrived after you left this morning."

Lawton would have given his right arm to know what it said and who sent it. The Gardiners, he imagined. He shuddered to think what fiendish torment the Snowbird and her passel of renegades had in store for him.

Having seen the thunderous scowl on Lawton's face, Cairo proceeded to tear the message into tiny pieces which flitted off in the wind. It pleased her no end that Lawton was irked by not knowing what was going on. Just to frustrate him, she refused to let him read the note or to reveal its contents. She hoped his curiosity killed him, bit by agonizing bit.

"What was that all about, Cleopatra?" Lawton demanded.

Cairo settled herself inside the mound of supplies that was perched atop the chestnut gelding. "A private matter," she replied belatedly. "Nothing for you to fret over, Mr. Stone."

"The name's Lawton," he corrected grouchily.

"A rock's a rock, no matter what name you give it," she said before tossing her head and reining down the street.

Lawton clamped his mouth shut and then was forced to open it to emit an annoyed growl when he heard Woody and Tucker snickering in amusement. "What's so damned funny?"

Both men grinned at him.

"Saucy little thing, isn't she?" Tucker's gaze followed the shapely blonde in breeches.

Lawton didn't reply. He gouged his steed and rode off.

Damn that woman. She must stay up nights, inventing new ways to get under his skin. She was the Snowbird, all right, Lawton convinced himself. She had received another secret message from her cohorts. Their plan had been set into motion, but Lawton would be damned if he fell into her trap! She was going to be his bait and his ticket to safety. The Gardiners weren't dealing with any greenhorn marshal who didn't know beans about protecting himself! They would have one helluva fight on their hands when they tried to dispose of him.

The first day of travel was not eventful, which didn't really surprise Lawton. He knew the Gardiners were biding their time, waiting for him to let his guard down. But Lawton refused to do that. He kept one eye trained on his surroundings, one on Cairo, and one hand resting on his holster. When the attack came, he would be prepared.

Day two was a repetition of day one. Nothing out of the ordinary occurred, except that Woody spent more and more time at Cairo's side, indulging in idle conversation. The poor man was becoming infatuated. Woody knew Cairo was as deadly as a loaded rifle, but he was still a sucker for a pretty face and a curvaceous figure.

Each time the foursome stopped to make camp, Cairo dragged out all her "necessities" for cooking and cleaning. She carried more pots and pans than a peddler and had equipped herself with more herbs, spices, and staples than a merchant boat from China. She also had enough clothing to change twice a day without having to do laundry for a week! She called it *necessity;* Lawton called it *extravagance.*

Despite her idiosyncrasies and her constant attempt to needle him, Lawton found his gaze straying to her at regular intervals.

Lawton could see Tucker and Woody becoming more and more entranced by her, too. They had let their guards down completely. They had convinced themselves that Cairo Calhoun wasn't the Snowbird.

Another of her clever ploys, thought Lawton as he whittled on a stick, his habit when he paused for the night.

"I'm going down to the stream to bathe," Cairo announced as she gathered her soap, towel, perfume and only God knew what else she had stashed in her knapsack of bathing "essentials."

Automatically, Lawton got to his feet to accompany her, but Woody grabbed his arm to detain him.

"I'll go," he volunteered enthusiastically. His hawkish gaze homed in on Cairo's shapely backside as she walked away. "We don't want you off by yourself . . . just in case the Gardiners decide to strike."

If Woody was expecting the Gardiners, Lawton would eat his hat, rattlesnake band and all! Woody had already decided Cairo was innocent. All he wanted was to spy on her while she was bathing stark-bone naked in the stream.

"I'm going," Lawton declared, his tone brooking no argument. "I'm the one who's getting paid two hundred dollars to ensure she doesn't meet with trouble."

"Hell, I'll take her to Oklahoma for free," Woody

insisted. "Lord, Law, isn't she the prettiest thing you've ever seen in all your life?"

Lawton rolled his eyes heavenward and sighed audibly. "Here, whittle yourself up a sweet dream to occupy you." He thrust his carved stick at the starry-eyed marshal. To his horror, he realized that he had unthinkingly whittled the figure of a woman who was every bit as shapely as Cairo. To his further mortification, Woody noticed, too.

Snickering, Woody rolled the figurine over in the palm of his hand. "A dandy likeness of her, Law," he teasingly complimented. "I never thought I'd see the day you fantasized about a woman. I didn't think females had any effect on you. I guess I was wrong."

Lawton snatched the tiny figurine away and snapped it in two. He stomped off in the direction Cairo had taken. It was bad enough that he had envisioned that treacherous minx in the altogether a zillion times, but to carve her delicious figure from a scrap of wood? Double, triple damn!

Cairo sank into the glittering stream. Although the water was a tad chilly, it was a refreshing change from the endless hours in the saddle. She also welcomed the privacy. It had been two days since she had been alone with her own thoughts.

Tucker and Woody had proved to be delightful company and they had entertained her with adventurous tales of their experiences in the Twin Territories, but Cairo needed solitude to sort out the myriad of emotions that had plagued her.

A dozen times a day, she found her mind and eyes straying to the muscular man who rode behind her, singing "Skip to My Lou." They seldom spoke unless absolutely necessary and never without the company of the other two marshals. She never thought she'd miss the snappy repartee that sharpened her wits and set fuse to her temper, but she did. Lawton Stone was stimulating in more ways than one. Yet, it was probably for the best that they were allowed no privacy to squabble and test their phenomenal physical reaction to each other.

Cairo squelched the warm tingles evoked by thoughts of Lawton's arousing kisses and caresses. There would be no more of that! she told herself fiercely. She'd suffered a temporary lapse of sanity, that was all. But now she would take herself in hand and put her emotions on an even keel permanently. Lawton Stone, Cairo begrudgingly admitted, was more man than she could handle. She wasn't going to complicate her life with silly romantic fascinations and wanton feminine curiosity. She and Lawton had shared a few fiery kisses and bold caresses, but that was the beginning and end of it.

Resigned, Cairo eased onto her stomach and glided across the creek. She marveled at the array of twinkling stars that seemed to be just beyond arm's reach. The Indian moon hung on the eastern horizon like a gigantic orange ball, preparing to make its ascent across the evening sky. Cairo absorbed the beauty of her surroundings and assured herself that she needed nothing more than nature's shadowed beauty and peaceful solitude. This restless need inside her would subside . . . eventually. Cairo was far too stubborn to identify the source of that need for fear it had a certain U.S. marshal's name attached to it!

* * *

Maybe Cairo had refused to admit who had caused the gnawing hunger inside her, but Lawton, at that very moment, was walking directly toward the source of his frustration. That sassy hellion had become like an itch he couldn't quite reach to scratch. Again he cautioned himself that Cairo's most compelling lure was also his greatest threat. He couldn't become emotionally involved with potential disaster.

Lawton braved a glance toward the stream when he heard a splash. Through the low-hanging branches of the trees, he could see the moonlight skipping over the water, randomly spotlighting objects until it came to rest on the gorgeous blonde in midstream. He could see Cairo gliding like a graceful swan in a river of sparkling silver, and it was a full two minutes before he could breathe normally. Any of his imaginings of her didn't compare to seeing her in the flesh! Her bare back and curvaceous hips were revealed in the silvery light as she floated beneath the dome of stars. A banner of blond hair drifted around her, reminding Lawton of a mermaid frolicking in the sea.

When Cairo rolled to her back, Lawton had to sit down before he fell down. Her moon-drenched body enthralled him. Diamond droplets sparkled on the full swells of her breasts and danced on her bare shoulders and slender arms.

Lord, he ached all over! He was punishing himself by enduring this sweet torture, but he couldn't drag his eyes off the luscious nymph to save his soul. He yearned to caress her, just as the moonlight did.

She couldn't possibly be the Snowbird, Lawton tried

to convince himself. No, a woman this gorgeous, this entrancing, couldn't be a bandit. He was simply mistaken about her identity and forced himself to believe the worst about her. He had treated her abominably because he was afraid to trust her, and more specifically, afraid to trust himself when he was so fiercely attracted to her.

Cairo Calhoun was just a bewitching young woman who had inadvertently walked into his life at a time when his mind was drowning in suspicion. She had no evil designs on him. She was simply battling this frustrating attraction, the same as he was. He had seen it in her emerald eyes each time she spared him a glance. She, like he, resented the sparks that flew when their gazes locked, when their bodies touched.

Lost in steamy fantasies, Lawton rose to his feet. He disengaged himself from the shadows and moved silently forward. Aroused by his luscious thoughts, he peeled off his gunbelts and clothes as he went. Try as he might, he couldn't shake the sensual and very vivid vision of taking Cairo in his arms.

Lawton glided across the water, his unblinking gaze focused on the lovely sprite who had dived beneath the surface, eluding him again.

When Cairo burst to the surface to inhale a breath of air, Lawton was standing chest-deep in the water, awaiting her. He felt her lure and it was all he could do to prevent pouncing on her.

Cairo gasped when she raked her waist-length hair away from her face to see the virile form of the man who stood a mere two feet away from her. Her eyes met those shimmering mercury pools and all her determination to avoid Lawton like the plague washed downstream. There was something in the way he stared at her that transformed her into a quivering jellyfish. Common sense cautioned her to back away and a dozen protests whizzed through her mind. But no words formed on her lips when his gaze wandered over her, making her tremble just as surely as if he had reached out to caress her.

"I want you, Cai." The passion in his voice sent Cairo's senses whirling like a carousel.

She felt his arm steal around her waist, drawing her body into intimate contact with his. As if he were silently making up for all the harsh words and biting insults he'd flung at her, Lawton held her tenderly in his arms. His silver eyes focused intently on her lips, fascinated by them. His head moved deliberately toward hers, seeking out her mouth, anxious to savor the sweet taste of her.

Again common sense made a valiant attempt to rescue her. Cairo heeded the warning signals and attempted to pull away.

"Don't go," he implored. His hands began to move of their own accord, massaging away the apprehension in her body.

Cairo braced her arms against his chest before he could tug her back into her arms and all would be lost, but even that was a critical mistake! The palms of her hands itched to measure his whipcord muscles, to explore his masculine contours.

Battling for composure, Cairo tilted her chin to meet those hungry silver eyes that devoured her with fierce intensity. "You don't want me," she contradicted, her voice quavering with the shock waves caused from being so close to temptation. "Any woman would satisfy you. I don't want to be the time you're killing, your object of lustful pleasure. I have much more respect for myself than that!"

He smiled tenderly as he slowly shook his head. "No, Cai. You're mistaken. You're the one I've wanted since the moment I laid eyes on you. I couldn't even bear to touch Molly Herman because she wasn't you."

When Cairo felt his arms tighten around her, tantalizing sensations crippled her mind and body. She forgot how to breathe, how to think. She found herself teetering on the edge of total abandon. When he touched her, her bones turned to liquid and her flesh to steam.

A soft moan broke from her throat when he fitted her petite body to his, caressing her breasts with his hair-roughened chest. The sheer impact of his flesh gliding against hers sparked a sultry flame. Reflexively, her arms glided over his muscular shoulders. His hips moved suggestively toward hers, and Cairo was bewildered and apprehensive. The potent force of this strong, virile man seemed to absorb her flesh and her will.

It had only been three days since she'd felt his hands discovering the most sensitive points of her flesh, since she'd felt his masterful kisses carrying her away from reality, but it seemed like an eternity. And yet, he had never held her quite like this, looked at her in such disturbing ways!

Why he appealed to her was no longer important, only that *he did* appeal to her in a way no other man ever had. Despite their bickering and mutual taunts, Cario suddenly wanted no more than this magnificent man could give. She was prepared to offer him what he wanted—anything to make this gnawing ache go away.

His slow explorations and sensual touch caused a sigh of pleasure to burst from her lips. His skillful hands swam over her flesh, learning more about her than Cairo knew about herself. She reveled in the feel of his warm lips coasting over her shoulder to tease the rosy peaks of her breasts. She thrilled to the feel of his caresses wandering to and fro, teaching her things she had never known about the magic of passion.

Cairo needed to return the exquisite pleasure that ribboned through her. Eagerly, she investigated the muscular planes and rock-hard columns of his body, igniting a fire in him that all the water in the rivulet couldn't begin to cool.

It shocked Lawton to realize that her caresses could so easily demolish his self-control. Making love to Cairo would be a deliriously wonderful experience, he was sure of it. But just touching her and kissing her seemed as vital to him as taking complete possession of her.

For the first time in his life he was vividly aware of the woman in his arms, aware of her needs as well as his own. Cairo wasn't just the object of his masculine desires, as she claimed. God, Lawton wished that was all she was! The truth was that this emerald-eyed tigress was the one woman who had the power to turn him wrong side out. She exposed the emotions that he concealed from the rest of the world. She caused a hot, sweet ache to pulsate through the core of his being, demanding more than physical satisfaction. His need for her seemed to penetrate the very foundations of his soul!

Inhaling a ragged breath, Lawton scooped Cairo

into his arms and carried her to the opposite bank. On bended knee he laid her down in the grass. His gaze glided over her, marveling at her exceptional beauty, at the divine sensations that merely staring at her evoked from him.

"I've never in all my life seen anything so exquisite," he whispered as his index finger trailed over the thrusting tip of her breast. His worshiping caress tracked along her ribs to the trim indentation of her waist. "The mere sight of you takes my breath away."

Compliments and confessions from Lawton Stone were rare. He was not a man who was easily moved or impressed. And even when he was, he didn't usually admit it. But the alluring sight of Cairo's curvaceous body sparkling with water droplets in the moonlight caused the words to flow from his lips.

Cairo felt a smile tugging at the corners of her mouth when Lawton peered down at her as if she were a treasured portrait that demanded his absolute attention. Any modesty had abandoned her. She adored having his eyes on her, his hands, his lips, and she delighted in studying him as blatantly as he studied her. She couldn't have dragged her gaze away from him, even if her life depended on it.

He was, she thought, the most incredible specimen of masculinity this side of heaven. She couldn't conjure up the vision of another man who could match him. Even the Greek gods were left standing humbly in his shadow.

Cairo had avoided any intimacy with men, assuring herself that she required no more than a man's companionship and conversation, but she wondered if she had deluded herself in thinking she was immune to passion. Or perhaps it was just that this enigmatic man was the only one who could awaken her desires and leave her trembling in eager expectation. It was as if she had been waiting all her life for him to come along and show her what she had been missing, to unlock the powerful emotions that lay deep inside her.

When his muscular leg glided between hers, Cairo felt a flood of pleasure gush through her. When his lips slanted over hers, she closed her eyes and mind to all except the raging need that consumed her. She felt his presence above her, beside her. She reached up to him, pulling him ever closer, wanting to satisfy this craving that tore at the very roots of her sanity.

His hands whispered across her flesh, acquainting himself with each sensitive point on her body. His languid caresses were embroidered with a surprising gentleness. He was doing the most wondrous things to her and she felt as pliant as bread dough beneath his questing hands.

When his butterfly caresses feathered over her abdomen to the silky flesh of her thighs, Cairo gulped air. Her nerves hummed; her muscles quivered. She was apprehensive of what was to come and yet unable to prevent him from doing whatever it was he intended to do to her.

His fingertips delved deeper, teasing and arousing her until she swore she was on fire. Cairo gasped at the pulsating needs that surged through every fiber of her being. With each skillful stroke of his hands Cairo felt the intense cravings multiply. And if his intimate caresses were not enough to drive her over the edge, his lips drifted over the rigid peaks of her breasts, leaving her throbbing in sweet, maddening torment.

"Lawton?" His name tumbled from her lips in a helpless whimper. Her naive body arched toward his, seeking an end to the torture of having him so close and yet so frustratingly far away.

It gave him immense satisfaction to know he had made this rebellious beauty want him as desperately as he wanted her. He had never been so gentle, so patient, with a woman before. And it mattered more than it should have that she was as eager to fulfill this monstrous need as he was.

When Cairo clutched at him, his body settled exactly over hers. A sharp stab of pain caused her to flinch involuntarily. Panic invaded the hazy world of pleasure, compelling her to push him away. Her eyes flew open to see Lawton staring down at her with a mixture of hunger and surprise.

He gently withdrew from her body. With patient tenderness, he moved toward her once again, whispering words of reassurance, promising pleasures that would overshadow the initial pain he'd caused her.

Cairo felt her body melt into his. Hypnotized by his coaxing words and titillating caresses, she surrendered to the warm tide of rapture that flooded through her. And suddenly she felt no pain, only a wild, compelling need that assumed control of her mind and body. She was matching his rhythm, feeling the mounting sensations swell until she feared they would burst. Cairo had become a wild thing in his arms, arching in urgent response to the demands of ecstasy. She felt as if she were reaching upward to grasp some mysteriously wonderful sensation that remained beyond her understanding.

And then she was there, beyond the moon, falling

through time and space. She was assaulted by the most phenomenal sensations imaginable. They rocked her very soul and put a cry of disbelief on her lips. Breathlessly, she clung to Lawton, afraid to let go of the one lifeline in a rapidly revolving universe of previously unexplored sensations.

When Lawton's body surged and shuddered upon hers, Cairo experienced a strangely satisfying brand of fulfillment. It seemed to take forever to return to reality. But she didn't care if she remained lost in this mystifying dimension of time. She had discovered bliss in the circle of Lawton's arms. If this wasn't heaven itself, Cairo was certain it was an incredible likeness to paradise.

Still weak from the devastating pleasures that numbed his mind and body, Lawton struggled to brace himself up on his forearms. His gaze dropped to Cairo's face and then slid over the silver-blond tendrils that sprayed around her. She was everything he'd expected and so much more, he thought shakily.

Cairo Calhoun definitely wasn't the Gardiner gang's paramour. He knew he had been this witch-angel's first man and that brought him immense satisfaction. The pleasure they'd shared beneath the sea of stars was incomparable. Whatever pleasure he'd experienced with other women was nowhere near what he'd felt when he made love to this enchantress. Even in her innocence, she had taught him things he hadn't known about desire. And here he thought he knew it all! She left him grappling with lingering sensations that truly astonished him.

Absently, Lawton combed his fingers through the silken tresses that sparkled like moonbeams and starlight. For the first time in his stormy relationship with Cairo he didn't feel belligerent, suspicious, or defensive. He didn't care that she knew how he reveled in loving her or that he took pride in being the man who introduced her to the magic of passion.

Cairo had forced him to reevaluate a few of his cynical opinions pertaining to women. She had sent his long-held theories into orbit, giving him a new perspective of life.

Cairo smiled as she traced the tiny lines that fanned from the corner of those mercury eyes that were surrounded with a thick fan of black lashes. Even in the aftermath of love Cairo wasn't certain what had caused the abrupt change between them. It boggled the mind!

She watched her hand drift over his broad shoulder to encircle his male nipple, adoring the feel of his hard flesh beneath her inquiring hand. Tonight Cairo had encountered a very different man than the one she thought she knew. Lawton hadn't taken from her; he'd given freely of himself. He had displayed a tenderness and sensitivity that had entranced her and left her helplessly responsive to his masterful touch.

That night in her hotel room had only hinted at the explosive reactions they set off in each other. It was as if the sultry spark transformed Lawton from a cynical, hard-bitten pistolero into a tender, sensitive lover. That mystical spark had also changed Cairo from a reserved lady into a receptive wanton!

Although Lawton could cut her to the quick with his razor-sharp tongue and demolish her pride with his penetrating barbs, he could also devastate her defenses with his loving touch. The moment he set his skillful hands upon her, she dissolved like snow in a blazing campfire. She and Lawton were not the same two people in private as they were in public. It left Cairo to wonder which personality reflected *her* true self and which man was the *real* Lawton Stone.

Cairo still wasn't certain Lawton would ever let a woman close enough to truly know and understand him. He seemed determined to keep her guessing, to keep her wondering what was running through his mind. Lawton was a baffling enigma—tough yet tender, fierce and domineering and sometimes incredibly receptive to her needs. Was he the man he had become in private because of *her* influence on him? Was *she* what Lawton transformed her into when he captured her in his arms?

It truly amazed Cairo that Lawton had allowed her to view this side of his personality . . . Or was it only a cunning charade? Was this beguiling transformation no more than a ploy to buckle her defenses in order to appease his male lust? Or could it be that Lawton truly felt something special for her that triggered emotions he kept buried deep inside him?

If only she knew for certain if this intriguing man was toying with her! And oh how she wished she could explain why she responded to him in so special and potent a manner! Was this passionate interlude the beginning of something magical between them or simply the appeasement of biological needs? She was so confused. Sometimes he seemed so close to her that he shared her very soul and other times he seemed an entire universe away!

"I didn't think you liked me very much," she murmured softly. "Now I'm not certain what to think."

A peal of laughter rippled through the air. "It seems

you've begun to grow on me, little minx," Lawton confessed before dropping a kiss to her lips. "Either that or I refused to admit that you had some magical hold on me all this time."

"And I must have liked you better than I knew. Or perhaps the truth is, I was afraid to discover *how much* I did like you." Cairo blushed at her own admission. It wasn't like her to hand out compliments, either. She, like Lawton, had always been difficult to impress and hard to please.

"Do you, Cai?" A slight frown creased his brow. Hesitantly, he trailed his forefinger over her cheeks. "Do you like me, I mean . . . ?"

Her arms slid over his granite shoulders, drawing his lips back to hers. She was surprised that he needed her reassurance. "I do, Lawton," she whispered against his lips. "I never dreamed it would be like this . . . with you . . ."

Lawton felt a sliver of suspicion. For a half-second, he found himself trying to read between the lines of her throaty confession, wondering exactly what she meant. But the feel of her pliant body beneath his smothered the lingering doubts temporarily. He didn't want to analyze this lovely creature, only to love her as long as the splendorous moment would last.

Slowly, reality was beginning to invade her foggy senses. "I'll probably live to regret this, and—"

His hand curled beneath her chin, forcing her to meet his level gaze. "*I* have no regrets, sweet witch," he rasped. His free hand mapped the silken curves of her body, reigniting the fires that had consumed them both. "What I have, instead, is this wild need to make love to you all over again . . ."

Lawton swore he had developed an addiction to this temptress. One kiss and he wanted her like hell on fire. One caress and he blazed like a human torch. Again he felt his body crying out to hers, longing for her to appease the burgeoning needs that threatened his sanity. He had given part of himself away when he first made love to her. Another corner of his heart crumbled when her untutored hands and lips sought to memorize his body by taste and touch.

He didn't care that Tucker and Woody were probably speculating on why it had taken Cairo so long to bathe. He could tolerate their taunts and snickers because he knew both his companions would have given anything to exchange places with him. But he alone had taken intimate possession of her luscious body and now she belonged to him. Lawton had never felt as if anything or anyone ever truly belonged to him before in his life. Knowing that he had taught Cairo about passion left him with an unfamiliar need to protect and preserve this bewitching nymph who had become a woman in his arms.

The thought of another man discovering all Cairo's charms bothered him. Lawton had never been a jealous person, but his new sense of possessiveness had taught him the meaning of the word. In fact, he was learning a lot of things he hadn't known about himself until Cairo came into his life.

That was the last sane thought to trickle through his mind before passion engulfed him again, catapulting him into a sensual world that defied rhyme and reason.

Chapter Seven

Tucker's grin was as wide as Indian Territory. So was Woody's. It was damned difficult for Lawton to amble back to camp and plunk down by the campfire as if nothing out of the ordinary had happened.

Feeling every bit as awkward, Cairo returned a few minutes after Lawton. Once the spell of passion had shattered and she had returned to her senses, feelings of shame had overcome her. The tenderness between her thighs was a constant reminder of her moonlight tryst with Lawton and guilt stabbed at her conscience like cactus needles. She, who had cautioned her female students to guard themselves against the lusts of men, had succumbed to the desires of her body. And the worst part of all was that she had surrendered to a man with eyes of granite, a heart chiseled from solid rock—a man of stone! Curse it, she seemed to have lost all her common sense. He had offered her no promises other than the pleasures of the moment. She was a tainted woman and an even bigger fool!

With humiliation staining her cheeks, Cairo busied

herself by repacking her supplies. She had managed to cast Woody and Tucker a faint smile, but she could feel their eyes on her, feel the waves of speculation that undulated through the air.

Cairo didn't dare spare the marshals another glance for fear they would look at her and realize she wasn't the same woman who had wandered off to the stream to bathe. Lawton had changed her forever and Cairo feared her body would reveal the effervescent glow caused by his ardent lovemaking.

"Mighty long bath," Tucker snickered to Lawton as he eased his head back against the saddle which served as his makeshift pillow.

"Mighty long indeed," Woody chimed in before sipping his coffee.

Lawton grimaced and then shrugged. "If she wanted to soak half the night away," he defended as he stared into his coffee cup, "that's her business."

"I'll just *bet* that bathing was all she's been doing," Tucker mocked. He flung Lawton a knowing glance. "Well, so much for the man with the will of iron and nerves of steel."

"Lay off, Tuck," Lawton muttered.

"Yeah, lay off, Tuck," Woody chortled. "Law just discovered women! Isn't it amazing how one special one can make such a difference to him?"

Lawton took his coffee and stalked into the shadows. He didn't want his ornery friends spoiling his memories. His partners were making a mockery of what he and Cairo had shared.

"Well now, since all you and I will be getting tonight is sleep, Woody, we may as well start," Tucker taunted as he rose to tether the horses, purposely veering toward Lawton. "And some of us probably won't sleep as well as others of us." He paused beside his brooding friend. "One thing good has come of this, Law. At least we can part company tomorrow and Woody and I won't have to worry about you. It doesn't appear that the Snowbird is out to trap you after all." Tucker gouged Lawton with his elbow. "Found a woman who changed your tune, didn't you, Law?"

"Don't you ever shut up?" Lawton growled.

"Nope," Tucker replied unrepentantly. "This is the most fun I've had in years—watching you buckle to a woman's charms. Damned gratifying to know you're human like the rest of us. For a while there, I was beginning to believe that legend about the invincible Lawton Stone."

Lawton sighed as Tucker walked away. He supposed this was his own fault. If he'd had any self-control at all, he wouldn't have left himself open to this kind of badgering.

A smile hovered on his lips as his eyes darted toward Cairo. He silently reminded himself that what they'd shared was worth the needling. He could feel his heart whispering Cairo's name. She had begun to earn his trust. The cloud of doubt that fogged his mind was drifting away. Whoever the Snowbird was, she wasn't the same intriguing woman who inflamed Lawton. Thank God for that! At least now he didn't feel like such a fool for wanting a woman who carried a death threat with his name written on it.

When Cairo wheeled around to grab her bedroll, the moonlight caught in her long blond mane, and the past suddenly collided with the present. The picture Cairo presented reminded Lawton of that night a year ago when he'd seen the mysterious female flying across the prairie with her band of renegades.

A smidgen of suspicion sprang back into Lawton's mind, but he pushed it away. He was going to force himself to believe the best instead of the worst about Cairo. After all, she was innocent until proven guilty, he reminded himself.

Tucker tipped his hat and smiled at Cairo. "It's been a pleasure sharing your company the past few days, ma'am," he declared with genuine sincerity.

Woody seconded that compliment before he swung into the saddle. His gaze darted to Lawton who had busied himself by piling part of Cairo's "necessities" on the back of his stallion. "Now you take good care of the lady, Law," he instructed. "Tucker and I wouldn't want to see anything happen to her."

Woody stared meaningfully at Lawton. "Tuck and I will find out what we can about . . . those renegades . . . we were trailing."

"If we have any news, we'll telegraph you at Webbers Falls," Tucker added.

Lawton nodded, knowing exactly what Woody had insinuated when he referred to "those renegades." Because of the dangers the marshals constantly faced, they had by necessity become suspicious and cautious. Although Tucker and Woody were convinced that Cairo wasn't the Snowbird, they were still careful about divulging information to anyone except each other.

When Tucker and Woody aimed themselves toward Salisaw to load their horses in a box car and make use of the train to reach their destination, Lawton nudged his steed due west. His gaze drifted skyward, studying the patch of clouds that had begun to pile up on the horizon like a mound of cotton.

A feeling of impending doom slithered down his spine, but he shrugged it away. Storm clouds were gathering on the horizon. Not that Lawton was the superstitious type, but he couldn't quite shake the feeling of trouble ahead that the weather seemed to portend. And although Lawton constantly assured himself that Cairo was innocent, the skeptical side of his nature refused to trust her completely.

He was tired of wavering back and forth between desire and doubt. He'd no sooner tell himself she was innocent than a suspicious voice inside himself whispered: *But what if she isn't?*

"Lawton? Tell me about yourself," Cairo requested, easing her chestnut gelding up beside his sleek black stallion. A faint blush crept to her cheeks. "Considering the things I do know about you, I know nothing of your past."

"Does it matter so much?" he questioned before ducking beneath a low-hanging branch that sought to snare him.

Cairo frowned. The previous night he had been warm, tender, and loving. But in the light of day he was as quiet and cautious as he'd always been. Cairo sorely resented it. His standoffish attitude made her feel ashamed and unwanted all over again.

"I didn't ask you to recite all the details of your wayward youth," she muttered in annoyance. "I was only curious about your place of birth and your background."

"You haven't volunteered any information about yourself, either," he pointed out.

"You could have asked," she snapped, and then sighed in exasperation. Why was he always picking fights with her? He put her on immediate defense. Because of her volatile temper, they always wound up in shouting matches. "Curse it, Lawton, what's the matter with you? I'm only trying to pass the time of day. Would you prefer that I keep my mouth shut and left you alone with your precious private thoughts?"

Silver eyes regarded her from beneath the brim of his hat. It took only one look at her face to cause the wall of ice around his heart to thaw once again. "I was born in Texas—if it matters so much," he elaborated. "I grew up on a farm until my—" He stared at the skirting of trees that lined the Canadian River. "I joined the cavalry when I was eighteen to battle the Kiowas and Comanches. Then, upon recommendation from my superior, Major Derrick Wright, I was chosen to ride with the Texas Rangers. A few years back, Judge Parker called me to service as a U.S. marshal. Since then I have served double and triple duty for Parker, the Rangers, and the courts of Oklahoma Territory."

Cairo frowned. From the sound of things, there were scores of various influences that had shaped Lawton Stone. He had been fighting everybody's battles most of his life. And what was very strange to her, he had avoided making reference to his family. Cairo was curious to know why.

"Are your parents still in Texas?" she prodded.

"Nope."

"Well? Where are they?" she wanted to know.

"What in hell is this? A cross-examination in a court

of law?" he grunted sarcastically.

"If you don't want to discuss your family, why don't you just say so?" Cairo all but yelled at him.

The man was making her crazy! Just when she thought she was beginning to know him, he crawled back into his shell. She wondered if she would ever understand Lawton Stone.

"I don't want to discuss my family," he declared with finality.

"Fine. I couldn't care less," she said flippantly.

"So . . . what about you?" He flung her a probing glance.

If he wouldn't reveal much about his past, then neither would she. She could be just as stubborn and contrary . . .

It suddenly occurred to Cairo that she wanted to make more of their amorous encounter than Lawton. This was his way of informing her that he wanted only her body and only when the mood suited him, that he wanted no lasting ties.

Silly fool! Cairo scolded herself. Did she think just because he had made love to her that it made a difference in their relationship? All his flattering confessions the previous night had been a ploy to get what he wanted, she realized. How could she have forgotten Lawton's low opinion of women? Nothing had changed . . . except that they'd been as close as two people could get for one night. Their intimacy had begun and ended when the lovemaking was over, and that's the way Lawton wanted it.

It stung Cairo's pride to realize that she wanted the affection Lawton was clearly capable of but that he offered it only in sparing amounts.

"I asked you a question," Lawton reminded her before the grumble of thunder shook the earth.

Cairo glanced skyward. "Maybe it will rain. We definitely could use some. This prairie grass is as dry as kindling."

Lawton stared at her long and hard. "Is there some reason why you don't want to discuss your past?" he prodded, giving way to that old familiar suspicion. "Is there something you don't want me to know about you?" Indubitably!

No answer, only another fierce clap of thunder. A gust of wind swept across the plains. The knee-deep grass rustled and the crisp autumn leaves rattled in the trees before they shook loose and danced across the ground.

Cairo clamped down on her hat, which was ready to fly off her head. The chestnut gelding shifted uneasily beneath her. Its nostrils flared to inhale the scent of rain and the steed nervously rolled the bit in its teeth.

"Whoa, boy," Cairo soothed her flighty mount.

The animal was wary of storms and didn't "whoa" at her command. When a lightning bolt flashed across the sky, the steed hightailed it for cover. Cairo felt as if her head had snapped off her shoulders when the frightened gelding plunged forward into a dead run. She considered herself a competent rider, but then, she had never been forced to cope with a runaway horse on an open prairie during a thunderstorm!

Stark fear shot through Cairo as her steed lunged through the sea of waving grass. Cairo knew that any second the spooked animal would step into an unseen hole and catapult her through the air and that would be the end of her.

The instant she clamped both hands on the reins and yanked back, her hat went sailing in the wind, but her effort to control the wild-eyed steed was in vain. Thunder boomed directly above them and the gelding ran hell-for-leather.

Lawton's heart slammed against his ribs as he watched Cairo unsuccessfully battle for control of her mount. Although he was in hot pursuit, fear had put wings on her mount's hooves and the gelding was impossible to catch. The animal had no intention of slowing down until it had put a safe distance between itself and the thunderstorm.

Another flash of light punctured the churning clouds. Lawton ducked. Cairo didn't. She was still trying to pull back on the reins when her panic-stricken steed reared up, startled by the nearby lightning bolt which struck the earth like an avenging warrior's spear.

The gelding's terrified whinny pierced the air and he spun about, trying to run in every direction at once. With a shriek, Cairo somersaulted backward. Her face was smashed against the horse's rump, startling him even more. When the steed came down on all fours, he lowered his head to kick at his stunned rider.

Cairo groaned as she was launched through the air. When a flailing hoof caught her in the thigh, her wail mingled with the howling wind. She landed facedown with a thud, knocking the very air from her lungs. Dazed though she was and afraid to move for fear she had broken every bone in her body at least once, she lay there like a slug. The faint smell of smoke infiltrated her nostrils as the world spun furiously around her. Her head throbbed in rhythm with her pounding heart and her stomach rolled like a tidal wave. With a tremulous sigh, Cairo collapsed into the swirling darkness that lured her away from the pain and nausea.

"Cairo!" Lawton's voice boomed like a cannon but the sound fell on deaf ears.

Lawton had spurred his steed to gobble up the distance between him and Cairo, but the blinding flash of lightning so close at hand had startled his stallion as well. Lawton found himself battling his own mount which had spun a tight circle to head off in the opposite direction. By the time Lawton regained control of the horse, Cairo's mount had galloped away without its rider. The prairie grass was so tall and it undulated so furiously in the wind that Lawton could see no trace of Cairo at all.

Frantically, Lawton stood up in the stirrups, staring at the rolling cloud of smoke that was sweeping across the dry grass, fed by the roaring wind.

Prairie fire! Before he even completed the horrifying thought of lightning igniting a blaze, sparks fanned out in all directions, turning the prairie into a sea of leaping flames.

The meadow would be engulfed in smoke and fire in a matter of minutes and he had yet to determine where Cairo had fallen! Although his steed violently protested, Lawton gouged his mount and rode into the path of the smoke and flames.

Over and over again, Lawton bellowed Cairo's name, but he could barely hear his own voice over the wailing wind and crackling fire. She was going to be burned alive and he would be helpless to save her! That grim realization rolled through his mind as he zigzagged through the cloud of smoke, feeling the intense heat of the fire searing his flesh and his composure.

When his steed snorted at the foul air that congested its lungs, Lawton grabbed his kerchief and tied it over his face. There wasn't much he could do for the stallion. Hell, there wasn't much he could do for anybody! He felt frustrated and helpless and . . .

"Lawton!"

Cairo had roused to consciousness on a strangled cough. Climbing onto all fours, she peered above the wall of grass to see flames rushing toward her. The instinct to survive put her on her feet, but her left leg buckled when she tried to dash away from the oncoming fire.

Lawton swiveled in the saddle just as Cairo collapsed on her injured leg. With a fierce yank, he wheeled his stallion around and gouged him in the flanks. The steed was thankful to be going anywhere until he realized he was headed straight toward the fire. Then he put up one helluva a fuss!

Lawton jerked on the reins. The steed could do as Lawton commanded or risk having his head yanked off. Lawton eventually won the battle of wills, but he did compromise by riding parallel to the fire before veering toward the spot he had seen Cairo.

Again Cairo tried to stand up. The fog of smoke clogged her dazed brain and she felt as if she were moving in slow motion as she tried to determine which way to run. Wobbling, she braced up on her throbbing leg. She didn't hear the thunder of hooves behind her because the howling wind and crackling fire drowned out all sound. She didn't see her knight in his red bandana and flannel shirt come charging through the thick cloud of smoke until the instant his arm hooked around her waist and yanked her off her feet.

Lawton hadn't had the time to be gentle in his rescue. He had leaned out from the saddle to pluck Cairo off the ground while his stallion raced along. And sure enough, the animal never broke stride as he whizzed past Cairo. She was left dangling in midair for what seemed eternity. The jolting movement of the steed beat against her bruised ribs as Lawton attempted to drag her onto his lap and still maintain control of his mount.

Cairo went into Lawton's arms like a homing pigeon returning to roost. Although she'd never been the crying type, this seemed the perfect moment for hysterics, if ever there was one. A choked sob erupted from her throat as she buried her face against Lawton's smoky shirt. She clung to him like a vine, afraid to let go for fear she would be trampled by the horse's thundering hooves.

Another crack of lightning sizzled overhead and thunder rumbled as they galloped away from the rushing wind that sent flames leaping toward the threatening clouds. Huge raindrops sizzled on the wall of raging flames. The sooty residue of smoke that covered Cairo's face became a grimy mask when the heavens opened up to send buckets of rain down to douse the prairie fire.

Lawton drew his winded stallion to a halt, still clutching Cairo to him. He watched the fire slow its swift pace across the prairie. Only when Cairo shivered in his arms did he give any thought to finding protection from the wind-driven rain that soaked his steed and both its riders.

"You okay, Cai?" he murmured as he cuddled her closer.

Cairo muffled a sniff and wiped the back of her hand over her face, smearing it worse than it already was. "Okay?" Faint laughter tripped from her trembling lips. "Aside from the fact that I can't walk and my head is beating like a drum and every muscle is screaming in pain, you mean? I came dangerously close to being burned to a crisp, but now I'm in splendid shape," she wheezed.

Lawton almost collapsed in relief. Cairo was lucky to be alive, even if she *had* been bruised and battered. For a while there, he didn't think she'd survive. He had come dangerously close to aborting his attempt to rescue her. In another moment he and his steed would have been too overcome by smoke to do anything except try to save themselves.

Reversing direction, Lawton rode across the charred acres toward the skirting of trees that lined the Canadian River. Halting his stallion, Lawton swung down and then reached up to retrieve Cairo.

"Can you stand up?"

"On one leg," she chirped. "Does that count?"

While she steadied herself on her right foot, Lawton ran his hand over her left thigh, feeling the fierce knot caused by her horse's flailing hoof.

"Ouch!" Cairo sucked in her breath and very nearly fainted when his hand investigated her tender thigh. "That hurts!"

Lawton jerked his hand away, scooped her in his arms, and deposited her beside a tree. Tugging the bandana from his neck, he hurried toward the river to saturate the cloth.

"Take off your breeches," he ordered abruptly.

Cairo's sooty lashes fluttered up to gape at him. He had been cold and remote for the better part of the day and she had no inclination to drop her breeches for the "other man" who shared Lawton Stone's brawny body.

"No," she replied, tilting her smudged chin to that defiant angle he had come to recognize.

"For chrissake, Cai," Lawton snorted impatiently. "It's not as if I've never seen you naked before. I need to know if anything is broken."

Only my heart, Cairo thought to herself. Lawton may very well be concerned about her but he hid his emotions so skillfully that it was difficult to tell. "There is nothing broken, only bruised," Cairo diagnosed herself.

"I'll be the judge of that."

"I didn't know you had a medical degree."

"I've doctored my share of wounds," he insisted as he squatted down beside her. "Now drop 'em, Cai. I'm not a patient man."

"Really? You could have fooled me," Cairo smirked.

The menacing look he gave her indicated that she could disrobe of her own free will or be forcefully divested of her garments.

Self-conscious and defiant though she was, Cairo wormed out of her breeches and draped them over her bare hips.

Lawton grimaced at the huge purple bruise and festered knot that rose up from her thigh like a ridge in the Rocky Mountains. Tenderly, he brushed his palm over her leg, checking for signs of fracture.

"You're fortunate. I don't think it's broken."

"I told you so," she grumbled.

Curse it, why did she feel so uncomfortable having those silver eyes on her? He'd done far more than look at her the previous evening and she had shamelessly welcomed his gaze and his intimate touch. But, she quickly reminded herself, he wasn't the same man who'd introduced her to passion. He was . . .

"Now take off your shirt," he commanded in a no-nonsense tone.

"I most certainly will not!" she spumed, green eyes flashing.

Lawton pounced. Buttons popped, flannel shirt gaped, and before she could formulate a protest, Lawton had removed the garment and rolled her over like a log to inspect her for other injuries.

"Bruised ribs, scraped thigh, and a bump on the back of your head," he reported.

Cairo snatched up her strewn clothes, but before she could don them, Lawton stilled her hands. The cold glitter in his mercury eyes had transformed into a warm rippling flame. Suddenly Cairo found herself staring at the man who'd seduced her the previous night. Lawton had undergone a startling metamorphosis right before her very eyes—again!

"I'd really rather you wouldn't put those clothes on just yet . . ." he murmured as his head inched toward hers, his gaze focused on her petal-soft lips. "I love looking at you, Cai . . ."

"Curse it, Lawton!" she exploded in frustration. "One minute you treat me as if we don't even know each other and you don't care if we do. And then, out of the blue, you act like—"

Her blustering complaint died beneath his possessive kiss. His embrace made demands that Cairo's traitorous body couldn't refuse. Even though she was so exasperated she wanted to pull out her hair, strand by strand, she felt her defenses crumbling beneath the onslaught of tantalizing sensations he aroused in her.

If she had a smidgen of pride and self-respect she would have shoved him away and raked him over the coals for taking unfair advantage. But she couldn't formulate her thoughts let alone put them to tongue when his kiss unleashed needs that she had only discovered so recently.

Suddenly Cairo was oblivious to the cold air, bone-chilling rain, and her own indignation. Her senses were filled with the smoky scent of the man who caused the world to shrink to fill a space no larger than he occupied. As if they possessed a will all their own, her hands delved inside his damp shirt to make arousing contact with his muscled flesh.

Lawton reached behind him to draw the Indian-rubber cloak over them, shielding them from the drizzle of rain that dripped through the overhanging branches of the tree. With exquisite tenderness, he kissed and caressed away her pains until she was burning with an entirely different kind of ache.

Her mind went blank as his roaming hands rediscovered every sensitive point on her flesh, unchaining needs that demanded satisfaction. His tender touch was like a balm that soothed her wounds and changed wrong into right.

"You're a most impossible man," Cairo sighed.

"And you're a most perplexing woman," Lawton whispered against her trembling flesh. "But that hasn't stopped me from wanting you . . ."

He could feel the hunger for her, feel the desperate

need emerging to consume him. White-hot fires boiled through him when Cairo returned his adventurous caresses.

Lawton had spent the day testing his resistance to Cairo, warning himself to proceed with extreme caution where she was concerned. His emotions had been waging war against each other—instinct battling desire. But he had come so close to losing Cairo in the prairie fire that he longed to hold her in his arms and disregard those nagging suspicions that still hounded him.

Over and over again, his caresses glided over her silky flesh. He swore he'd somehow become obsessed with touching her. He just couldn't seem to get enough of this alluring sprite. Lawton wasn't sure why he'd stepped out of his customary rut to find himself so lost in a woman.

Although it went against his grain to be bewitched by a woman, he couldn't have moved away from her, even if his life depended on it. And that worried him to the extreme—that his life *might* very well depend on it!

"Aw, to hell with it," Lawton muttered to himself. A woman who made him feel this good couldn't be all bad. Could he have been such a poor judge of character?

Lawton ached to take possession of her exquisite body again, to chase away those frustrating demons of suspicion. He needed to . . . No, he realized suddenly, he *had* to have this silver-haired temptress, just as he had to have air to breathe. And he wasn't going to be able to think straight until these desperate cravings ebbed.

Lawton rolled sideways, pulling Cairo above him.

The fire of desire flickered in his eyes and a rakish smile curved his sensuous lips. Without guarding his stare, his gaze flooded over her body, marveling at her unsurpassed beauty. He chuckled when he realized Cairo was looking at him with a mixture of innocence and confusion.

"If we do this the same way I taught you last night, I might aggravate your injuries," he murmured as he forced her to straddle him and drew her hips suggestively against his.

A hot blush stained her cheeks when she digested his meaning, when the velvet warmth of him glided intimately against her parted thighs.

"I can't help but wonder if *you* would be as careful about hurting *me,* sweet witch . . ."

When he drew her down to flick his tongue against the taut peaks of her breasts, Cairo lost all interest in interrogating him about his strange comment. His hands settled on her hips, guiding her to him, setting the hypnotic cadence that swept her into the churning clouds of passion. She wasn't sure which was more devastating—the thunderstorm that had wreaked havoc on the prairie or the firestorm of desire that bombarded her from all directions.

Sensations sizzled through her like lightning bolts, setting every nerve and muscle to tingling. Her heart thudded against her chest, and she was aware of nothing except the feel of his hair-roughened body molded intimately to hers, of the wind-swept pleasure of loving this enigmatic man.

Cairo could feel herself spinning. The world whirled as he thrust deeply into her, appeasing needs that left her completely out of control. A cry of ecstasy tumbled from her lips when each one of the incredible sensations that buffeted her converged all at once. It was as if she were flying into the sun, burning alive in the intense heat of passion's wildfire.

Lawton was amazed at what a short walk it had been from hell to heaven. One minute he was doubting Cairo's intentions and battling the fierce prairie fire that was about to take her away from him forever. The next instant he was soaring toward the horizon on a pastel rainbow, engulfed by the most fantastic feelings imaginable. When the last shudders of ecstasy riveted his body, his mind was paralyzed by the lingering sensations that loving this green-eyed woman aroused in him.

Lawton nuzzled against her neck. His hands languidly glided down her hips, reveling in the luscious texture of her skin. This was no evil sorceress come to do him harm, Lawton reassured himself. This was an angel who was made for love. Inexperienced though she was, she had the power to stir him the way no other woman ever had. He had begun to care for her, even though he fought the unfamiliar feelings of possession and affection.

Cairo crossed her arms on his broad chest and rested her chin on her wrists. Her passion-drugged eyes drifted over Lawton's face, committing each feature to memory. When she peered into those rippling pools of silver and reflected on the intimate encounter they had shared, she could barely recall her crusade or what life had been like before Lawton.

"You have the most remarkable way of making me forget why I'm here." She reached up to trace the line that bracketed his full mouth. "You are a most distracting man, Lawton Stone."

Hell's bells, there he went again, reading meanings into her comments. Just *why* was she here? he asked himself worriedly. To lure him into a trap? Or was she honestly trying to rescue this father she claimed to have from trouble? And what about those two mysterious messages she'd received in Fort Smith that she had refused to explain? If she had nothing to hide, why had she been so mysterious about those notes and the wilted flowers she kept strapped to her saddle?

Lawton didn't know what to believe, but he wasn't about to confront Cairo with his suspicions. That would be worse than aiding and abetting one's enemy . . . which she very well could be. Who knew how far a woman would go to extract her bizarre brand of vengeance? How could he know what thoughts were tripping through her mind? He had never bothered with women often enough to understand what made them tick.

Grappling with his troubled thoughts, Lawton eased Cairo down beside him. With no regard for modesty, he rolled to his feet and strode toward his horse.

Cairo sighed appreciatively at his lean, muscular physique. Lawton Stone was the essence of masculine grace and elegance. She had touched his body, savoring each caress, but long before she tired of lying in his arms, he had moved away, leaving her feeling cold, alone, and unwanted. Again.

Grabbing some dry clothes, Lawton shrugged them on and then pivoted to survey the frown on Cairo's face. She didn't seem to understand his change of moods, or at least she didn't want him to think she did. And Lawton wasn't about to explain for fear of leaving himself vulnerable to danger.

"I'll see if I can round up your horse. He has to be around here somewhere," he mumbled, staring at the air above Cairo's head.

"If you find him, kick him a couple of times for me," Cairo requested.

When Lawton stepped into the stirrup without casting her another glance, Cairo sighed. Confound it, there he went again, from lover to stranger, she thought.

"You know you're a fool," Cairo chastised herself as she huddled beneath the makeshift tent of his rubber rain slicker and shivered from the chill of the inclement weather and Lawton's frosty mood.

All she was, and would ever be, to that exasperating man was the time he was killing. If she were smart, she'd never let herself forget that again! There wasn't one woman on the planet who had been able to chisel her initials in Lawton's heart of stone. Why in the world had she thought she could?

Foolhardy arrogance, she supposed. Lawton was a thirty-one-year-old woman-hater who had only one use for females. He wasn't going to change just because she had developed this hopeless fascination for him.

Of all the men she could have had, she had become bewitched by this insensitive cad. Maybe this was her punishment for turning her previous suitors away and refusing to become involved in anything more than a platonic relationship. Now she knew how it felt to be rejected, to be cast aside like a worn shirt. It felt *awful,* and her feminine pride was smarting far more than the knot on her hip and the bump on her head.

From now on she would put a respectable distance

between herself and Lawton. There would be no more passionate trysts. And she vowed she would not become sentimental when he exhibited that gentle side of him. When he assaulted her with his rakish smile and tantalizing caresses, she would remind herself how cold and uncaring he could be when he wasn't in the mood to feed his male lusts.

Cairo had paid Lawton to guide her into Oklahoma and that would be all she would expect from him from this moment forward. She was a fool to waste a smidgen of affection on him. That was the last thing a man like Lawton wanted from a woman!

He doesn't mean a thing to me—no more than I do to him, Cairo told herself. She had simply been overcome by the needs Lawton had awakened in her. He was no more than a careless experiment with passion. This reckless business was over and done and Cairo had learned a valuable lesson. Romance had been grossly overrated. It was, as far as she could tell, an experience in frustration.

"Curse you, Lawton Stone," Cairo muttered to the world at large and to Lawton's tormenting image in particular.

Chapter Eight

Since the moment Lawton returned from retrieving Cairo's runaway gelding, she had barely acknowledged him. He'd had another heart-to-heart talk with himself, and decided Cairo was innocent of his suspicions. He'd felt guilty about abruptly dismissing her and was ready to apologize for his callousness. That he'd even *considered* apologizing for his behavior to a woman was new to him. But he suddenly had no inclination to voice any admission whatsoever when Cairo had given him the cold shoulder the instant he rode into camp.

The next morning Lawton dared to ask why she was still so short and curt with him and the verbal battle was on.

"I have been reminding myself why I am here in this territory with you," she'd said. Then the sassy blonde had kindly thanked him to keep his distance when next he felt lust overcome him because, as she had put it "if there is any *killing* to be done around here, it was not going to be the killing of *your* time with *my* body!"

"Just what the hell is that snide remark supposed to mean?" Lawton had countered.

To which Cairo had replied, "Figure it out for yourself since you think you're so damned smart, Mr. Law and Order Stone!"

Lawton had reminded Cairo that he had saved her life and the very least she could do was be civil and not bite his head off.

"Consider yourself thanked," Cairo had snapped back and nudged her horse across the rolling prairie without looking back.

That was the last conversation they'd had. Cairo had stared in every direction except Lawton's and he practiced the same tactic of ignoring her. Despite the fact that Lawton suddenly wished that perplexing female a stay in perdition, he had aimed them toward Webbers Falls and the luxury of bedding down in a hotel room instead of the cold ground.

Lawton was aware that Cairo was still in considerable pain, even though the stubborn woman would have died long before she admitted it to him. He had seen her grimace each time she put weight on her left leg, when she squirmed restlessly in the saddle. He shouldn't even have considered her discomfort since she was probably sitting atop her horse, devising new ways to torture him before the Gardiner gang murdered him.

For the past few days, Lawton had been droning the words to "Skip to My Lou" as he and Cairo rode over hill and dale. After listening to him croon for hours on end, she had had enough.

"Will you cease that caterwauling," she demanded. "Unlike you, I'm not tone deaf."

"Tuck and Woody never complained about my singing."

"They must have been exceptionally good sports if they listened to you howl like a wounded tomcat," Cairo snapped. "You couldn't hit a high note, even if you had a hammer!"

"Well, you aren't perfect yourself," Lawton smirked. "You have more than your fair share of flaws."

"Such as . . . ?" she questioned, and then wished she'd kept her mouth shut.

"Such as your annoying habit of carrying so many necessities that you look as if you're sitting between the humps of a camel instead of on a horse's saddle," he declared. "And it irritates the hell out of me when you dip food onto your plate and refuse to let one category of food touch any of the others."

"What is wrong with wanting to enjoy one type of food without its flavor getting mixed up with the others?" Cairo challenged. "That is hardly as bad as scrambling *all* the food together the way you do!"

"The way you separate your food and lug all those *unnecessary* necessities suggests you are overly particular," Lawton parried, glaring daggers at her. "What you need is a Conestoga wagon to cart around all your supplies and a stove to cook all your meals!"

"How I wish I had a wagon," Cairo hurled at him, returning his glare, dagger for dagger. "Then I could wrap a pillow around my head and bury myself in the wagon under a pile of blankets so I wouldn't have to listen to you wail in that annoying voice of yours!"

Lawton granted Cairo her wish. He stopped singing. Now he spitefully *hummed* the chorus of "Skip to My Lou" . . . over and over and over. He knew it grated on

Cairo's nerves, but her haughty remarks had grated on *his* nerves.

Although Cairo voiced no further complaint about his inability to carry a tune, she was silently seething. She knew Lawton was purposely trying to irritate her and he was doing a bang-up job of it, damn him.

Cairo wracked her brain, anxious to devise some tactic to get even with him. She supposed she was being childish, but she needed revenge!

To counter his off-key humming, Cairo began hammering a wooden spoon against one of her cooking kettles. It took her steed a while to grow accustomed to the racket. It took Lawton a good deal longer. The louder she played on her improvised drum the louder he hummed.

The citizens of Webbers Falls knew the twosome was approaching long before they arrived. A curious crowd had gathered outside the train depot to monitor the peculiar behavior of the man and woman. Cairo tucked away her spoon and pasted on a smile to greet the amused faces that peered up at her as she rode by.

"I need to stop at the telegraph office to check for messages," Lawton declared, drawing his steed to a halt.

"I'll be at the hotel, enjoying a few minutes of privacy," Cairo informed him before giving him a sarcastic smile. "I'll be counting the minutes before I see you again."

When Lawton ambled into the telegraph office, the attendant was staring through his thick spectacles at the shapely blonde who sat regally atop her chestnut gelding.

"Is that the same lady who was through here a few weeks back?" Angus Ford questioned Lawton. "Sure looks like her."

Suspicion leaped up like goblins from the dungeon of his mind. Lawton pivoted to watch the attendant stare appreciatively at the curvaceous sprite. "Could be. Did you speak to her the last time she was here?"

Angus adjusted his glasses on the bridge of his beaklike nose and hobbled back to his desk. "Nope. I just saw her ride through town, same as everybody else."

"Was anyone with her?" Lawton demanded.

The elderly man shifted uneasily beneath Lawton's probing stare. The irritation in Lawton's voice left him to wonder if he hadn't broached a touchy subject with the giant of a marshal who passed this way on occasion. Angus had the feeling he had made trouble for the comely woman and that had not been his intention. He had only meant to make idle conversation.

"The lady and a blond-haired man came through town and stopped at the dry goods store for supplies and then they rode out." Clearing his throat, Angus tried to smooth over his blundering comments. "Now don't get me wrong, Marshal Stone. I can't swear she's the same woman. They look alike to me. Of course, my vision isn't what it used to be, you understand." He shrugged. "The two women probably just resemble each other and it wasn't your lady friend. My mistake . . ."

Lawton seriously doubted that any mistake had been made. If there had been, Lawton had made it himself when he first began giving Cairo Calhoun the benefit of the doubt!

"I've got a couple of messages for you." Gladly, Angus changed the subject. "One telegram arrived just this morning. The other one . . ." He frowned at the message. "It's been here awhile. Maybe you can make some sense of it. I couldn't."

Lawton gnashed his teeth when he read the brief, unsigned message.

Fate summons you. . . . All in good time . . . The debt will be paid—in our own way. . . .

Lawton knew who had sent the message and what it meant. The Gardiners were assuring him that they hadn't forgotten that Lawton had killed their youngest brother.

After tucking the message in his pocket, Lawton read the other telegram from Woody and Tucker.

The Gardiners have abandoned their favorite haunts. Guard your back, good friend.

Lawton strode out the door and stalked down the street to the dry goods store to interrogate the clerk. The rotund storekeeper nodded in recognition when Lawton quizzed him about the blonde who had accompanied the marshal to town.

"I didn't get a real good look at the woman either time," Geoffrey Muldoon insisted. "Last time she never climbed down from her horse and the sun was blaring through the window. Her wide-brimmed hat shaded her face, but she looked like a pretty little thing from where I stood."

"Can you describe the man with her?" Lawton

attempted to prevent his anger from seeping into his voice.

Geoffrey nodded. "He was tall and thin and blond. He walked with a limp and he had icy blue eyes and a hardened face. He wasn't the friendliest customer I ever had, I can tell you that!" He pulled the ledger in front of him, moistened his index finger, and flipped back the pages. "The man bought enough supplies to feed an army. I remember wondering if the man and his female companion planned to consume all that food by themselves or if they were having a party."

Lawton's suspicions of Cairo had mounted. From all indication, the Gardiners had made camp in the area before the Snowbird traveled to Fort Smith to lure out her victim. Unless he missed his guess the strike would come as soon as he and Cairo reached an isolated spot that was suitable for ambush.

Lawton marched toward the hotel, knowing his days were numbered. To add to the evidence that Cairo was someone other than whom she claimed to be, he found her in a squabble with a burly brute in the hall. Lawton realized Cairo Calhoun, despite her sophisticated airs, was no average woman. She was perfectly capable of defending herself.

Garbed in one of her fashionable gowns, Cairo had whizzed out the door of her room in search of the hotel restaurant. She was anxious both to appease her hunger and to be conveniently out of the way when Lawton returned. When one of the hotel guests, sporting a rakish leer, made a lurid suggestion to her, Cairo had snubbed him. The foul-smelling hooligan had latched onto her arm when she tried to brush past him.

That was when Lawton had arrived. In astonishment, he stood at the top of the steps, watching the prim and proper Miss Cairo Calhoun become all fists, feet, and flying fur. She possessed spunk and style—a dangerous combination for a woman, he reminded himself bleakly.

To Lawton's amazement, Cairo had doubled her fist and punched the pudgy miscreant in the midsection when he tried to grope at her. She kicked the man's shins to splinters and then planted her fist squarely between his eyes. With a startled grunt, her assailant stumbled back, only to find himself staring down the barrel of the .41-caliber, snub-nosed Remington pistol she had retrieved from her purse.

"If you dare to touch me again, I'll blow your hands off at the wrists," Cairo promised. "Do you understand me?"

The man nodded his head meekly. Casting her an apprehensive glance to make sure she wasn't planning to shoot him in the back, the scoundrel slinked into his room and closed the door.

Cairo tucked the pistol in her purse, shook the sting out of her knuckles, and wheeled around to continue on her way. It was then that she saw Lawton lounging against the railing, regarding her with a wary frown.

Cairo glared at him as she breezed toward the staircase. "You could have come to my assistance," she snapped. "After all, that's what U.S. marshals are paid to do, isn't it? Protect citizens from the unseemly individuals of society."

"I suppose so," Lawton murmured, giving Cairo the once-over twice. "If only I could tell the unsavory elements of society from the decent citizens."

Cairo looked as if she wanted to hit him.

"Besides," Lawton continued, "I saw no reason to interfere. You were managing quite well by yourself." Another dubious frown puckered his forehead. "Where did you learn to fight like that?"

That Lawton had stood back without lending assistance infuriated her. The fact that he insulted her and then wanted to know where she'd learned to take care of herself when he refused to speak of his past compounded her irritation.

"That is none of your business," she snapped, her chin jutting out to a stubborn angle.

His arm snaked out to capture her as she whizzed past him. "Damnit, answer me!" Lawton growled.

Lawton, who packed two ivory-handled Colts on his hips and a variety of concealed weapons on his person, always looked *vaguely* dangerous. At the moment, sporting that glittering silver glare and angry snarl, he looked *positively* dangerous. Cairo had the unsettling feeling that he would have shaken the information out of her if she didn't supply it of her own free will.

"My father taught me to protect myself, if you must know," she grumbled as she pried his fingers from the crumpled sleeve of her dress.

"The same father, I suppose, who is fending off the prostitutes in Canadian Station as we speak," he said in a sardonic tone.

"Of course that father," she hurled at him. "Most folks have only one, you know."

"Some have more," Lawton contended, still glaring silver bullets at her. "And some folks don't even know who their natural father is."

She would never understand Lawton Stone. After all they had been through together, he still seemed leery and mistrusting. Maybe it had something to do with his remark and something questionable about his heritage.

Scowling at himself for blurting out that comment, Lawton laid his hand against the small of Cairo's back and propelled her down the steps. He may as well feed his frustrations, he decided. His stomach was growling and wary trepidation was gobbling him alive. He had never been more certain that Cairo was Snowbird and yet he was still strung by his illogical attraction to her. This turmoil which raged within him was wearing him out.

"I don't know why you are lashing out at me," she muttered, jerking away from him. "I am hardly to blame for whatever misfortune you may have endured."

"I've learned to live with my past." Lawton clamped onto her arm and led her into the hotel restaurant. "It's my future that concerns me most."

Cairo decided there was no way to carry on an intelligent conversation with Lawton. The man talked in riddles and he leaped from one topic to another like a grasshopper. She never knew what he was driving at with his cryptic insinuations.

Leaving her to seat herself, Lawton plunked down in his chair and stared at the menu that was painted above the counter. He yearned to blurt out his suspicions about Cairo's ties to the Gardiner gang. How he wished he were wrong about her. But after hearing what the telegraph operator and storekeeper had to say, Lawton knew she was guilty as sin. And after watching her repel the advances of her overzealous admirer Lawton knew there was nothing clumsy about Cairo's battle tactics. She was too skillful and resourceful to be a novice at fighting. If she was just a prim and proper schoolmarm from Missouri he was a crowned prince!

Although Lawton had never trusted Cairo less, he wondered if he hadn't been employing the wrong strategy with her. Instead of antagonizing her, hoping he would annoy her to the point that she blurted out her wicked plans, maybe he should have been trying to win her affection as Woody suggested. If Cairo began to care for him, even a smidgen, she might come to his defense during the Gardiners' ambush.

Cairo was still his bait, Lawton reminded himself. But if he *did* play his cards right, this beguiling witch might stand between himself and certain death.

Resolved to that sensible theory, Lawton pasted on a disarming smile and asked what Cairo wanted for supper.

"Your heart boiled," she countered.

Curse it, Lawton was transforming before her eyes again! One minute he was growling at her like a grizzly bear, the next second he was oozing with charm. Did he anticipate returning upstairs for a tumble in the sheets? Most likely, lusty varmint that he was!

Well, Cairo would have none of that! She was furious with him and she was determined to hold a grudge. Their problems could never be solved in a bed, only postponed. There was a vast difference between *wanting* a woman's body and truly caring for her. Obviously Lawton Rock-Hearted Stone didn't know that. The only thing he was going to get from Cairo Calhoun was a very bad time!

Lawton sighed. "I'm trying to be congenial," he

replied to her sassy remark. "My heart isn't on the menu. Settle for something else."

Begrudgingly, Cairo did. Within a few minutes she sank her teeth into a thick, juicy steak. It didn't curb her irritation but it did appease her appetite. And to her further confusion, Lawton became the picture of devotion during their dinner. He had never been a sparkling conversationalist, but suddenly he was rattling on about a myriad of interesting subjects. He was communicating with Cairo almost as if she were his equal! My, wasn't that a switch!

Despite the decision to hold her grudge, Cairo found herself voicing her opinions on all the topics Lawton brought up. She found him to be very knowledgeable. He was civic-minded and he imparted scads of information about the newly formed territory of Oklahoma. He cited his recollections of the area during his travels.

Cairo enjoyed their evening together until they reached the door to her room. There, his footsteps and his conversation halted.

"Thank you for the meal and the stimulating conversation," she said, feeling awkward all of a sudden. She and Lawton had been bedding down together on the ground for a week, spending every moment together. And now she was going to closet herself in her room and he would be locked in his.

"I want to stay with you," he murmured, staring down at her with his veiled gaze.

If there was one thing a body could say about Lawton Stone it was that he never minced words.

Cairo was bound and determined not to humiliate herself a third time. She had resolved to keep a respectable distance between them and she was going to do exactly that, even if her wanton body did crave the pleasure of his touch.

"If it's physical satisfaction you want, I'm sure there are several women hereabout who earn their living by making men happy," she managed to say in a civil tone. Her chin tilted to a proud angle. "I thought I made it clear that I have no wish to be the time you're killing."

His hand curled beneath her chin, bringing it down a notch. He stared at her for a long deliberate moment, forcing her to meet his unblinking gaze. "I think I'm falling in love with you, Cairo. Finding another woman to accommodate me wouldn't satisfy what I really want."

The caressing huskiness in his voice and his admission left Cairo gaping at him in disbelief. Of all the things she expected this confusing man to say, that wasn't even on the list! His conduct had indicated he felt nothing but lust for her. Why should she believe he loved her? If he honestly did, he had the most peculiar way of showing it. Most likely, his words were a ploy to get him where he wanted to be—in her bed again. Hell would sooner be encased in a glacier!

"You can love me just as well in your own room," Cairo bit off, incensed that he thought she was so foolish as to believe his confessions of affection.

The sparks that flashed in Cairo's emerald eyes assured Lawton he had wasted his breath. He hadn't meant what he said, of course. He was never going to fall in love and he never wanted to. Women didn't deserve a man's affection, especially this lying little thief. All he wanted was Cairo's protection when the Gardiners tried to bushwhack him. But this was no simple-minded twit who melted in a man's arms when plied with phrases of love.

Still determined to soften Cairo's heart, Lawton inched toward her. His lips slanted over hers, intent on kissing away her resistance. He kept telling himself he didn't really love her, even when his body began to catch fire and burn. He could feel his heart leaping into triple time when he drew her reluctant body against his. He could feel desire pulsating through his loins when her breasts brushed against his chest and he brought her hips into familiar contact with his.

When love words tumbled from his lips between kisses, Lawton assured himself that it was just part of his scheme to win Cairo's allegiance and save himself from disaster. She would become the pawn that he played for his defense. That was all.

Words didn't mean a thing, and neither did these wild bubbly sensations that touching her always aroused in him. She stirred him because she was a beautiful woman, and just because Cairo Calhoun stirred him more than any other female he'd held in his arms only indicated that she possessed incredible powers over the male of the species. Woody and Tucker hadn't been able to resist her charms, either, he consoled himself.

Cairo felt her defenses melting into a puddle when his sensuous lips rolled over hers and he pressed her into his muscular contours. Her pride and her nagging conscience battled the desires of her betraying body. She wanted to hug him closer and push him away, all in the same moment.

When another hot tide of passion crested upon her, Cairo felt herself being tugged by the currents of pleasure that lured her deeper into his spell and her arms glided over his powerful shoulders to toy with his curly raven hair.

For those breathless seconds that accompanied her momentary lapse of sanity, Cairo wanted to believe Lawton's confession. She wanted him to return the affection she had begun to feel for him, but his unpredictable behavior left her doubting his sincerity. She knew for a fact that men would say anything to get what they wanted from a woman. Lawton was no different.

Pride and conscience rallied to save her in the nick of time. She would not mortify herself! Lawton Stone wouldn't know love if Cupid drew his bow and shot an arrow clean through his granite heart!

"No!" Cairo gasped as she flung away from him. "This isn't what I had planned." Her voice wavered with longing and desire that she refused to appease, even when denying him meant the agony of denying herself.

Lawton, of course, misinterpreted her comment. He knew exactly what this hellion had planned: his funeral. She intended to decorate his chest with those stupid damned wilted flowers she left draped over her saddle! Damn it, was there no way to worm into her wicked heart? Was there no way to earn her affection, just to save his own neck? Apparently not. But Lawton vowed to die trying. She was, as he saw it, his only salvation against the Gardiners.

Bracing his arms on either side of her shoulders where she stood plastered to the door, he gazed into her enchanting face. "I love you, Cai," he whispered in his most convincing tone. "I think I have loved you since the moment I laid eyes on you. I've been fighting the feelings. Maybe that's why I've been hateful one minute and congenial the next. I'm not accustomed to love. It's unnatural to me. But no matter how hard I've tried to deny my feelings, they're still there, lurking just beneath the surface to torment me. I don't want to hurt you. You mean too much to me."

Let her chew on that thought a while to see if her conscience would hound her! Perhaps she would feel something for him that would refuse to let her be a party to his ruthless murder.

Lawton pushed away from the door and sighed melodramatically. He was turning out to be every bit as good at theatrics as she was! "If loving you means sleeping alone to prove I'm sincere, then that's what I'll do." He summoned his most engaging smile. "I won't like sleeping alone, of course. I'd much rather communicate my affection in ways that require no words. You would know how I feel in the way I touched you, the way I showered you with adoring kisses . . ."

When he swaggered down the hall to let himself into his own room, Cairo clutched the doorknob to prevent collapsing. That swarthy giant was the devil's own temptation. Sentimental fool that she was, she longed to believe every word he said, to reverse her decision and call him back to her. But Cairo yearned to do more than share Lawton's bed. She wanted his respect and devotion as well as his passion. No other man had made her think in terms of forever, but Lawton made her ponder hundreds of thoughts she'd never before entertained!

A pensive frown knitted her brow as she ambled into her room. Did he truly care for her in his own way? Cairo mulled over that question as she pulled the pins from her hair, allowing the silver-blond tendrils to tumble down her back in disarray. Cairo doubted he had uttered love words to every woman he met. Maybe he wasn't the type who plied females with empty phrases to get what he wanted. He didn't have all that much respect for women in general, and no doubt his promiscuous mother was responsible for his cynicism.

She peeled off her gown and carefully folded it before putting it away. Only time would tell if Lawton was sincere. If, in the days to come, he continued to treat her with consideration and respect, she would allow herself to start believing him.

Cairo had never been one to cast caution to the wind and leap into deep water. She clung to the sensible part of herself and sorted out her emotions one at a time. Except when it came to her irrational affair with Lawton Stone, that is, she reluctantly reminded herself. In that instance she had definitely lost her head, but she would never let go completely until she was sure of his feelings.

Stifling the lingering sensations of Lawton's potent kisses and caresses, Cairo tucked herself beneath the quilts. After cuddling in Lawton's arms all week long while they lay beneath the canopy of twinkling stars, the hotel bed felt incredibly empty.

She was sorely tempted to sneak into his room and follow the call of her heart. She swore she deserved a medal for refusing to succumb to her whims. But Cairo was awarded no medal, only fitful hours of begging for sleep.

Trying not to think about how much she wanted him was exhausting, so exhausting in fact that she was entirely too tired to sleep!

Chapter Nine

It had been unseasonably dry until the previous week. Now it had become unseasonably cold. Cairo had learned that the weather in the Twin Territories was subject to drastic change, very much like the moods of her traveling companion.

Cairo shivered as she drew the collar of her jacket around her neck. She stared west, wondering how long it would be before they reached the border of Oklahoma Territory. Another shiver ricocheted down her spine when the wind slapped her in the face.

Gray clouds blanketed the sky like layers of dingy wool. Fall had abruptly given way to a prelude of winter and Cairo huddled atop her steed. The crisp wind blew through her jacket, and her ears and nose were so numb she feared they would drop off if she dared to touch them.

After a full day of riding, Lawton had finally called a halt to set up camp. He had paused by the embankment that was clumped with blackjacks and cottonwood trees which protected the location from the icy north wind. With a thankful sigh, Cairo swung from the saddle. Her foot had barely touched the ground when the rustle of leaves behind her steed caused him to sidestep skittishly. An unfamiliar noise erupted from the mound of leaves and Cairo swiveled her head around to see two beady black eyes and a mouthful of deadly teeth confronting her. The badger, whose den in the side of the tall embankment they had disturbed, hadn't taken kindly to the intrusion and had lunged toward the horse's leg, determined to discourage the creature from stamping on the entrance of the den.

The chestnut gelding's whinny pierced the frosty air when the badger's sharp teeth sank into his leg. Cairo was instantly mashed between Lawton's steed and her frightened mount that had instinctively kicked at the badger. Lawton, who had yet to dismount, felt Cairo's shoulder collide with his leg when the horses rammed each other broadside, squeezing Cairo between them.

"What the hell is going on?" Lawton growled, twisting in the saddle.

The commotion and the retaliation of the chestnut gelding provoked the badger to launch his second attack. The steed reared up, thrashing the air with its front legs, preparing to lunge away from danger.

Lawton leaned over to retrieve the gelding's reins and bring him under control. To Lawton's surprise, he felt Cairo clawing at his boot. To his further amazement, she snatched up the long-barreled Barns 50-caliber pistol he didn't know she knew he kept stashed in his right boot!

Cairo cocked the trigger and aimed in one fluent motion. As the badger scurried forward to clamp its teeth around the gelding's leg, Cairo blew him away with deadly accuracy. With one last growl, the furry animal expelled its last breath and collapsed in a motionless heap.

Lawton's eyes bounced to the woman whose skills with a pistol were as obvious as the wart on the end of one's nose. Not only could Cairo counter the attack of a man with her fists and brandish a pistol in the offender's face, but she could also draw and fire at a speed which indicated she was no stranger to handling firearms. What was even more unsettling to Lawton was the fact that this blond-haired spitfire knew the exact location of every weapon he carried on his person! If she ever found the need to disarm him, she was capable of retrieving every pistol and knife he carried, leaving him defenseless.

"Who taught you to shoot like that?" He fired the question like the bullet which had brought a quick end to the attacking badger.

Cairo tucked the long-barreled pistol back into Lawton's boot before he swung from the saddle. "My father, of course," she responded, miffed by the frown he was bestowing on her. "Is it a crime in Indian Territory for a woman to be as capable with a pistol as a man?"

Crime? Hell, the only crime Lawton was concerned about was the one that the Snowbird and the Gardiners were about to commit against U.S. Marshal Lawton Stone! As swift and accurate as Cairo was, Lawton knew he wouldn't have so much as a prayer when the shooting started. If the Gardiners didn't gun him down, Cairo certainly could. She was *that* good with a pistol. He shuddered to think what she could do with a knife. No doubt, Idaho Joe had taught her to be as deadly with a dagger as he was.

Lawton well remembered what had happened to the half-breed George Tinsley when the Gardiners had ambushed the farmhouse. George had never known what hit him. Idaho Joe's talents of hurling stilettos had earned him the begrudging respect of every marshal in the Twin Territories and their surrounding states. The Gardiners had added to their ranks men who were masters with dynamite, knives, and a variety of firearms. And from the look of things, they had each taught the Snowbird to match their unsavory skills.

Lawton continued to gape at her. She frowned in confusion. "Lawton? What are you staring at?"

Certain death, Lawton thought bleakly. With each passing day he was learning more about Cairo's abilities, becoming more aware of how deceiving looks could be. Holy hell! He didn't stand a chance unless he convinced this charading female outlaw that she would like him better alive than dead!

Lawton stepped from the stirrups to tether the horses. If he were smart, he would dedicate the next few hours to convincing her of his affection for her. He desperately needed her loyalty and devotion.

Lawton strode toward Cairo, who was still studying him bemusedly. Before she could protest, he pulled her into his arms and kissed the breath out of her. Cairo found herself bent over backward and molded to his rock-hard contours. Even if she had attempted to fling herself away from him she would have wound up on the ground with him following her down. But the potent magic of his unexpected kiss kept Cairo paralyzed. As cold as she had been five minutes earlier, she was on fire in less than a heartbeat. She could feel her traitorous body absorbing Lawton's masculine warmth, feel her wanton needs burning like glowing coals. Every nerve and muscle in her body danced with the pleasure of his fiery kiss and intimate caresses. His hands had delved beneath her jacket and shirt to make titillating contact with the taut peaks of her breasts. And then his greedy lips followed, tasting her as if she were the meal he wanted to devour.

She moaned deep in her throat when his wandering hands seared her quaking flesh, causing another flame to flicker in the core of her being. Cairo hadn't meant to respond so ardently to his amorous assault, but it was impossible not to.

What made it even more difficult to resist his charm were the quietly uttered words of love he offered. She not only heard the confession, but she felt it hovering on her skin as he greeted every inch of flesh he exposed to his moist kisses. In a bed of grass and leaves, Cairo found herself returning his confession. The words tumbled from her lips in the heat of passion, blocking out any logic.

As his hand speared beneath the band of her breeches to caress her hips and thighs, Cairo moaned in sweet torment. She delighted in his skillful touch, she yearned to shed the hindering garments and lie flesh to flesh with him, sharing the passion that exploded every time they were in each other's arms.

Lawton told himself it was the winning of Cairo's untamed heart that provoked the surge of pleasure that rippled through every fiber of his being. By gaining her love he had acquired an ally with whom to face the inevitable battle against the Gardiners. But it wasn't victory alone that caused this onrush of heady satisfaction. He knew he was a fool to be so entranced by a woman, especially this woman, but each time he touched her, he ached up to his eyelashes. She was a poison in his blood, he knew, and yet he couldn't control the hunger that mushroomed inside him when she was in his arms.

He groaned when her fingertips probed beneath his shirt to encircle each male nipple. Another moan rumbled in his chest when her inquiring hands set out on their arousing journey of discovery. Cairo had become an incredible seductress in a short time. She now knew where and how to touch him to spur his passion and demolish his self-control.

When her hand glided into his breeches to stroke his swollen manhood, Lawton swallowed a pail of air. Over and over again she caressed him and Lawton felt himself melting. He wanted her so badly that no other thought could penetrate his mind.

As nightfall settled over the canopy of trees that protected them from the icy wind, Lawton swore his garments, as well as Cairo's, had split at the seams and fallen away, leaving them lying naked in each other's arms. When he stared down at her luscious body, a shudder of anticipation pulsated through him. And when he met those animated green eyes that flickered with desire, he lost every ounce of sense.

"I do love you . . ." Cairo murmured, searching the rugged features of the face that hovered only a hairbreadth above hers. "Only you cause this sweet ache and only you can make it go away . . ."

Her words brought him eagerly to her. The gentleness he'd displayed with his kisses and caresses transformed into savage urgency. Her confession clipped the string that freed his raging needs and his emotions burst loose like floodwaters tumbling over a collapsing dam.

With a groan of torment, he clutched Cairo's body to his and thrust deeply within her, forging them into one essence. He inhaled the sweet fragrance of her hair and reveled in the dizzying rapture of making wild sweet love to the only woman who could turn his emotions wrong side out. He could feel his overworked heart pounding the beat of a mystical melody that played in his soul. He clutched her to him, aching to appease this gigantic need.

Torrents of rapture spilled through Cairo as she felt herself lifted from one soul-shattering plateau to another. She swore she'd die before she found an end to these maddening sensations.

Making love to this magnificent man was just as it had been the very first time, yet it was completely different. She discovered a maelstrom of delicious sensations which were wondrous and new. She reveled in the kaleidoscope of feelings that swirled about her.

And then, Cairo felt all those miraculous sensations recoil upon her, burning in her mind and body like a hot sweet flame. She knew for certain she was dying in the splendor of it all. Her body shuddered time and time again as she held on to Lawton for dear life. Tingles of lingering pleasure sparkled on her skin and trickled through every nerve as Lawton trembled above her in passion's shuddering release.

For what seemed forever, Cairo lay there, numb to the exquisite ecstasy that enveloped her. The heavy weight of Lawton's body seemed no burden nor did she feel the chill of the night or the brittle leaves beneath her. She had discovered heaven without leaving the circle of Lawton's arms.

Lawton had enjoyed the same spine-tingling sensations. The only difference was that he was fighting like the devil to regain command of his mind and body. The vulnerability he always felt when he made passionate love to this enchanting woman frightened him.

And what really scared him most was that there were times, like now, when he was afraid he really had fallen in love with her, that his words were no lie he'd voiced to win her allegiance.

Mustering his depleted strength, Lawton rolled away to gather his clothing. Good God, wouldn't it be the crowning glory if he *did* fall head over heels for a woman who had evil designs on him? The Snowbird and her outlaw gang would have the last laugh, and fool that he was, Lawton would cling to the hope that Cairo would be his salvation, even when he was breathing his last breath.

Lawton cursed himself as he stalked off to gather wood for the campfire. He thought he could travel across Indian Territory with the Snowbird in tow and elude the Gardiners. Now he wasn't so sure. He wondered if Cairo meant what she had said, wondered if she would protect him in the face of calamity. Maybe she had employed the same sly tactic of trying to win his allegiance. Maybe her words of love were all a sham, aimed to strip him of his defenses.

Time to switch tactics, Lawton decided as he squatted down to ignite the kindling. He would try to appeal to her sense of decency and steer her away from her life of crime.

"Belle Starr, the bandit queen of Indian Territory, is buried south of here, near her hideout at Younger's

Bend," Lawton said out of the blue.

Cairo paused from fastening the buttons of her jacket and peered at him. What a bumfuzzling man Lawton was! He had seduced her and declared his love. And then, abruptly, he was telling her about a female bandit. Talk about hopping from one unrelated topic to another like a leaping mountain goat!

"Belle's most recent husband, Jim July Starr, is rumored to have bushwhacked her in February of this year. Unfortunately, that hasn't been proved conclusively," Lawton went on to say as he added logs to the fire. He hoped Cairo was taking his words to heart. "Jim tried to pay Milo Hoyt two hundred dollars to kill her. But Milo liked Belle, obviously a lot better than her second husband did. When the attempt to have Milo murder Belle failed, Jim tried to frame his neighbor, Edgar Watson, by borrowing his rifle, the same one which supposedly brought Belle to a bad end. But Watson had an alibi and he found the tracks of Jim's boots near the scene of the ambush. Judge Parker dismissed the charges against Watson and some of the marshals are scouring the country to locate Jim to arrest him."

Lawton stared levelly at Cairo. "Belle's death only proves that crime doesn't pay," he said philosophically. "The very man Belle trusted was the one who betrayed her. There seems to be no code of ethics among outlaws. Sure glad I'm not one," he added in what was meant to sound like an off-handed remark. "They'll shoot you in the back if you give them the chance—even if you are one of their own kind."

Cairo wanted to discuss her love for Lawton, not Belle Starr's ambush. If Lawton could bounce from one unrelated subject to another like a jackrabbit, so could she! "Lawton, there's something I want to—"

She was unable to wedge in a full sentence before Lawton went off on another tangent.

"And that brings to mind another female bandit named Ella Watson, alias Cattle Kate. And no, she wasn't related to the Edgar Watson who was framed for Belle's murder," he assured Cairo before she could pose the question. "Kate was suspected of stealing herds of livestock and selling them for a profit of one hundred percent." Lawton stirred the fire before focusing on Cairo. "But Kate got to see her end coming. She and her lover, Jim Averell, were dragged from their cabin on the Sweetwater range in Wyoming this very year. They were hanged side by side. That was the end of the gun-toting rustler queen and another example of a good woman gone bad."

"Lawton, this is all very interesting, but I—"

Again Cairo was cut short. Lawton was determined to discourage the Snowbird from her life of crime, for her benefit as well as his own. "But I would have to say the most brutal female in the West has to be Katie Bender of Kansas. She was not only a beauty but also the brains of her household. In the seventies, Katie and her family sold groceries to travelers and offered them room and board. After several people disappeared, including a local physician, a posse searched the Bender farm and came upon the victims Katie had robbed and buried in the vegetable garden."

Cairo shuddered. She was all the more determined to change the grisly subject and quickly! "Curse it, Lawton," she interjected, in a firm tone. "There are several things we need to discuss and now is the time—"

The bark of an unseen rifle suddenly sent a bullet zinging through the trees. Lawton dived to the ground, but pelleting gunfire danced in the dirt so close to his head that he swore he saw fragments of his life pass before him.

This was the moment of doom that he had anticipated! The Gardiners had sneaked up on him while he was babbling about female bandits who had died as they had lived. Cursing his predicament, Lawton rolled sideways to clutch his rifle and pump lead at the sparks that revealed his assailants' hiding places in the underbrush. Lawton had no time to pay heed to what Cairo was doing, only time to cover himself as he fired a barrage of bullets and crawled toward a nearby tree.

Another volley of rapid-fire bullets kept him pinned down, but the instant a distant rifle exploded, he took aim at the flash of light caused by the discharging weapon and he blasted away at the bushwhacker.

The yelp which erupted in the distance indicated he had found his mark. Lawton quickly turned his attention on the sparks to his right and sent a round of lead whizzing into the brush. The rustle of the bushes and the suddenly silent rifle indicated he had met with success a second time.

Only then did Lawton dare to allow himself to become distracted. His gaze swung to the spot where Cairo had stood two minutes earlier. She suddenly emerged from her hiding place behind a blackjack tree with a pistol in her hand—one of his Peacemakers, no less! Lawton didn't want to believe his eyes when Cairo turned the weapon toward him, her jaw clinched, her frown menacing.

God Almighty, she intended to finish him off while she thought him to be distracted by the gunfire! Lawton hesitated for a split second, rebelling against the idea of having to shoot Cairo before she could cut him down. Later, he would deal with this emotional turmoil that bombarded him, but not now, not when he was staring death in the face—a lovely but treacherous face!

The click of the trigger put Lawton's survival instincts into action. When Cairo took aim at him, he had no choice but to shoot. Like a lunging panther he dropped his rifle and snatched up his pistol. He fired at Cairo's right shoulder, hoping to wound her and cause her shot to go astray. Pistols simultaneously screamed in the night and it was an agonizing wait to discover who had hit whom.

The disbelieving look on Cairo's face when she realized Lawton had shot her in the arm would haunt Lawton throughout eternity. Pain and horror were etched in her shadowed features as she spun about and collapsed, clutching her bloody arm.

The shot Cairo had fired had whizzed over Lawton's head. He had been so tormented by what Cairo intended to do to him and what he had been forced to do to her that his brain was momentarily paralyzed. It was only seconds later that he became aware of the thrashing in the bushes, even though time seemed to hang in haunted limbo for countless hours.

Lawton lurched around to see his wounded attacker charging from the underbrush with his rifle cradled against his injured ribs. Too late Lawton realized that Cairo had set her mark on the third bushwhacker who had sneaked up to ambush him in the dark.

While Lawton was focusing on his assailant, Cairo was clutching her pistol in her left hand to fire again. Three bullets discharged in unison—Cairo's, Lawton's and the bushwhacker's.

The scalawag staggered forward, still attempting to pull the rifle to his shoulder and pump Lawton full of lead. Before his finger could clench on the trigger, his eyes glazed and, bleeding profusely, the assailant pitched forward on the ground, never to rise again.

Lawton was still crouched, his pistol poised in his hand. His tormented mind shouted curses at him. God, he had really shot Cairo! She had taken aim on the third bushwhacker who had used his friends to provide cover while he sneaked up on Lawton's blind side. Cairo hadn't attempted to kill him. Her bullet was meant for his assailant and she had hit her target and slowed the man down long enough for Lawton to recover. She had tried to protect him from catastrophe and he had shot her!

His head swiveled around to see Cairo doubled over. The unspoken questions in her misty green eyes had Lawton suffering all the torments of the damned. He knew she would hate him now and forevermore. But damn it, he thought she was going to blow him to smithereens!

Like a condemned prisoner marching to the gallows, Lawton approached the wounded, sobbing beauty.

Lawton cringed at the unsettling thought of what he'd done, but before he could open his mouth to apologize, Cairo blasted away at him.

"Are you crazy!" she railed through the scalding tears that boiled down her cheeks. "I tried to save your rotten, miserable life and you tried to destroy mine!

Damn you, Lawton, one minute you say you love me and the next second you try to blow off my arm."

Cairo glared flaming arrows at him. "Curse it, with a lover like you, I have no need of mortal enemies. What happened? Did you regret your words of love so much that you thought the ambush would be the perfect excuse to get rid of me permanently?" Bitter laughter tumbled from her lips. "No doubt you planned to write up a tidy little report that indicated I was killed by bushwhackers instead of the legendary Marshal Lawton Stone himself!"

While Cairo wept a river of frustrated tears, Lawton dropped to his knees to inspect the wound he had caused. "I'm sorry, Cairo. I thought—"

Cairo jerked away as if she had been stung by a scorpion. "Don't touch me ever again, you maniac!" she sputtered furiously.

"Let me take a look at your wound," Lawton requested.

God, he felt horible. He had marred this exquisite beauty for life. Shooting Cairo was the worst torture imaginable. Realizing, too late, that she had only tried to protect him was unholy torment.

Cairo was still irate. With an angry jerk, she split the seam of her shirt-sleeve to gesture to the seeping wound Lawton had inflicted on her. "There, look at it," she spluttered through her tears. "Are you satisfied now that you know you've drawn blood?" Cairo gulped down the nausea that threatened to crack her composure. Then she burst into another choked sob that tore Lawton's heart out. "I hate you. I loathe you. I—" Her voice broke completely and the dam of tears burst forth like a roaring river.

Lawton managed to drag his feet beneath him and stand up. Dismally, he strode over to collect his first-aid supplies from his saddlebags. When he returned to Cairo she had regained a smidgen of her composure. Her moist lashes swept up, regarding him with blatant hatred and mistrust.

"Don't you want to shoot me once more for good measure?" she questioned. "Or do you simply plan to patch me up just enough for gangrene to set in?" She laughed resentfully as she cradled her throbbing arm against her side. "No doubt you'll derive demented pleasure when you get to amputate my arm—"

"Stop it," Lawton snapped. He made a valiant effort to contain his own guilt, but Cairo's well-aimed barbs lodged under his skin. "Damnation, I thought you were trying to shoot me and I reacted in self-defense."

"Shoot you?" Cairo howled in pain and astonishment. "Why the blazes would I do that? You're the lunatic around here, not me." She dragged in a deep breath and glared mutinously at him. "While you were blasting away at the other two bushwhackers in the clump of brush, I saw the silhouette of the third man darting through the trees. I shot him before he could bury a bullet in your back. I wish I hadn't interfered!" she all but yelled at him. "It's a shame you didn't take the bullet. But I'm sure you would have only bled ice water and the wound would have frozen up in no time at all."

His head dropped in a humble gesture. "I didn't realize what you intended until it was too late." He sank down to tend her wound. "In this profession there are damned few allowances for mistakes. A man doesn't get second chances. Knowing that, I reacted instinctively. I'm truly sorry about what happened."

"Aren't you just!" she smirked, trying to scoot away.

Although she protested his touch, Lawton poured antiseptic on the gash on her arm and listened to her yelp of agony. "It's only a flesh wound," he diagnosed while he packed poultice on her injured shoulder.

"Lucky me! I suppose you could have put a bullet clean through my heart if that had been your wont."

"I could have," he agreed.

It wasn't a boast, only a simple statement of truth. She had seen Lawton in action. He was deadly and accurate and lightning-quick with both pistol and rifle. But what upset Cairo beyond words was that Lawton had so little faith in her that he believed her capable of murdering him.

What a miserable judge of character she had turned out to be. The man she thought she loved was a trigger-happy shootist who would unload his pistol on anything or anybody who walked, crawled or flew—including her!

Lawton bandaged Cairo's arm and tied a sling over her shoulder while Cairo glared at him. If she had known how terrible he felt about what he'd done to her, she would have enjoyed immense satisfaction. But if he uttered one word while she was in this murderous frame of mind, he knew she would have cheerfully killed him. Not that he didn't deserve to be lambasted with insults and blown to kingdom come, but Lawton had already called himself every name in the book and endured nine kinds of hell. Nothing Cairo could do to him could make him feel worse than he already did.

When Lawton finally identified his dead foe, Cairo glared holes in his buckskin jacket. "What do you plan to do now, gather the dead and shoot them again for sport?"

The hateful remark found its mark. Lawton flinched and broke stride. With considerable effort, he clamped down on his tongue and ambled off to locate the bodies of the men who had attempted to murder him. He knew he had made a critical mistake when he inspected the three desperadoes. Although they fit the descriptions of marauding horse and cattle thieves who had preyed on the Creek Nation, none of them were members of the Gardiner gang.

Again Lawton was tormented by indecision. For the past few days he had been certain Cairo was the Snowbird. Her comments seemed to carry double meanings. Her skills with weapons proved she could be resourceful and deadly. But the men who had tried to kill him *weren't* the Gardiners and the sensible side of his brain insisted he had misjudged the green-eyed hellion.

But what if Cairo had taken advantage of opportunity? the hounds of doubt barked at him. Maybe she had seen her chance to dispose of him without the Gardiners' help and she had only fired at his assassin when she feared Lawton was wise to her. Maybe the Gardiners were still out there somewhere waiting, just as their taunting telegrams suggested.

That was certainly within the realm of possibility, Lawton mused. But he still couldn't figure out why these three rustlers had come gunning for him.

Lawton had a million questions and not one logical answer. He began the unpleasant task of burying his would-be murderers. He hoped the time it would take him allowed Cairo to cool off.

When Lawton returned to camp, Cairo had rolled into her blankets as if they were a protective cocoon. She didn't speak or even acknowledge his presence. First she had ranted and raved at him. Now she was giving him the silent treatment.

Wrestling with his own troubled thoughts, Lawton crawled into his bedroll. He had the unshakable feeling he wouldn't get much sleep this night, what with all the torment that haunted him. And sure enough, Lawton was right. He hardly slept a wink.

Chapter Ten

Cairo wasn't certain if the temperature had dropped again or if the chill in her body and soul had caused her to shiver inside her coat. She had donned several layers of clothing to counter the biting wind as she rode west behind the man she had once loved and now hated with the same fervent passion. Cairo was annoyed to the extreme when he even dared to look in her direction. Lawton could do no right in her eyes. And when he began to hum "Skip to My Lou" for the umpteenth time, Cairo exploded.

"I already told you that you couldn't carry a tune, even in a gunny sack," she snapped. "Your incessant humming is no better!"

"Since you refuse to speak to me, I have to do something to occupy my mind," he defended.

The iciness between them and the dropping temperature was spoiling Lawton's mood, too. To compound that, he was battling guilt and regret. What he needed was to put some space between himself and Cairo until he could think clearly once again. But that was impossible. If he let her out of his sight she would probably sneak up and shoot him when he wasn't looking. She still appeared to be *that* furious with him.

"Occupy your mind?" Cairo countered "*What* mind? As far as I can tell, you don't have one."

"Damn it, I said I was sorry!"

"Sorry?" Cairo smirked. "Do you think you can offer an apology and wave your arms and magically make everything right again?" She glared at Lawton. "Well, you can say you're sorry ten dozen times and it won't soothe the pain in my arm." *And in my heart,* she silently tacked on.

"What do I have to do to convince you that I regret jumping to the wrong conclusion and shooting you?"

"You *jumping* off a towering cliff into a dry riverbed ought to do it," she sniped.

Lawton sighed. "Did you ever stop to think that you looked guilty when you aimed that pistol at my head?"

"I was aiming *over* your head," Cairo clarified, her voice rising with each word. "If you weren't so blessed suspicious you might have noticed!"

"It was damned difficult to tell who was trying to shoot whom, especially when bullets were coming at me from all directions," he snapped back at her.

"It's a wonder to me that you haven't shot Woody and Tucker before now," she parried caustically, just before a pained groan erupted from her lips. Her chestnut gelding had leaped over the gully in front of them and the jarring motion aggravated her tender shoulder.

"Do you want to stop to rest?" Lawton asked her when he noticed the grimace that whitened her elegant features.

"What? And force myself to spend extra time in your disgusting presence? No thank you. I'm counting the minutes until I'll be rid of you permanently!"

"I'll just bet you are," Lawton grumbled. The Snowbird was probably back to plotting his murder again. If she didn't think she had cause to kill him before, she certainly did now!

Flipping his ivory-handled Peacemaker from its holster, Lawton leaned out to place the weapon in her hand. "Here. Why don't you go ahead and blow me to kingdom come and get this over with. I'm sure we'll both feel a helluva lot better."

"The only thing that will make me feel better is having you feel worse," she flung at him, along with a venomous glower.

When the snowflakes began to fall from the dense gray clouds that had blanketed the sky for the past two days, Cairo groaned. "Curse it, an early snowstorm. I swear the weather in these Twin Territories changes every other day."

Lawton pulled the brim of his hat low on his forehead to ward off the snowflakes that drifted from the heavens. As if there wasn't enough chill in the air from Cairo's arctic tone, it had to go and snow! Now it would be a simple matter for the Gardiners to track him. The hoofprints that were beginning to stretch out behind him were as obvious as a map.

Making a mental note to keep a careful watch on his back, Lawton trekked west toward the farmhouse of a Creek Indian who had always offered him a room and food and plenty of conversation. Lawton welcomed the opportunity of putting a buffer between him and the fire-breathing witch who had chewed him up one side and down the other so many times that he had become thin-skinned. He couldn't wait to be greeted by a friendly face!

Although fear and distrust prevented most Indian and white residents of Indian Territory from lending assistance to U.S. marshals, Possum Hitke was an exception. In some areas, Lawton had come upon entire communities that provided asylum for fugitives from justice in exchange for immunity against the thieving hordes. There was also a borderline class of individuals who weren't above thieving and peddling whiskey to Indians, who eagerly lent their assistance to known criminals. But unlike most folks, Possum worked his farm without outside interference from Indians or whites. His log cabin was off the beaten path and was often used by respectable travelers and fleeing desperadoes. It stood on a ridge of ground, surrounded by a clump of trees. He could see the comings and goings of travelers before trouble landed on his doorstep. Lawton wasn't sure what technique Possum utilized to disappear into thin air when outlaws did veer toward his farm to attempt to steal supplies or take cover. Lawton didn't ask, either. He knew it was better for Possum to simply evaporate when an ill wind blew outlaws in his direction.

Most Indians in the territory spoke very little to the whites. Some only made gestures with their hands and grunted when questioned for information. But most of the Indians, Lawton had discovered, were amazingly honest—more so than the whites of the region. When an Indian imparted information to a marshal, he could depend on the statements to be truth. And if an Indian made a promise, he kept his word. If an Indian liked an officer, he would even risk his life for him. And the misinformed whites called Indians heathens! Some white folks would have done themselves a favor if they had taken lessons in honesty from the Five Civilized Tribes.

Possum Hitke had taught Lawton the invaluable techniques of tracking outlaws across the plains. According to the experienced Possum, a marshal could ride to a lone tree or rock ridge and pick up a trail. Everyone in the area used singular trees and high peaks of ground as landmarks. Many a time, when a wily band of thieves had eluded him, Lawton found the tracks converging at just such landmarks. Possum was a wealth of information, but he was particular about who he called friend. Lawton was honored to be one of the chosen few.

When Possum, toting his Winchester, emerged from his cabin, Lawton greeted him with a wide smile. He was rewarded with Possum's answering grin, which lacked two front teeth!

"Saw you comin', Law," Possum declared. His obsidian eyes shifted to assess the blonde who cradled her arm in a sling. He frowned, then refocused his attention on the imposing figure of the man who sat upon his black stallion. "Unfill yer saddle, Law. The fire is cracklin' and supper's cookin'."

Lawton swung to the ground. He would have attempted to assist Cairo down, but he'd had his hands slapped away so many times the past few days that he'd abandoned his attempt at courtesy.

Lawton could tell by the way the stout Creek Indian

kept stealing glances at Cairo that he recognized her. The instant Cairo went inside the cabin to warm herself by the fire, Lawton turned his questioning gaze on Possum.

"You've seen her before, haven't you, Pos?"

Possum's massive shoulders lifted and then dropped beneath his buffalo-hide coat. "Maybe yes. Maybe no. Can't say for certain."

"When?" Lawton prodded.

"A month ago, maybe more. I lose track of the days," he answered honestly. "Three men and a woman passed through here." He gestured toward the rise of ground to the north. "I smelled trouble and took to my hidin' place with my supplies so nobody could steal them."

Lawton was no closer to the truth than he had been the day Cairo had swept into his cottage in Fort Smith.

"Who shot the woman?" Possum asked.

"I did."

Possum's black brows jackknifed. "Is she wanted?"

"I'm not sure," Lawton hedged, shifting uncomfortably from one foot to the other.

"Then why'd you shoot her?" A mischievous smile pursed Possum's lips. "Did you think she needed it?"

"I guess I must have," Lawton mumbled, staring at the door instead of Possum's ornery grin.

Possum didn't lay claim to much with his modest farm and scant number of livestock, but he did possess an expansive sense of humor. He laughed heartily. "Wish I'd thought of that when my woman ran off with a white man. Might've at least slowed her down, though I can't say I wanted to stop her. She did me a big favor when she left. One contrary, ill-tempered mule around here is enough. No need to feed two."

Lawton grinned. Didn't he know what it was like to put up with a muleheaded female! Maybe he'd save himself a peck of trouble if he let Cairo ride off alone.

The instant Possum and Lawton entered the cabin, Cairo turned back to the blazing hearth. She didn't want to seem rude to the Indian, but she could barely tolerate the sight of Lawton. Cairo had never believed it possible that a man could break her heart. She simply couldn't understand Lawton. But the one thing she *did* comprehend was that he had plied her with false phrases of love, and she vowed never to fall prey to those empty words again.

"Do you want something to eat, Cai, or do you plan to survive on your hatred for me alone?" Lawton asked as he came to warm himself by the fire.

Cairo flashed him a poisonous smile. "Although despising you is nourishment enough to last me a month, I am planning on eating. Hopefully, it will smother the bitter taste that thinking about your treachery leaves in my mouth."

Possum dipped up a steaming cup of stew from the kettle that hung in the hearth. He moved silently toward the table and gestured for Cairo to join him. When Lawton went to fetch his own cup and stew, Possum graced Cairo with a toothless grin. His dark eyes twinkled devilishly as he dropped into the seat beside her.

"He's a mean son-of-bitch," Possum confided, still grinning mischievously. "Outlaws hate him, but I like him." His gaze shifted to her wounded arm. "It might be better for you if you liked him, too."

Cairo didn't quite know how to take Possum Hitke.

He had an ornery gleam in his opaque eyes and a wry smile on his lips, but she supposed the comments were his way of taking the edge off the brittle silence that filled the room.

Finally, Cairo buckled beneath his contagious smile. Since she was a guest in the Indian's home, she decided to call a truce in her war with Lawton.

"Thank you for the stew, Possum, and the chance to ward off the chill." One delicate brow arched questioningly. "You wouldn't, by any chance, have such a soft spot in your heart for Lawton that you would consider changing places with me, would you?"

Possum gave his head a negative shake, sending his black hair rippling over his shoulders. "Nope. I can only take him in small doses. I might not like him so much if I had to ride with him." He leaned closer to convey a private comment. "He don't sing so good. Reminds me of a dyin' coyote."

Cairo couldn't contain her giggle. It seemed she wasn't the only one who took offense to Lawton's off-key crooning.

The Indian's remarks eased Cairo's sour mood and the stew warmed the frozen place that had once been her heart. Feeling better than she had in days, she sat in the crude homemade chair and listened to Lawton and Possum converse. The Indian compensated for his long weeks of lonely isolation by talking Lawton's legs off. Cairo, however, would have settled for shooting them off. She might have set aside her anger temporarily, but she still wanted to see that big handsome gorilla suffer for hurting her.

If only he had a heart, she sighed defeatedly, she would do all within her power to break it so he would know how deeply he had hurt her with his loving lies and his painful shot in the arm!

When the sun peeked through the clouds the following morning, Cairo looked out the window to see a thick carpet of snow blanketing the prairie. The world didn't appear quite so bleak, but there was still a chill in the air and in her heart.

After Lawton had thanked Possum for the hospitality and dropped a few coins in his hand to express his gratitude, he accompanied Cairo outside. Stubborn to the core, Cairo struggled into the saddle without his assistance.

Possum stifled a grin when he witnessed Cairo's belligerence. He ambled off the porch to make an offer to Lawton, who had paused to check his worn saddle cinch. "I could keep the white woman for you," he volunteered. "Maybe she'll thaw out, come spring."

"I doubt it," Lawton grunted as he reached under the stallion to fasten the girth.

"If she stays with you, she may be frozen up till summer," Possum predicted.

Lawton couldn't argue with that. In fact, he thought Possum was being a mite optimistic.

Lawton waved farewell and reined his steed west, plodding through the blinding white snow. Just as he suspected, Cairo reverted to her icy demeanor the instant they left Possum's cabin. Having time to mull over what Possum had told him about spotting Cairo, or her lookalike, in the area the previous month, Lawton felt the old familiar suspicions digging another trench in his mind. Was she the Snowbird or wasn't she?

They rode in silence all day, pausing only a few minutes at a time to rest their horses and tend their needs. When Lawton announced that they were halting for the night, Cairo beat him out of the saddle to gather wood for a campfire.

Curse it, she was freezing to death! The fact that Lawton showed no visible signs of discomfort assured her that the cold-blooded snake was immune to the winter chill. Nothing fazed Lawton Rock-Hearted Stone—not rain, hail, sleet or snow, and certainly not a woman's scorn.

After munching on canned beans, dried fruit, and sourdough biscuits, none of which, Lawton noted, Cairo allowed to touch each other on her plate, he grabbed the shovel, and began to dig a hole. Since Cairo had cursed him for singing and humming "Skip to My Lou," Lawton now whistled the tune while he dug.

Cairo frowned as she watched him, ignoring the annoying sound. "I hope that isn't my grave," she commented sarcastically. "I had visions of being put to rest in a less secluded place where passersby could pause to read your name on my tombstone as my cause of death."

Lawton slammed the short-handled shovel into the ground and punished her with a steely glance. "For chrissake, will you knock off the snide remarks! I'm digging you a pit for coals so you can stay warm through the night!"

"I'll dig my own pit, thank you very much." Her chin jutted out to that stubborn angle.

Lawton thrust the shovel at her. "Fine, then," he said gruffly. "I'm sure you think you can do a better job of it anyway, even with one arm in a sling."

Cairo regretted allowing her stubbornness and volatile temper to get the better of her. It was difficult to dig in the half-frozen ground with only one good arm, but her pride encouraged her to complete the task, exhausting though it was.

Huffing and puffing, Cairo paused to watch Lawton scrape the glowing coals from the campfire and insulate them. Cairo copied the procedure, unfamiliar though it was to her. When Lawton opened his mouth to offer advice, she flung up her hand to silence him.

"I'll do this myself," she announced.

He shrugged a broad shoulder. "Have it your way."

"I intend to."

And she did.

Three hours later, when the chill of the night settled over the prairie, Cairo realized she hadn't *insulated* the coals; she had *smothered* them. She had been chilled for more days than she cared to count, and now the earth beneath her was as cold as the air above her.

Cairo snuggled down into her bedroll and shivered until her teeth chattered. When she glanced at Lawton, he levered himself onto an elbow and flipped back the quilt in invitation for her to join him in his cozy coal bed.

It was on the tip of her frozen tongue to tell him exactly where he could stuff his glowing coals, but Cairo quickly decided to swallow her pride. She could either lie there and freeze to death or sleep with that snake. Her instinct for self-preservation overpowered her chilled pride.

With as much dignity as she could muster, Cairo bridged the space that separated them and slid beneath the quilts. "I want it understood here and now that I intend to do nothing more than share your warm pallet," she said in no uncertain terms.

"I didn't ask for anything more, did I?" Lawton muttered.

"No, but I can see that devious mind of yours working," she accused as she cuddled up against his toasty chest.

"Pleasant dreams," Lawton murmured against the curve of her neck.

Cairo told herself that the glowing coals beneath her were setting sparks to her latent desires. Whatever the source of the fire, instant flames scorched her body. She was burning inside and out from the moment she nestled against Lawton and inhaled the scent of him. She could feel her pulse leapfrogging through her blood when Lawton did something as harmless as draping his arm over her hip. They lay on their sides, her back molded to his chest, her hips meshed familiarly to his lean, powerful thighs, his knees tucked beneath her derriere. She could feel his warm breath caressing the ultrasensitive spot beneath her ear and she trembled, but not from the cold air that hovered above her!

Cairo had assured herself that Lawton's touch would repulse her, in light of what he'd done to her. The pain in her shoulder was a constant reminder of that bitter incident. But Cairo realized that she was not immune to his touch, no matter how much she wanted to be. Despite her wounded pride and bruised heart, he still had the power to stir her. The feel of his masculine body lying next to hers triggered memories of their lovemaking. Each time Lawton moved, her body tingled. Each time his moist breath caressed her neck, she trembled with awakened desire.

Curse it! Didn't she have an ounce of willpower, a tittle of sense? This man had tried to *kill* her, for crying out loud! And what was every bit as bad was that he believed *her* capable of killing *him*. How could she still want him?

If Cairo thought she was having difficulty battling her traitorous body, Lawton was in double trouble. Cuddled against this shapely minx, all he could think of was the wild ecstasy they had shared when they set their conflicts aside and responded to the ardent needs they aroused in each other. The feel of her voluptuous body against his was driving him mad. He could feel the hunger of wanting her burgeoning inside him, throbbing in his loins.

What the hell, thought Lawton. He wasn't going to get any sleep with her lying in his arms anyway. He had no willpower. Each time he had resisted his attraction for her it only intensified his craving. He had grown accustomed to her hatred but he couldn't live without her lovemaking.

While Lawton was mulling over his thoughts, his hand glided over Cairo's hip in an absent caress. When he realized what he was doing it was already too late. Gigantic needs engulfed him. His lips sought out hers, hungry to lose himself in the sweet taste of her kiss. His body covered hers, though he took care not to aggravate her injured arm. His knee slid between her legs, guiding them apart before his hands wandered over her belly to swirl over her inner thighs.

Cairo hadn't meant to gasp at the feel of his

fingertips skimming the fabric of her breeches. Nor did she intend to arch toward his seeking hand. But she did, and most shamelessly. She knew Lawton was aware of the effect he was having on her—the same devastating effect she seemed to have on him.

Her brain broke down when his exploring hands slid beneath her shirt to caress the roseate buds of her breasts. She struggled to inhale a breath when his greedy lips suckled at the taut peaks. His hands were everywhere at once—teasing, sensitizing, arousing. With masterful seduction, he peeled away her garments, granting himself the freedom to explore her silken flesh.

His passionate touch and heart-stopping kisses demanded her response, and Cairo returned the heady pleasure kiss for kiss, caress for caress. Her hands were never still as they investigated the whipcord muscles that covered his chest, the hard, lean columns of his thighs and hips. But touching him and having him touch her suddenly wasn't enough to satisfy the white-hot ache that burned in the core of her being. She longed to be flesh to flesh and soul to soul. She yearned to soar toward that pinnacle of rapture she had discovered when they were one beating breathing essence.

"Lawton, please . . ."

He knew what she wanted without her having to voice the words, but he was governed by a need to caress away every ounce of her hatred for him, to shatter every smidgen of her reserve. In their stormy relationship he wanted this to be the one sweet moment that transcended their conflicts.

Cairo swore she would burn herself into a pile of

frustrated ashes long before Lawton satisfied the burning needs he had evoked from her with his seductive caresses. Over and over again his hands and lips sought out each sensitive point on her body and set it aflame. He was teaching her about passion, things that left her senses reeling in delight. Her body quivered beneath his intimate assault until she was shuddering.

Finally, Cairo could endure no more of this maddening torment. Impatiently she drew his lips back to hers and guided his body to hers. She stroked his velvet warmth, urging him to take complete possession, to end the sweet agony of having him so close and yet so far away.

Lawton had held his own raging desires in check to arouse her to the limits of sanity. But when her hand folded around him, he could feel restraint fighting its chains of captivity. His taut body uncoiled upon hers to take absolute possession, but *he* quickly became *her* possession, a mindless puppet who responded to the cadence of lovemaking she had set.

His body surged toward hers, matching the throb of pleasure that pulsated through his heart and echoed back from hers. Wave upon wave of splendor crested over him as they rode out the storm of passion. Lawton could feel himself losing all control over his mind and body, driven by the intense pleasure that riveted him.

Spasms of ecstasy undulated through him as he plunged deeply within her. The world turned black. He felt as if he had become like the blazing stars that flamed in the midnight sky—burning from inside out, consumed.

With a groan of satisfaction, Lawton clutched Cairo

to him so tightly that he feared he would injure her mending arm, but he couldn't ease his grasp to save his life. Only when the last shudders of splendor shot through his body did he feel himself loosening his hold on her.

Cairo's long, curly lashes fluttered up as she pressed a kiss to his neck. "You are a devastating lover," she complimented and then blushed at her confession. The words had flocked to the tip of her tongue and flown off before she could think to bite them back.

Although his energy was depleted, sheer will allowed Lawton to prop himself up on his forearms. He stared down into Cairo's face. "Am I?" A roguish smile quirked his sensuous lips. "What did I do to earn such praise, sweet witch?"

Cairo wondered if Lawton had any idea how sensual and devastating he was when he smiled. There was a natural aura about him that tugged on her heartstrings and lured her to him. Cairo couldn't think past this delicious moment, didn't *want* to think about their stormy past and frustrating conflicts. With an impish grin, she scooted away and eased onto her hip.

"This is what you did, if memory serves . . ." she murmured as she set her hands upon his steel-hard flesh.

Cairo traced a path around each male nipple before she tracked a path down the dark matting of hair that covered his belly and beyond.

Lawton choked on his breath and caught her adventurous hand in his own. "Perhaps witches can revive quickly after such devastating passion, but mortal men cannot," he croaked. "I need time to regain my strength."

One delicately arched brow elevated as her eyes glided over his muscular flesh. "I think perhaps you underestimate yourself."

Lawton didn't think so. At the moment, everything he did demanded extreme effort. "You still have a lot to learn about men," he told her, his voice ragged with the aftereffects of passion.

A seductive smile pursed her lips. She wormed her hand free to continue her explorations. "Indeed I do," she agreed. "And there is no better time to learn than now . . ."

When her brazen kisses and caresses swam over his flesh, Lawton was the one who discovered a thing or two he hadn't known. He could have sworn the fires of desire had burned themselves out, but her tantalizing touch regenerated him. When her body glided over his in a long, sensual caress, Lawton groaned in astonishment. Suddenly he was back to wanting this woman in the worst possible way.

She employed the arousing techniques he had used on her and she invented a few of her own that left Lawton's palpitating heart climbing the ladder of his ribs. The numbing pleasure that had engulfed him moments before became a tingling sensation that expanded until it affected every fiber of his being. She was doing incredible things to his body with her butterfly kisses and whispering caresses. One soul-shattering sensation after another assailed him, causing him to sink into the web of rapture she had spun around him. She stroked him until he gasped for breath. She teased him until he arched toward her and groaned in sweet torment.

Cairo had replenished his strength and left desire

gnawing at him, as if it had been days instead of minutes since they had made wild sweet love. She had proved her powers over him and made a liar out of him. He didn't need to rest after all, he realized as her kisses and caresses wandered over his body to locate each sensitive point. He needed this green-eyed temptress with hair like moonbeams and eyes like polished emeralds. She made him whole and alive.

With a tormented groan, Lawton guided her curvaceous hips to his. His tongue flicked at the rose-tipped crests of her breasts as she moved above him, fanning the flames of a fire Lawton swore would never burn itself out.

"You win . . ." Lawton gasped. "Do with me what you will . . ."

Cairo marveled at the satisfaction she felt in seducing this iron-willed man. It was gratifying to know she could shatter his self-control as thoroughly as he had shattered hers. She had initiated their lovemaking and aroused him to the point that he actually trembled with the need of her.

"You want me then?" Cairo taunted playfully.

"*Want* you?" Lawton drew her ever closer. "I swear I'll die if you don't come to me!"

Lawton settled her intimately above him. And suddenly they were setting sail across the starlit heavens. Ineffable sensations of splendor ribboned through him. He was like a shooting star blazing toward the earth, scorched by the flames that he knew would soon consume him.

Much later Lawton emerged from the wild dimensions of ecstasy. And there, peering down at him with a mischievous smile on her petal-soft lips was the one woman who could affect him like no other. He had suddenly acquired the ability to read her mind. The challenging expression on her face prompted him to give his head a negative shake.

"Oh no you don't," he protested, his voice not as firm as he'd hoped. "Not again . . ."

"Oh yes I do," Cairo contradicted as her hand glided over the scar on his ribs to trek along his hip. "Again . . ."

"I can't . . ."

His feeble protest died beneath her breath-stealing kiss. And lo and behold, Lawton discovered that he *could,* over and over again, each time she set her skillful hands upon him. There seemed to be no limit to his power when this witch began to kiss and caress him. Suddenly he and Cairo were making up for each night they had slept alone, appeasing needs that blazed anew with each intimate touch.

Lawton dozed off a time or two, but that was about the extent of it. He thought sometime during the night that he and Cairo could get enough of each other. It was the damnedest thing he'd ever experienced and he didn't dare think about why he had so lost himself to this woman.

Chapter Eleven

It was as if Lawton and Cairo had silently agreed to a truce. Cairo had pushed the tormenting events of the past aside. The night she'd shared in Lawton's arms on his bed of coals blurred the unpleasant memories. During their recent days of traveling, Lawton had become the essence of gentlemanly devotion and Cairo kept bursting into radiant smiles without knowing why.

Well, actually she did know why, even though she didn't vocalize her feelings. Cairo longed to discard their conflicts and begin their relationship from this point in time. The closer they came to the boundary of Oklahoma Territory, the more precious each moment she spent with Lawton became.

Cairo was uncertain of the future. There was still the problem with her father to resolve. She hadn't the faintest notion what she'd find when she arrived in Canadian Station. She only hoped Rylan Calhoun had been able to hold onto his hotel, despite his difficulties. But Cairo quickly reminded herself that Rylan was a very determined man. After all, she had inherited her persistence from him. Rylan wouldn't let anyone force him out, Cairo assured herself. He would dig in his heels and fight to save his dream of a new beginning in Oklahoma Territory or would die trying.

Determination . . . Cairo frowned. If she prided herself in being so determined, why was she such a coward when it came to confessing her love for Lawton and assuring him that she had never meant him any harm? And why was he so leery of her betraying him? It didn't make sense. Lawton seemed hell-bent on thinking the worst of her. Was it because he had no faith in women and had become too set in his ways to change?

Cairo suddenly felt herself being jerked out of the saddle. Her wide eyes focused on the rugged face above hers as Lawton settled her on his saddle facing him. Cairo was forced to straddle his hips, her thighs draped suggestively over the lean columns of his legs. The gliding movement of the stallion brought their hips together and apart and Cairo was vividly reminded of the potent magic of the intimate moments they had shared each night since their silent truce.

"Mmm . . . this is much better." Lawton's voice rumbled with disturbed passion. He, too, was aware of the provocative motion. "I don't like it when we're so far apart."

"We were only a horse away," she teased as she linked her fingers behind his neck.

His hair glistened blue-black in the bright sunlight when he gave his head a contradictory shake. "You were farther away than that, little nymph," he contended. "There was a distant look in your eyes.

Where were you?"

She tossed him a seductive smile as she pressed her supple body closer to his. "I'd prefer to discuss where I am now . . ."

When her honeyed lips parted in invitation, his curiosity melted into liquid desire. When that faraway look had glazed her eyes earlier, Lawton had felt as if she had abandoned him. Suspicion spurred him to pry into her private thoughts. But Cairo had distracted him so completely that he didn't care what she was thinking, only that she was back in his arms, offering him a kiss as intoxicating as wine.

"I wonder how difficult it would be to make love to you on the back of my stallion . . . he drawled.

But that wasn't the time to find out, Lawton soon discovered. The crack of a rifle suddenly shattered the silence. If Lawton hadn't been in the process of dipping his head toward Cairo's tempting mouth, he was sure the bullet would have parted his hair instead of merely sailing over his head.

Lawton plastered himself against his horse, squishing Cairo between him like sandwich meat between two slices of bread. The pommel of the saddle stabbed her in the back while the stallion thundered toward the cover of trees.

Another shower of bullets rained through the air from an embankment of rocks that protruded from the rolling plains. Lawton cursed himself for being so distracted. From what he could determine from his past experiences in shootouts, two gunmen were trying to fill his hide with lead. And they had come damned close to doing just that! A spray of buckshot splattered against the black stallion's rump, causing him to emit a shrill whinny and lunge off in fear.

Lawton had only regained control of his steed and bounded to the ground when another volley of bullets hissed through the air at closer range. Suspicion leaped up in Lawton and he glared at Cairo. Damn it, his weakness for this woman had almost gotten him killed a second time. He had barely dodged the barrage of bullets and found cover.

When more gunfire pelleted the melting snow beneath his feet, the startled stallion decided to hightail it to safety, leaving Lawton without a shield of defense. Before Lawton dived for cover, he recognized one of the two bushwhackers who had scuttled into the row of trees to the north.

Panhandle Dick, the notorious gunslinger who had joined the Gardiners in their most recent robbing sprees, bounded to his feet to snap his Winchester against his shoulder. Lawton didn't recognize the young scalawag who followed suit by bracing his rifle in position to fire. Lawton didn't have time to decide if the second man fit the descriptions of one of the dozen bench warrants he carried in his saddlebag. He was short on time and his life was at stake.

To Cairo's disbelief, Lawton yanked her in front of him as if she were his shield of armor! To her further astonishment, he rammed the barrel of his Winchester under her arm, aiming it directly at Panhandle Dick.

The two desperadoes were momentarily stunned by Lawton's action. Panhandle Dick, who had been staring down the sight of his rifle, preparing to fire, jerked his head up to peer bewilderedly at the woman who was clamped in Lawton's arms.

"Drop 'em," Lawton growled.

He was certain the bandits wouldn't try to get to him through Cairo. She was, after all, one of them! But Lawton had committed an error in judgment. He had forgotten that Cairo stood only five feet two inches tall and that he towered over her at six feet four. That left, according to Panhandle Dick's calculations, a foot of bulky shoulders and head as a possible target.

Dick aimed at his target. But because he had so little room for error, he was overly deliberate in staring down the rifle sight. That allowed Lawton the precious time needed to cock his rifle and shoot from the hip.

Cairo screeched in horror when two rifles discharged. Lawton hurled himself and Cairo from the path of the speeding bullet. Cairo was squished into the snow, an experience made infinitely worse because two hundred twenty pounds of steel-honed muscle landed on top of her. Her tender shoulder burned like fire, but Cairo couldn't relieve the strain on her arm while Lawton was smashing her into the ground, leaving her to sputter curses into the snow.

Kid Fontain watched in horrified disbelief when his partner stumbled backward—a fatal victim of Lawton's unerring aim. When Panhandle Dick collapsed in a lifeless heap, Kid scrambled behind a tree before he wound up in the same condition Dick was in—no condition at all, unless dead counted.

Lawton noted the frightened expression on the young outlaw's face. He was an inexperienced amateur at best, Lawton decided. Losing his partner had taken the wind out of the young renegade's sails in a damned hurry!

Using Cairo as a springboard, Lawton vaulted to his knees to snatch up the Peacemakers that hung on each hip. Before Kid Fontain could grab his Colt to protect himself from what he swore was certain death, Lawton had drawn and fired. It was then that Kid Fontain realized he wasn't as quick and accurate as he thought he was! Hell, he was still thinking about shooting at Lawton and the marshal was already pumping lead out of both pistols!

One of Lawton's bullets plunged into Kid's thigh, and he was so shocked that he didn't have time to consider firing. He was still staring at his bloody wound when Lawton bounded to his feet and charged at him, both pistols blazing.

Kid Fontain had the inescapable feeling that any of the bullets that splattered snow on his breeches could easily have found the target of his heart if that had been Lawton's wont. Marshal Stone was every bit as good as Kid Fontain had heard he was.

"Drop that weapon!" Lawton ordered with deadly venom.

Wide-eyed and blanch-faced, Kid did as he was told. Lawton stalked forward. With an angry jerk, Lawton shoved one Peacemaker back into its holster while keeping the other one trained on Kid's heaving chest. Kid waited until Lawton was almost upon him before he kicked snow in his captor's face and made an attempt to escape.

Kid had only wheeled and taken one step before the pistol barked at his heel. He panicked! Clashing with Lawton Stone was a living nightmare. His instinct to fight for his life was raging and he pivoted on his injured leg to kick at the Peacemaker. Kid threw himself toward Lawton to deliver a right cross. He did manage to get in two unanswered blows while Lawton was trying to wipe the muddy snow from his eyes, but when Lawton regained his balance and cleared his vision, the battle was on and Kid found his challenger to be more than a handful.

The young bandit wasn't sure which hurt worse—the gunshot wound in his thigh or the doubled fist that mashed his belly against his backbone. An agonized grunt exploded from his lips when Lawton's blow picked him up off the ground and sent him staggering backward. But that wasn't the worst of it, Kid soon found out. He became the recipient of two more bone-jarring blows that left stars revolving around his head. He found himself sprawled in the snow before it even registered in his spongy brain.

"Get up!" Lawton snarled ferociously.

Kid couldn't rise quickly enough to suit the furious marshal. He felt himself yanked up by the lapels of his jacket and slammed back against a tree.

"Why'd you try to shoot me?" Lawton sneered, his eyes sparking like pounded steel.

Kid couldn't speak. He swore Lawton had punctured both his lungs with his powerful blows.

"Answer me, damn you!" Lawton roared.

Kid flicked at his swollen lip and attempted to explain, but Lawton had no patience. With a muted growl, he shoved Kid back into the tree, putting a knot on his head.

Kid stared at the towering giant who looked tough enough and vindictive enough to tear his opponent limb from limb, if he had a mind to.

"We tried to bushwhack you for the money," Kid chirped when his voice finally began to function.

"What money?"

Kid had only to look as if he wasn't going to answer and Lawton encouraged him to sing like a bird. The painful blow to Kid's midsection loosed his lips.

"The bounty money," he sputtered. "The Gardiners sent word around the Twin Territories that they'd pay a ten-thousand dollar reward to anyone who killed you." Kid found meager satisfaction when Lawton cursed at the startling news. "They turned the tables on you, Marshal, and made a contest of it. For once you're the marked man with a price on his head. Every outlaw in the country will be trying to pick you off for the bounty."

Kid was unprepared when the burly marshal clamped his fingers into the collar of the muddy jacket and faced him toward the woman who had rolled to her feet to nurse the injury to her arm that had become reactivated.

"Do you know who she is?" Lawton spat in question.

"Sure, don't you?" The snippy retort earned Kid a painful jab in the ribs. For some reason the marshal was sensitive about the female. Kid didn't know for certain, but he thought that Lawton assumed the woman to be Jarita Gardiner. The two women certainly looked alike, especially at a distance. Kid had mistaken the woman himself when he'd first seen her with Lawton. Even Panhandle Dick had hesitated when Lawton dragged the woman in front of him for protection.

Jarita Gardiner and this shapely female were almost the same height, and both had curves in all the right places. Even though the woman with Lawton was covered with mud and snow she was even more beautiful than Jarita. And their hair and complexion were amazingly alike in hue.

It suddenly dawned on Kid that Lawton had yanked the woman in front of him because he thought she *was* Jarita Gardiner and that the bushwhackers would recognize her. Mulling over that revelation, Kid wasn't sure what to say to help his precarious predicament, so he said nothing more.

Lawton had the uneasy feeling the young rascal had recognized Cairo. Kid had hesitated too long in assessing the treacherous blonde not to know who she was.

Lawton propelled Kid toward the black stallion that had returned, sensing the trouble had passed. After retrieving his shackles, Lawton clamped them on Kid's wrists. Once Kid had been tethered to a tree to ensure he stayed put, Lawton went to inspect Panhandle Dick.

Lawton couldn't muster much sympathy for the scalawag who'd sustained a fatal shot. Dick had been wanted for robbery and murder, not only in the Twin Territories but also in Missouri, Texas, and No Man's Land.

By the time Lawton returned, Cairo was livid. Her glare was as hot as the hinges on hell's door. Lawton couldn't imagine why *she* was so upset with *him.* After all, she was the one who set up this entire charade to lure him cross-country while every bastard in the area took turns trying to bushwhack him!

Damn her wicked hide! Time and time again, Lawton had allowed himself to forget who she was, but he wasn't going to let himself forget again. The Snowbird was escorting him through the territory like a sitting duck!

While Lawton was thinking the worst about her,

Cairo was silently consigning him to the fiery reaches of Hades. He had used her as a shield during his showdown and then flung her to the ground as if she were a sack of feed.

It was glaringly apparent that she meant absolutely nothing to Lawton Solid-Rock Stone. She was nothing to him except his armor of defense and his object of lust. She was going to hate him until her dying day, which would probably be soon if he kept using her as a human barricade for his own protection!

"I hate you," Cairo spewed when Lawton stalked past her.

"The feeling is mutual," he snapped gruffly.

"I can't imagine why it should be." She wrapped the words around her tongue and hurled them at him. "I'm perfectly harmless and you're the one who—"

"Harmless!" Lawton hooted. "Woman, you are as harmless as a loaded shotgun with a hairpin trigger! I'm surprised you didn't shoot me in the back while I was pursuing your friends."

Cairo gaped at him. *"Friends?"* She glanced at the young fugitive who couldn't have been more than a year older than she was, if even that. "I never saw either of these men before in my life!"

"Haven't you?" His lips curled as he regarded her with mocking disdain. "Funny thing, this one hesitated in admitting he didn't know you, either. Trying to protect each other, no doubt!"

"Lawton Stone, you're an absolute idiot!" Cairo hissed.

"I must be if I let myself get mixed up with you," he countered.

"I hope you roast in hell!"

"I'm sure I will if you have anything to do with it," he parried.

The heated exchange hadn't gone unnoticed. Kid Fontain was all ears. It dawned on him that Lawton was sweet on this sassy minx, even though he suspected her of being Jarita Gardiner.

Kid smiled slyly. He was on his way to jail for running whiskey to the Indians and acting as an accomplice for Panhandle Dick, but Jarita Gardiner would be safe from Lawton's wrath. When Kid got the chance to send word to the Gardiners, he would pass on this interesting information.

Panhandle Dick hadn't been able to bring Lawton Stone down, but Kid could make the marshal's life a living hell by feeding him a pack of lies about this woman. Hell, he might even be able to buy himself a reduced sentence if he played his cards right.

Savoring that devious thought, Kid allowed Lawton to tend his leg wound without complaint and watched the curvaceous blonde fling Lawton poisonous glares at regular intervals while she cradled her tender arm against her ribs.

"Are you ready to talk?" Lawton prodded while he administered first aid to his prisoner. "How long have you known her?"

"I'll tell you all you want to know about Jarita Gardiner if it will get me off the hook," Kid bartered.

The comment made Lawton's blood boil. For more than three weeks he had suspected Cairo of being the mysterious Snowbird. He had interrogated several individuals who couldn't positively identify her, but this young renegade was offering conclusive proof. Lawton's darkest suspicions had proved correct. He felt angry and betrayed, even when he'd warned himself a dozen times not to expect anything but the worst from that blond-haired hellion.

"What's your name?" Lawton demanded as he doctored the wound.

"Kid Fontain."

"There are better ways to make a living than the devious profession you're pursuing," he said as he rose to retrieve the bench warrants from his saddlebag. He thumbed through the papers to locate information about the young bandit. "It says here you are wanted for peddling whiskey in the Cherokee Nation."

Kid nodded in confirmation and then shrugged. "I was running short of cash a few months back. Panhandle Dick came to town, though I didn't know who he was at the time. We had a few drinks together and I was complaining about farmhand wages not paying much." Kid paused to stare at the blond woman who had swung into the saddle, anxious to be on her way. "Dick asked me if I wanted to make some fast money by hauling stolen whiskey into the Cherokee Nation. The Gardiners had set up a deal with some of the Indians and I was to deliver the goods. That's when I met the Gardiners."

"And Jarita?" Lawton prodded, cursing under his breath.

"She was with them, but she doesn't hang out with her brothers much of the time. I'm surprised you even knew they had a sister who sometimes rode with them. Vance and Nate are mighty careful about protecting her . . . in case they come to a bad end. But she's a clever one who can take good care of herself."

The young fugitive was telling Lawton what he

wanted to know but hated to hear. The Gardiners didn't allow their younger sister to join them in the robberies, but she was guilty of spying and casing prospective sites for holdups.

"Are you going to let me go since I told you what you wanted to know?" Kid asked hopefully.

"You haven't told me much of anything yet." Lawton wrapped the bandage in place and assisted Kid to his feet.

"Jarita isn't wanted for anything. She just rides into town to look the places over, jots down train schedules, and checks on the time of payroll deliveries to forts and Indian agencies," Kid elaborated.

"Why did she seek me out at Fort Smith? To draw me out so the outlaws could take pot shots at me?" Lawton demanded to know.

Kid shrugged after he'd mounted his steed. "I'm not bosom buddies with the Gardiners, Marshal. I only met them twice . . . briefly. When the Gardiners put a bounty on your head, Panhandle Dick asked me if I wanted to ride along with him since he thought I was pretty good with a pistol." He stared at Lawton. "But I found out there's a difference between taking target practice at whiskey bottles and squaring off against a man like you. I never killed anyone before and I'm beginning to think being a farmhand might be better work for me after all."

"You've got that right," Lawton assured him as he effortlessly swung onto his stallion.

Kid sighed heavily as they wove through the trees. "Look, Marshal, I only committed a minor offense. If you let me go, I swear I'll never—"

Lawton had heard those solemn vows a hundred

The Publishers of Zebra Books
Make This Special Offer
to Zebra Romance Readers...
AFTER YOU HAVE READ THIS
BOOK WE'D LIKE TO SEND YOU
4 MORE FOR FREE
AN $18.00 VALUE
NO OBLIGATION!
ONLY ZEBRA HISTORICAL ROMANCES
"BURN WITH THE FIRE OF HISTORY"
(SEE INSIDE FOR MONEY SAVING DETAILS.)

times before. Half the fugitives he captured promised to walk the straight and narrow, given a second chance. Some did. Most didn't.

"You can spend two weeks in Guthrie's jail, thinking how you fouled up when you started running with the wrong crowd," Lawton replied. "If you don't cause any trouble there, then we'll talk."

Kid breathed a sigh of relief. All he had to do was mind his manners for fourteen days and then he could waltz off scot-free.

While Kid was thanking his lucky stars that things hadn't turned out worse for him, Lawton was cursing his vulnerability to Cairo . . . Jarita Gardiner, he bitterly corrected himself. What was he going to do with that treacherous spitfire? She deserved to be locked behind bars and yet he didn't have a warrant for her arrest. And unfortunately, Kid Fontain's testimony was hardly garnered from concrete information. He had passed on hearsay himself. He certainly hadn't witnessed Jarita breaking any laws and he insinuated that she didn't take part in the robberies and killings. Kid had only told Lawton enough to torment him.

Damn, of all the women in the world, why did he have to get tangled up with this devious witch? Lawton grappled with that baffling question for two full days. And forty-eight hours later, he still didn't have an answer, other than the fact that he was just damned unlucky!

Chapter Twelve

Lawton couldn't believe he had arrived in the same town he'd passed through four months earlier. He had traveled to Guthrie soon after the land run. At that time, the infant community had been a city of tents and stock piles of furniture, lumber, and livestock that had been shipped to the railroad depot. Now the streets had been marked off and more than twelve hundred business buildings and fifteen hundred residences had been erected.

Lawton smiled as he rode down the main thoroughfare. Rome might not have been built in a day, but all the towns in Oklahoma Territory had been born in one afternoon. And a few months later, most of the tents had been replaced with timber, brick, and stone buildings. There were lawyers' offices, barber shops, and surveyor offices on every street corner. The bustling town of four thousand boasted five banks, fifteen hotels, and ninety-seven restaurants and boardinghouses.

Although Lawton was marveling at the drastic

changes in Guthrie, Cairo was too busy brooding to care about much else besides her wounded pride and bruised heart. For almost a week she had cursed Lawton at regular intervals. He had begun to treat her as if she were the criminal and Kid Fontain his chum. She did have to admit that the young outlaw was very personable. He seemed to have learned his lesson after his crucial mistake of squaring off against the formidable Lawton Stone. When he was near Cairo he treated her with humble respect.

Yet, all things considered, Cairo was still so frustrated she wanted to pull out her hair. She had been living on false hopes and foolish dreams. Cairo shook her head at her obvious inability to judge character and the inconsistency of the male species in general. Marshal Stone was supposed to be competent and sane. Lord, he was anything but sane! And Kid Fontain was supposed to be the lowest form of life on earth. The young bandit had turned out to be more of a gentleman than Lawton! Talk about inconsistency!

Perhaps Cairo wouldn't have been so exasperated if she understood why Lawton had become leery and mistrusting of her. But he was as close-mouthed as a clam and as unapproachable as a coiled rattlesnake.

To counter her anguish, Cairo had turned her thoughts to her father. Since her rocky affair with the marshal had evolved into disaster, Cairo had begun to formulate her future plans. She had every intention of helping her father resolve his problems with his enemies in Canadian Station.

Cairo planned to apply for a teaching position in the area. Her modest savings were running low and unless she sought gainful employment, she would have to depend on her father for support. Too bad she didn't know about the bounty on Lawton's head, for she could have shot him as she had been tempted to do and collected the reward.

Cairo swung from the saddle to survey the crowded streets of Guthrie. If she knew what was good for her, she would purchase a train ticket and head south to locate Canadian Station.

Giving the matter second consideration, Cairo decided that was exactly what she was going to do. If she spent any more time with that impossible man, she would be as crazy as he was! There were other marshals in the area, Cairo reminded herself sensibly. Lawton had informed her that Chris Masden had left his position with Judge Parker to accept an assignment as one of Oklahoma's "Guardsmen." Masden had headquartered at Elreno, which was southwest of Guthrie. And if Masden was too occupied chasing lawbreakers, perhaps he could suggest a competent deputy to assist her.

When Cairo marched off without announcing her destination, Lawton stared after her. He couldn't help but wonder if that devious minx was on her way to send a message to her bandit brothers. Lawton wouldn't have put it past her.

"Come on, Kid," Lawton muttered, distracted by his troubled thoughts. "You have a date with a jail cell."

Without protest, Kid stepped from the stirrup and hobbled along on his bum leg. He had changed in the week he rode with Lawton Stone. Kid had had every intention of making trouble for the legendary marshal who worked for Parker, but there was one thing Kid hadn't counted on. He had grown to like the brawny giant. Lawton's lectures on the life of crime not paying had begun to sink in and Kid found himself admiring the dynamic marshal. Lawton had even suggested that Kid, after he paid his debt to society, consider putting his talents with a pistol to a far better use: upholding the law instead of breaking it.

Unfortunately, Kid had never been allowed a moment alone with Lawton. He wanted to confess that he had purposely lied about Cairo after the shooting incident which left Panhandle Dick dead. But he was guilty as hell and felt awkward about dredging up the past, especially when he knew Lawton would be furious with him.

"Law, I want to ask you something." Kid quickened his pace to keep up with Lawton's long, gliding gait. "Do you honestly think I could hire on as a deputy somewhere in these parts after I serve my time?"

Lawton broke stride to peer into the youthful face of Kid Fontain. The sincerity in his baby-blue eyes held Lawton's probing stare. Lawton had spent the week hoping to make the young man aware of the error of his ways. Kid was a likable sort, even if he had made a mistake by getting mixed up with Panhandle Dick. Watching Dick meet his violent end had definitely made an impression on Kid. There was a lot of good in the young man. With guidance, Kid could be a credit to his name instead of a black eye to his family.

Lawton recalled the stern major in the Texas cavalry who had taken him under wing a decade earlier. Lawton had been bitter about his stepfather's death and his mother's heartless abandonment. Lawton had been out to show the world that he didn't need family or friends to make his own way. Major Derrick Wright had knocked the chip off Lawton's shoulder and ensured that he channeled his energies in beneficial directions. Derrick taught Lawton how to handle himself with his fists, pistols, knives and rifles. He had also been a friend—a critical one at times but always dependable and sincere. Because of Derrick Wright's positive influence, Lawton had been recommended to serve with the Rangers and Derrick had been instrumental in ensuring that Judge Parker received his impressive credentials.

Lawton stared at Kid Fontain long and hard. "You still have a lot to learn," he told the young man in a straightforward manner.

Kid nodded his shaggy brown head. "I know that, but do you think I've got a chance of making something of myself?"

The very fact that Kid wanted to be something besides a sketch on a wanted poster was encouraging. "Yes, but you'll have to be good, just like the rest of us who uphold the law."

Kid broke into a lopsided smile. "I'll never be an angel, but raising hell wasn't all that much fun, either. I'd settle for plain ole respectable."

The Kid had grown on him to the point that Lawton was considering giving him a second chance. "You'll have to drop that nickname," he advised. "Kid Fontain sounds too much like an outlaw on the run. What's your real name?"

Kid blushed and his gaze dropped to the scuffed toes of his boots, as if something there had suddenly demanded his attention. "You promise you won't poke fun?"

"I promise," Lawton vowed.

Kid glanced self-consciously at Lawton. "Alphonso Peabody Fontain."

Lawton bit back an amused grin. No wonder the young rascal went by the name of Kid. "Al Fontain will be name enough," Lawton announced. "Now let's see what we can do about getting your sentence reduced for volunteering information to a law official."

When Lawton pivoted to stride toward the sheriff's office, Al hesitated, dreading the topic that had haunted him for the past few days. "Uh . . . Law, there's something else you have to know."

Al wasn't anxious to inform Lawton he'd lied about the striking blonde. Never once had he been alone long enough to broach the topic. Now was his one and only chance. He knew he might jeopardize his chance to make a new start in life, but Lawton's influence on him had caused his conscience to nag him continuously.

"Whatever it is, it can wait," Lawton insisted impatiently before glancing in the direction Cairo had taken. He noticed that she had scurried into the train depot and his curiosity was killing him. What was she up to? And how was it going to affect his future . . . or lack of it?

"No, I don't think this can wait," Al protested as Lawton propelled him along at a fast clip.

"It'll have to." Lawton guided Al into the office and planted him in a vacant chair.

Drawing Sheriff Tom Peters aside, Lawton explained the circumstances of Al Fontain's arrest and his unfortunate but brief association with the Gardiners. Then Lawton requested that the sheriff hold Al for two weeks. At the end of that time Lawton intended to return so that Al could be released into his custody.

The sheriff nodded agreeably. "Suits me fine. You know as well as I do that the punishment for hauling whiskey to the Indians isn't as severe as plotting the illegal sale and gathering of cash from it. Besides, we've got far more important cases to be tried in court. I can barely keep up with the paperwork as it is. If you are willing to take responsibility for the boy, you won't hear any complaints from me or the judge."

With that settled, Lawton quizzed the sheriff for information about the Gardiners.

Tom nodded glumly. "I received a wire three days ago that two men fitting their description, plus five other known criminals robbed the bank at Kingfisher and spirited off with twenty thousand dollars. Marshal Chris Masden took a posse and is trying to trail them, but the Gardiners are experts at covering their tracks."

Lawton digested the news. The Gardiners had moved their area of operation from the Cherokee Nation to Oklahoma Territory. They had put a bounty on his head and were waiting to see if their renegade friends could pick him off before Cairo—Jarita Gardiner—led him into a fatal trap. Armed with that knowledge, Lawton lurched around to trail Cairo. He'd probably left that sneaky witch to her own devices too long already.

"Law, wait a minute!" Al called after him. "There is something you have to know!"

"You can tell me about it in a couple of weeks. Behave yourself, Al," Lawton threw over his shoulder, immediately before the door slammed shut behind him.

"Lawton, wait!" Al bounded from his chair and

charged toward the door, but Tom Peters latched onto his arm before he could escape.

"Don't spoil your chance to make good, Kid," Tom scolded as he tugged Al toward the cells. "Lawton spoke up for you. You should feel privileged. He doesn't do things like that very often." He opened the cell and guided Al into it. "If I were you, I wouldn't want to disappoint Lawton Stone. It's a helluva lot safer and healthier to be his friend than his enemy." Tom stared through the bars at the disappointed prisoner. "Whatever you had to say to Lawton will keep. You heard him, son. Just behave yourself."

Al slumped on his cot, feeling guilty as hell. He was personally responsible for allowing Lawton to believe the blonde was Jarita Gardiner. By the time Al was permitted to speak his piece, Lawton would never forgive him for imparting false information. Damn, now he wouldn't get his second chance. Not only didn't crime pay, he realized, but lying could get a man in all sorts of trouble!

Damn it. Him and his big mouth. He had thought himself such a cocky rake the first time he confronted Lawton Stone, hell-bent on having his own private revenge. Well, now it had backfired in his face and there wasn't a thing he could do except bide his time.

Al stared at the narrow confines of his cell. When he was finally allowed to tell Lawton the truth, the fuming marshal would let Al sit here until he mildewed or rotted . . . whichever came first!

To Cairo's dismay, she was informed by the ticket agent in the train depot that Guthrie and Elreno had yet to be connected by steel rails. The agent directed her down the street to the stage company to make her travel arrangements. Cairo was told that the southbound coach was scheduled to depart in less than fifteen minutes.

Without hesitation, Cairo plunked down the money for her ticket and went to retrieve her menagerie of supplies from her steed. In a flurry, she gathered her belongings and even found an anxious buyer for her horse, a man who offered her more than she had paid for the mount in the first place!

Scuttling back to the stage station, Cairo closeted herself in the ladies' dressing room to change into her gown. And within a few more minutes she found herself wedged into the coach with four men.

Cairo forced herself to consider the past month with Lawton Stone as one stupendous mistake she would never repeat. She was going to get over that infuriating gorilla if it was the last thing she ever did!

How hard could it be to fall out of love with him? she asked herself. It had been easy to fall in love with him when she hadn't even tried. Now that she was making a dedicated effort to forget him, it should only require a few days . . . a week at the most. It was nothing but a simple conquest of mind over body. Why, by the first of next week, she probably would barely recall his name.

Resolved to that noble thought, Cairo scrunched between the broad-shouldered men who filled the coach to overflowing and endured the rough ride over rutted roads. And if she never saw that impossible raven-haired, silver-eyed cad again that would be more than fine with her!

Even though Lawton's memory stuck in her mind

like porcupine quills, she would extract them one and all. She would forget her feelings for him, forget the hell he'd put her through. She was determined! And that was, after all, her most notable trait—determination.

After interrogating the ticket agent, Lawton had stormed from the railroad depot and stalked to the stage office. Oh, yes, the railroad agent had vividly remembered the curvaceous blonde whom he had directed down the street. And yes, the stage agent was also quick to recognize Cairo's description, but he was sorry to report that the lady had left fifteen minutes earlier and the connections to Elreno were making their only run of the day.

Muttering a string of obscenities, Lawton stomped back into the street. He'd had visions of staying the night in Guthrie, of treating himself to a warm bath in a real tub and enjoying a succulent meal at one of the local restaurants. But from the look of things, he and his black stallion were going to be sharing several more hours of each other's company.

Lawton debated whether to do himself a favor and say good riddance to that devious vixen or hunt her down. Common sense bade him to thank his lucky stars he was still alive and let Cairo go her own way. But damnit, he couldn't make himself let that green-eyed firebrand go, especially when she could lead him to her outlaw brothers who had put a bounty on his head.

If Vance and Nate Gardiner were as protective of their little sister as Al Fontain said they were, Lawton could use that to his advantage. That was the only reason he planned to track the ornery minx, Lawton assured himself. It wasn't because he still had a romantic interest in her. If he found himself in need of female attention he would search elsewhere. It was for damned certain that any other woman on the continent was safer than the treacherous Snowbird!

Lawton had it figured that his life wasn't worth a damn until the Gardiners were standing on Judge Parker's gallows. Now that the Gardiners had made him a marked man, Lawton would need eyes in the back of his head to prevent being bushwhacked for the bounty.

Calling Cairo every name in the book, Lawton strode down the street to gather supplies for his journey. The stagecoach would set a swift pace and he would have to ride hell-for-leather if he intended to catch up with Cairo before she made contact with her thieving brothers.

Damn her hide, why couldn't she have been what she said she was? It had been difficult enough to cope with his feelings for her when he wasn't certain if she was guilty or innocent. Knowing for sure now that she was an accomplice to a variety of crimes tore Lawton to agonizing pieces.

What an accomplished liar she was!

What a blind fool he was!

Nate Gardiner rocked back in his chair and plunked his feet on the edge of the table. He rolled a cigarette, lit it, and watched the cloud of smoke rise above him.

"Panhandle Dick should have been here long before

now," Nate grumbled between draws on his cigarette.

"Maybe he isn't coming back," Vance muttered. "We shouldn't have let him take Kid Fontain with him. The boy is too damned green."

"I'll go after that bastard marshal for you," Idaho Joe volunteered before he hurled his sharp-bladed knife across the room and envisioned burying the dagger in Lawton's back.

"No!" Vance declared sternly. His hatchetlike features puckered and his close-set eyes narrowed on Joe. "We need you for the job at Darlington Indian Agency. The tribal funds are due to arrive next week. According to Jarita, we stand to make a big haul." A sinister smile pursed Vance's lips as he studied the glowing end of the cigarette he had rolled for himself. "Once we have enough money to tide us over for a few months, I'm going after that son-of-a-bitch myself. Then maybe Billy can rest in peace."

"Killing is too good for that miserable bastard," Nate muttered. "He put bullets in Vance and me. And I want him to suffer the way we did when we lost Billy."

"Stone would have shared part of our torment if we'd gotten a few good shots at his partners when they found us on the Grand River," Vance grunted. "I'd like to take something precious away from Stone and let him bleed before we send him leaping into hell."

"And then I get to carve out the heart of Stone," Idaho Joe snickered as he retrieved his dagger and tested its sharpness. "The devil will have to piece that bastard back together before hanging his carcass over the fiery pits."

Vance and Nate were certain their cohort would do just that. Idaho Joe had a fiendish fascination for his dagger. If Joe hadn't been so indispensable in the past two strikes, the Gardiners might have sent him to track Stone. But his skills with a pistol and knife had proved instrumental in securing their booty.

Now the Gardiners were nestled comfortably in their hideout in southern Oklahoma Territory and they had buried the gold they had stolen in Kingfisher. Once they had settled their feud with Lawton Stone, they could slip over the border to prey on the communities in Indian Territory while the posses searched high and low for them in Oklahoma.

Vance pulled out his timepiece and frowned. "I thought Jarita would be back by now. Maybe we should go look for her. She's been gone longer than she planned."

Nate nodded in concern. "She said she would wander around Darlington to purchase a few supplies before she met us here. But if she isn't back by tomorrow, I'll go find her. Losing Billy was bad enough. Losing Jarita would be . . ." His voice trailed off into a wordless sneer. "I'd sure as hell turn Joe loose with his knife if any man caused trouble for Jarita."

"I'd cut him in strips. Don't think I wouldn't," Joe growled, his eyes glittering murderously.

The creak of the door caused the men to spin around with their pistols poised. Although they were prepared to blast the intruder, they relaxed the instant Jarita waved her white handkerchief in the partially opened door.

Vance and Nate shoved their pistols back into their holsters and scurried forward to greet their sister. She gestured for the men to follow her outside to unload the wagon of supplies she'd brought with her.

"You certainly look pleased with yourself, Sissy." Vance noted her smug smirk as he carted in a box of supplies and ammunition.

"I've had a very successful trip," she announced. "You'll never guess who I saw riding past the Indian Agency this morning."

The men in the cabin fixed inquisitive stares on her.

"None other than Marshal Lawton Stone." The room suddenly became as silent as the grave.

Vance and Nate snarled maliciously. If Lawton was still alive, chances were Panhandle Dick wasn't. Another member of their gang had fallen beneath Stone's blazing pistols.

"Maybe we should postpone our strike at Darlington to settle our score," Nate suggested.

Jarita gave her blond head a contradictory shake. "If the folks in these parts know we're in the area, they'll have Marshal Masden sniffing around like a bloodhound. As much as I want to see Stone dead, the timing isn't right. If we kill him now, every posse and law official in the territory will be hot on our heels. We have to take the tribal pay wagon first and then we'll concentrate on Stone. Once we have plenty of cash, we can go wherever we choose until the posses abandon their attempts to find us.

"Besides," Jarita added as she unpinned her bonnet and shook out the silken locks of silver-blond hair, "Marshal Stone was riding alone. He'll be an easy target when the time is right."

"You always did have a good head on your shoulders, Sissy," Nate complimented her. "You run along to bed now and we'll stash the supplies."

When Jarita swept toward her private room, Vance's

gaze swung to Idaho Joe who surveyed her with hungry eyes. In deliberate strides, Vance crossed the room to stare directly at the scraggly renegade who had propped himself against the wall. "I've known for a long time that the main reason you're riding with us is because of Jarita." A deadly gleam flickered in Vance's blue eyes. "I know you've taken a fancy to Sissy. But if you ever touch her . . ." His mouth hardened in a grim line. "If you ever touch our sister, Nate and I will use your precious knife on you and there won't be enough left of you to feed a starved coyote."

Two pair of stormy blue eyes bore into Idaho Joe's whiskered face.

To emphasize the point, Nate ambled over to force Joe back into the corner. "You damned well better heed what Vance said," Nate warned with a menacing sneer. "We would take turns carving on you if you didn't treat Sissy with the respect she deserves. We may ride on the wrong side of the law, but we have strong feelings for our sister and she will always be treated with consideration. Is that understood?"

Idaho Joe nodded bleakly before he wedged past the Gardiners to grab a breath of fresh air. He'd wanted that shapely beauty for so long that he ached every time she appeared at their hideout for one of her infrequent visits. Joe lived for stolen glances at her, thrived on the fantasies of taking her over and over again until he had satisfied his craving. But Vance and Nate never let him within ten feet of Jarita. Hell, he was barely allowed to speak with her and never in privacy!

But one day, Joe vowed silently as he scanned the dome of stars . . . One day he was going to enjoy his lusty dreams.

Chapter Thirteen

Cairo hadn't believed it possible to be courted simultaneously by four men in a stagecoach, but she had been. All four of them were eligible bachelors and they were the picture of manly devotion during the overland journey. The rough roads caused the passengers of the coach to be flung around as if they were packed in a butter churn. The men were constantly inquiring about Cairo's discomfort, of which there was plenty thanks to the washboarded roads. And each time they paused at a stage station to harness a fresh team of horses and take a meal, Cairo had more assistance getting in and out of the coach than she knew what to do with.

She had listened to the story of each man's life and heard his hints of taking a wife to serve him and share dreams of a new life in Oklahoma. Cairo could have had her pick of available husbands, had she been in the market for one. She could have become the instant bride of a land surveyor, carpenter, freighter, or physician. Considering she was still nursing a bruised and battered heart, she could have rebounded from her tormenting affair with Lawton into a hasty marriage, but she couldn't bring herself to accept the offers. Matrimony would ensure she never had to tempt herself with Lawton Stone again. But, as Cairo had learned this past month, the solution to one problem only created a new set of problems.

Lawton Stone was the prime example of that theory, Cairo reminded herself. She had singled out Lawton to resolve her father's crisis and she had been confronted with a new passel of problems. And even after all her lectures to herself she still hadn't recovered from Lawton Stone.

"Let me help you down, Miss Calhoun," Frederick Pullman eagerly volunteered. The handsome young doctor set Cairo to her feet, allowing his hands to linger on her trim waist longer than necessary. "I recommend the Del Norte Hotel for your stay in Elreno."

Reluctantly, Frederick let her go to gesture toward the two-story building. His admiring gaze strayed back to her for the umpteenth time. "As has become the custom in the new towns, there will be a party held at the site of recently constructed homes and businesses." He indicated the mercantile store with its fresh coat of paint. "I would like to escort you to the dance tonight and to familiarize you with our community."

Frederick leaned closer to Cairo. "I hope that you will be so taken with Elreno—and me—that you will want to make it your permanent home."

Cairo peered at Frederick and, as she had done for the hundredth time already, compared him to Lawton. She hadn't meant to, truly she hadn't, but she did it nonetheless. Kind, respectful, and courteous though

Frederick was, he didn't spark fires in Cairo's blood. Her pulse merely loped along at its normal pace.

"Thank you for the invitation, but it has been a dusty, exhausting trip and I—" Cairo tried to decline, but Frederick pressed his forefinger to her lips to shush her.

"I'm sure you will feel refreshed after a bath and a rest at the hotel," he diagnosed. "You can meet me at the party after I've checked on some of my patients, who must feel they have been neglected while I was retrieving medical supplies from the train depot in Guthrie."

"I'll see how I'm feeling by dusk," Cairo hedged, and then graced him with a disarming smile. "And if I don't come, I'm sure there will be a harem of young ladies anxious to take my place."

"None will be as welcome, I assure you," Frederick murmured, giving her hand an affectionate squeeze.

Cairo stared into his handsome face that was capped with sandy-blond hair and wished she felt some stirring of her heart. But again, nothing happened. The physician's lean physique and attractive features paled in comparison with the rugged, intimidating image of Lawton Stone.

After Frederick took his leave, Cairo gathered her belongings and struggled down the street to the hotel. There she found a half-dozen more men who were willing and eager to assist her. With great relief, Cairo eased the door shut to her room and collapsed on the bed to await her bath.

Men! They were everywhere. A woman couldn't turn around without tripping over or colliding with one of them. And if she hadn't found herself comparing all of them to that infuriating Lawton Stone, perhaps she might have noticed that all men weren't as insincere as that raven-haired varmint!

"Get out of mind, Lawton Stone," Cairo muttered.

The rap at the door jostled her from her thoughts. With her luck, Lawton would be standing on the other side of the door, waiting to torment her again.

Hesitantly, Cairo approached the portal and eased it open a few inches. To her relief, she was greeted by the hotel attendants who had carted hot water upstairs for her bath. When the three men had come and gone, ogling her as if she were a feast they had come to devour, Cairo peeled off her dusty garments and sank into the steamy tub.

Ah, this was heaven! Cairo sighed in contentment as she sponged the water over her skin. She wished she could cleanse away not only the grime but also the lingering memories of Lawton—

Another knock rattled the door. "Curse it, I have plenty of hot water," Cairo blurted out. "I don't need any more."

But it wasn't the attendants returning with more water as an excuse to gape at her. Lo and behold, the door swung open and a noticeably dusty and blatantly annoyed Lawton Stone filled the entrance.

Cairo gasped as she scrambled to cover herself with the towel before any passersby in the hall got an eyeful.

"Thanks one helluva lot for not having the courtesy to say goodbye before you flew off on your broom, witch," Lawton growled into her crimson-red face.

Against his will, his silver gaze flooded over her scantily concealed figure, noting the water droplets that sparkled on her satiny skin as they had the first night he had made love to her on the streambank. Lawton grimaced when his eyes fell on the scar that marred her left shoulder. He was annoyed with himself for tearing off on this wild-goose chase and at this woman for forcing him to do it. But even his anger couldn't overshadow the guilt he experienced when he glanced at her scarred shoulder. She deserved all the tortures of the damned, he knew. Yet, it was no less painful to think he was responsible for the one flaw on this exquisite creature's luscious body.

"Close the damned door!" Cairo hissed when Lawton simply stood there as if he had been planted on the spot.

Shaking himself from his meandering thoughts, Lawton kicked the door shut with his bootheel. "Done. Now, why didn't you tell me where you were going? Didn't you want me to know?" he questioned harshly.

"No." Her glower was hot enough to ignite a prairie fire. "I really didn't think you cared where I went, so long as I was away from you."

Lawton regarded her with a calculating stare. "I thought you were dead set on solving your daddy's problems," he mocked as he sauntered across the room, unwillingly drinking in her beauty and hating himself for still being so distracted by her.

Cairo tilted her head to a proud angle and swiveled around in the tub to present her back to him. "Your services are no longer required. I have decided to seek the assistance of a law official who isn't quite so sadistic as to shoot me in the arm and use me as his shield against oncoming bullets." Without bothering to fling him the murderous glare he so richly deserved, Cairo hitched her thumb over her shoulder. "Now please leave. I'd like to live long enough to enjoy my bath and see my father again. When I'm with you, I'm left to wonder if I'll even see the dawn of another day."

"Those are my exact sentiments," Lawton scoffed, unwillingly savoring the silky skin of her bare back and the delectable curve of her hips. Damn, he knew who and what she was and yet he was still stung by needs that had no business clouding his thinking.

Cairo turned in the tub to glare at the towering giant whose stubbled face indicated he hadn't taken time to shave before chasing after her. *"Me?* Harm *you?"* she crowed in disbelief. "You haven't sustained so much as a scratch because of me. I wish I could say the same!"

When Lawton squatted down beside the tub, Cairo shrank away. Valiantly, she battled her hopeless attraction to the man she swore she'd never understand and no longer cared if she did, even if she could.

Lawton would have been better off if he had turned around and walked out when he found Cairo frolicking in her bath. He'd spent the better part of two days telling himself he despised her for what she was and what she intended to do to him. But when he saw her sitting there amid the fragrant bubbles, his heart almost burst. All he could think about was what he wanted to do to her, how he yearned to touch her, to feel her supple body responding to his.

It was damned hard on Lawton's male pride to realize that he still ached for this sassy minx, even when he knew the truth about her. She was his fatal curse, a deadly atraction. Why couldn't he settle for a female who was safe and devoted and doting? Oh, no, fool that he had become, he was obsessed with a spiteful sorceress who carried his death warrant.

However, she really couldn't cause his death while she was steaming in her bubble bath, now could she? She was no threat to his life now. She was only his mindless obsession.

Lawton stared into those lively emerald eyes that dominated her elegant face and he wanted her so badly he ached all over. His gaze caressed her velvety flesh and his senses reeled with lusty anticipation.

"Aw, the hell with it," Lawton muttered, half aloud.

Cairo gaped at Lawton in astonishment when he began to shuck his clothes. He was crazy if he thought he was going to plop down in her bathtub while she was still in it and do what he looked as if he were contemplating doing to her! She was still furious with him and he wasn't going to seduce her into submission. She wasn't going to have anything to do with this maniac, ever again, even if her body was already tingling in pleasure from watching him expose his muscular physique to her betraying gaze. And she would stitch her eyelids shut to keep from noticing his masculine elegance . . .

So much for Cairo's noble convictions as Lawton stepped into the tub, positioning her between the long columns of his legs. Her back brushed against his hair-matted chest as he situated himself more comfortably behind her.

Her body had suddenly become more demanding than her floundering mind. Traitorous sensations undulated down her spine, causing her to tremble in helpless response to his devastating nearness. A feeble protest formed on her lips, but the words died a quick death when his arms slid around her waist, bringing her quaking body into closer contact with his. When he whispered along the pulsating vein of her neck, Cairo swore that she and her bubble bath were dangerously close to going up in a cloud of steam.

It didn't seem to matter that she had her heart set on hating Lawton forevermore. The instant this infuriatingly impossible man walked in and filled up her world, she lost every grain of sense she'd been collecting the last twenty-one years. Suddenly, her wanton body was taking command of her senses and making demands of its own. And when his experienced caresses swirled around her waist to trail over the throbbing tips of her breasts, Cairo felt forbidden desire plucking at her taut nerves like a musician's deft fingers hovering over harp strings.

Twice Cairo thought she had marshaled her defenses well enough to vault from the tub and take refuge behind the dressing screen. Twice her willpower fell short of saving her from humiliation. Lawton assaulted her with another round of bone-melting caresses and kisses. He hadn't apologized to her. He simply engulfed her in his swarthy arms and made her forget everything that had any semblance to reality. Cairo found herself toppling over the edge into total abandon, burning in the sweet hot ache of desire.

In less than a heartbeat Cairo became a captive of his raging passions, as well as her own longings. Lawton touched her in tender ways that were far more devastating than sheer force. He kissed her with a hunger that had gone unappeased for more than a week, and Cairo responded without thinking, exulting in the divine torture of his skillful touch.

A surrendering sigh escaped from her kiss-swollen lips as his hand glided over the pale-pink tips of her breasts to track a tantalizing path over her abdomen and down to the sensitive flesh of her thighs. Cairo swore she would have sunk into the bubbles if Lawton hadn't shifted her onto his lap.

For days Cairo had alphabetized Lawton's extensive faults and dwelled on his peculiar behavior, hoping to fall out of love with him. And then, here he came again to turn her world upside down and leave her craving what she'd discovered with no other man.

He knew just where and how to touch. He made her melt into senseless mush and riveted her body with bulletlike sensations that embedded themselves in her very soul.

Lawton gloried in the feel of her silky flesh beneath his bold caresses. He couldn't keep his hands off her, no matter how wicked this lovely witch was. His caresses wandered of their own accord, rediscovering each voluptuous curve and swell, each sensitive point, each luscious peak. Entranced by the pleasure he derived in reacquainting himself with her delicious body, Lawton explored her to his heart's content. His lips seared across her shoulder and arm. He turned her to face him so that he could press his cheek against the soft mounds of her breasts. With a muffled groan he took the soft bud into his mouth, savoring the taste of her as if she were a long-awaited treat. And all the while his hands roamed and aroused, leaving Cairo writhing helplessly in his arms.

Lawton heard the rush of water that cascaded over the rim of the tub as he twisted to trace a path of ravenous kisses over her belly, but he didn't care that they were sending streams of water coursing across the floor. All he knew was that he had to satisfy this fierce craving or he would go mad. His emotions had been battling a fierce tug-of-war while he thundered toward Elreno to find her. He had wanted to curse her on sight and yet the sight of her was his tormenting curse. He had but to look at this spellbinding beauty and he remembered each moment of splendor they had shared while they trekked west through the wooded hills and rolling plains.

Gasping for breath, Lawton scooped Cairo into his arms. In three strides he had reached the bed and fell upon it, tumbling Cairo onto the cotton bedspread. He couldn't bear to waste even a second before he caressed her again and again and again.

Cairo struggled to inhale a breath of air, but her heart was pounding so wildly that she feared she would faint from oxygen deprivation. Her quivering body arched to meet his prowling hands and greedy lips. Shamelessly she gave herself up to the tumultuous needs that churned inside her. All the while he was caressing her, her hands were coasting over the hair-roughened terrain of his chest and thighs, longing to return the intense pleasure that mushroomed until it was almost beyond bearing.

When she caressed him so intimately Lawton could feel his trembling body inching steadily toward hers. He felt like a puzzle that made no sense at all until he was one with this silver-blond witch who had tormented his days and haunted his nights. He ached to be flesh to flesh. He wanted to feel her pliant body beneath his, around his, enveloping his like a cloud of ineffable pleasure. He wanted to share the same ragged breath, the same wild heartbeat, the same soul for that glorious space in time that could span eternity . . .

That compelling thought brought Lawton to her. Her name was on his lips—his curse, his dream—as he drew her luscious body beneath his and glided over her. Tingles of rapture trickled through his blood as he molded her body intimately to his and cradled her in his arms.

And yet, even when they were one, moving in perfect rhythm to a melody as ancient as time itself, Lawton wanted more. He wanted to know that despite her grudge against him, she needed him as desperately as he needed her.

"Love me, Cai," he rasped against her parted lips.

"I do," she whispered without thinking. She was so lost in him that she was unaware of all else except this fervent need to hold him until the world came to an end.

A gasp of ecstasy broke from her throat as the crescendo of pleasure built inside her. Cairo could feel the last of her self-control eroding like sand scattering in a cyclone. Rapturous sensations swirled around her like a circling wind that blew the stars around. Cairo dug in her nails and held on for dear life. One wild exhilarating sensation after another pummeled her as Lawton drove into her. When he clutched her to him and shuddered uncontrollably, Cairo found sweet, satisfying release as the clouds of passion parted and she was soaring on pinioned wings, sliding over rainbows.

The last ounce of energy seeped from Cairo's body as Lawton eased down beside her. For more than a week she had survived on raw nerves and fierce determination, vowing to overcome her ill-fated attraction to this silver-eyed devil. But Lawton's masterful lovemaking had drained all her pent-up emotions and left her drifting into a land of passionate dreams that took up where reality left off.

Cairo sank into a peaceful sleep. And Lawton, who could scarcely hold his passion-drugged eyes open, followed her. They lay cradled against each other, the tormenting thoughts of mistrust scattered, leaving them captives of their emotions.

Neither of them understood the mystical lure for each other, but it was always there, like the moon whispering silently to the tides. And nothing seemed quite right unless they were in each other's arms, sailing through that magical dimension of time that only lovers shared.

Cairo came slowly awake. Her tangled lashes fluttered up to see the strong, commanding features of the face that was a hairbreadth away from hers. Before she could dwell on the sublime rapture of losing herself in Lawton's embrace, stinging pride scolded her lack of willpower.

How could she have surrendered when she had vowed only two days ago that she was done with Lawton Stone? A dozen times over, she had reminded herself that Lawton only wanted her body, wanted her heart only as a conquest. She would never earn his respect or devotion and still she had yielded to him like a shameless trollop! Curse it, he made her hate herself.

Cairo inched away and eased off the bed. Quietly, she fished into her satchel to retrieve some clean clothing. She had to locate Marshal Chris Masden and make the necessary arrangements before Lawton roused to interfere in her life again.

Cairo retrieved the snub-nosed pistol from her breeches pocket. For a moment, she stood on the opposite side of the room with the pistol dangling in her fingertips and stared at the magnificently formed man who made the large bed appear undersize while he was sprawled on it.

While Cairo stood there, reflecting on her stormy courtship with Lawton, he cast her a discreet glance. His heart hung in his chest like an anchor when he spied the pistol in her hand. From where he lay, it looked as if Cairo was debating whether to blow him to kingdom come. Lawton knew he didn't have a snowball's chance in hell if she decided to blast him. His pistols were tangled in his discarded clothes beside the tub. They might as well have been in Fort Smith for all the good they would do him if Cairo decided to shoot him to pieces.

Cairo turned away and tucked the pistol into her purse. Lawton breathed a sigh of relief without alerting Cairo to the fact that he was awake and watching her every move. It appeared she didn't have the heart to blow him to smithereens.

When Cairo slipped out the door, Lawton rolled out of bed and got himself into his clothes. His first order of business was to track Cairo's movements and then retrieve his gear so he could don fresh garments.

Lawton realized he had given Cairo too much of a head start. By the time he stepped onto the street she had disappeared from sight.

Lawton grabbed his gear and went back to the hotel, taking the steps two at a time in his haste to change clothes. When he returned to the street, there was still no sign of Cairo. His keen gaze swept both sides of the crowded street as the sun dipped behind the horizon, bathing the world in crimson and gold.

And then he saw her, weaving in and out of the crowd. A muddled frown clouded his brows, wondering which building Cairo had emerged from. The telegraph office? The bank? Was she casing Elreno for a possible strike?

While Lawton was speculating on her activities, Cairo was mustering her determination. She had barged into the sheriff's office to inquire about Chris Masden and was told that the marshal and his posse were combing the area around Kingfisher, hoping to track down a gang of outlaws and that he wasn't expected back for several days. Disappointed but hardly discouraged, Cairo had decided to proceed to Canadian Station, which was located on the southwest border of the territory. She would assess the situation there and then return for assistance.

But no matter what, Cairo was going to send Lawton Stone on his way once and for all! Even if she and her father needed Lawton's expertise, she wasn't going to ask for it now. Her sanity would crack wide open if she didn't put some space between them. Lawton would always manage to hurt her one way or another.

Her thoughts and her footsteps came to a screeching halt when she spied Lawton propped against the outside wall of the hotel. Curse it, Cairo didn't want to confront him just now. She was still deeply ashamed that she had succumbed to him. She needed time to compose herself before encountering Lawton.

The sound of music and laughter wafted from the door of the mercantile shop, catching her attention.

Frederick Pullman had invited her to join him at the grand opening party for the newly constructed business. Frederick would be her salvation and she could distract herself. And with any luck at all, Lawton would tire of waiting and wander off before she returned to her room.

And if worse came to worst, Cairo would even agree to marry the physician despite the fact she'd only known him two days. It would be a rather drastic measure of avoiding Lawton, but she was desperate!

With a determined tilt of her chin, Cairo squared her shoulders and propelled herself into the shop that was teeming with people and vibrating with lively music. If Frederick wasn't there, Cairo thought as she meandered through the crowd, she was going to have to latch onto the first stranger she met in hopes of avoiding Lawton Heartbreaker Stone.

Chapter Fourteen

Frederick smiled in delight when he spied Cairo, garbed in a fetching green gown. Like a bumblebee he buzzed through the crowd to intercept the voluptuous blonde before any of the men who were admiring her could strike up a conversation with her.

Relief washed over Cairo's face when Frederick materialized before her to clasp her hands in his. Now, with any luck at all, she could distract herself for a couple of hours and Lawton would go away so she would not have to face him after she'd given in to her wanton desires.

Cairo pasted on a cordial smile when Frederick led her around the shop to introduce her to the citizens of Elreno. After several rounds of how-do-you-do's, a glass of alcohol-laced punch was thrust into her hand and Cairo downed the drink in one gulp. Although Cairo had always been a teetotaler, she drained every glass that found its way into her hand. After half a dozen drinks the anxiety of facing Lawton flitted away.

The evening was proceeding superbly. The punch

had taken the edge off her nerves and the starch out of her stubborn pride. Cairo found herself giggling like a schoolgirl as Frederick twirled her around the floor in rhythm with the folk tune that filled the air.

"You seem to be having a good time, my dear," Frederick observed as he drew Cairo's body ever closer to his.

"I'm having a marvelous time," she enthused, her tone a mite sluggish.

Her nose tingled and her eyes couldn't seem to catch up with her when Frederick swung her in a tight circle. Odd, she never remembered feeling quite so giddy before. Apparently the punch had packed quite a wallop.

"Dr. Pullman!"

A frantic voice sliced through Cairo's dazed brain. She swiveled her head to see a middle-aged woman scuttling through the throng of dancers to single out Frederick.

"My husband fell off the roof while he was constructing our hay barn," the woman explained breathlessly. "I fear he's broken his arm or leg—or both!"

Frederick stepped away from Cairo and sighed. "I'm sorry, my dear. I had hoped we could spend the evening together. But when emergencies arise . . ."

Frederick glanced at the tall Irishman who saw his chance to beat the physician's time with the attractive woman.

"Don't you worry about a thing, Doc," Eric O'Brien insisted as his arm circled Cairo's trim waist. "I'll see to it that the lady has plenty of attention."

"I'm sure you will," Frederick muttered as he shoved

his spectacles back on the bridge of his nose. "I'll come back to check on you in the morning, Miss Calhoun. We can have breakfast together."

The doctor's departure seemed to signal open season on intoxicated blondes. Cairo found herself swarmed by eager dance partners who stepped on her toes and talked her ears off. When she adjusted to the feel of one man's arms around her, another unfamiliar set of hands clamped around her waist and she was spun in dizzying circles. Each new suitor came equipped with a glass of punch to quench her thirst. Cairo drank and danced until her feet ached and her stomach sloshed like a keg of whiskey.

"I really must sit down," Cairo slurred. Before she could locate a wooden barrel which served as an improvised chair, her knees buckled beneath her.

"Just one more dance, honey," Eric cooed, wrapping a steadying arm around her. "I've waited five dances to have my next turn with you."

Before Cairo could reject the offer, Eric had her circling the room in rhythm with the high-stepping polka. The neat bun Cairo had pinned atop her head fell lower down her neck with each jarring movement. Eric O'Brien obviously hadn't mastered the art of dancing. He was like a kangaroo who bounded around the room, dragging his inebriated partner with him. Cairo was getting dizzier by the second. Her heart was pounding with the music and her stomach rolled like the laughter that undulated across the room.

"I really must sit down. Now . . ." Cairo insisted.

Eric, who had been hovering around the punch bowl a tad too much himself, refused to relinquish his hold on the shapely nymph for fear another man would latch onto her again. "Come on, honey. You and me were just getting acquainted."

Before Cairo could protest, Eric propelled her in another whizzing circle. When Cairo finally caught her breath, she *did* protest. Her legs felt like cooked noodles and her head was spinning like a top.

"I can't dance another step until I catch my breath," she wheezed.

"Sure you can," Eric declared as he wrapped his burly arms around her.

"The lady said she'd had enough."

Lawton Stone's voice boomed over the sounds of the piano, the fiddle, and the harmonica.

Cairo lifted droopy eyelids to see Lawton cutting his way through the crowd of dancers. Eric pulled her possessively against him and glared at the intruder.

"Now look here, mister," Eric growled drunkenly. "I found her first. If you want your turn with her, you'll have to stand in line like everybody else."

Lawton, who had been watching while Cairo was passed through her endless rabble of admirers like a hot potato, had lost the grip on his temper. He was in no mood to be sassed. He'd been stung by jealousy and it was playing havoc with his disposition.

Lawton stalked forward to loom over the stout Irishman. "Unless you want to wind up in jail for disturbing the peace, you'll turn the lady over to me . . . now!"

Since Lawton hadn't flipped back his jacket to expose his badge, Eric didn't know he was arguing with a U.S. marshal. "Hell, all I was doing was having a little fun. I just wanted to dance. There's no law against that.

Now why don't you run along and mind your own business, sonny."

Cairo was so tipsy that she couldn't concentrate on one thought for more than a second before becoming hopelessly sidetracked. Mumbling to herself, she wobbled between the two glaring men. "Go ahead and dance with him, Lawton," she said sluggishly. "I don't mind. I just want to sit a spell . . ."

When her legs folded at the knees without a chair to support her, Lawton snaked out an arm to catch her. Even though he was annoyed with the persistent Irishman, Lawton felt an amused smile tugging at his lips. It was a new experience to watch Cairo—Jarita Gardiner—staggering around like a newborn calf. Her hair was all atangle, her eyelids drooped, and her gown had been twisted around her waist from one too many fast polkas. Cairo was behaving nothing like the sophisticated young lady he had first met in Fort Smith.

"Come on, Cai, we better put you to bed," Lawton murmured.

Eric O'Brien had been entertaining his own visions of putting the intoxicating beauty to bed and he misinterpreted Lawton's remark. "That's just what I thought. You're planning to take unfair advantage of her."

As if Eric wasn't, Lawton thought peevishly. Lawton had only completed that thought when a doubled fist came plowing toward him. Eric O'Brien was as strong as an ox and the unexpected blow caused Lawton to stumble back against Cairo who was having enough difficulty standing erect as it was.

Cairo slammed against the wall of humanity that

had formed around the threesome. Her forward momentum set off a chain reaction, causing the ring of men to collide with one another.

Pandemonium broke loose. While Lawton answered Eric's blow to the jaw, another fight broke out on the other side of the room and spread toward the middle. Suddenly fists were flying in all directions at once. Women rushed in from the perimeters of the room to bring their husbands and sweethearts under thumb, but several attacks had been launched before the brawl could be stopped. Even while the womenfolk spouted demands to cease the battle, fists were still connecting with jaws and midsections. Just when one corps of females quelled the disturbance on one side of the store, war broke out on the other.

Meanwhile, Lawton and Eric were pounding each other flat. Lawton found himself equally matched against the hot-tempered Irishman who knew how to utilize his fists. Every time Lawton thought he'd leveled the "final blow," Eric bounced back to his feet and charged like a mad bull.

Lawton finally managed to bring Eric to his knees and keep him there for a moment—long enough to scan the room in search of Cairo. But she was nowhere to be seen. The proprietor of the store, fearing his merchandise was about to be damaged, leaped onto a wooden keg to fire a shot with his pistol. His bellowing voice demanded attention and he threatened to target a few heads if the fighting didn't cease.

Outside the store, Cairo had found relief from the colliding bodies and clog of smoke. She had eased down on the back of a wagon that stood in the street while its owner stopped in to enjoy the opening celebration. Unfortunately, the explosion of the proprietor's pistol startled the team of mules and they took off like cannonballs.

Cairo felt herself tumbling pell-mell around the back of the runaway wagon. Her head was already whirling and her stomach pitching. The jostle of the wagon, as it rumbled down the rutted street, left Cairo's mind and body in a nauseated tangle. A terrified yelp burst from her lips when the mules veered around the corner, flinging her against the other side of the wagon.

Although Lawton had recognized Cairo's voice, it took him a few moments to elbow his way through the crowd to locate her. Lawton had just sailed out the door when he spied the runaway wagon careening around the corner on two wheels.

With a curse that turned the air blue, Lawton bounded onto the nearest steed to give chase. The thin sliver of the moon and fleeting clouds made it difficult for him to tell where he was going, much less the direction of the runaway buckboard. The fact that Cairo was screaming for all she was worth wasn't helping matters since she had startled the mules even more than they already were. They plunged into the darkness, veering from the trodden path. Each bump they hit sent Cairo catapulting from one side of the wagon bed to the other, eliciting another eardrum-shattering screech.

Cairo was too intoxicated and her coordination too shaky to attempt to clamber onto the seat to retrieve the reins. She simply rolled and tumbled, unable to take control of her destiny. She swore that if she did survive this catastrophe, she would never partake of so much as a drop of whiskey, ever *ever* again! Cairo's dilemma gave her no time to wonder what had become of the raven-haired lawman; she was too busy battling to prevent being ejected from the bumping wagon and thrown to the ground.

Lawton cussed another blue streak when the team of mules plowed through a creek bed, splashing water as they went. He was all set to jump the creek, but too late he realized the steed on which he sat had an aversion to jumping. The horse set its front feet the instant it spied the water glistening in the dim moonlight. Lawton, unprepared to stop, soared over the steed and nose-dived into the creek.

Cursing furiously, Lawton picked himself up, grabbed the reins, and dragged the steed across the stream before mounting up to give chase.

He was soaked to the bone, angry with Cairo for traipsing off to the celebration in the first place and scared as hell. In her inebriated condition, Cairo wasn't competent enough to take command of the team of mules. And Lawton had found himself on a flighty steed that refused to jump gullies and leaped sideways at shadows.

Tugging off his belt to whip his steed into a faster pace, Lawton finally began to close the distance that separated him from the thundering wagon. Although the animal protested drawing up beside the buckboard in which Cairo was screaming at the top of her lungs, Lawton crouched on the saddle.

He leaped onto the speeding wagon and groped for the trailing reins. Gritting his teeth, he yanked back on the leather straps, forcing the mules to give up their mad dash.

Bruised, battered, and soaked to the bone, Lawton

stamped on the brake and then spun around to see Cairo crawling onto her hands and knees. She took one look at Lawton's plastered black hair and dripping clothes and began giggling.

"What in hell is wrong with you?" Lawton scowled at the inebriated young woman. "You very nearly met your death and you're laughing. I can't imagine what you could possibly find amusing about this."

Cairo's mind was still in a whirr and her high-speed ride hadn't sobered her as she had expected. Only an act of God could have done that before the effects of the whiskey ran their course.

"Damn it, quit cackling unless you're planning on laying eggs and answer me!" Lawton ordered. "What's so funny?"

Cairo glanced over her shoulder and laughed some more at the brawny figure of the man whose clothes clung to his virile torso like an extra set of skin, whose hair was mashed so thoroughly to the sides of his face that it looked as if he had a square head. "You haven't figured it out?" she questioned between giggles.

"Hell no!" Lawton exploded as he stepped over the seat and plunked down beside her.

Cairo peered up at him through bloodshot eyes. "I find it laughable that the very man who has twice tried to kill me has twice saved my life." She burst into another intoxicated laugh. "And you should see yourself! Dripping wet doesn't become you."

Lawton decided he'd have had to have been drunk himself to appreciate her warped sense of humor. Considering her near brush with death, she was certainly taking the incident exceptionally well. Lawton supposed her strange mood was the result of the liquor. Some people got mean when they drank. Some folks stumbled and fell all over themselves. Others, like himself, chattered like a magpie, and some became pensively silent.

Cairo, however, was a giggler whose pickled brain left her snickering at things which were nowhere near funny. She could have been killed a half-dozen times in the past thirty minutes! Now how funny was that?

Cairo took another look at Lawton and burst out laughing again. He looked ridiculous with his splotched face and wet garb. A glob of mud was perched on the end of his nose like a wart and another wad was smeared across his cheek. Impulsively, Cairo reached over to flick the clump of mud off his nose, but her aim was off the mark and she thumped his nostrils. Cairo giggled at her own clumsiness and Lawton grunted in discomfort.

Rolling his eyes at Cairo's outrageous antics, Lawton hopped off the back of the wagon. "You stay put while I round up that spooked horse I was riding," he ordered.

The terse demand slid off Cairo like water down a duck's back. When Lawton disappeared into the darkness, Cairo eased from the wagon to wander along the creek east of Elreno. She was still in a most peculiar mood after having all her thoughts twisted like a tangled jungle. Her brushes with calamity gave her such eagerness to live every moment to its fullest. She felt like a carefree child as she ambled along the shallow stream that was sheltered by cottonwood trees. The whiskey still had a mighty hold on her spongy brain and she was left to wander and giggle at every fleeting thought that breezed through her head.

Despite all the heartache Lawton had caused her the past month, Cairo realized she had done more living and encountered more adventure than she had experienced in all her lifetime. Chances were she would return to her uneventful, well-organized life after Lawton went on his way. Things just seemed to happen when he was around. He was one of those men who naturally attracted excitement.

Cairo paused to ponder the outstretched limbs of the tree that towered over her. She reflected on how many times she'd found herself out on a limb during her dealings with Lawton Stone. That fleeting thought prompted another impulsive giggle.

Cairo clutched at the branch above her head and hooked her leg over it like a chimpanzee. It had been eons since she'd climbed a tree. And in her present frame of mind, it didn't occur to her that she was behaving in a most unladylike manner. The whiskey had warped her thinking, leaving her a creature of reckless instinct who reacted simply because she felt like it.

And so Cairo tripped along the tree limb to latch onto another branch, just to see if she could still climb after all these years.

Chapter Fifteen

"Cai?" Lawton called to the darkness at large and then pricked his ears to the sound of her voice.

Nothing.

"Curse it," Lawton scowled, unaware that he had resorted to using her favorite expression. "Didn't I tell her to stay put? But did she listen? Hell no, she just wandered off, and where she is only God knows!"

When Lawton stopped talking to himself long enough to listen, he heard a faraway giggle and the slurred words to "Skip to My Lou." He stamped toward the sound. When he'd walked to the spot he'd calculated as the source of the noise he found nothing but vacant space beside the stream. Another chortle wafted through the tree and Lawton glanced skyward.

He stared in shock when he spied the oversize bird in her emerald-green gown tripping along a tree limb high above him. Lawton clamped his mouth shut before he bellowed at the idiotic woman and startled her so much that she tumbled to her death.

Good Lord, he thought he knew this frustrating female, but it was glaringly apparent that he didn't know her at all. She was positively outrageous when she was intoxicated. Her inhibitions had taken her as high as a kite, leaving her vulnerable to her dangerous antics. Her conduct this evening lent testimony to the fact that Cairo Calhoun—Jarita Gardiner—was capable of just about anything. Beneath her sophisticated image was a wild-hearted hellion who was as much the daredevil as Lawton himself.

His breath froze in his throat when Cairo's skirts snagged on a branch, causing her to teeter precariously. Lawton positioned himself beneath her to break her fall, but, in the nick of time, Cairo clutched a higher limb and steadied herself. Bursting into another giggle, she tripped on her merry way to swing over to another branch.

"And *she* called *me* crazy!" Lawton grumbled as he hooked his leg over the low-hanging branch and chased after Cairo who was practicing her aerial maneuvers high atop the tree.

The thrashing in the limbs below and the snapping of twigs drew Cairo's attention. Straddling a branch, she peered down at the bulky form of a man who climbed toward her.

"Lawton? Is that you?" she asked sluggishly.

"Who the hell did you expect?" he grunted as he hoisted himself onto a higher limb.

Cairo tittered recklessly. "Certainly not you. I never expected you to behave like a child. If the truth be known, you probably hatched from an egg, full grown at twenty years of age."

"Come down from there," Lawton snapped

grouchily. "I'm tired of your idiotic games."

Cairo threw back her head, sending the silver-blond tendrils trailing across her shoulder. "What are you going to do if I don't?" she taunted him. "Shoot me, Mister Marshal?"

Lawton gnashed his teeth, hissed a few choice oaths, and levered himself onto another towering branch. But Cairo appeared intent on making a game of this chase through the trees and he remained several limbs behind her.

"Damn it, Cai, I've had enough of this!" Lawton all but yelled at her.

"Good," she called down to him. "Why don't you trot back to town and cram your fist in Eric O'Brien's face a few more times. He certainly seemed willing enough to spar with you. I, on the other hand, prefer to climb trees—"

When Cairo lost her footing and was left dangling by her fingertips, Lawton's heart stalled in his chest. "Blast it, woman, you're going to break your damn fool neck if you don't watch where you're going."

"It's *my* damn fool neck." She looped her leg over the limb and hung upside down, enjoying a different view of the world.

"I hope you like your neck broken in fifty pieces," Lawton scowled as he scampered toward her.

Before Cairo could right herself and walk the tightrope of limbs again, Lawton clenched his fist in the nape of her gown and yanked her up. "We're climbing down this instant. Do you hear me?"

Who couldn't? He was yelling loud enough to rouse the dead.

Cairo swayed toward him while he steadied himself

against a nearby limb. She purred like a kitten as she looped her arms around his broad shoulders and cuddled up against him.

Lawton's brows jackknifed in response to her unexpected swing in mood. He had anticipated that she would resist his touch and he had braced himself in case she put up a fight. He had always found himself battling his way through her defenses, but this time Cairo did the unexpected. She planted a steamy kiss to his lips and molded her body into his.

"Do you know what an irresistible temptation you are, Mister Marshal?" she slurred as she ruffled the damp strands of raven hair that clung to his head.

He peered down into her droopy eyes and he felt a smile spread across his lips. "No, suppose you tell me, minx."

Cairo hadn't realized the whiskey could work as a truth serum, but it did. She sighed heavily and then traced the lines that bracketed Lawton's sensuous mouth. "I never thought I'd meet a man who would have a lasting effect on me," she admitted in a slurred voice. "But you have a definite effect on a woman, whether she prefers you to or not."

The feel of her delicious body meshed familiarly to his ignited a fire that could have set the tree ablaze. Lawton cursed his instantaneous reaction to this high-spirited woman who had him behaving as outrageously as she was. And Lawton hadn't even had a drink, for crying out loud!

"You need to be standing on solid ground," Lawton advised, his voice wobbling from the potent effects of her kiss.

"I'd rather stay up here with you," Cairo murmured

as her wandering hands mapped the planes of his virile body.

Lawton rolled his eyes skyward. Cairo was saying the most ridiculous things and behaving in an even more ludicrous manner. Lord, when she was sober she would be mortified beyond words by her conduct. *If* she even remembered the things she'd said and done under the influence of liquor, Lawton quickly amended. But *he* wasn't likely to forget this wild escapade.

In the course of three hours Lawton had experienced the entire spectrum of human emotions—anger, fear, amusement, arousal—for a start. Not only that, but he had observed Cairo while she was surrounded by eager suitors. He'd gotten himself into a brawl because of her. He'd wound up on a high-speed chase before being ejected from the saddle and into a creek for an unplanned bath in his clothes. And now, to top it all off, he'd fluttered up into a tree to find himself seduced by a most tempting witch.

Cairo sighed melodramatically as she slumped against Lawton's chest. "But temptation though you are, I suppose I should marry Frederick," she said out of the blue.

"Who the blazes is Frederick?" Lawton demanded to know.

"The physician," she replied, as if that explained everything. It didn't, at least not to Lawton's satisfaction.

"Why are you going to do that?" Lawton was amazed at the sting of jealousy that needled him. It shouldn't have mattered what Cairo did with the rest of her life, but it did. He had sworn he didn't want her and yet the thought of another man claiming her turned him inside out.

Cairo peered up at him, trying to decide whether to dignify the foolish question with an answer. "Well, because he asked me, of course."

"If you'd married every man who asked you, how many times would you have wed?" Lawton questioned.

Cairo thought about it for a minute. "A dozen times or more, I suppose."

Lawton gnashed his teeth, biting at the jealousy that was gnawing at him. "Then what's so terrific about Freddie?"

Her shoulder lifted in a nonchalant shrug. "Nothing. But at least he doesn't despise women the way you do."

"I've got good reason," Lawton muttered in self-defense.

Cairo exhaled a breath and found herself distracted by her wayward hand. Her fingertips had delved beneath his soggy shirt to make contact with his cold flesh. "You have a magnificent body, Lawton."

"Thanks, I'm glad you like it." He was amused by her abrupt change of topics and the silly grin that dangled off the corner of her mouth.

"I like it too much for my own good," Cairo mused aloud. "And I shouldn't since you won't be around much longer."

The careless remark clouded Lawton's suspicious mind. For the past few hours he had allowed himself to forget her desire to see him dead for murdering her outlaw brother.

Lawton cupped her chin, tilting her face to his probing stare. "Would you still do what you're planning to do if I loved you and you loved me back?"

The whole thought was too complex for Cairo to

comprehend in her present condition. All she could concentrate on was the "if I loved you and you loved me back."

Cairo let out her breath in a long sigh. "You couldn't," she responded drowsily. "You don't even have a heart. And anyway, love isn't all it's cracked up to be, so far as I can tell."

Lawton shook his head in dismay. He didn't know why he'd bothered to broach the subject. Cairo was too sauced to think straight. He doubted she even knew what she was saying.

"Let's just forget it," he muttered. "We're going back to town to put you to bed."

Before Cairo could argue, Lawton hooked his arm around her waist and picked his way down the tree. During those few minutes required to reach the ground, Cairo's giggles gave way to tears—of all things. Lawton hadn't expected that! Cairo had been snickering halfway down the tree—laughing harder and harder until she was sobbing in great gulps.

"Stop that!" Lawton growled when he finally set Cairo to her feet so he could shake her back to her senses.

The tactic just served to jerk more tears out of her petite body. A steady stream of them boiled down her flushed cheeks, frustrating Lawton to no end.

Cairo had no idea why she was crying her eyes out. She couldn't control the tears any better than the laughter. When Lawton shook the stuffing out of her, water erupted from her eyes like a geyser and the stream wouldn't stop flowing.

"Confound it." Lawton carried Cairo over to plunk her down on the wagon seat. "I'm wet enough already without you bleeding tears all over me. What the hell's the matter with you?"

His scolding had no effect whatsoever. Cairo simply sat there and cried. The turmoil of emotions she'd endured the past few weeks came pouring out and nothing, not even a dam, would hold them back.

Halfway back to town the convulsive tears gave way to loud unladylike hiccups which Cairo had no control over, either. She expelled a shuddering sob, hiccupped loudly, sniffled, and then hiccupped again.

Lawton muttered under his breath when he felt Cairo slump against him. She had draped her right arm over his shoulder in case her body-wrenching hiccups catapulted her off the wagon. Her head lay against his shoulder and the tangled tresses of her long blond hair cascaded over his arm like a waterfall.

Annoyed with her antics though he was, Lawton couldn't suppress the grin that slid across his lips when he glanced down at her. Cairo was pathetic but utterly adorable. She had moved into the final phase of inebriation: sleep. But each time she dozed on his shoulder, the buckboard hit a rut and her head rolled down his arm, bringing her awake with a start. Then she'd hiccup loudly and nod off again.

After Lawton returned the wagon and horse to the store, he scooped Cairo's limp body into his arms and carried her to the hotel. Once he had situated her on her bed, he shucked his wet clothes and waited for the bath water he'd ordered from the hotel clerk. Within a few minutes, a string of attendants appeared to fill the tub.

Lawton sank into his bath to ward off the chill of tromping all over the countryside and along tree limbs in his soggy garb. While he lathered himself and shaved the stubble from his face, his eyes kept straying to the sleeping bundle of green satin and petticoats that lay upon the bed.

Lawton shook his head in wonder. In all his thirty-one years, he had never met a woman who had come remotely close to evoking so many emotions from him. She'd brought him a little bit of heaven and a lot of hell. Even now that Al Fontain had positively identified her as the Gardiners' kid sister, Lawton still wanted her. She had become a poison in his blood and he couldn't get her out of his system . . .

A mumbled moan drifted from Cairo's lips, jostling Lawton from his reverie. He got out of the tub and absently dried off. All the while his gaze remained fixed on the shapely nymph whose exquisite features were soft in repose. The flickering lanternlight bathed her flawless face in shades of gold and sparkled in the silken mane of hair that tumbled over the pillow like a molten river.

Lawton ambled across the room to scrutinize her, marveling at the crosscurrents of emotions that washed over him.

"Ah, what an enigma you are, little Snowbird," Lawton murmured as he eased down to peel off her hindering garments.

That, Lawton instantly realized, was a mistake. The more flesh he exposed, the more enticed he became. Cairo was in no condition to resist his amorous assault. His initial intention had been to make her more comfortable but disrobing her was discomforting him in a most arousing way. His eyes roamed over her creamy flesh and he felt as if he were unwrapping a precious gift that belonged only to him. No matter what Cairo was, she was his—his lover, his torment, his antagonist, his deadly curse.

The feel of tender caresses migrating over her bare skin brought Cairo from the depths of her dreams. And yet the lingering effects of the alcohol prevented her from completely returning to reality. She hovered in a dark dimension of time that swirled with tantalizing images and sensations. Involuntarily, she moved toward the warmth that hovered above her.

Lawton's pulse leapfrogged when Cairo cuddled against him. His hungry gaze swept over her luscious body. On their own accord, his hands skimmed over her on a journey of intimate exploration. He had touched her before, but never as reverently as he did now. He had slanted his lips over hers before to taste the sweet nectar of her kiss, but he had never been as gentle with her as he was now.

Lawton couldn't comprehend the flow of emotions that streamed through him. This exasperating female drew upon a well of hidden feelings that he had buried deep inside him. What he felt for her went against the grain, defied common sense, invited danger.

When Cairo sighed and draped her arm over his hip, Lawton felt another wave of desire tumble over him. He could feel her moist breath against his cheek, feel the tips of her breasts boring into his ribs. When her silky leg slid between his knees and she cuddled closer to employ him as her pillow and blanket, Lawton went hot all over.

"Lord, will I ever recover from this insatiable craving for you?" he whispered hoarsely.

Not any time soon, he decided as his body inched nearer to her. There was no fighting the wondrous feelings that spilled through him when he took Cairo in his arms and she instinctively responded to the firm pressure of his hands and lips.

The image of glittering mercury eyes and a rakish smile materialized in the fog of Cairo's mind. The familiar and intimate passage of his hands over her submissive flesh infiltrated her cloudy senses. Spontaneously, she arched to meet his hungry kiss and the titillating caresses, giving him free access to her body.

His name tumbled from her lips in a groggy sigh and Lawton groaned in unholy torment. It was happening again, just as it always did when he dared to touch her. He became so lost in his need for her that nothing else mattered.

How easily he had dismissed the other women who drifted in and out of his life. But how impossible it was to turn his back and walk away from this sorceress who was both the cause and cure of the greatest torment Lawton had ever experienced!

With a defeated sigh, Lawton allowed himself the pleasures of spreading kisses and caresses over her smooth flesh. He longed to instill the same cravings in her that had consumed him. In his desire to take complete possession of her, Lawton explored Cairo's delicious body to his heart's content, eliciting responses that assured him he had taken control of her flesh and soul—at least for this one glorious instant.

There had been a time in his life when appeasing his own needs was all that concerned him. But with Cairo, that was never enough. He placed pleasuring her above his own needs. He had to know he could shatter her as easily as she shattered him. The rapture he enjoyed while he was with this beauty doubled when she returned it. He yearned for the splendor of passion that swelled and blossomed to envelop both of them, as it had in the past.

Drowning in arousing thoughts, Lawton showered Cairo's body with worshiping kisses and reverent caresses. He left no part of her pliant flesh untouched in his crusade to pleasure her, and when he drew her quaking body beneath his to take final possession, his flesh, as well as hers, was a mass of sublime spasms that demanded fulfillment.

Lawton buried himself within her, feeling the sultry flame leap through his body, mind, and soul. The tenderness changed to a savage urgency that exploded and rippled through every fiber of his being. His muscles flexed as the surge of uncontrollable passion gripped him. And still he couldn't get close enough to the raging fire that scorched him, inside and out. He moved in the ageless rhythm of love, clutching Cairo to him as if he never meant to let her go, reveling at the feelings that crashed down upon him. He shuddered beneath the nerve-shattering needs that had found release. And still he couldn't let her go, even when the strength drained from his body, leaving him nothing more than a trembling shell.

Exhausted and appeased, Lawton slumped against Cairo. Impulsively, he dropped a kiss to her petal-soft lips. Her thick curly lashes swept up for a moment and she graced him with a lazy smile, but she spoke not a word before her eyes closed and her body relaxed beneath his.

When he felt her shallow breathing, Lawton knew his angel had slipped back into her intoxicated dreams. What a hellish headache she was going to have in the morning, he thought with an amused grin. As gentle and relaxed as Cairo was now, she was sure to become an irritable tigress in the light of day. He wondered if she would even recall the wild splendor they'd shared.

Lawton combed his fingers through the lustrous mane of silver-blond hair that tumbled over his pillow. "One of us will wind up hurting the other before this is all over," he mused aloud. "And if you don't succeed in killing me, I will eventually be forced to condemn you."

Lawton pushed that grim thought from his tormented mind. He didn't want to dwell on where this would all end. He only wanted to drift on the tide of bliss. Tonight he would wander through sweet satisfying dreams and relive the rapture he had found in this perplexing beauty's arms. He would let tomorrow take care of itself until he could gather his energy and thoughts to deal with the frustrations that were sure to come.

Chapter Sixteen

When Cairo awoke she swore a couple of centuries had passed her by. Piercing sunlight like sharp-edged daggers penetrated her swollen eyelids. The bed—or whatever supported her, she wasn't sure at the moment—seemed to pitch and roll and swirl like a rudderless ship on an angry sea. An agonized moan rattled in the air and it was a second later before Cairo realized it was her own voice that broke the silence. The noise vibrated through her head, which felt like an overly ripe pumpkin about to split wide open.

Cairo groaned again when excruciating pain plowed through her skull and hammered on her aching brain. Lord, she felt as if she'd died during the night and no one had bothered to tell her. No, she thought sickly. Death had to feel better than this! This was a torture worse than hell. Even her eyebrows ached. Her insides were gnawing at each other and her mouth was as dry as cotton. Cairo desperately needed some water, but the thought of pushing into an upright position to fetch a drink was out of the question!

A devilish smile quirked Lawton's lips as he watched Cairo flounder in bed. Her face was as white as the sheet under which they lay. Her silver-blond hair looked as if it had been arranged by a cyclone and her lips were a pale shade of blue. Having endured a few horrendous hangovers himself, Lawton recognized all the symptoms. Cairo would have gladly given a fortune for some relief from her pounding head and pitching stomach.

Deciding to dress and fetch Cairo a cup of coffee, Lawton rolled out of bed. When he did, the sagging mattress caused her to tumble sideways. She gave out with another howl of anguish when her sensitive stomach sloshed against her ribs. The groan of discomfort sent another drumroll crashing through her brain and Cairo begged to die a quick death.

"Sorry, princess," Lawton whispered as he bent over to brush a kiss across her waxen forehead. "But she who partakes of too much whiskey must suffer for her sins."

Cairo was in no mood for Lawton's taunting lecture. "Just go away and let me die in peace," she croaked and then grabbed her throbbing head, trying to hold it at an angle that didn't hurt. But there wasn't one.

"I'll fetch you some toast and coffee," he volunteered.

Cairo didn't want food or drink. She wanted immediate relief. She felt horrible, and having Lawton see her in this disgraceful condition humiliated her to the extreme. "Why don't you just shoot me as you're so fond of doing and put me out of my misery."

Lawton shook his head. "It wouldn't help. You'd have to be dead a week to feel better."

Cairo wanted to bawl like a baby but she feared that would give her an even worse headache. Already her mind was an empty slate. The liquor had distorted her memory, and she couldn't recall anything except dancing on a cloud and guzzling alcohol-spiked punch at the party. From that point her brain was a blur. She could only assume she had wandered out into the street where Lawton had found her and returned her to her room. The fact that she lay abed, naked as the day she was born, suggested Lawton had . . .

A frown puckered her brow when fleeting images soaked through her spongy brain. Cairo faintly remembered feeling as if she had been tumbling helter-skelter and then flying through space. She also recalled experiencing a multitude of sublime sensations that she felt only when she and Lawton were . . .

"You seduced me when I wasn't in command of my senses," she realized and said so.

"That's all you remember?" Lawton chuckled. It left him with an odd feeling of pride to know that his lovemaking was all that had made an impression on Cairo. Considering her wild escapades the previous night, that was quite a compliment!

"So you admit you seduced me against my will, you loathsome scoundrel," Cairo spluttered, her ashen face flooding with a crimson wave of embarrassment.

"Against your will?" Lawton shoved a muscular leg into his breeches. "You were very responsive, as I recall."

"I was drunk!" Cairo blared at him and then howled at the pain that pummeled her tender head. "I hate you, Lawton Stone!"

"Of course you do," he countered as he fastened his breeches.

Cairo was all set to fling another insulting remark at him but the rap at the door interrupted her. "Answer that," she demanded crossly.

Lawton flashed her an ornery grin that made his eyes sparkle like polished silver. "It's your door. You answer it . . . unless you want to further humiliate yourself by allowing the residents of Elreno to know you're not only an inebriate but that you also entertain men in your room."

The remark served its purpose, just as Lawton anticipated it would. He wanted Cairo on her feet instead of lounging on the bed, dwelling on the unpleasant effects of her hangover.

Sick as she was, angry resentment spurred Cairo to stand up. After flashing Lawton a look that was meant to maim, she wobbled toward the door and braced her arm against the wall.

"For God's sake!" Lawton snatched up the sheet and tossed it at her.

Cairo blushed a dozen shades of red when she realized she had almost answered the door without wearing a stitch.

After she wrapped the sheet around her like a toga, Cairo inched open the portal and craned her neck to peer at Frederick Pullman standing in front of her. She suddenly remembered that Frederick had promised to come by to escort her to breakfast before he made his rounds to visit his patients.

Frederick took one look at Cairo's splotched face and puffy eyes and gasped in shock. The expression on his face testified to the extent of his concern. "My goodness, Cairo, are you all right? Of course you aren't all right," he muttered. "I can see that for myself. I had better examine you."

Frederick pushed his way into the room without invitation. He had only taken three steps before he saw Lawton sitting bare-chested on the chair, tugging on his boots. Frederick's eyes widened behind his wire-rimmed spectacles as his bewildered gaze jumped back and forth between the shapely nymph draped in the sheet and the partially dressed rake in the chair.

Cairo wished the floor would open so she could have dropped out of sight. She was so humiliated she wanted to die! Lawton's presence in her room and her lack of clothing had Frederick speculating on what had left these two people in this awkward situation. As if he didn't know!

"I thought you and I . . ." Frederick's deflated voice trailed off into brittle silence.

One look at the tall, lean gentleman who clutched a medical bag in his left hand was all the identification Lawton needed. This was Freddie the physician who was entertaining thoughts of making Cairo his wife. And if this little minx hadn't wanted to see Lawton dead for gunning down one of her brothers, he might have even felt sorry for her when her would-be fiancé arrived upon the scene. But Lawton couldn't muster much sympathy, even when Cairo looked humiliated. To Lawton's way of thinking, Cairo was getting exactly what she deserved.

What really annoyed Lawton was that this sly vixen had gone around the country, collecting men who could be of some use to her if her true identity was ever discovered. First she had bedazzled the powerful Judge Parker. Then she had lured Daniel Siler, the upstart lawyer, into her spell. Now she had a physician following on her heels. But judging by the look on Freddie's face, his bubble had burst. The woman of his dreams hadn't turned out to be quite what he expected. Too bad for Freddie, Lawton thought with a devilish grin.

Pasting on a cordial smile, Lawton stretched out his hand. "The name's Lawton Stone," he introduced himself. "I brought the lady back to her room after the shindig at the mercantile store." Mischief danced in his gray eyes as he nodded toward Cairo. "Maybe you should examine her, Doc. She doesn't look as if she's feeling up to snuff to me, either. Maybe she's coming down with something."

Feeling awkward and irritated, Frederick brushed his palm over Cairo's clammy forehead. Then he stared into her puffy, red-streaked eyes. A quick investigation of the scrapes and bruises on her elbows and forearms had him frowning curiously.

Cairo couldn't explain the bruises, nor did she dare try. Lawton was probably the only one who knew how she'd acquired them and he was too busy being ornery to divulge that information.

Gathering her shattered dignity, Cairo retreated a step and clutched the sheet self-consciously around her. "There is nothing wrong with me except a slight hangover," she insisted.

"Slight?" Lawton crowed. "If this is *slight,* I'd hate to see *severe!"*

Frederick, who had been doing a valiant job of controlling his frustration, wheeled on Lawton. "You, sir, are no gentleman for taking advantage of the lady," he blustered. "And to make matters worse, you have the unmitigated gall to mock her condition. If the truth be known, you're probably responsible for seeing that she got that way in the first place so you could compromise her!"

Frederick presented his back to Lawton and focused his attention on Cairo whose complexion wavered between a humiliated red and a pea green. "Cairo, despite what happened, I still want you to be my wife. No one else needs to know about this disgraceful incident, over which I'm sure you had no control." He glanced over his shoulder to fling Lawton a disdainful glare.

"Thank you, Frederick." Cairo was unable to meet his eyes. "You are very understanding and noble to propose in the face of such—"

"Now wait just a damned minute!" Lawton pushed his way in front of the doctor to confront Cairo. "You can't marry Freddie and you know it."

Cairo's chin tilted to a rebellious angle. "I can do anything I please and you aren't going to stop me. I want you out of my life." She indicated the door. "Get out and don't come back!"

Lawton didn't budge. He simply glowered at the headstrong, belligerent minx.

"You heard the lady," Frederick piped up. "You have done enough damage."

Lawton stomped over to retrieve his shirt. He gestured toward the badge. "I happen to be a U.S. marshal and this woman is my prisoner. If you know what's good for you, you'll take a wide berth around her. She's nothing but trouble and you're lucky you found out before you married her."

Frederick's jaw swung on its hinges and Cairo gaped at Lawton as if he had sprouted another head—

equipped with devil's horns.

"She escaped me in Guthrie and took the stage to Elreno," Lawton went on. "I caught up with her last night while she was celebrating her freedom by guzzling alcohol-spiked punch. Then she tried to seduce me to bribe me and—"

"That's a lie!" Cairo screeched furiously.

Curse that Lawton Stone! He didn't want her but he was spiteful enough not to want any other man to have her. He had already made her life hell and still he wasn't satisfied!

"Do you deny telling me that I was your temptation and that you were attracted to my—and I quote—magnificent body?" Lawton delighted in watching her face turn a bright shade of purple. "I suppose you're going to tell Freddie you don't remember draping yourself all over me when I tried to cart you back to your room." He laughed when Cairo looked as if she had just swallowed her Adam's apple. "You can plead momentary insanity, but I was there and I know exactly what happened."

"I think I had better leave." Frederick pivoted toward the door.

"Wise decision, Doc," Lawton agreed before the door slammed shut behind Cairo's former-future husband.

Cairo was so outraged she couldn't think straight, and her hangover wasn't helping matters, either. In a burst of fury, she snatched the pitcher off the commode, wishing it was Lawton's head. The missile sailed across the room, colliding with his shoulder before it crashed to the floor.

"You're the worst excuse for a law official I've ever

met!" she spewed as she buzzed toward her satchel to retrieve a fresh set of breeches. "First you stole my virginity, then you shot me, and now you've ruined my life and what's left of my reputation. I hate you. I despise you. I never want to see you again!"

Lawton wasn't sure what had prompted him to twist the truth for his own convenience to get Freddie the physician out of the room. He supposed his jealousy had gotten the best of him. Lawton had found himself faced with the possibility of having Cairo leap into a marriage with a man who couldn't handle her. And Cairo *had* been a criminal in his custody from the very beginning of this trek across the Twin Territories. He had been careful not to let her know that he was wise to her deadly scheme. And even now, she thought he'd dreamed up that excuse, just to get rid of Freddie.

Lawton had lingered too long in thought. He'd been staring after Frederick, finding excuses for his unethical behavior. Taking Cairo Calhoun for granted while she was in a fit of temper was a costly mistake. Lawton didn't realize she had pounced on him until it was too late.

Before Lawton knew what hit him, something had! Cairo clubbed him over the head with his Peacemaker. Like a giant redwood falling beneath a lumberjack's ax, Lawton pitched forward and crashed to the floor.

Cairo felt ever so much better after she'd taken her frustrations out on their true source. Lawton Stone could lie there until he mildewed for all she cared. She wanted nothing more to do with that sly weasel! He was by far the worst mistake she had ever made in her life!

"Magnificent body indeed!" she scoffed as she

stepped over his crumpled form. After stuffing her belongings in her satchels, Cairo confiscated Lawton's boot pistol and Colt for extra protection.

Quickly, she unfolded the map her father had sketched to direct her to Canadian Station, then marched toward the door. To satisfy her lingering irritation, she retraced her steps to walk down the middle of Lawton's back, leaving her footprints all over him.

"You, Lawton Stone, can go straight to hell. I never plan to see you again as long as we both live!"

Cairo flung one last glare at Lawton and stalked out. Lawton's devious attempt to turn Frederick against her was the last straw. The man was a spiteful, heartless maniac and she regretted every emotion she had wasted on him. Cairo vowed to set fire to the mental scrapbook of memories which had Lawton's name on it. In her mind, he would cease to exist. She would forget the way he looked, the way he talked, his awful singing, the wondrous way he made her body hum when he . . .

Cairo smothered the traitorous tingles that trickled down her spine. She detested Lawton Stone! All she wanted was to forget him and find her father and begin her new life.

And that is exactly what I'm going to do, Cairo assured herself fiercely. She would rely upon the Calhoun brand of determination to see her through. It had never failed her before and it wouldn't fail her now!

Lawton propped himself up on an elbow to inspect the goose egg on the back of his head. He cursed colorfully when he cast a fuzzy glance around the room to find it empty. Although his body and his throbbing head complained, Lawton pushed upon his hands and knees and finally managed to stagger to his feet.

Inhaling a steadying breath, he wobbled over to retrieve his gear and then propelled himself toward the door. When he trudged downstairs and into the street, he expelled several more expletives. Not only had Cairo knocked him silly but she had also stolen his black stallion! He wasn't all that surprised, considering her unseemly profession, but the inconvenience of haggling with the blacksmith for another mount would slow down his pursuit. Cairo would be miles away before he gave chase.

Lawton broke stride when he asked himself why Cairo had gone to such drastic extremes to elude him. If her brothers had put a price on his head, why hadn't she gunned him down when opportunity knocked? Lawton reminded himself that it would have blown the Snowbird's cover if she had shot a U.S. marshal in a hotel room. No, Cairo was too smart to put a posse on her trail. That would have caused trouble for the Gardiner gang.

Anxious to pursue Cairo, Lawton thundered out of Elreno at breakneck speed. He hadn't ridden more than three miles when he met a fashionably garbed man who had "gambler" written all over him. Knowing that type had an eye for high-stake card games and pretty women, Lawton halted the traveler.

"Did you happen to pass a blonde in breeches, riding a black horse?" Lawton quizzed the man.

The gambler grinned and nodded confirmation. "Indeed I did." He drew his gold timepiece from the pocket of his gold brocade vest. "It was two hours ago to be exact. When I tried to pause to pass the time of day with her, she pulled a pistol on me and told me to be on my way because she had a low tolerance for men, especially ones with black hair." He swept the hat from his head and then regarded Lawton, whose head was capped with the same color hair. The gambler stroked his goatee and grinned wryly. "I suppose she was referring to you," he speculated.

"I suppose she was," Lawton mumbled, staring into the distance.

After squirming to a more comfortable position in the saddle, the gambler chuckled. "She was a pretty little thing, but too damned feisty for my tastes. If you don't mind a piece of advice, friend, I wouldn't ride up on that hellion without a shield of armor," he warned. "The lady seemed angry enough to shoot."

The gambler raked his hands through his dark hair and then replaced his hat at a jaunty angle on his head. "I always did say a pistol-packing female was a lot more dangerous than a man. Most men pride themselves in being able to outdraw an opponent, fair and square. But not women. They don't care if a fight is fair, only that when it's over, they've won."

That just about summed up Lawton's theories on the female of the species, too. A man couldn't trust a woman and he was a fool to try. Just look what had happened to Lawton when he took Cairo for granted for one moment? She'd cracked his skull and stolen his horse!

With a nod of farewell, Lawton nudged his steed into a gallop and tore off down the road in search of the sassy spitfire. He still wasn't sure why he was bothering with her. He should have aimed himself in the opposite direction to release Al Fontain from Guthrie's jail.

With careful guidance Al Fontain could make something of himself. But Cairo? Lawton scoffed cynically. Her thieving brothers had probably sabotaged her thinking at an early age and their constant influence had ruined her for life. She could portray the sophisticated lady when it met her whim, but she'd always be an outlaw at heart. The only thing that would reform the Gardiner clan—Jarita included—was a well-aimed bullet.

Lawton grimaced at the gloomy thought. He had the sickening feeling that sooner or later, he was going to have to betray his affection for that wild-hearted firebrand, would have to choose between *his* life and *hers*.

"Damn you, Cairo Calhoun," Lawton scowled. "I'm going to hate what you're going to force me to do to you before this feud is over."

Chapter Seventeen

Feeling positively miserable, Cairo slid from the saddle to wash her face in the creek that meandered through the rolling prairie. She was still plagued with a nagging headache, sour stomach, and a bleeding heart.

As she toweled off her face and hands she thought how she couldn't wait to reach the border community called Canadian Station to be reunited with her father. According to the map Rylan had sketched, the town was only three miles south of her present location. Once she was in the protective circle of her father's arms, she would be safe from Lawton's haunting memory. And if he dared to show his face, Cairo would threaten to blow him to kingdom come if he didn't turn right around and walk out of her life forevermore . . .

The crackling of twigs along the creek jolted Cairo from her spiteful musings. She shot toward the stallion that had ambled downstream to help himself to a drink. When Cairo made her frantic dash toward him, the steed jumped sideways. In her haste to snatch up the reins, she startled the stallion and he bolted through the creek and up the steep bank.

The crackle of brittle leaves prompted Cairo to clutch at the Colt she had stashed in her belt. Before she could wheel to take aim at whoever or whatever had jumped her, she felt someone plow into her, shoving her forward. Her breath came out in a rush when she slammed into the ground and a man's heavy frame sprawled on top of her.

Cairo bucked and writhed to unseat the scoundrel. Like a winding snake, Cairo contorted her head and body so she could take a blind shot at the varmint who was squishing her into the mud.

A steely hand clamped over her pistol, causing the bullet to zing through the overhanging trees. Determined to fight with her last dying breath, Cairo lifted her elbow, catching her unseen assailant in the ribs.

Craning her neck, Cairo glanced over her shoulder to see none other than Lawton Stone snarling at her. When he tried to jerk the Colt from her hand, she hung on tight, refusing to allow him control of the weapon. Cairo expected him to shoot her if he got the chance. She was not about to give him another chance!

"Gimme that!" Lawton snapped as he tried to grab her swinging arm.

"You're welcome to it as soon as I shoot you with it," Cairo hissed at him.

While they struggled over possession of the Peacemaker, Cairo's left hand slid toward her boot to retrieve the long-barreled pistol she'd swiped from Lawton. Although he managed to wrestle the Colt from her fist and turn it on her, he found another of his weapons staring him in the face.

Stalemate.

Cairo sucked in a ragged breath and cocked the

trigger when Lawton simultaneously cocked his Colt.

"Put it down," Lawton snarled.

"You put yours down first," Cairo demanded in the same threatening tone.

Impasse.

Lawton expelled a frustrated breath. "I won't shoot you if you drop the gun."

"I'm not making any such promises," Cairo sassed him.

Lawton blinked incredulously. "You'd shoot me, even when you know damned good and well you wouldn't live to enjoy any satisfaction? Woody and Tucker would track you down and hang you by your skinny little neck!"

"Killing you would be the ultimate satisfaction after all the hell you've put me through."

"What *I*'ve put *you* through?" Lawton repeated sarcastically. "You've got that exactly backward."

"You're not the one with battle scars all over you," she erupted. "Even if I shot you, I still wouldn't consider us even . . ."

Cairo made the crucial mistake of involving herself too deeply in an emotional conversation and employing gestures with the hand that held the pistol. And while she was busy raging at Lawton, he struck, catching her off guard. He'd squeezed the trigger of his Peacemaker, which he'd aimed at the long barrel of her pistol. The weapon flipped out of her hand and landed in the mud.

Flinging his Colt aside, Lawton shoved Cairo's shoulders to the ground and straddled her belly to glower into her outraged face.

"Get off me!" she spluttered, infuriated that she had been bested by this trigger-happy lunatic. The helpless frustration of realizing she could never win against Lawton caused a knot of anger to coil in her belly. She felt like screaming and crying and cursing, but she knew it wouldn't have any effect whatsoever on this towering mass of granite.

Admitting defeat, Cairo slumped against the ground. "Why can't you just go away and leave me alone?" Her voice cracked with tormented emotion. "I can find my own way from here."

"I'm sure you can," Lawton scowled, despising his own vulnerability to this green-eyed terror. "But why did you suddenly decide to leave without me? I thought you needed me to solve your father's dilemma." *As if she had a father who had a dilemma,* Lawton thought.

Cairo refused to meet his accusing gaze. And why was he glaring condemnation at her anyway? Because he was a hopeless cynic and a total lunatic, she reminded herself. "I'll find someone else," she muttered.

"Don't you always?"

"What is *that* supposed to mean?" Cairo was thoroughly confused by his comments.

"Just forget it," he mumbled as he bounded to his feet. None too gently, he hoisted Cairo up beside him. "I ought to haul you off to jail for stealing my stallion."

Cairo's head was spinning. Lawton was hopping from one topic to another again like a cricket and it was too damned hard to keep up with him.

"I didn't steal your horse; I borrowed him because I was in a hurry to reach my father."

"Of course you were," he snorted caustically.

"I *was!*" Cairo all but screeched at him.

"Then prove it," he challenged as he grabbed her arm and dragged her toward the mount he'd tethered in the trees. "I'm anxious to see for myself if you really have a father."

Cairo was completely miffed by his remark. She couldn't think of one reason why he should question the existence of her father, other than he was the most mistrusting human on the planet.

When Lawton scooped her up and set her atop his steed, Cairo stared straight ahead. Her back was as stiff as a flagpole. She refused to speak as Lawton picked his way through the trees and brush to locate the black stallion that grazed in the meadow.

Cairo sighed. Why was it that when she was with Lawton, her emotions felt as if they'd been tossed in the back of a runaway wagon and flung pell-mell? Now why would she make a comparison like that? she wondered as fleeting images skittered across her mind without settling into place.

Lawton dismounted and pulled Cairo's saddlebags off his stallion and then strapped them on the other horse. Then he swung onto his own steed. "This mount is yours, even if I did threaten to cart you back to jail for horse stealing," he growled.

In silence, Lawton followed Cairo south. He glanced in every direction at once, expecting to find the Gardiners leaping out to ambush him, but nothing out of the ordinary happened.

As they rode upon the high rise of ground that overlooked Canadian Station and the Canadian River south of it, Cairo gaped in disbelief. There *was* a community situated by the river, just as it had appeared on her father's map, but there was nobody in it! It was glaringly apparent to Cairo that her father no longer had the need for assistance. Curse it, where had everybody gone?

The sight of the ghost town in the distance came as no surprise to Lawton, being the suspicious soul he was. He knew it had to be a trap. This was the perfect place to bushwhack a marshal with a death threat on his head. Lawton wasn't about to ride into the valley of doom to be picked off by the Gardiners.

While Cairo gaped in bewilderment, Lawton leaned out to cup her chin, forcing her to meet his somber stare. There was a glitter in his silver eyes as he stared into the exquisite face that had been tormenting his dreams.

"You can ride into that ghost town to join your own kind, minx, but I'll be damned if I'm going with you. I have no doubt that we'll meet again, and under very different circumstances, I expect. And when we do, what's between us will be of no consequence. I'll have a job to do and I'll see it done. I'm sure you understand my meaning . . ."

She understood perfectly. Cairo had no doubt that Lawton Stone was a bona fide lunatic!

When Lawton wheeled to thunder off in the direction he'd come, Cairo stared after him. Just what *did* he *think* she understood? And what was all that mumbo-jumbo about meeting again under different circumstances? Damned if she knew!

Cairo's shoulders slumped. She had spent more than a month with this lunatic marshal and she had finally arrived at her destination only to find a ghost town. What the sweet loving hell was going on? Curse it, where was her father?

Cairo nudged the bay gelding down the slope. Her spirits scraped rock bottom as she clomped down the abandoned street. Along the way she passed a vacant farmhouse, blacksmith barn, post office, dry goods store, and finally the two-story hotel. Cairo peered at the establishment, battling the turmoil of emotions that very nearly reduced her to tears.

What she needed was to fling herself into her father's comforting arms and forget the past month. How she hoped Rylan was there waiting for her. And if he wasn't, surely he'd left a note at the desk to explain what had happened and where to meet him.

Cairo swung to the ground and ambled inside, but she was met with deafening silence. After thoroughly searching the lobby, Cairo found no message with her name on it.

A frown knitted her brow as she pushed open the door that led to the quaint home that was attached to the back of the lobby. She found evidence that her father had been living in the chambers. His clothes hung in the closet and his pipe rested on the tray beside a wooden rocking chair. The cabinets in the kitchen had been stocked with food and the extra bedroom had been prepared for her arrival. No matter what had happened to the other citizens of Canadian Station, it appeared that Rylan had remained behind to await his daughter.

Cairo plunked down in the rocking chair and stared at the portrait of her that Rylan had brought from Missouri to place on his mantel. Well, there was nothing to do but wait until he returned, Cairo decided. Perhaps her father had ventured to a neighboring farm or community to gather supplies. She would simply busy herself by preparing a meal and surprise him when he returned. It would occupy her mind, she hoped. The last thing Cairo wanted was to be alone with her agonizing thoughts of Lawton Stone.

When Lawton's befuddling comments buzzed in her

ears again, Cairo shrugged them aside. She wasn't going to spare that peculiar man another thought. Damnit, he just wasn't worth all the torture he'd put her through.

An unidentified whining and scratching noise dragged Cairo from her musings. When she opened the door of the hotel to retrieve her supplies, she found a shaggy hound staring up at her. The creature wagged its tail as if it was delighted to see her. Of course it was, Cairo realized. There wasn't much activity to be found in a ghost town and the stray dog was eager to adopt anyone who happened along.

Squatting down, Cairo stroked the mutt's head and received a lick on the hand for her attention. "Come along, friend, you and I will rustle up something to eat."

The dog seemed elated with the prospect of finding both a friend and food. As Cairo ambled off the steps to unload her saddlebags, the furry creature followed obediently at her heels.

Within a few minutes Cairo had arranged her belongings in her new room. And in an hour she had rummaged through the cabinets to gather ingredients for a stew.

After finishing the tasty meal that her father never showed up to eat with her, she tidied up the kitchen, then heated some water for a welcome bath and soaked to her heart's content.

Still her father hadn't returned. Grumbling at the thoughts of Lawton Stone which kept creeping into her mind and heart, Cairo thumbed through the two novels she had purchased before leaving Missouri. Sinking down in the rocker, Cairo decided to start reading one of them until her father arrived.

Devotedly, the dog plopped down at her feet while

Cairo waited and waited and then waited some more.

Sheriff Jubal Newton glanced up from the stack of papers on his desk when the door creaked open. A faint greeting smile touched his lips as he stared at the stony-faced stranger.

"Can I help you?" Jubal Newton questioned.

"I need information." Lawton flipped open his jacket to reveal his badge.

Jubal blinked in surprise. "You must be the man Doc Pullman came in here asking about this morning," he declared. "And you must have made a distinct impression on the doctor because he wanted to know everything I knew about you, which wasn't anything except that I received a telegram that was to be delivered to—"

Lawton was in no mood to hear that Freddie the physician had been checking up on him. With a dismissive gesture of his hand, he interrupted Jubal and cut to the heart of the matter. "What happened to that town on the southwest border of Oklahoma Territory?" he wanted to know.

"You mean Canadian Station?"

"The ghost town," Lawton growled impatiently.

Jubal frowned at Lawton's demanding manner but he supplied answers nonetheless. "It was a thriving little community until three weeks ago when the railroad surveyors came through there to plot their line across the Canadian River into Indian Territory. The townspeople tried to persuade the railroad to run their tracks beside their community, but the high bluff and treacherous quicksand along that stretch of the river was unsuitable for a bridge. The surveyors decided to construct their line two miles east, so everyone packed up their belongings and moved to the new site to begin again."

Jubal eased back in his chair and crossed his feet on the edge of his cluttered desk. "The migrating citizens of Canadian Station had a squabble with the man who originally claimed that half-section of ground during the land run. He didn't want to share his space with a town or the approaching railroad. But after they offered him a sizable sum to relocate, he found a fertile piece of ground to the northeast of the new town site."

The sheriff's shoulders lifted in a casual shrug. "Canadian Station isn't the only hazard of this new territory," he went on. "Even Elreno had the same trouble. The first town site was located on the banks of the North Canadian River and it went by the name of Reno City. When folks learned where the railroad planned to lay tracks, they up and moved over here."

Jubal frowned as he assessed the brawny marshal. "If you don't mind my asking, what did you do to upset Doc Pullman?"

"It was a personal matter," Lawton answered cryptically.

"Well, the doctor was sure in a snit when he sailed in here to find out about the marshal who'd showed up with his prisoner."

"I actually did the man a favor," Lawton responded enigmatically before glancing at the crisp new wanted poster requesting information about the Gardiner gang.

"Frederick didn't act like anybody had done him any favors," Jubal snickered. "His hands were shaking so badly I wouldn't have wanted him operating on me . . ." Suddenly he sat straight up. "I almost forgot!"

Jubal pawed through the stack of papers on his desk. "Here's your telegram. The attendant brought it over this morning when he couldn't figure out who to deliver it to."

Lawton frowned in confusion when he read the brief message.

Heard discouraging news at Webbers Falls. Thought you might need help. We'll wait for you in Guthrie.

Woody and Tuck

The note did more to pique Lawton's curiosity than appease it. Wheeling around, Lawton aimed himself toward the door.

"Hey, aren't you going to tell me what went on between you and Doc? I'm dying to know," Jubal called after him.

Lawton turned, his expression grim. "If I were you, I'd be more concerned about the Gardiner gang. They're somewhere in the area. I'd bet my life on it. They are notorious for making three or four quick strikes while they have the posses going around in circles. If I were sheriff here, I'd deputize a few men to guard the bank and stage lines. You could easily find yourself short-handed and in the middle of a gun battle."

Jubal watched Lawton stride out the door. Suddenly, his curiosity about the conflict between Frederick Pullman and Lawton Stone was the least of his concerns. He knew for a fact that Marshal Masden was, at this moment, scouring the countryside in search of the outlaw gang that had invaded the area. But he had expected the renegades to hightail it back to the

Cherokee Nation to hide out. Apparently, Lawton Stone didn't expect them to do that.

As a precautionary measure, Jubal decided to wire Guthrie and request a few more deputies to keep surveillance on the town. The last thing he wanted was to face that ruthless gang without reinforcements.

After sending a telegram to Woody and Tuck to inform them of his return, Lawton had lit out of Elreno like a house afire. It had been over a week since he'd left the temporary territorial capital at Guthrie, but it seemed like a month. His emotions felt as if they'd been put through a meat grinder and betraying thoughts of the treacherous blonde still tormented him.

As if it had happened only an hour ago, Lawton recalled his tussle with Cairo on the creekbank. He'd seen the hatred flashing in her green eyes and heard the anger in her voice. He had never let on that he was wise to her scheme of leading him west while an array of outlaws tried to pick him off. Lawton thought he'd even managed to earn her affection for a time, but the unspoken conflict between them had severed the fragile bond.

It was over and done, Lawton told himself determinedly. He'd probably still go on wanting Cairo, but he knew she was poison. He was a helluva lot better off without her. Someday, they would clash again and he wanted no sentimental attachment when he hauled her to Judge Parker's court with her renegade brothers. She'd be just another criminal who had been unable to outrun the long arm of the law . . .

His thoughts trailed off when Woody and Tucker emerged from one of the saloons to greet him.

"Damn, it's good to see you're still in one piece." Woody expelled a relieved sigh. "After all the reports we've heard along the way, we were afraid we'd arrived too late."

"Too late for what?" Lawton queried as he swung to the ground.

"Too late to rescue you from your own funeral, of course." Tucker gestured for Lawton to join them for a drink. "The prisoners we picked up in the Cherokee Nation asked if you were still alive after the Gardiners put that bounty on your head for killing their little brother. And when we arrived at Webbers Falls we heard there had been an ambush and three men were killed."

Tucker sank into his chair. "Woody and I were worried sick until we saw the graves for ourselves. We knew you were still alive when we noticed you marked the outlaws' resting places with an X."

The instant Tucker had seen the graves, he knew Lawton was the one who had launched the renegades into eternity. Lawton always maintained that murderers and thieves didn't deserve to be buried beneath a cross, only an X. As Lawton had said many a time: "When the Lord looks around for prospective angels, he won't have to waste His time thumbing through these devils' credentials because I've already checked these scoundrels off the list."

Woody stared grimly at Lawton before filling three glasses of whiskey. "We found another grave along your trail. You must have had one hell of a trip." He chugged the liquor in one swallow. "What did you do with Cairo?"

"There *is* no Cairo Calhoun," Lawton muttered, and then washed the bitter taste of her name away with a gulp of whiskey. "She is really Jarita Gardiner and by now she's probably back with her pack of thieves."

Woody and Tucker peered at their stubble-faced partner for a long moment. "Are you absolutely sure?"

"Positive," Lawton confirmed before pouring himself another drink. "One of the renegades who rode with Panhandle Dick identified her when I took him prisoner."

"Well, I'll be damned," Woody groaned. "I could have sworn she was genuine. She didn't seem that bad to me. Feisty, yes, but—"

"You thought she was genuine because you always give women the benefit of the doubt," Lawton grumbled.

"She fooled me, too," Tucker interjected. "I believed her tale about her pa, too."

Lawton's stare revealed none of the emotional turmoil Cairo had caused him. "It's over and done. Next time we meet up with that lying minx, she'll be indicted as an accessory to crime. And sooner or later she'll make the mistake of being seen in the company of her brothers and their cohorts during a strike."

"Speaking of cohorts," Woody muttered. "We heard the Gardiners picked up a few more scavengers to ride with them. Chris Masden and his posse lost the Gardiners' trail on the river after the robbery at Kingfisher. But, according to reports, there were more riders in the gang than there were when they were terrorizing the Cherokee Nation. A farmer and his wife who homesteaded near Kingfisher spotted the renegades circling back to the east. They took cover without being spotted, but they counted seven men on horseback, leading two pack mules."

"And speaking of posses, we were volunteered to

form one of our own to pursue the Gardiners after we reported to the territorial marshal's office," Tucker informed Lawton. "Looks like we're back to serving double duty again. With all the squabbles over land claims and trouble with border outlaws, Oklahoma is short-handed."

"And until the Gardiners are brought to justice, you'll have a bounty on your head," Woody added. "The way I figure it, you won't be safe until we track the Gardiners down."

That's the way Lawton had it figured, too. After chugging his drink, Lawton rose from the table. Although Al Fontain hadn't served his full two-week hitch in jail, Lawton intended to have the young pistolero released into his custody. Al had seen the Gardiners face-to-face on one occasion. He might prove helpful.

"Where are you going?" Woody called as Lawton breezed out the door.

No answer.

"Lawton never was much to say what he was planning," Tucker scowled before he swallowed down one last drink and vaulted to his feet. "He just expects us to trail after him and find out what he's up to."

With Woody and Tucker a few strides behind him, Lawton marched across the street to the sheriff's office to sign the necessary papers for Al's release.

While Lawton made the legal arrangements, Woody and Tucker fired questions like bullets. Briefly, Lawton explained the incident that had left Panhandle Dick dead and Al Fontain wounded. He also informed his partners that Al had volunteered information about Cairo and had requested the chance to prove himself worthy of riding on the right side of the law.

"Are you sure you can trust this kid?" Tucker questioned. "He wouldn't be the first one who promised to uphold the law just to spring himself from jail."

"I think he regrets his mistake," Lawton declared with conviction. "I spent a week with the kid and I even tested him a few times. I turned my back and made it easy for him to escape and he didn't seize the opportunity. And even if he does decide to abandon us, there will be three of us to keep an eye on him."

"Lawton!" Al breathed a relieved sigh when Sheriff Peters led him into the front office. "God, am I glad you're back. I've been through hell waiting to tell you what I tried to before you left!"

The kid certainly had a one-track mind, Lawton decided. Al had been determined to impart some mysterious piece of information, but Lawton had been in such a rush to catch up with Cairo that he had refused to be waylaid. And the first thing out of the kid's mouth when they met again was his reference to that unfinished conversation.

"The first order of business is to get you a new set of clothes and a bath," Lawton announced. He gestured to his partners. "Woody, Tucker, meet Al Fontain. If he steps out of line, you have my permission to shoot him. I already took a crack at him myself," he added teasingly.

"But Lawton, I—" Al tried to interrupt, but his guardian only allowed him to squeeze in three words.

"Kindly thank the sheriff for keeping you until I got back," Lawton prompted Al. "And it wouldn't hurt to assure him that he'll never see you on the inside of his jail again, either."

Al sighed. It seemed his confession was to be delayed

again. "My thanks, Sheriff Peters, but I don't plan to enjoy any more of your jail's hospitality."

After Woody and Tucker left with Al to have him fitted for some clothing appropriate for his new role as deputy and then to arrange for him to bathe and shave to further improve his appearance, the sheriff nodded thoughtfully. "The kid's all right, Lawton. I only wish some of the other men who came through here had the chance to make good. Al proved himself two days ago when somebody slipped a knife to one of the prisoners during a visit. I could have been stabbed to death when the thief tried to make his break, but Al jumped him, wrestled the knife away, and then lectured him on the evils of crime."

Lawton was glad to know he had been a good judge of character in Al Fontain's case. He only wished he could have had a positive influence on Cairo Calhoun.

Don't think about that little witch, Lawton chided himself as he strode into the street. He was still too raw inside to contemplate that beguiling vixen without feeling as if his heart was ripping apart. She'd have her day of reckoning. And when she did, Lawton would render her up for punishment without regret. Cairo Calhoun—*Jarita Gardiner,* Lawton quickly corrected himself—would get exactly what she deserved!

Lawton walked toward the restaurant to appease his growling stomach. He plunked himself down in the restaurant and gobbled his meal like a python. But even that didn't help curb his frustration. No matter how much food he consumed, the gnawing ache in the pit of his belly didn't go away. Unwanted thoughts of Cairo kept creeping into his mind to taunt him. Damn it, he just wanted to forget her!

"She's a female bandit, for chrissake," Lawton

scowled at his plate. *But she's an intriguing one,* a quiet voice whispered inside him.

"And that's what makes her so damned treacherous," Lawton muttered before he wolfed down another forkful of fried potatoes.

"Do you talk to yourself often, Marshal?" the waitress teased. She leaned over to refill his coffee cup and her appreciative gaze wandered over the badge and the broad chest on which it was pinned. The look she flashed him assured Lawton that she was openly inviting his attention.

And maybe Lawton would have accepted the silent offer if the wench hadn't been a blonde. Feeding his frustration over Cairo with food hadn't helped one whit, and Lawton doubted that loving her tormenting memory away would, either.

Lord, he could use another drink . . . or three. Maybe whiskey would numb his brain to thoughts of that sassy hellion.

Lawton tucked a coin in the buxom waitress's hand. "Woman trouble," he grunted to explain his conversation with himself. He gestured toward the money he'd given her. "All I want for that is the guarantee that you won't cause a man the anguish I'm going through right now."

The woman rolled the coin in the palm of her hand, cast him a seductive smile, and returned the coin. "Are you sure you don't want to forget your woes with one woman by distracting yourself with another?" she purred in question. "I don't want your money, only you."

"I'd better just settle for a drink."

"If you're that taken with her, I doubt a drink will help, either," the waitress predicted as she watched

Lawton move toward the door. "But if you change your mind, I'll be off work in two hours . . ."

Two hours later Lawton found the waitress's prediction coming true. He'd tried to drown Cairo's memory in a bottle, but her enchanting image rose to haunt him all over again.

What would it take to exorcise her memory from his mind? Even when he knew that Cairo preferred to see him roasting in hell, he hadn't been able to smother his fascination for her.

Lawton Stone, the man who prided himself in refusing to fall victim to any woman's charms, was bewitched. But he wasn't about to make the humiliating confession to Woody and Tucker. They'd never let him hear the end of it!

Cairo was right, Lawton realized disparagingly. He really was crazy! But damn it, she was the one who had driven him over the edge!

Chapter Eighteen

While Lawton retraced his path to Elreno and Guthrie, Cairo had spent three days waiting for her father to return. Her only conversations had been with the shaggy hound that constantly followed at her heels. All this solitude had Cairo on the verge of climbing the walls without a ladder. She decided to write her father to inform him of her arrival in case they missed each other coming and going. Her only recourse she decided was to form a one-woman search party to track Rylan down.

Cairo gathered a few supplies and headed east with the faithful hound trotting along behind her. She had ridden only two miles when she came upon a bustling settlement whose inhabitants were all busy constructing homes and businesses to replace the tents that were scattered around the area.

After quizzing the postmaster, Cairo learned the community had migrated east from Canadian Station in anticipation of the railroad. And yes, the postmaster knew Rylan Calhoun. But no, he hadn't seen him in two weeks. According to the man, Rylan had purchased a new site to establish another hotel, but he had remained in Canadian Station to await his daughter's arrival.

The postmaster speculated that Rylan might have traveled to Guthrie to arrange shipment for lumber from Kansas. He also suggested that Cairo journey back to Elreno where Rylan often traveled to gather supplies that were unavailable in the new community that was still under construction.

Relieved to learn that Rylan was in the area, Cairo returned to the hotel at Canadian Station. She waited another day but there was still no sign of her father.

Exasperated, Cairo decided to venture back to Elreno in hopes of encountering her father. Even if that did not occur, she would at least be able to communicate with other forms of human life. A woman could only converse with a dog for so many days before she toppled off the deep end!

Cairo mused that something good had come of her solitude as she aimed herself north. She had finally put her tormenting affair with Lawton Stone into proper perspective. He had been like a severe case of the grippe. She'd had him and now she was getting over him. By listing all the abominable things he'd done to her, Cairo honed her hatred for that raven-haired rake with the glittering mercury eyes. He was a woman-hater, a hopeless skeptic, and a raving lunatic, in addition to being blunt, inconsiderate, and mistrusting. She regretted the day she met him!

It had been nothing more than a physical attraction, Cairo told herself firmly. He had awakened her feminine desires, that was all. It didn't mean a thing. Lawton Stone was rugged, virile, and attractive and it was natural for her to be attracted to him. She and

Lawton had been convenient for each other while they trekked westward. It was a normal reaction for a man and woman in close proximity to let their emotions overcome them, especially when they found themselves facing constant danger.

Her experience with Lawton had taught her several valuable lessons. From now on she would respond to the logic of the situation instead of her foolish emotions. Never again would she become physically involved with a man. It tormented the mind and wounded the heart. Never again would she mistake fascination for love. And she would spin no more whimsical dreams. She would make only sensible plans for the future.

Cairo was prepared to resume her life . . . such as it was. She had yet to make connections with her father, but at least she wasn't carrying a torch for that infuriating, impossible man who plied her with loving lies and used her to satisfy his lust!

"Love indeed!" Cairo sniffed distastefully. "Lawton Stone doesn't know the meaning of the word. When he's finished with a woman, he would just as soon shoot her as look at her. And didn't he do exactly that!" She glared at the haunting image that floated above her. "I'll never forgive you for that, Lawton. I despise you!"

The hound whined in response to Cairo's explosive soliloquy, but he never broke stride as he followed at her heels. He was determined not to lose track of his only friend in the world!

Al Fontain was so nervous he couldn't sit still. He'd been led around like a dog on a leash for more than two hours. His arms had been crammed into the sleeves of jackets which suited the tastes of Lawton's partners. Al had been fitted for a hat, breeches, and boots, all of which bore Woody and Tucker's stamps of approval.

In the gunsmith shop Al had been equipped with double holsters and ivory-handled Peacemakers which came highly recommended by the marshals. Toting his new pistols and wardrobe—all of which he was informed would be paid for when he received his first month's salary—Al was herded into the barber shop. Under Woody and Tucker's careful scrutiny, the barber clipped Al's shaggy mane of brown hair and shaved off his beard and mustache. Then Al was propelled to the hotel, stuffed into a tub, and ordered to cleanse away the stench of the jail.

Al had scrubbed himself until he shined, fastened himself into his new clothes, and still Lawton hadn't returned. Between his nagging conscience and his apprehension, Al was pacing the confines of the room like a caged tiger, dreading his inevitable conversation with Lawton.

"Sit down, Kid, you'll wear the soles off your new boots," Tucker grumbled after watching Al circumnavigate the room for the umpteenth time.

"When's Lawton coming back?" Al questioned.

"He'll be here when he gets here, Kid," Woody muttered. "Now plant yourself in a chair and stay there."

Al obeyed but he kept flinging expectant glances at the door at regular intervals. When he heard footsteps in the hall, he was on his feet in a single bound. He couldn't wait to bare his soul and listen to Lawton rake him over the coals for lying. Lawton would retract his offer to make a respectable deputy out of him, he was sure but Al no longer cared, just as long as he got this frustrating confession off his chest. The weight of his guilt was about to crush him!

Lawton noted the transformation in Al's appearance immediately despite his inebriated state. The young man looked quite handsome and very respectable in his new attire.

"That's better," Lawton slurred as he swept the Stetson from his head and recklessly tossed it toward the bedpost. He missed his target and the hat plunked upside down on the floor. "You look the part of a deputy, Al."

Al had no time or inclination to wallow in the praise. His nerves were in knots. "Law, I tried to tell you before you left the first time," he blurted out of the blue.

A muddled frown creased Lawton's brow and drew the curious gazes of Tucker and Woody.

"After Panhandle Dick tried to bushwhack you, you asked me if I knew the lady who was riding with you." Al curled his index finger in the collar of his new shirt to relieve the mounting pressure. "I said I did, but I didn't. I was only trying to have my own brand of revenge on you."

When Lawton's face fell like a rock slide, Al plunged ahead before he lost his nerve. "Cairo Calhoun did look a lot like Jarita Gardiner," he squeaked. "When I first saw her in the distance I thought she *was* Jarita. And after you roughed me around I said she was, just to spite you."

Al's rapid-fire confession had a sobering effect on him though Lawton would have preferred to remain drunk to take the sting out of what he was hearing and feeling! All this time he'd been spinning his sticky theories about Cairo like a damned spider only to learn he couldn't have been more wrong about her.

"I tried to muster the courage to tell you during our ride to Guthrie, but I never got you alone," Al rushed on. "And with each passing day I regretted lying to you because I found myself liking you a lot more than I anticipated."

Al went back to his pacing, drawing three pair of narrowed eyes as he wore a path on the rug. "When we reached the jail I tried to clear my conscience, even if it meant that you got mad and left me there to rot, but you went tearing off and I didn't get the chance to tell you."

"Damn you!" Lawton snarled as he stormed toward Al.

Al tilted his chin and braced himself for the devastating blow he was sure he was about to receive from Lawton's doubled fist. "Go ahead and hit me, Law. I know I deserve it. But it can't hurt worse than living more than two weeks with this guilt. I've done a lot of things I regret, but lying about the lady has haunted me more than anything else I've done in my whole life!"

Swearing a blue streak, Lawton reared back and clobbered Al with a powerful right cross. The new young deputy slammed into the wall and slid to the floor. Tentatively, Al inspected his stinging jaw and peered up at the towering mass of raw fury that was poised above him.

"I was wrong," Al mumbled out of the side of his mouth that wasn't pulsating in pain. "Your fist hurts every bit as much as my guilt. And I wouldn't blame you if you hauled me back to jail and left me there until the end of my days."

"He does regret his lie," Tucker murmured in defense. He studied the young man who was sprawled on the floor. "Al was as jittery as a gun-shy rabbit while we shuffled him all over town."

When Lawton burst into another round of curses Woody frowned at him. "So Al made a false identification. What's the big deal? It's not like you dragged Cairo to jail and sentenced her to life in prison because of it. You let her go scot-free. You should be relieved to know the truth and thank Al for clearing up the last of your suspicions."

"Relieved? Thankful? You two don't know the half of it!" Lawton raged as he turned on Woody and Tucker like a fire-breathing dragon. "For chrissakes, I shot her and then I used her as a shield against Panhandle Dick. Then I treated her as if *she* were the criminal and *Al* was my best friend!" He wheeled on Al, who instinctively shrank back when Lawton punished him with a murderous glower. "Damn you, you half-grown little brat! I ought to strangle you!" His booming voice ricocheted off the walls like a resounding cannon.

Woody and Tucker's eyes bulged. "You did *what?*" they trumpeted in unison.

Lawton slammed his fist into the palm of his left hand. Now he was the one who was bearing the burden of a nagging conscience. It made him physically ill to think of all the hateful remarks he'd made, the cruel things he'd done because of his own suspicious mind and Al's lie.

Woody and Tucker glanced back and forth between Lawton and Al. Noticing the mist in his eyes, they almost swore the younger man felt so bad that he was going to break down and cry.

That Lawton Stone was overwrought with regret

and frustration knocked Woody and Tucker off balance.

"Good Lord, you really did fall in love with Cairo," Tucker realized and said so.

Lawton said nothing. He merely gave himself a few mental kicks and cursed his skeptical mind. Cairo did indeed have every right to despise him, every right to think he was a raving lunatic. But damn it all, he couldn't have confronted her with his suspicions. That would have been disastrous if Cairo had really been Jarita Gardiner. Only a fool would have openly accused her, knowing she would panic and dispose of him the first chance she got!

"Well I'll be damned," Woody breathed in disbelief as he stared at Lawton's tormented expression. "I think you're right, Tuck. Of course Law would never admit it to us, but if he hadn't been in love with Cairo he wouldn't be in such a snit now. He would have shrugged off Al's confession and let the matter drop.'

"I'm really sorry," Al bleated, suffering all the torments of the damned. "If you'll kindly hand me my new pistol I'll go ahead and shoot myself and get this over with."

Lawton obliged, much to Woody and Tucker's amazement.

Tucker lunged across the room to retrieve the pistol. "Gimme that, for crying out loud! Nobody's going to get shot in this room. I'm not cleaning up the mess!" He wheeled on Lawton. "If you took a shot at Cairo and used her as your shield of armor, it had to have been *before* Al plied you with the lie. Now you can go on blaming the kid if you want to, but you know damned good and well that you suspected Cairo since the moment she walked into our cabin in Fort Smith.

And unless I miss my guess, you probably invited Al to make the identification. He didn't volunteer that information right out of the blue, now did he?"

Lawton knew Tucker was right, but he hated like hell to admit it. He was looking for somewhere to place the blame because he felt like such a fool for treating Cairo so shamefully. Now that he knew she hadn't lied to him he felt thoroughly ashamed of his accusations and suspicions. There weren't enough words to describe how much he regretted treating Cairo like a criminal.

Lawton dropped onto the edge of the bed to hide his face in his hands. He recalled how he'd pounced on Cairo at the creek south of Elreno and then deserted her on the rise of ground that overlooked the ghost town. Her father was probably long gone and Lawton had abandoned her to a community with nobody in it! He'd sentenced her to solitary confinement. And to make matters worse—he had broken all ties by announcing that if they ever met again he was going to pretend they were strangers.

Damnation, he had behaved like a maniac and Cairo didn't have the foggiest notion why he'd been so suspicious and mistrusting of her.

Well, there was only one thing to do, Lawton decided as he surged off the bed and headed toward the door. He had to go back to Canadian Station and apologize. He had to explain why he'd behaved like such a fool. Cairo hated him, with good reason, but she was going to hear the truth. Then she could consign him to hell again, even if he was already there.

"Now where are you off to?" Woody questioned Lawton.

Again, no answer.

"Hell's fire, Law! If you don't tell us where you're

going this time, we'll chase you down and beat it out of you!" Tucker threatened.

"I'm going to find Cai and explain," he tossed over his shoulder.

"Damn it, we've got a band of desperadoes to track," Tucker reminded him. "Your love life is going to have to wait until we find the scoundrels who put that bounty on your head. You won't be safe until we do."

"We've been chasing the Gardiners for almost a year," Lawton strode down the hall in long swift strides. "They'll wait another week. And if they ambush me and put me out of my misery I might just thank them!"

Little did Lawton know the Gardiners waited for no one. They were making preparations to strike the Darlington Indian Agency which was located a few miles north of Elreno. If Lawton had been looking, he wouldn't have had to look very far to find his arch enemies.

Woody hoisted Al to his feet and tossed him his satchel of new clothes. "Come on, kid. We just left town."

"But Law won't want me riding with him after what I did," Al mumbled as he was propelled down the hall, bookended by Woody and Tucker.

"I think Law blames himself more than he blames you," Tucker declared.

"Maybe you should tell Lawton that. I don't think he knows it." Al sighed disheartenedly.

"He just used you as his scapegoat to relieve his frustration." Tucker reassured him. "He'll come around to apologize when he cools off."

Al wasn't so sure about that. Lawton Stone looked like a man pursued by the hounds of hell as he rode out of town. The threesome left Lawton to himself for several hours, allowing him to turn his tormented thoughts over in his mind before he faced his friends again.

The ride from Guthrie to Elreno was the worst trip of Lawton's life. He kept thinking how he'd left Cairo to fend for herself in a ghost town, how he'd baited her, goaded her, shot her, and used her as his shield. She was never going to forgive him or forget what he'd done to her. She would carry the scar from his bullet for the rest of her life. He'd treated her like a condemned prisoner. He'd betrayed her in the face of danger and used her so many times that it made him sick just thinking about it.

Ten miles later, Lawton slowed his pace to allow the threesome to catch up with him. Dawn had spilled over the rolling Oklahoma hills and dewdrops sparkled like diamonds in the golden light. Grimly, he stared into Al Fontain's blanched face, knowing he was seeing the same expression he would be wearing when he confronted Cairo: guilty regret.

When Al paused his steed to voice his shame once again, Lawton spoke first. "I'm sorry, Kid," Lawton mumbled apologetically. "I had no right to take my frustrations out on you. Like Tucker said, I had judged Cairo guilty long before you falsely identified her."

"I'll make it up to both of you somehow. I swear it," Al vowed. "Hell, I'd cut out my own tongue if I could take it all back."

"Well, Lover Boy," Woody teased, saddling Lawton with the nickname that had been foisted on him for the past two years. "How do you plan to get yourself back in Cairo's good graces? Crawl to her on your knees?"

"Don't call me that," Lawton snapped.

"You deserve it and you know it," Tucker declared unsympathetically. "For all the years and all the times you've cast women off like worn shirts, you've finally come across one whose opinion matters." Tucker stood up in the stirrup to give his aching backside a rest. "Why don't you just admit you're in love with Cairo Calhoun."

To admit to his friends that he loved was to confess he was human. At the moment Lawton didn't think he was, not if he could have treated Cairo so horribly.

"Well, even if you can't admit it to us, you better confess it to Cairo." Tucker snorted, glaring at Lawton's back. "Cairo should enjoy some sort of consolation after all the rotten things you did to her. Hell, I ought to tell her pa and then see to it that you marry her. She can give you hell for the rest of your days."

"She wouldn't have me," Lawton grumbled sourly.

"And that's the only reason I'll keep my mouth shut," Tucker sniffed. "She's too good for the likes of you anyhow. You don't have enough love in you to fill a thimble. A woman like Cairo deserves to be loved well and loved often, if you ask me."

"Nobody asked you," Lawton growled. "Christ! Don't you ever get tired of hearing yourself rattle?"

"If you weren't so muleheaded to begin with, you might have given Cairo the respect she deserved," Woody piped up. "Now, I'm the kind of man who would treat Cairo right while you're—"

"Go soak your head in the creek, Lover Boy," Lawton bit off testily.

"You're the one who's earned that title," Woody ribbed him. "My sap hasn't been rising near as high and fast as yours has. Never met a woman you couldn't forget?" He burst out laughing. "Famous last words, Law . . ."

The parting shot died beneath the clatter of the black stallion's hooves. Lawton spurred his steed and thundered down the road, wishing he could erase the past month.

"You were pretty rough on him," Al scolded, watching Lawton disappear over the rolling hill.

"He had it coming," Tucker insisted. A wry smile flicked across his lips before he took a sip from his canteen. "If you're going to ride with Lawton, you've got to learn how to deal with him, Kid. He won't tolerate weakness in you that he doesn't possess himself. And he'll be a lot happier when he realizes he's human, too. Even the mighty Lawton Stone isn't immune to Cupid's arrow. And I can safely say Lawton has met his match. If Cairo could crack Lawton's rock-hard heart wide open, I'd say she's entitled to him."

The threesome trailed behind Lawton. If he had expected sympathy from his partners, he certainly hadn't received a smidgen of it. But then, Lawton was feeling so miserable that he doubted compassion would have helped to lift his spirits. He'd done Cairo wrong so many times he didn't expect her forgiveness, but he knew he wasn't going to feel better until he had apologized, even if she refused to accept his humble words of regret.

Chapter Nineteen

With the devoted hound trailing behind her, Cairo whizzed into the dry goods store in Elreno to ask questions about her father. She received the same information she'd heard from the postmaster in the newly established community east of Canadian Station. Yes, the proprietor was acquainted with Rylan Calhoun. And yes, he'd been in the area two weeks earlier, but not in the past few days.

Disheartened, Cairo stepped back onto the street. She froze like a block of ice when the last man she ever wanted to see reined his stallion to a skidding halt in front of her.

A few paces behind Lawton sat Al, Woody, and Tucker. Upon seeing the comely blond, Al prepared to dismount and unburden his tormented conscience, but he wasn't allowed the chance to speak his piece. Al found his progess halted when both marshals grabbed him by the shoulders and shoved him back into the saddle.

"Stay out of this, Kid," Tucker whispered. "Law has

to make his peace first. You'll have to wait your turn."

It was as if the bustling town of Elreno had faded into oblivion. The instant Lawton spied Cairo emerging from the store, the world shrank to fill a space no larger than she occupied. The sound of clomping hooves, jostling wagons, and jingling harnesses didn't reach Lawton's ears because his heart was hammering so hard and loudly he was aware of nothing else.

Lawton hadn't expected to see Cairo in Elreno, but there she was, staring at him as if he were a snake that had just slithered out from under a rock. She was exactly as he remembered her in his haunted dreams—a vision of flawless beauty with hair like moonbeams and eyes like polished emeralds. The plain calico gown she wore didn't detract from her curvaceous figure. Her natural beauty always shined through.

"Hello, Cai . . ."

His voice was soft as he drank in the alluring sight of her. Not that it did him one whit of good to be friendly and polite. Cairo had vowed to despise Lawton forevermore. That was one promise she was determined to keep!

Ignoring the rush of betraying tingles that assaulted her, Cairo tilted her chin to a proud, defiant angle. She didn't return Lawton's pleasant greeting. She merely presented him with a venomous glare. Cairo sorely wished she could snap her fingers and he would disintegrate into a puff of smoke.

Lawton hadn't forgotten the way Cairo jutted her delicate chin, the way her eyes flashed when she was angry. She was stubborn defiance personified.

Cairo flung her nose in the air and swept across the street narrowly escaping being run down by a speeding wagon. She had been so oblivious to everything except the man she was trying to ignore that she found herself in harm's way before she knew she was there. But she recovered nicely, and agilely leaping backward, waited for the wagon to zoom past and then marched toward the hotel to rent a room for the night.

She was not about to risk riding off cross-country and giving Lawton the chance to pursue her and confront her alone on the prairie! Cairo vowed to avoid any situation that would put her alone with Lawton. The mere sight of that muscular giant sitting upon his strapping black stallion had sent invisible shock waves through her that caused her heart to lurch and her legs to buckle.

Despite all her sermons, she was still vulnerable to that horrible man. Cairo didn't dare risk experimenting with her reactions to Lawton because she had the inescapable feeling she would fail miserably. It was too soon and she was still too tender inside. Maybe in a hundred years she could face him without her body betraying her with forbidden sensations, without the deep resonance of his voice triggering bittersweet memories of unrequited love. But not yet! It would be too easy for him to break open the unhealed wounds in her heart.

"My, isn't she thrilled to see you, Law," Woody taunted his friend. Not often could a man get Lawton Stone's goat. "If she was any happier to see you she would have thrown herself beneath that wagon's wheels."

"Your tongue is overworked. Give it a rest," Lawton growled as he swung from the saddle.

Lawton had to admit he had never seen anyone make

such a spectacular display of ignoring anyone as well as Cairo had. She had made it perfectly clear that he was as welcome as the plague.

Lawton tossed his reins to the grinning marshals. "Take care of my horse until I've had the chance to talk to her."

"We'll be here waiting . . . until hell freezes over," Tucker chortled. "And I'll wager that even then, she won't listen to you."

Al was feeling more miserable by the second. He held himself personally responsible for the conflict between Cairo and Lawton. When he impulsively tried to squirt from beneath Woody and Tucker's grasps, they yanked him backward and held him in place.

"You aren't going anywhere, Kid," Tucker muttered. "Cairo looked as if she'd like to blow Lawton's head off. You might get caught in the crossfire."

Al blinked like a disturbed owl. "Do you really think she'll shoot him?"

Woody chuckled at Al's naiveté. The kid had oodles to learn, and not just about how to meet the rigorous demands of a deputy. The kid didn't know beans about love or women, either.

"That's the way romance is, Al," Woody explained between snickers. "Sometimes a woman loves a man so much that when he betrays her or angers her she gets so mad she'd like to kill him and be done with him. There's a fine line between love and hate when it comes to affairs of the heart." He glanced at the shapely nymph who was sailing through the door of the hotel. "I'd say Cairo Calhoun is tripping on that borderline right now."

Woody was right. Cairo was being bombarded by a

barrage of conflicting sensations. She kept telling herself she didn't want anything to do with Lawton Stone, but her body didn't agree with the good advice sent out by her brain. Lawton's ruggedly handsome face superimposed itself on the ledger where she had hastily scribbled her name. She flinched when the specter leaped up at her; she winced when she felt Lawton's looming presence behind her.

"Cai, I've got to talk to you."

Lawton's voice was so close to her ear that Cairo very nearly leaped out of her skin. Gnashing her teeth, she extended her trembling hand to grasp the key from the clerk.

"Cai . . . ?"

Still refusing to acknowledge his presence, Cairo flew up the steps two at a time in her haste to reach her room and lock herself inside. Despite her artful dodging she was unable to escape Lawton. He was upon her like rust on a nail. She had only clutched the doorknob when his hand folded over hers, searing her flesh and sending her pulse hopping like migrating frogs.

Cairo felt as if she had latched onto a lightning bolt. Dagger-like sensations shot up her arm and vibrated through every fiber of her being. She felt suffocated by Lawton's nearness and she was overcome by the masculine scent of him. Curse it, why wouldn't he go away and leave her alone? She had been managing just fine without him until he reappeared to remind her of what she was trying so hard not to remember.

"Get away from me," Cairo hissed, marshaling her sagging defenses.

"I can't." His hands lifted to cup her face, forcing

her to meet his unblinking gaze. "I love you, Cairo."

Saying the words and knowing he meant them with all his heart brought an unexpected feeling of inner peace. "Nothing has ever hit me so hard. I love you . . ." he repeated softly.

His confession was not well received. Although he sounded more sincere than he had the first time he'd uttered those words a few weeks earlier, Cairo reminded herself that he'd had more practice. He still didn't mean what he said, of course, and she wasn't about to fall for his wicked lies.

"Liar!" Cairo whacked him on the head with her purse and then twisted the key to gain entrance into her room. "You wouldn't know love if it jumped up and bit you!" In swift, precise strides Cairo marched inside and then wheeled to glower at him. "Now get away from me before I scream these walls down and the sheriff comes to haul you to jail. And that's where you belong, lunatic that you are!" She eyed him with marked disgust and blatant contempt.

Lawton disregarded her demand to make himself scarce. He stared hungrily at her pouting lips, remembering the taste of them. He swaggered forward, kicking the door shut behind him.

"I mean it!" Cairo blared threateningly. "I'll scream bloody murder. So help me I wi—"

Lawton captured Cairo in his arms and his mouth swooped down on hers before she could do as she threatened. But Lawton had a full-fledged fight on his hands. Cairo was one determined woman. She refused to allow herself to succumb to his seductive spell. She might be stubbornness personified, but Lawton was iron will in flesh.

Although Lawton kissed the breath out of her, Cairo refused to buckle to the warm flood of pleasure that trickled through her veins. She might burn herself into a pile of frustrated ashes, but she would be damned if she humiliated herself by melting in his sinewy arms and kissing him back!

"I do love you," Lawton rasped as his arms glided over her hips, bringing her trembling body into familiar contact with his. "Believe it, Cai. It's the truth . . ."

How big a fool did he think she was? Cairo had heard those empty lies from those poison lips before—right before he shot her. That in itself was enough to discredit the loudest and longest declaration of affection he could voice! Lawton had obviously been without a woman too long. Cairo had accidentally turned up, right under his nose. So naturally, he decided to ply her with his loving lies and tumble her in bed. Over her dead body!

"I despise you!" Cairo spat, giving him a jab in the ribs with her elbow to emphasize her declaration.

"You have every right to," he conceded as his head came toward hers. His silver eyes riveted on her sensuous lips. "But that doesn't change the way I feel about you . . ."

With an indignant squeal, Cairo dodged his kiss. She preferred Lawton's blunt honesty to these calculated lies of affection. If he'd simply have said he wanted her, she would have believed him because she knew full well that lust was second nature to a man like Lawton No-Heart-Whatsoever Stone.

"Of course you love me," she scoffed. "That's why you shot me and then shoved me in front of an oncoming bullet."

"I thought you were someone else," Lawton tried to explain.

Cairo peered at him as if he had tree roots growing out of his ears. "What do you mean you thought I was somebody else?"

Lawton had more arousing things on his mind than long-winded explanations, but he hadn't been able to crumble Cairo's wall of defense. She was still as stiff as a fence post in his arms, yielding only because he had overpowered her with his superior strength.

God, how he longed to relive the splendor-filled moments they'd shared when they both surrendered to their passion for each other. How he wanted to make up for the pain he'd caused her. He yearned to replace her torment with pleasure.

Although Lawton was entertaining romantic notions, Cairo was still stuck on the fact that he thought she was somebody else. He was making absolutely no sense. But then, when did he ever? she asked herself as she wriggled for freedom.

"Go find yourself a trollop," Cairo erupted. "I want nothing to do with you."

Lawton wasn't throwing in the towel. He intended to prove to her that she was the only woman on the planet who'd ever gotten under his skin, the only one who fascinated him to total distraction.

Cairo probably wouldn't ever love him back, but by God, she would accept the truth of his affection! For the first time in his life, Lawton Stone realized he was totally and completely in love and wanted this fiesty spitfire to know it.

Growing more frustrated by the second, Lawton

gave Cairo a fierce shake, spilling the silver-blond curls from the bun that set atop her stubborn head. "Curse it, woman, I love you," he thundered.

"That is *my* favorite expression and I'll thank you not to steal it," she spewed angrily. "And you do *not* love me. You wouldn't know love if it marched up and sat down on top of you!"

"I would and it did!" Lawton blared into her contemptuous frown. "Now what the hell do I have to do to prove it to you?"

Cairo glared poison arrows at him and then gestured toward the window. "Throw yourself through the glass pane," she suggested. "That should be proof enough of this devotion you claim to feel for me."

"Hell and damnation! I'm being perfectly serious and you're cracking jokes."

"You think I'm kidding?" She glowered at him. "Well, I'm not." Her glare was a direct challenge. "If you love me, you'll jump."

"You're crazy," Lawton growled in exasperation.

"I'm crazy?" she parroted. "I have miles to go before I get as crazy as you are. You're the one who saved my life, shot me, and then patched me up so you could try to kill me again. Now you've come riding in from out of nowhere and profess to love me because I wasn't the somebody else you thought I was!"

Cairo had the facts so tangled that Lawton barely recognized them himself. "If you'll sit down, I'll try to explain."

When Cairo stood there like a marble statue, Lawton shoved her into a chair.

She popped up like a jack-in-the-box. "You can talk yourself blue in the face, but it won't change anything because it doesn't matter anymore. You just aren't worth all the trouble you've caused me," she assured him disdainfully. "You are a page from my past, Lawton Stone. I just don't give a damn about you anymore," she lied.

"Don't you?" One black brow arched to counter her earlier challenge. "If you don't care, then kiss me."

Her chin jutted out. "What will that prove?"

"Suppose we find out . . ."

His arm stole around her waist to draw her resisting body against his muscled contours. The searing imprint of his body burned her inside and out and her defense backslid, exposing the naked emotion beneath them.

"Are you afraid you care more than you'll admit?" he whispered against her neck, sending a skein of goose bumps flying across her flesh.

"I don't care one whit," Cairo declared stubbornly.

A taunting smile quirked his sensuous lips. "You know there has been a lot more going on between us besides that trek across the Twin Territories."

"Was there?" Cairo smirked in a haughty tone. "I really hadn't noticed."

Talk about intractable defiance! thought Lawton. But instead of rising to the bait and losing his temper, he countered with, "Here's your chance to prove there's nothing left between us . . ."

If he had yanked her to him to roughly assault her with a bruising kiss, Cairo was certain her instincts to survive would have leaped to her defense. If he had ravished her, if he had ground his hips into hers, she was sure she would have been stung by revulsion. But Lawton did none of those things. His lips courted hers like a butterfly fluttering above a flower petal. His masculine body brushed provocatively against hers, luring her deeper into his spell.

These familiar feelings leaked out of the cracks in her armor of reserve, setting off a chain reaction of wondrous sensations that had lain dormant for more days than Cairo cared to count. All her self-inspiring lectures whizzed off in the wind, leaving her vulnerable to her own betraying desire for this impossible man who could arouse her as no other could. Suddenly she was as pliant as bread dough and she couldn't remember the meaning of self-control.

Her brain malfunctioned the instant his mouth slanted over hers, taking no more than she offered, demanding no more than she freely gave. As her resistance crumbled, her arms went up. Her fingertips delved beneath his chambray shirt to caress his rock-hard chest. On their own accord, her hands glided down his ribs and swirled across his belly.

"Mmmm . . . I adore what you do to me, Cai," Lawton murmured against her petal-soft lips. "Do it some more. It's been an eternity since I've felt your caresses and drowned in your sweet kisses."

Lawton could honestly say that he had never purposely tried to seduce a reluctant woman before Cairo came along. Most females came into his arms without invitation and without coaxing, but Cairo Calhoun was a different matter entirely. She was always a challenge—and no greater challenge than at this very moment. Lawton knew that all too soon Cairo's own mistrust and suspicion would force her back inside her shell. But before she escaped him and hid behind her shield of anger and pride, he wanted to love her in all the right ways, to make amends for unjustly wronging her. He wanted to worship her luscious body with kisses and caresses, to convince her he did have a heart and that it did belong to her.

Cairo decided she was nothing but foolish and arrogant. Oh, she had delivered herself all the consoling platitudes and sworn off men—Lawton Stone in particular. She had assured herself a hundred times over that she wanted nothing more to do with this wildly sensual lady killer—literally. But when he touched her, offering his sensual temptation, Cairo realized she was a hopeless cause.

Lawton was still her mindless obsession. She touched his finely honed body and her brain broke down. She returned his soul-shattering kisses and needs as compelling as survival itself flooded out of her. He was a hunger that she could never fully appease, a fever she could never cure.

"I hate what you do to me," Cairo groaned before her lips were instinctively drawn back to his. "I know I'll regret this. I always do. But like a senseless moth, I fly into the flame . . ."

"Feed the fire," Lawton rasped, his body trembling with need. "I want you as I've wanted nothing else. I touch you and nothing else matters."

Lawton was spinning a web of delicious pleasure with his words. And after that, Cairo couldn't manage a sane thought to save her wayward soul. She was so lost in the feel of his body moving suggestively against hers that she became a prisoner of her own wanton desires. She suddenly couldn't get enough of him. His kisses breathed new life back into her. His caresses became her addiction.

Her surrendering moan bubbled beneath his possessive kiss. Cairo felt herself melt into a bubbling pool of pleasure. She felt giant needs clamor through her body and echo back from his and she lost the will to resist. Although Lawton had wooed her with tender kisses, they were suddenly devouring each other with desperation. Urgency rippled through both of them, washing away the last remnants of reserve.

Cairo didn't know how they came to be on the bed, but they were there, peeling away the garments that had deprived them of lying flesh to flesh. Her hands were everywhere at once, as were his. They rediscovered each other, aroused colossal cravings that screamed for release.

Cairo was swamped by the most fervent desires imaginable, shattered by Lawton's wildly intimate caresses and kisses. He taught her things about lovemaking that she had never dreamed possible. He made her feel wanted and cherished and incredibly feminine.

Shamelessly she arched to meet his exploring hands and lips. He discovered the most secret places of her body—teasing, touching, eliciting wondrous sensations that pulsated through the core of her being. Spasms of ineffable pleasure riveted her body, driving her into breathless abandon.

Finally Cairo could endure no more of the rapturous torture that left her entire body humming like a tuning fork. She twisted away to return the intense pleasure until she had him moaning with the want of her.

Cairo invented new ways to please him. She caressed him with her body, her tongue, her hands, her lips. She whispered her need for him, letting him hear the words while she spread them over his bronzed skin. She courted him; she teased him; she stroked him until he cried out in torment.

Lawton drew her to him, begging her to end the tormenting ecstasy. With a growl of wild desperation, he rolled sideways, pulling her supple body beneath his. Savage urgency consumed him as he settled himself above her, forging them into one beating, breathing entity.

Cairo swore the world had exploded in a zillion pieces, and she along with it, when Lawton came to her. She could feel his virile body absorbing hers. He took possession of her body, her heart, and her soul. She marveled at the tremors that coursed through her as he drove into her, setting the wild cadence of passion. She could feel him moving with her, unleashing sensation after splendorous sensation. She could feel his heart thumping against her cheek as he clung to her.

She was flying higher and higher still, drifting on moonbeams and sailing past the galaxy of twinkling stars. Each sublime sensation that had sent her skyrocketing through space suddenly converged. She was engulfed by the hot sweet ache that left her shuddering in rapture. When Lawton clutched her fiercely to him and trembled in wild release, Cairo was again assaulted by tremors that rippled through the very core of her being and expanded to completely engulf her.

Lawton smiled with satisfaction in the lazy aftermath of passion. He had felt Cairo tremble beneath him and dig her nails into his back when they reached the pinnacle of ecstasy together. This wild-hearted vixen had defied him and cursed him, but she had not denied either of them the intense pleasure he only experienced when he held her in his arms.

Tenderly, he brushed his lips over her brow and uttered those three words that now tumbled so easily from his lips. He had faced the truth of his emotions and had accepted his feelings for her. Lawton had said the words before, but he'd convinced himself it was a ploy to gain Cairo's loyalty. Yet, he supposed he'd always known he loved her, even if he was too proud and stubborn to admit it. But he knew it now and he wanted Cairo to believe him.

As the sun dipped on the western horizon and darkness crept silently into the room, Lawton felt the fire rekindling itself, burning hot against the night. He didn't allow Cairo time to regret falling into his arms. He yearned to love away her mistrust and her doubts. Headstrong and determined though Cairo was and always would be, he dared her to deny this potent magic between them.

And Cairo couldn't deny it. Lawton wove a tapestry of passion around her, leaving her prey to the emotions she had desperately tried to control. When she was wrapped in his wondrous spell, it was as if her willpower was nonexistent. And when he came to her, tantalizing her with bone-melting caresses and heart-shattering kisses, Cairo instinctively responded.

This love was her curse in life and yet nothing could counter the incredible pleasure that loving Lawton evoked from her. Lawton Stone, she knew, was her heaven and her hell. Cairo feared she would never get over him, even if she was granted an eternity to do so.

Chapter Twenty

Tucker stared bleakly at the darkened window in the upper story of the hotel. "Are you going to go fetch him, or do I have to do it?"

Woody was staring at the same window from which Cairo and Lawton's voices had blared an hour earlier. "You do it, Tuck," he said with a sigh.

"Coward," Tucker grumbled as he squared his shoulders and propelled himself toward the hotel lobby. "I hope Law and Cairo have worked things out. If they haven't, Law isn't going to appreciate being dragged away so soon."

"I'll go," Al volunteered. "I've got an apology to make to the lady."

Woody clamped his fingers around Al's arm before he burst forward to overtake Tucker. "We've already put off telling Lawton as long as we dare. We've no time for your long-winded apologies to Cairo."

"But I—" Al tried to protest.

Good-natured though Woody seemed to be, Al realized this wasn't the time to test the marshal's temper. The grim report from Sheriff Newton's office had put all three men in a bleak state of mind. Although Al was bursting with the need to apologize to Cairo, he sank down on the bench and assured himself that one day soon he would have the chance to beg Cairo's forgiveness for all the trouble he'd caused her.

The unwanted rap at the door had Lawton scowling under his breath. "Go away!" he growled.

"I wish I could, Law," Tucker muttered at the door. "But this won't wait. I'm afraid I'm the bearer of bad news."

Lawton swore out loud as he rolled off the bed to don his breeches. Glancing over his shoulder, he made certain that Cairo had covered herself as best she could. Then he muttered again. They had resolved nothing, as of yet. Tucker's timing was terrible! Lawton and Cairo had allowed their hunger for each other to sweep them away, but he still hadn't had the chance to make her understand why he'd behaved so strangely.

When Lawton whipped open the door, Tucker peered somberly at him. "The Gardiners just robbed the pay wagon that was to be unloaded at Darlington Indian Agency. Sheriff Newton is trying to round up a posse." He paused to inhale a shallow breath before he plunged on. "There was a shootout and two men were killed trying to protect the payroll."

"Damn . . ." Lawton swiveled his head around to stare at the bewitching blonde who held the quilt beneath her chin. If he went chasing off after the Gardiners there was no telling how long he'd be gone. There was so much he wanted to say to Cairo and now there was no time to say it. Double damn.

"I'll be right down," Lawton grumbled before he eased the door shut.

The interruption had brought Cairo to her senses and humiliation burned her cheeks. It infuriated her that she had submitted to Lawton and mortified her that Tucker knew what they had been doing for the past hour.

"Cai, I—"

Cairo's muttered hiss interrupted him, but it didn't matter. Lawton wasn't sure what he wanted to say now that he was forced into offering a condensed explanation of the past two months in fifteen seconds. That wasn't even enough time to collect his thoughts, much less spit them out.

"Just go." She turned her back and pulled the quilt tightly around her. "You got what you wanted anyway."

"What I wanted was—" Lawton expelled a frustrated curse. Confound it, he didn't know what he wanted or what Cairo would accept after the abominable way he'd treated her. He hadn't expected her forgiveness to begin with, but he—

"I don't want to see you ever again," Cairo burst out, wiping away the tears with the back of her hand. "You have your life to lead and I have mine."

She had made it easy for him, though, damned if she knew why. Lawton Stone deserved no consideration. Let him go thundering off to chase criminals. Cairo didn't want to have to stew over when and if he'd come back. If she didn't break the ties between them here and now she would drive herself crazy.

"This thing between us isn't over yet," Lawton

scowled as he shouldered his way into his shirt.

"Oh yes it is!" Cairo contradicted in a voice that wavered with conflicting emotions. "I don't even know what to call *this thing* between us, but it's definitely over. I'll not humiliate myself again!"

"Why not? Don't you think I'm good enough for a citified schoolmarm?" Lawton hurled at her without thinking. Damn it, he was as frustrated as she was and his tongue had outdistanced his brain, making matters worse than they already were.

"No, I don't," she flung back, wanting to hurt him the same way she was hurting. "You're better at tracking down fugitives than courting women. You should stick with things you're good at and I'll follow the same sensible policy."

"Fine," Lawton stuffed his feet into his boots in angry jerks. "I came to apologize and I did that already. I guess that's that."

"Your apology is rejected." Cairo didn't dare look at him for fear he'd see the love shimmering in her eyes and know he had enjoyed the ultimate victory over her. "Just get out of my room and out of my life, Lawton Stone!"

"I'm gone!" he snapped before he slammed the door behind him, then abruptly he realized he'd made his exit without his pistols. Mustering his dignity, he reversed direction to retrieve his weapons. It was for damned certain he'd need to be armed to the teeth when he confronted the Gardiners.

When he burst back into the room, Cairo was sitting in bed, pointing his Peacemakers at him. There had been a dozen times in the past when he'd expected this firebrand to blow him to kingdom come, but never had she looked quite so intent on doing it as she did at this moment. But to his relief, she didn't squeeze the triggers.

"Here." Cairo tossed his weapons on the foot of the bed. "You almost left your best friends behind."

Lawton scooped up his pistols. His attention riveted on Cairo's misty green eyes and the cascade of silver-blond hair which was highlighted by the moonlight that splintered through the window. "I *am* leaving my best friend behind," he murmured before he pivoted toward the door. "Trouble is, she has a certain tendency toward stubbornness and she refuses to believe it. Goodbye, Cai. I'm sure you'll be a lot happier knowing I'm walking out of your life for good."

"Happy?" Cairo enthused with commendable acting ability. "I'm elated!"

The slamming door shattered Cairo's composure. Torment knotted her stomach the instant Lawton turned and stalked away. She broke down and cried her heart out. Pride had kept the tender words of love locked in her soul. She'd prefer to die than to allow that silver-eyed scoundrel to know he'd broken her heart so many times in the past that it would never mend. He was gone and he wasn't coming back and she was glad of it!

Liar, her wounded heart wept. *You sent him away, but you're never going to forget him—not in this lifetime leastways.*

That depressing thought caused Cairo to cry even harder. Curse it, for a woman who'd never been prone to tears, she had suddenly sprung a leak! A man like Lawton Stone could turn a woman wrong side out. She had become defenseless prey to a maelstrom of sentimental emotions but Lawton's core of solid rock remained uncracked by their stormy affair.

Flinging herself across the bed, Cairo saturated the pillowcase with tears. If she purchased nothing else while she was in Elreno she would have to buy a few dozen hankies. Already, she had cried a river of tears and she wasn't half done yet!

Tucker didn't take time to question Lawton about his encounter with Cairo. Lawton's annoyed frown told Tucker there was still trouble between them. The relationship between Cairo and Lawton wasn't going to have the chance to improve while he was off chasing the Gardiners, Tucker reckoned.

Lawton barely noticed the flurry of activity around Sheriff Newton's office when he rode past. But then, he'd never expected much help from inexperienced posses, either. All Lawton could think about was the expression on Cairo's shadowed face and the burning ache in the pit of his belly when he'd walked out.

He'd told himself long before he located Cairo that she wasn't going to be receptive to his apology or his declaration of affection. He'd bared his heart to her and she'd trampled all over it. She'd been hurt, confused, and angry with him and with herself. Lawton knew that Cairo would curse herself for submitting to her feminine desires and to his hungry needs. To cope with her humiliation, Cairo had nurtured her hatred for him and demanded that he walk out of her life.

And she was probably right in wanting me gone, he mused. What had he ever brought to her except trouble and torment? If he were Cairo, he wouldn't have had much use for Lawton Stone, either.

But damn it, how was he supposed to know how to behave when he was in love for the first time in his whole life! And worse, he hadn't known how to cope with that unfamiliar emotion when he'd found himself falling for this woman whom he had erroneously assumed to be his enemy.

Lawton's wandering thoughts evaporated when he came upon the grisly scene that lay before the Darlington Indian Agency. Two federal guards lay dead beside the wagon that was riddled with bullets. Two other men were being tended by Dr. Frederick Pullman.

Frederick wheeled around to fetch antiseptic from his medical bag and froze when he spied Lawton. The incident with Cairo in her hotel suite had hit Frederick squarely between the eyes and he scowled at the unpleasant memories and the man responsible for them.

Lawton wisely chose to steer clear of the physician. Instead, he interrogated the injured guards.

"They ambushed us when we came through the clump of trees to the east," John Hanley responded to Lawton's question. "One of the bastards must have climbed atop a tree to wait until we rumbled past." His gaze strayed to the man who lay on the ground, covered by a blanket. "Henry took a knife in the back and pitched forward while he was driving the wagon. When he slumped over, bullets started flying like buzzing hornets and the horses bolted."

"Idaho Joe," Woody muttered sourly. "He delights in hurling knives. It's his trademark."

"We thought we could outrun them and reach the

agency, but a whole passel of gunmen closed in around us. We got off a few good shots and I think we wounded one of them," John elaborated while he absently massaged his wounded arm. "But they chased down the runaway wagon and took the gold, even while we tried to blast away at them."

"How many were there?" Lawton asked quietly.

"Near as I could tell in the dark, maybe six or seven," John speculated. His gaze swung back to the remains of his longtime friend. "I want to ride with you, Marshal. Henry was like a brother to me."

Lawton shook his head, denying the request. "We'll be traveling at a swift pace. You'll be needed here to make the final arrangements for him."

Once Lawton had determined which direction the renegades had taken, he stepped into the stirrup. For a split second his gaze locked with Frederick Pullman's. It was a long moment before Lawton responded to the unspoken question in Frederick's eyes.

"I let Cairo go. She wasn't really my prisoner," he murmured as he reined his horse to the east. "She's in town. You'd be damned lucky to have her, Doc. It's for certain she wants nothing more to do with me."

The news caused Frederick's shoulders to slump in relief. After he'd recovered from the torment of finding Cairo with Lawton Stone, he realized he still cared for her. Obviously, she wasn't guilty of anything except getting mixed up with this marshal. Frederick hoped that he would have the chance to woo Cairo without Lawton's unwelcome influence.

Tucker gaped at Lawton in disbelief as they trotted across the prairie. "You just about gave the doctor permission to court Cairo. Why the hell did you do that?"

"Because it's over," Lawton grumbled bitterly. "That's the way she wants it. And after the hell I put her through, it's probably best for both of us. As the lady said, I'll never be more than I am and we'd never fit into each other's worlds."

"That's a crock of malarkey," Woody scoffed. "A man always has room for a woman in his life."

"Maybe you do, Lover Boy. But as Cai reminded me, this is what I do best. And I'm not worth a damn at romance."

"Quit calling me Lover Boy," Woody demanded hotly. "You're the one with the messed up love life!"

"Maybe *I* should marry the lady," Al pondered aloud. "I'm the one who started the trouble."

"Clam up, Kid," Tucker ordered brusquely. "You've still got a lot of growing up to do before you tangle with a woman. And besides, Cairo Calhoun is too much woman for a normal man to handle." His probing gaze landed squarely on Lawton who was quietly droning out the words to "Skip to My Lou," just as he always did while he was riding and thinking at the same time. But now the song had a melancholy sound to it. "Even that doctor won't stand a chance with Cairo. Even he can't treat what ails her. Only Lawton can and he doesn't have the guts to try again after he got rejected."

"Lay off, Tuck," Lawton scowled. "I've got more important things on my mind than a stubborn, hot-tempered woman."

"Not more important," Tucker qualified. "Only more pressing."

"End of discussion," Lawton snapped, his voice like a pounding gavel.

"My, what a sourpuss Law is turning out to be," Woody said confidentially to Tucker.

Tucker chuckled. "He's never been in love before. He's so frustrated that he doesn't know what to do with himself."

The foursome had ridden five miles before the tracks led them to a log cabin located beneath a canopy of trees and beside a winding creek. The farm belonged to Eric O'Brien, the burly Irishman who had taken several punches at Lawton before he learned he was squaring off against a U.S. marshal.

A more subdued Eric O'Brien emerged from his cottage, cradling his rifle across his arms. "If you're looking for those renegades, they've already come and gone." He gestured toward the corral that held a herd of winded horses. "They stole my stock and left me with these broken-down nags."

The foursome lit their torches and followed the trail the gang had left behind them. A mile later they were forced to part company because the tracks diverged in all directions. Lawton sent Al and Woody south to scout one trail while Tucker rode east. Lawton followed the two sets of hoofprints that circled back to the northwest.

Difficult though it was, Lawton neatly folded the tormenting memories of Cairo and tucked them in the closet of his mind. This was not the time to dawdle in thought. On several occasions, outlaws had been known to split up so they could bushwhack members of a posse while lawmen lacked the strength of numbers. Lawton would be a setting duck if he didn't keep his wits about him. And knowing there was a bounty on his head, he could expect to be gunned down the first chance the Gardiners got.

Lawton slid his Colt from its holster, just in case he found himself in the middle of an unexpected showdown. After the disappointing reunion he'd had with Cairo and her demand that he walk out of her life, Lawton wasn't expecting the rest of the night to progress much better. Cairo had showed him the door and the Gardiners wanted him dead.

Frederick Pullman gasped when he spied the comely blonde standing on his doorstep. "Cairo . . ."

The young woman on the stoop drew her scarf from her head to reveal the mass of silver-blond curls, but it wasn't until she stepped into the light that Frederick realized it wasn't Cairo Calhoun who had come to pay him a late-night visit at his cottage.

"I'm sorry, ma'am, I thought you were someone else. When Marshal Stone told me . . ." His voice trailed off and he glanced the other way, missing the flare of hatred in the woman's pale green eyes.

Jarita Gardiner fought down the anger that threatened to spoil her charade. "I came to you because my husband was wounded when he tried to stop those bandits from stealing our horses."

It was a lie, of course. The truth was that Vance, her oldest brother, had been shot during the raid at Darlington. She and Vance had circled back toward Elreno and came upon an abandoned dugout north of town. While she went to summon the doctor, Vance had sprawled on the cot to recuperate from the shot in the arm. Learning that Lawton Stone was still in the vicinity was another brand of torment for Jarita. She vividly remembered what had happened the last time Stone had descended on the Gardiners.

"I know the hour is late, sir." She paused to grace him with a beseeching smile. "But my husband requires immediate attention. Will you come?"

While Frederick scurried to fetch his bag, Jarita peered thoughtfully after him. "Is Marshal Stone chasing after those thieves who stole our horses?"

Frederick grabbed his coat and shrugged it on as he strode out the door. "Indeed he is," he replied innocently. "And I hope it keeps him occupied. Cairo doesn't need him entangling her life any further. He isn't good enough for her."

A curious frown knitted Jarita's brow as she listened to Frederick. Mulling over what she had learned, Jarita swung onto her steed to lead the doctor to the dugout. "Marshal Stone is sweet on a woman hereabouts?" she quizzed in a conversational tone.

Frederick wished he'd never brought up the topic. "She would have been my fiancée if he hadn't showed up. But with any luck at all, I'll convince her to marry me and forget about him. His rough edges are better suited to chasing fugitives."

Jarita smiled secretively. She had happened onto valuable information while she retrieved the physician to treat her brother's wound. Knowing the legendary Lawton Stone had an Achille's heel by the name of Cairo could work to the Gardiners' advantage.

While the gang was lying low, waiting for another

strike at Fort Reno, she could locate this Cairo, who obviously shared Jarita's coloring and stature. The news would make Vance feel ten times better. It could very well be that she had discovered a way to draw Lawton Stone out and exact vengeance for Billy Gardiner's death. The invincible Lawton Stone was going to discover just how it felt to lose someone special to him!

A devilish smile quirked Jarita's lips as she trotted toward the dugout that was built into the side of a hill. Her brothers would see to it that Lawton Stone paid in full for wounding them and taking Billy's life. The cocky marshal would rue the day he'd tangled with the Gardiners!

While Frederick patched Vance's shoulder, Jarita skillfully pried information from him about the four men who were combing the countryside in search of the gang. She also discovered that Sheriff Newton had sent for two seasoned deputies from Guthrie and, with their assistance, had formed a posse from eight inexperienced men who had left town only an hour earlier.

When Dr. Pullman climbed back into his buggy to drive to town, Jarita turned to her brother who was dragging himself off the cot to fetch their horses. "I have some very interesting news." Jarita pulled her cloak tightly about her to ward off the evening chill. "If things work out as I visualize them," she assured Vance, "we're going to lead Lawton Stone into a death trap."

And sure enough, when Jarita imparted the information about Cairo, Vance felt considerably better. Sweet revenge was the soothing balm that took the sting out of Vance Gardiner's wounded shoulder.

* * *

The distant rumble of thunder caused Cairo to nudge her steed into a faster clip. Once she had gathered her composure, she left her room at the hotel despite the late hour. With the flop-eared hound padding along behind her, Cairo had aimed herself toward Canadian Station. She prayed her father had returned from his mysterious trek! Cairo desperately needed comfort and an understanding friend.

Thoughts of Lawton Stone followed in her shadow, causing her to shed a few more buckets of tears. And here she thought she'd cried until she was completely devoid of emotion! But memories of Lawton were like thorns. Their prick was painful when they lodged in her heart and they were every bit as painful when Cairo tried to extract them.

"Damned Lawton Stone anyway," Cairo muttered at that darkness at large.

The hound barked in agreement, hollow solace though it was for Cairo.

"I'm not going to see him ever again," Cairo told herself determinedly. "He and his poison lies of love!" Cairo angrily wiped away the tears that boiled down her cheeks. "Isn't that just like a man to ply a woman with such a confession if it gets him where he wants to be—in her bed."

The hound barked again.

"Oh, clam up, you bag of fleas. You don't have to agree with everything I say," she snapped and then slumped when the dog tucked its tail and slinked along behind her. "I'm sorry. I'm turning out to be as mean and hateful as What's-his-name."

Thunder rolled across the sky and the low-hanging clouds swallowed the moon. Cairo nudged her steed into a gallop. If she didn't set a swift pace, she'd be drenched before she reached her father's hotel.

When cold raindrops splattered about her, Cairo veered toward the abandoned blacksmith barn. Since the past week had been unseasonably warm, Cairo had allowed her mount to graze without penning him up. With the threat of rain in the air, she decided to tuck the horse in the barn.

Dismounting, Cairo led the steed into one of the stalls. While she unfastened the saddle, the hound trotted off to sniff around in search for food. His abrupt howl prompted Cairo to clutch at her pistol. With her heart beating ninety miles a minute, Cairo inched along the darkened path that ran the length of the barn.

After overhearing Tucker announce there was an outlaw gang on the loose, Cairo was extremely cautious. The way her luck had been running lately, she expected to find a whole passel of murderers and thieves crouched in the corner of the barn . . .

The thought brought Cairo's head up with a decisive jerk. What the devil was she doing? She should have turned tail and run the other way instead of investigating the noise in the barn. Common sense prompted her to pivot on her heels and dash toward safety, but she had taken only four steps when the hound's mournful whine froze her in her tracks.

There were no scuffling noises in the straw, no sign that a band of outlaws was lying in wait. Drawing a courageous breath, Cairo reversed direction to track the whining mutt.

Cairo had to feel her way along the stalls in the darkness to reach the dog. When her foot collided with an unidentified object, Cairo leaped backward. She was unable to contain her scream of alarm. Instinctively, she clutched her pistol and backed away from the object she had stumbled over, scurrying toward the faint light that filtered through the open door of the barn.

As she darted toward the hotel to fetch a lantern, Cairo tried to breathe normally, but the air was heavy with moisture and her heart was still hammering with the vigor of a carpenter driving nails.

Once she had located the lantern, she rushed back to the blacksmith barn, wishing curiosity didn't have such a fierce hold on her. Cairo knew she wouldn't sleep a wink until she discovered what had been lying in the hay.

Gathering her unraveled composure, Cairo strode toward the far end of the barn and rounded the corner. A bloodcurdling scream erupted from her lips when the lanternlight sprayed across the remains of the man who had been stabbed in the back and had lain facedown in the straw for what Cairo feared had been at least two weeks.

"Oh my God . . ." Her breath caught in her throat and her hands shook so badly she very nearly dropped the lantern and set the barn afire. "Papa!"

The shock of finding her father lying dead caused her soul to wrench and her heart to wilt inside her chest. Gasping for breath, Cairo dropped to her knees and wept. She was certain now that she had been trapped in the arms of a living nightmare. She had come all this way, battling the emotional turmoil of loving a man who had sailed in and out of her life like a cyclone. She had endured pain, danger, torment, and disaster. And before she had learned to cope with the gigantic hole Lawton had left in her heart, Cairo was forced to endure the anguishing torture of discovering her father had been brutally murdered. She had trekked through hell and she had arrived too late to save Rylan from catastrophe. Never again would she bask in the warmth of her father's smile or hear his hearty peal of laughter. All she had were the memories of their life together before he chased his dream of a new beginning in Oklahoma.

While tears bled down her ashen cheeks, Cairo collapsed in the straw to troll through a sea of tender memories from days gone by. As if it were only yesterday, Cairo could visualize her father grasping her hand and leading her out to the field beside the barn on their small farm in Missouri. He had instructed her on how to handle firearms and made her take target practice until she had become proficient with both pistol and rifle. Time and time again Rylan had stood behind her, offering guidance, teaching her the art of self-defense.

"Daughter," Rylan had said in that firm but loving way of his. "There will come a time when you discover the world can be cruel. You have to be prepared to deal with it and with those who might wish to do you harm."

Oh, how right he had been! Cairo thought as she trembled with bitter despair.

"I won't always be there to protect you and you must learn to defend yourself." Then Rylan had set the weapons aside and taught his young daughter to fight with her fists and her feet. He had laughed when Cairo had punched the straw-filled gunny sack he had hung for her target.

Even now, Cairo could almost hear him chuckling as he cuddled her close to give her an affectionate hug after her lessons in self-preservation. But, even with all Rylan had learned from his experiences, nothing had saved him from the dagger wound that discolored the back of his jacket . . .

The wailing wind that whipped through the barn was a mere whisper compared to the high-pitched scream of outrage and sorrow that came from Cairo's lips. Her body shuddered as if besieged by an earthquake and her soul shriveled inside her.

How much more torture must she endure? And why was she the one who was left behind instead of her father, who had wrapped himself in his hopes and dreams? And what unforgivable sin had she committed to deserve this hell on earth? What unpardonable crime had her father committed to deserve a senseless death in this deserted town?

When the hound crawled onto her lap to comfort her, Cairo clutched him to her in desperation. She sat there for what seemed forever, attempting to come to grips with the grief of losing the only family she had left in this cruel world. It was all she could do to gather her feet beneath her and trudge back to the hotel. And all the while, the vision of her father lying in the straw rose like a specter to haunt her.

She had made this tedious journey from Missouri to begin a new life with her father and share his dream of prosperity. Now she had to see to his burial. Cairo tackled her grim task with a heavy heart. She was so overwrought with sorrow and torment that she couldn't bear to think, only to perform mechanically the gloomy deed that lay ahead of her. In the mist and fog, she did what had to be done because there was no one there to assume the dismal task for her.

No one there . . . The depressing thought echoed through her mind until she swore she would go mad. Fighting back the tears, she dug the grave where father was to be buried.

Cairo muffled a sniff as she stared at the simple wooden cross she had driven into the damp earth on the high rise of ground that overlooked the Canadian River. Now she was the last of the Calhouns. She had no one except the scrawny hound who had befriended her. If she leaped into the quicksand that swirled below the cliff, no one would weep for her and no one would care.

With her spirits scraping rock bottom, Cairo trudged back to her room, just as dawn feathered through the cloudy sky. The quaint home that was attached to the hotel was safe. It was all she had. Inside the rooms were all the things that had belonged to her and her father. After the world had been pulled out from under her, Cairo needed to wander among the keepsakes her father had brought with him to Oklahoma. It was all the security she had left, her cherished link with the memories of the past.

Sleep, Cairo thought as she collapsed on the edge of the bed. She was totally exhausted and completely drained of emotion. All she wanted was to close her eyes and mind and sleep the entire day away so she didn't have to think anymore.

Cairo suddenly didn't care if she ever woke up because the bitter memories would be there to greet her. The grief that engulfed her was suffocating and her heart was so heavy that Cairo wondered if it had the strength to keep beating.

Although Cairo swore she had depleted every emotion, another flood of tears came to wash her into the dreary currents of her disappointed dreams. Yet, the dreams were too much like reality to be classified as anything except what they were—tormenting nightmares.

Chapter Twenty-One

Lawton sighed wearily as he swung to the ground to tether his stallion in front of the hotel. He had followed the two sets of tracks to an abandoned dugout north of Elreno, only to find the tracks of a horse and a buggy coming and going toward town. The drizzling rain had erased what was left of the tracks and Lawton had cursed when he lost the renegades' trail.

Although he knew he was probably dashing to a cliff to leap to a wrong conclusion, he wondered if the wounded outlaw and his companion had sought out a doctor. That was Lawton's only lead and he was determined to interrogate Frederick Pullman, whether the physician wanted to see him again or not.

Before seeking Frederick out, Lawton ambled inside the hotel to see if Cairo was still around. According to the clerk, Cairo had hightailed it out of town soon after Lawton had galloped toward Darlington. It seemed she had dashed back to her father's protection and away from Lawton.

If Lawton had known the agony Cairo had endured

upon her return to Canadian Station, he would have ridden hell-for-leather to find her. But all he knew was that she never wanted to see him again.

When Lawton reached Frederick's cottage, he was forced to wait almost two hours before the physician returned from his evening rounds. And when Frederick did rein his carriage to a halt, he didn't even bother with a civil greeting.

"If you're looking for Cairo, she isn't here," Frederick bit off in a most unpleasant tone.

Lawton ignored the contempt in Frederick's voice. Even though he was thick-skinned and didn't much give a damn what the rest of the world thought of him, he wasn't a blind fool. It was glaringly apparent that Frederick had no use for him whatsoever.

"I need to ask you a few questions, Doc," Lawton said as he got up from the porch step.

"No, Cairo isn't going to marry me," Frederick burst out, erroneously anticipating the question before Lawton could ask it. "I haven't seen hide nor hair of her in over a week . . . thanks to you. I thought she had come to me last night, but the woman only *looked* like Cairo."

Lawton felt his heart slam against his ribs and stick there. The elusive Snowbird . . . It had to be her. Cairo had been mistaken for Jarita Gardiner a dozen times before.

"This woman who came to see you . . . What did she want?" Lawton was impatient to know the answer that very second.

"My, aren't you the suspicious one," Frederick mocked. "For your information, Marshal, the woman requested that I patch up her husband after he'd been shot by the notorious outlaw gang that *you* are supposed to be hunting down instead of lounging on my stoop, pestering me with questions."

Frederick unlocked the door and let himself in, not inviting Lawton to follow him inside. "If you had been doing your job, the woman's husband wouldn't have required my medical attention at such a late hour."

Lawton was prepared to bet his badge and fortune that Frederick had bandaged one of the desperadoes and hadn't even known it. The Snowbird had obviously batted her eyes and pleaded with Freddie to come with her. And Freddie, devoted to his profession, had trotted along behind her. That would explain the buggy tracks at the dugout.

Lawton invited *himself* into the physician's home. Knowing the Snowbird's uncanny knack for dredging up valuable information to aid her outlaw brothers, she'd probably discovered everything Freddie knew about the manhunt. Double damn.

"And what did this supposed sodbuster look like?" Lawton questioned the back of Frederick's tawny head.

Frederick lit the lantern and spun around to counter Lawton's sarcastic inquiry with a mutinous glare. "He was about our age, maybe a little older. He had blue eyes and blond hair, but I couldn't call him attractive. *Weathered* would be a better description," he snapped, obviously annoyed with the interrogation and his unwanted guest. "He didn't look like a hardened criminal, if that's what you're thinking. And he had a very lovely wife."

Lawton regarded the doctor who had puffed up with

so much indignation that he very nearly popped the buttons off his shirt. "I suppose you're an authority on what hardened criminals look like," he snorted. "Well, I've got news for you, Doc. You just described Vance Gardiner, as well as his younger brother Nate. Vance was wounded in the holdup and you patched him up and sent him on his way. Thanks one helluva lot for the help."

Frederick sat down before he fell down. "It couldn't have been," he blasted. "Not with that pretty wife of his."

"That wasn't Gardiner's wife, it was his sister who acts as a spy and informant for the gang," Lawton growled into the doctor's face. "The woman is one of the reasons the Gardiners have been so successful. She had pretended to be a schoolmarm, a newspaper woman, and only God knows what else to aid her brothers."

Frederick's face turned a remarkable shade of blue and he gasped and grunted while Lawton continued his explanation.

"I suspected Cairo of being the woman you met last night. I don't have to tell you what a striking resemblance they share since you've seen them both face-to-face. You know that better than I do, in fact," Lawton muttered as he paced the confines of the parlor like a caged tiger. "I made the mistake of thinking Cairo was Jarita Gardiner and you made the mistake of swallowing her tale about a husband who had been shot by outlaws. Hell, he *was* the outlaw!"

The comments took the wind out of Frederick's sails and he sagged on the couch with a dismayed groan. "So that's why you were acting so strangely around

Cairo . . ." he pondered aloud.

Lawton loomed over the deflated doctor, his eyes probing into Frederick like slivers of steel. "Now what did you tell Jarita and her brother?"

Frederick gulped hard as he peered up at the towering mass of barely controlled irritation. "I . . . mentioned . . . uh . . . the fact that you were giving chase and—"

Lawton was furious. That was just what he didn't need! The Gardiners would probably regroup and come gunning for him. "What else?" He hated to ask but he had to know if he intended to come through this crisis alive.

"I told them there were three other marshals riding with you," Frederick croaked like a sick bullfrog.

"Did you name names?" he demanded impatiently.

"I didn't know the names, only the numbers," Frederick reported gloomily. "And she asked about the sheriff's posse—"

"And being the witless chatterbox you are, you volunteered information about the size of the posse," Lawton speculated sourly.

Frederick reluctantly nodded.

"Damnation."

"Well, how was I suppose to know who they really were?" Frederick muttered in self-defense. "I'd never seen the Gardiners before in my life. When someone is wounded, I don't ask questions." He glared at Lawton. "I'd patch *you* up if you were bleeding and I don't even like you because of what you did to Cairo!"

Lawton didn't need to be reminded of all the abominable things he'd done to Cairo. He was carrying that painful memory around in his conscience like a thorned rose since the day Al Fontain confessed the truth.

Lawton turned on his heels and stormed away. He had the feeling the Gardiners would hole up in the area to allow their leader time to recuperate and to plan another strike, There was no telling where they were. They could have been anywhere. There were abandoned cabins and dugouts all over the area. After the land run, the citizens had built temporary homes before migrating to better locations.

Although Tucker, Al, and Woody had yet to return to town, Lawton didn't expect they'd had much success in trailing the desperadoes, either. The rain had covered their tracks and the bandits were clever enough to take to the creeks to elude their pursuers.

Maybe he couldn't track the Gardiners down immediately, but he could retrieve Cairo and her father and bring them back to Elreno. If the Gardiners decided to use the ghost town as a hideout, the Calhouns would be in bad trouble.

The thought of Cairo meeting with disaster scared the living daylights out of Lawton. It was a good thing the Gardiners didn't know he and Cairo were . . .

Lawton's thoughts froze in their tracks. His hand stalled in midair before he could grasp his stallion's reins and swing into the saddle. Icy dread settled over him. Like a condemned prisoner trudging to the gallows, Lawton reversed direction. Without knocking, he barged inside the physician's home to find Frederick still slumped dejectedly in his chair.

"One last thing, Doc." Lawton's voice dropped like stones in the silence. "You didn't happen to mention Cairo or the fact that she and I knew each other . . . ?"

Lawton didn't even finish his question before Frederick's face turned a lighter shade of pale and he grimaced uncomfortably. Frederick didn't utter a word in explanation. He just sat there, looking sicker by the second. Lawton knew the foolish doctor had indeed imparted vital information to the Snowbird.

"I'm a marked man, Doc. The Gardiners put a ten-thousand-dollar reward on my head because I killed their kid brother in a shootout in the Cherokee Nation," Lawton scowled at Frederick. "Would you like to venture a guess as to what those murdering bastards will do to Cairo if they think it will draw me into a trap to exact their revenge?"

Frederick sank a little deeper in his chair.

Lawton snarled resentfully. "You may get your chance to decide if you want to stitch me back together after the Gardiners get through with me." His glittering silver eyes bore into Frederick's like heated daggers. "But knowing the Gardiners and their butchering cohorts as I do, your skills as a physician may not be enough. Cairo and I may both require the services of an undertaker. I won't hold a grudge if you turn out to be my cause of death, Doc. But if anything happens to Cai—"

Leaving the remark hanging in the air, Lawton stalked back to his horse. Damn it to hell! Just when he thought things were about as bad as they could get, they managed to get worse! If the Gardiners got hold of Cairo and used her as bait for a trap, neither of them stood an icicle's chance in hell of emerging alive. The Gardiners were a vindictive pack of wolves who thrived on revenge and were very protective of their own.

Cairo was on a collision course with disaster and she

didn't even know it. If the Gardiners captured her . . .

Lawton rattled off every obscenity in his vocabulary. The prospect of Cairo being held prisoner and tortured for information turned his blood to ice. He had to get to her before the Gardiners did! Her life wouldn't be worth a tittle because the Gardiners were out for Lawton's blood and they didn't care who they had to hurt in the process of exacting revenge.

Lawton galloped back to the hotel to leave a message for his partners. He wished for a winged stallion as he thundered toward Canadian Station in search of Cairo. He prayed he could reach her before the Gardiners went searching for her. She would order him out of her sight, but by God, he would bind, gag, and tote her back to Elreno if he had to! She wasn't staying in that ghost town unprotected, even if she did know how to use firearms. She wouldn't stand a chance against the Gardiners and their newly gathered reinforcements.

Lawton plunged over the plains. Images of Cairo kept leaping up to torment him. Cairo had been through hell because him and his cynical misconceptions. But the worst was yet to come if he didn't reach her in time!

Lawton was too sick at heart to even contemplate what he would do if Cairo had already been taken captive. All he could think about now was reaching Canadian Station before the Gardiners discovered where she was. Damnation, *Lawton* wasn't even sure where she was! She and her father might have taken up residence elsewhere. In Elreno Lawton had been too intent on apologizing for the atrocities he'd committed against her to ask about her father and her future plans.

And when he'd gotten her all alone he had been too consumed by his need to communicate his love to think of anything else.

Lawton wasn't living up to his reputation. All those glowing accolades of his skills and resourcefulness hadn't done him a whit of good where Cairo was concerned. He was going to get her killed and she was an innocent victim who'd been unjustly accused and punished—by Lawton Stone himself! If anything happened to her, Lawton would never be able to forgive himself.

He would outsmart the Gardiners—somehow. He'd take Cairo into protective custody before those bastards got their murdering hands on her! She would be safe in his arms and he wouldn't let anything happen to her ever again.

Clinging to that comforting thought, Lawton galloped toward Canadian Station as fast as his stallion could carry him. Cairo would be alive and as fiesty as ever when he found her. Of course, she would spout off at him and call him every disrespectful name in the book, but he didn't care as long as she was safe. He wouldn't leave her unattended for a moment until the Gardiners were behind bars.

Things would work out, Lawton encouraged himself as he rode through the night. By dawn of the new day he would reach the ghost town and cuddle Cairo protectively in his arms, even if that was the very last place she wanted to be!

The clatter of hooves roused Cairo from fitful sleep. It sounded as if the U.S. Cavalry had thundered into the ghost town. Voices echoed in the still evening air and Cairo stumbled from her bed. She had indeed slept the entire day away, either that or the world had turned black as pitch to mourn her father's passing. Now, to make matters worse, unidentified visitors had swarmed in on her . . .

The hound's yelp prompted Cairo to grope across the dark room to retrieve her pet. Cuddling the mutt to her, Cairo veered around the maze of furniture to stare out the window, monitoring the activity outside. Eight riders dismounted in front of the spacious farmhouse on the outskirts of the ghost town. The abandoned home was strategically located on a rise of ground that granted an unobstructed view of the surrounding area. It was also well equipped with a tackroom and corrals to pen their horses.

Intuition told Cairo that the outlaws Lawton had been chasing had made the ghost town their headquarters. Intuition also whispered that one of the thieving, murdering bastards was responsible for her father's death. No doubt Rylan Calhoun had been determined to remain in Canadian Station until Cairo had arrived from Missouri. Rylan had purchased a new site for his hotel in the new community to the east, but he had spent most of his time in the ghost town—waiting. Fate had frowned on him when the bandits arrived to claim their hideout. They had obviously spotted his horse and . . .

Cairo gulped over the lump of fear that leaped to her throat. Her mount was in the blacksmith barn. If the desperadoes decided to venture into it, they would come looking for its owner.

She wondered briefly if that wasn't better than

having her horse tethered outside the hotel. That most certainly would have given away her exact location. And it was most fortunate that she had been asleep and the lantern had been snuffed out. The outlaws might have seen the light glowing in the window and come to investigate. She would have wound up just like her father . . .

Although it was laughable that Cairo considered herself lucky to have penned up her horse, it was indeed the first stroke of luck she'd enjoyed in a month. Since she'd met Lawton Stone her life had been jinxed by one disaster following closely on the heels of another.

Her bitter thoughts trailed off when she spied three of the bandits carting strong boxes and heading toward the river. Cairo moved away from the east window when the threesome disappeared from sight. After rushing to the south window, she drew back the curtain to watch the men scurrying toward the cliff that overlooked the river . . .

Her heart stalled in her chest. She feared the outlaws would spot her father's fresh grave. Luckily, the men veered a good two hundred yards away from the plot and Cairo breathed a sigh of relief.

Squinting, she studied the renegades as they dropped their loads and began digging beside the lone cedar that stood apart from the clump of evergreens that rimmed the cliff. Cairo would have bet her life the desperadoes were burying their booty.

Cairo prided herself in having a good head on her shoulders. If she found herself trapped and eventually discovered in the ghost town, there was only one way to make sure she stayed alive long enough for someone to track the bandits to their hideout. If she recovered the stolen money and hid it, the thieves wouldn't be so hasty in killing her since she would then hold vital information.

That thought spurred her into action. Quick as a wink, Cairo tied a muzzle around the mutt's mouth and locked him in the closet. Hurriedly, she wormed into her breeches and shirt. As soon as the buscaderos trotted back to the cabin to celebrate, Cairo eased open the back door and darted toward the underbrush with a gunny sack in hand. Slipping like a shadow around the trees and bushes, Cairo crept along the bluff until she reached the lone cedar. Since the ground was soft from recent rain, digging wasn't difficult. Cairo pawed at the ground like a dog unearthing a previously buried bone. To her amazement, she found a fortune at her fingertips. Casting a wary glance at the lighted cabin, Cairo stuffed the money and gold into her sack. Beneath the strong boxes was yet another cache that was laden with more money—money that had been stolen from the bank in Kingfisher.

It seemed the thieves had twice buried the loot from their robberies. All the better, Cairo thought spitefully. They wouldn't be in an all-fired hurry to dispose of her if she confiscated every cent they'd stolen. They might eventually kill her, just as they had killed Rylan, but she would take the secret to her grave, along with that Calhoun brand of stubborn determination. It would be small consolation to know she had duped those murdering bastards, but that was probably all the solace Cairo would enjoy.

Huffing and puffing, Cairo dragged her booty and then paused at regular intervals to sweep away the tracks she'd left behind. She glanced around her, trying to decide where to stash it. Her gaze landed on the hotel's stone foundation.

A triumphant smile pursed her lips as she hauled her loot toward the small opening at the back of the foundation. Dropping onto her belly, she slithered into the dark damp niche, thankful this wasn't the season for snakes to be out and about.

After digging a trench on the inside of the foundation, Cairo placed the stacks of money and gold coins in their new hiding place and covered them with layers of dirt. After packing the earth, Cairo stuffed a roll of bills in her pocket. Her funds were low and she probably wouldn't live to spend the money she'd confiscated, but just in case she did need it . . .

Having accomplished her task, Cairo inched open the back door and tiptoed back to her room to retrieve the mutt from the closet.

Now there was nothing to do but wait and hope the renegades thundered off at dawn. Then Cairo could hightail it to safety. She would seek out Lawton and . . .

Cairo floundered on the thought when a pair of flashing mercury eyes rose above her. Lawton's image was followed by a score of bittersweet memories. Lawton . . . She could visualize him towering over her, taunting and ridiculing her. She could see him bending over her in one of his gentler moods, whispering promises of pleasures to come. And then he was rolling across the ground to retrieve his Colt and turn it on her as if she were his mortal enemy. Cairo winced. She could still hear the whine of the rifles and pistols, feel the searing pain that had exploded in her shoulder.

How many times had that hard-hearted man

betrayed her and then seduced her? And through it all she had loved him, hated him, and then wound up loving him again. But if there was one thing she *wasn't* going to do, it was go to her grave carrying a torch for a man she had never been able to understand and trust. His deeds and words were tormenting conflicts that confused her. He was as hard and callous as the criminals he pursued and he didn't know the first thing about love, even if he said he did!

And he wasn't such a hotshot marshal, either, Cairo thought resentfully. *She* was the one who had found the bandits, not *him*. Lawton Stone was probably tucked in bed with a trollop at this very moment, unwinding after a long day of manhunting, which had obviously been unsuccessful since the whole damned lot of scoundrels had practically landed on her doorstep!

Even while Cairo perched on the edge of her bed, pumping out spiteful thoughts about the raven-haired rake, her heart was somersaulting in her chest. "Horrible, impossible man," she muttered at the taunting image that floated above her like a black cloud.

Cairo had secretly yearned for him to be there to comfort her when she found her father's body in the blacksmith barn. Having his sturdy shoulder to lean on would have made her grief easier to bear. But there had been no one to cling to, no one to reassure her that the world wasn't as gloomy as it appeared . . . It was, though, Cairo thought when she heard a round of guttural laughter wafting toward her from the farmhouse. She was sitting on the fringe of hell!

Cairo cuddled the mutt closer to rest her chin upon

its shaggy head. "I would have loved you long and well, Lawton Stone," she whispered to the taunting image that swirled around her. "But you wouldn't give me the chance. Now you'll never know what we could have had together because I won't be around much longer . . ."

If she didn't think she would get caught, she would have sneaked to the barn, mounted her steed, and ridden away from this doomed town. But the most sensible thing she could do was wait it out, praying the thieves would tire of celebrating and venture off again.

Chapter Twenty-Two

Idaho Joe ambled back into the cottage and propped himself against the doorjamb. The thought that had brought him back inside faded from his mind when he caught sight of Jarita. His lusty gaze swung to the shapely beauty who was tucked protectively beside Vance, who was nursing his injured shoulder.

How he longed to get his hands on that luscious beauty! Bloodthirsty and ruthless though Joe could be at times, he had a soft spot for a beautiful woman. At the moment, his fascination was fixed on Jarita Gardiner.

In annoyance, Joe peered at the outlaws who had joined the gang two weeks earlier. They had all been casting speculative glances at Jarita, even though Vance and Nate had previously listed the strict limitations that were to be observed where their sister was concerned. Jarita had always been off limits and would always be as long as Nate and Vance were there to protect her. But Joe had the sneaking suspicion that Jarita wasn't as pure as her brothers wanted to believe.

She seemed to know how to seduce a man with the sway of her hips, with that slow languid stare that tempted and tormented . . .

"Something bothering you, Joe?" Vance queried, watching the renegade ogle his sister.

The question snapped Joe to immediate attention. "Maybe, maybe not," he mumbled as he pushed away from the door and swaggered over to retrieve the bottle of whiskey that was being passed around the table. "I was wandering around the blacksmith barn a while ago. I found a horse and saddle inside, but the old man I killed a couple of weeks back is gone."

"Got up and walked off, did he?" Hank Forbes smirked before guzzling another drink. "Maybe he wasn't as dead as you thought he was."

"He was dead all right," Joe scowled. "Somebody must have found him and buried him. But that don't explain the horse."

Jarita frowned. "Nate, you better go check around. Someone may be spying on us."

Jarita was always cautious. Although he and Vance ruled the outlaws' roost, Jarita's close attention to details and her talents of observation had saved them from disaster many a time. Nate never questioned her feminine intuition. If his kid sister was concerned, then he would relieve her fears.

"Hank, come with me," Nate commanded as he grabbed his jacket and ambled toward the door. "We better have a look around, just to be on the safe side."

When Nate and the lanky young desperado exited, Vance settled himself more comfortably on the couch. His curious gaze swung to Jarita, who sat beside him. "Are you still planning to ride into Elreno to search for this mysterious woman who caught Lawton Stone's eye?"

Jarita nodded. "She shouldn't be too difficult to find if she looks like me."

Affectionately, Vance cupped her chin, lifting her face to his wry grin. "She can't be as pretty as you, Sissy," he murmured before he brushed the back of his hand over her tanned cheek. "You can go, but be careful. I can't say for certain if Stone knows about you, but I don't want to take any chances."

Vance scowled. "I wish I knew what the hell happened to Kid Fontain and Panhandle Dick. They were supposed to be tracking Stone. They might be able to tell us what that son-of-a-bitch has been up to."

"Before long, it won't matter what Lawton Stone has been doing." Jarita smiled spitefully. "When we get our hands on Cairo Calhoun, he'll find himself up to his neck in trouble. At long last we can put Billy's memory to rest and settle this feud with Stone."

"I want you to take a couple of men with you when you ride into town to round up that little bitch," Vance ordered. "I'm not sure I trust any of these hooligans alone with you, though. They have yet to prove themselves." His wary gaze swung back to the clump of men who were passing the whiskey bottle around the table.

"I can take care of myself," Jarita assured him as she smoothed away his worried frown.

"Maybe you can, Sissy, but with Stone in the area, I'm just not going to risk any trouble." He gestured his good arm toward the bedroom. "You better get some sleep. We've been riding most of the night. I'll make sure the men keep their voices down so they won't disturb you."

With a nod of compliance, Jarita rose from the sofa and sauntered away. To Vance's chagrin, four pair of eyes lingered on his sister's shapely hips.

"Sissy needs her sleep," Vance announced, staring each man down for their lusty thoughts. "Don't disturb her, not now . . . not ever . . . if you get my meaning."

Their eyes dropped back to the glasses of whiskey on the table, but not one man could rein in the arousing thoughts of the comely chit. And the provocative blonde knew it, too. She delighted in teasing and tormenting the members of the gang while her brothers kept a watchful eye on her.

Nate Gardiner inched along the boardwalk toward the hotel with his pistol cocked and ready. He and Hank Forbes had searched every nook and cranny in all the other buildings in the ghost town and had turned up nothing. Nate wasn't sure there was anyone around, but he wasn't going to declare the town abandoned until he'd checked every room in the hotel.

The board beneath his foot creaked and somewhere within the confines of the hotel a dog barked. Gesturing with his head, Nate silently ordered Hank to scuttle back to the cabin to bring reinforcements. One horse suggested that only one rider was somewhere about, but he couldn't be absolutely certain. Nate wasn't taking any unnecessary risks. With a trigger-happy brigand at his disposal there was no sense in searching for the intruder alone.

Like cats stalking the darkness, five men surrounded

the hotel. With a wave of his hand, Nate motioned for his men to sneak in the front and back door of the building on cue. With pistols aimed in all directions at once, the desperadoes homed in on the mysterious intruder.

Cairo was shaking in her skin! The hound's bark had given her away. She had heard the creak of boards, but she had been unable to clamp down on the mutt's mouth before he let out a loud bark. Cursing her misfortune, she snatched up her pistol and backed into the closet with the hound tucked under her arm.

This was the beginning of the end, Cairo told herself bleakly. The bandits were coming for her. Sinking down with her knees tucked under her chin and her Colt aimed to fire, Cairo waited. She was sure they would have no trouble locating her because her heart was thumping like a brass drum. They'd have to be stone deaf not to hear it.

Stone . . . A bitter smile flitted across her trembling lips. Wouldn't Lawton Stone be disappointed to learn someone else had shot her down? These bandits would steal Lawton's thunder and he'd track them to the ends of the earth. Of course, by then, she'd be just another victim of these bastards, but they would pay retribution when Lawton Stone lowered the boom on them . . .

Although Cairo had clamped her free hand around the hound's mouth, he attempted to bark when the bedroom door whined. Cairo realized the desperadoes had just entered her room. With her fingers clenched on the Colt, Cairo waited for the closet door to whip open and bullets to fly.

When the door hinges creaked, all Cairo's instincts of self-preservation burst to life. Her senses were tuned to imminent danger. It was a technique she had learned from Lawton—act now, feel and think later.

As the lanternlight curled around the partially opened door, Cairo heard a low growl. The sound didn't come from the hound but rather from a man on the opposite side of the door. When the gleaming barrel of a pistol inched forward, Cairo panicked. Her fingers clenched on the trigger of her Colt and she fired three quick shots through the wooden door.

Howls and growls erupted in the room and the clomp of more footsteps scurried toward the bedroom. It occurred to Cairo that if she intended to divulge the information about the stolen money, now was the time! The murderers would riddle the closet door with a barrage of bullets and she would be too dead to tell anyone anything!

"I stole your stolen money!" Cairo yelled at the top of her lungs.

Nate Gardiner, who had dived into the room immediately after the pistol blasts, rose to his knees on the far side of the bed. The sound of the woman's voice put a scowl on his face. The clever bitch had outsmarted them before she blasted the first wave of men who had located her. Quickly, Nate assessed the two men of Spanish decent who lay sprawled on the floor—victims of the woman's deadly ploy. His gaze flicked to Hank, who was clutching his bloody knee.

"Don't shoot her," Nate ordered as he appeared from behind the bed.

Hank snarled as he clutched his leg. His wild-eyed

gaze swung to the desperadoes who had tried to open the closet door and found themselves in the middle of a battle. It was the last battle his companions would ever fight, thanks to that murdering bitch!

"Throw out your pistols," Nate ordered brusquely.

Cairo tossed the weapon out of the closet. She drew her feet beneath her and stepped forward. "I'm coming out."

The men who were left standing took aim, in case the daring minx had more than one weapon in her possession. To their disbelief, Jarita Gardiner's look-alike emerged from the closet, cuddling a wriggling hound in her arms.

Nate glanced at the curvaceous blonde who lingered in the shadow of the partially opened closet door. With her face concealed by the slanting shadows, he almost mistook Cairo for his sister. One look at her and Nate knew he had stumbled onto the woman who had bewitched the legendary Lawton Stone.

Nate Gardiner wasn't the only one who had been thrown for a loop by the shocking likeness. Hank and Idaho Joe stood there gaping. Cairo had no idea why the scraggly renegades were peering at her as if she were a creature from outer space, but she took advantage of the silence.

Like a discharging cannon, Cairo zoomed out the door, slamming it behind her. Setting the hound to his feet, Cairo left an obstacle course of furniture behind her when she made her escape. Her ultimate destination was the blacksmith barn. If she could reach her horse she might be able to thunder out of the ghost town before the bandits caught up with her. It was risky, but it was all the hope she had.

Like a herd of elephants, the desperadoes gave chase. They cursed vehemently as they stumbled and fell over themselves and the maze of chairs and tables Cairo had left in the dark lobby.

As dawn streamed across the sky flinging red-gold streamers over the horizon, the bandits burst through the door to see Cairo dashing toward the barn.

When Hank raised his pistol to take aim, Nate backhanded him across the cheek. "You idiot! She's got the money. We may never find it if she isn't alive to tell us where she stashed it."

Growling at the woman's daring, Nate and Joe gave chase, leaving Hank to hobble along behind them. The rumble of hooves caused Nate to leap sideways before Cairo ran him down in her haste to escape on horseback.

"Shoot the horse out from under her!" Nate whipped out his pistol and growled the order to his men.

Cairo was certain the desperadoes intended to shoot her in the back, even if she did have their money. The instant three pistols barked, she braced herself to meet her violent end. Her terrified scream pierced the morning air when she was catapulted over the stumbling steed to skid through a mud hole.

Although Cairo had the wind knocked out of her, she dragged her wobbly legs beneath her, but before she had taken two steps, all three men descended upon her. Cairo's furious screech echoed through the abandoned town and sailed off in the breeze. A half-dozen hands clamped around her in an attempt to subdue her.

While she fought like a wounded wildcat, the hound put up a loud protest. Though the mutt snarled and nipped at the scuffling bootheels, he didn't have the slightest influence on the three man who had wrestled Cairo to the ground. Despite her efforts, Cairo had been taken captive by the Gardiners, and all that would temporarily keep her alive was the fact that she was the only one who knew where the stolen money had been buried. Although Cairo continued to wrestle for freedom, she found herself hoisted to her feet and chained in Nate Gardiner's arms. Determined to fight to the bitter end, Cairo rammed her elbow into Nate's midsection and kicked his shins into splinters with her bootheels. When he tried to grab her arm, she bit a chunk out of his hand.

"Damn you!" Nate snarled as he blocked her next attack of a well-aimed knee to the groin.

With another ferocious curse, Nate flipped his pistol in his hand to clamp hold of the barrel. With a quick snap of his wrist, he clubbed Cairo over the head. When she wilted like a fragile flower buckling beneath the scorching summer sun, Nate scooped her into his arms and marched toward the farmhouse.

"Wildcat," he growled into Cairo's pale features. "That'll teach you to give me trouble!"

Stark terror riveted Lawton to the saddle. He had halted on the hill that overlooked the ghost town when he saw Cairo sail from the hotel toward the barn. He had witnessed her bold escape attempt and his heart flipflopped in his chest when he heard the blaring pistols. In anguish, he watched her fly off her fallen horse. His very soul split asunder when he saw the three bandits subdue the blond-haired tigress who fought with every ounce of strength she possessed.

Never had Lawton felt so frustrated, so utterly helpless. He was still too far out of rifle range to pick off Cairo's captors. And even if he *had* been within range, he wouldn't have risked hitting her with a stray bullet. Charging blindly ahead and with both his pistols blazing wouldn't have accomplished anything, either, he told himself. He had been forced to hold his position and watch from afar, and that was worse than suffering for every sin he'd committed in life.

Lawton would have preferred to exchange places with Cairo rather than sit here in the distance. He'd defied danger a hundred times in the line of duty, but it scared him witless to watch Cairo fight her futile battle alone. He could feel her anger and frustration coiled in his belly. Adrenaline pumped through his veins as if he had been the one to make the daring dash to the barn to retrieve a steed, as if he had been the one straining against the arms of captors.

When Nate hammered Cairo over the head with the butt of his pistol, high-riding emotions urged him to whip out every weapon in his possession and plunge down the hill to attack, despite all odds. But his instincts and his well-seasoned talents bade him to keep his wits about him. Infuriating though it was, Lawton *made* himself sit still while the outlaws carted Cairo to the farmhouse.

When the bandits and their hostage had disappeared inside, Lawton slumped in the saddle as if the weight of the world had been heaped on his shoulders. He couldn't even draw a breath without his heart thumping frantically against his ribs. His mind raced, desperately seeking a solution, still warring against the compelling need to rush blindly ahead to rescue Cairo at all costs.

Lawton had thought the most difficult thing he'd ever done in his life was shooting Cairo. He was wrong! Wheeling his steed and riding off in the direction he'd come, leaving Cairo to the wolves, was positively the worst! Damnation, he couldn't even offer her comfort or compassion now. He couldn't lay seige to the ghost town without planning a mode of attack and he knew it. He would get Cairo and himself killed unless he sought assistance.

When the idea hatched in his mind, Lawton spurred the black stallion into a gallop and thundered toward Elreno. He had only one chance of rescuing Cairo from certain disaster, but he was going to have to be dead to do it. That thought caused a faint smile to hover on Lawton's lips. Only in dying would he have the chance to save that emerald-eyed spitfire's life.

"No, absolutely not!" Tucker McGuire shouted at Lawton as if he were deaf and dumb. "You've had some wild ideas in your time, but this is absolutely the worst!"

"I second that!" Woody glowered at Lawton as if he were the world's biggest idiot. "Al Fontain has yet to prove that he'll walk on the right side of the law. And besides that, he's just a green kid. Hell's fire, Law, if you put Al under that kind of pressure he might crack and you'd be dead twice!"

Lawton had anticipated his partners' negative reaction after he explained his plan, but he had no intention of backing down. "This is the only chance

Cairo's got," Lawton argued. "We can't wait for the Gardiners to come to us with their own deadly scheme. They don't know that Al has turned over a new leaf."

"I don't think that he has either," Tuck muttered sourly.

"For chrissake, Law, if you give the kid a chance to turn bad again he could easily betray you to save his own hide," Woody pointed out. "You'll sure enough get yourself killed twice and I'm not going to attend your funeral if you go through with this ridiculous scheme!"

"Me neither," Tuck chimed in, glaring furiously at Lawton. "But I'll damned sure see that stupidity is listed as the cause of death on your certificate."

Lawton sighed impatiently. While he was debating with his partners, Cairo was immersed in a frightening nightmare. Every second he tarried caused him and Cairo another instant of agony. "I don't have a week or a month to test Al's abilities in the face of a crisis. He's the only one who can get me into town without arousing suspicion. Al knows the Gardiners. If they think he shot me down and has come to collect the bounty on my head, they'll let him inside without unloading their rifles on him."

"And while you're draped over your horse like a damned corpse, the Gardiners may decide to fill you with lead, just for good measure," Tucker grimly predicted.

"I thought of that already," Lawton grumbled.

"Well, you must not have thought about it very long or you would have rejected the hare-brained idea yourself," Tucker grunted sarcastically. "If you ride into death valley, sprawled over the back of your horse like a limp carcass, the Gardiners will riddle you with bullets the instant you try to raise your damnfool head!"

"Then Al will collect the bounty and explain that you weren't as dead as you looked and join up with the Gardiners," Woody snapped in frustration. "If you think that's going to save Cairo, then you've been out in the sun so long that it fried your brain."

"As near as I can tell, this is my only . . ." Lawton's voice trailed off when Al trotted toward them, carrying the raw steak he had been ordered to fetch from the butcher shop.

"Is somebody gonna tell me why I was sent for this steak?" Al asked when he paused beside the three marshals who waited for him a mile south of town. "What the hell's going on?"

Lawton swung from the saddle and peeled off his buckskin jacket. Draping the garment over a tree limb, he fired his rifle into the back of his jacket, leaving a noticeable hole and powder burns.

Al gaped at Lawton and then his owl-eyed gaze swung to Tucker and Woody. "What was that all about?" Before an explanation could be offered, Lawton snatched the package of meat from Al's hand, unwrapped it, and smeared it over the hole in his jacket.

"Why would he want to go and mess up a perfectly good coat?" Al asked in disbelief.

Having accomplished his task of making his jacket look as if he'd been shot while he'd been wearing it, Lawton shrugged into the garment. While Al peered incredulously at him, Lawton swung back into the saddle.

"The Gardiners are holed up in a ghost town south of here," Lawton grimly reported to Al. "They have taken Cairo captive."

Al's face turned white as chalk.

"You're the only one who can ride into town without the risk of being shot on sight," Lawton went on. "Since you and Panhandle Dick were sent to ambush me, they won't be so suspicious when you ride in with my body slung over the saddle."

"But what if—"

Lawton stared into Al's young face, his expression bleak, his eyes like brewing storm clouds. "You're the only chance Cairo's got, Kid. You have to convince the Gardiners that you're still on their side. You've been wanting to apologize to Cairo for falsely identifying her. Now you can go one better than saying you're sorry for all the trouble you've caused her." He paused for dramatic effect. "Without your help, she won't live to see tomorrow."

Al looked as if he were about to melt out of the saddle and drip into a pool on the ground. "But I—"

Lawton refused to allow Al to waver. "We'll have the element of surprise on our side when I arise from the dead. I'll take care of the Gardiners, but it will be up to you to get Cairo to safety."

"You're going to take on all seven men?" Al croaked.

"Tucker and Woody will be hiding in the brush to add confusion with a barrage of bullets," Lawton informed him.

Al choked on the lump that threatened to strangle him.

Tucker glanced at Woody, who looked doubtful about the success of this daring mission. Woody's expression mirrored Tucker's wary trepidation.

Lawton didn't give Al time to voice another reservation or express his anxiety. He simply reined his steed south, forcing Al to accept the task that had been foisted off on him. The kid needed time to collect his wits and rehearse what he intended to say when he confronted the Gardiners.

"If the kid sticks his foot in his mouth, Lawton's and Cairo's lives won't be worth a damn." Tucker scowled as he trotted alongside Woody.

"Our aim better be as good as our eyesight," Woody sighed. "If we bring down two men apiece, that will still leave Lawton to square off against three of them."

"All that while he's worming off the back of his horse," Tucker added in a deflated tone. "Damned lousy odds, if you ask me."

Tucker nudged his steed up beside Lawton, who was staring into the distance. "If we'd have known you had your heart set on getting yourself killed, Woody and I would have shot you ourselves. At least it would have been quick and painless."

"Hell, I wouldn't even have charged you for gunning you down," Woody called, having overheard Tuck's remark.

"You boys have a better idea, do you?" Lawton asked.

"Well, no but—" they chorused.

"You know as well as I do that Al is Cairo's only salvation," Lawton remined them.

"Yeah, and whose gonna be *your* salvation?" Tucker asked.

Lawton smiled wryly as he paused to swing from the saddle. "I guess it's up to the two of you to decide whether you want me to come out of this dead or alive."

"That's a strange thing for a man to say when he's going into this confrontation draped over his horse *dead!*" Woody snorted. "I never claimed to be the crack shot you are, Law."

Lawton's smile vanished as he retrieved a rope to tie himself over the back of his horse. His silver eyes lifted, drifted from Tucker's poker face to Woody's worried frown. "If I don't . . ." He stared at the silhouettes of the building that set in the distance. "Tell her I . . ." Lawton inhaled a deep breath. For a long moment he peered at Woody from beneath the shaded brim of his hat. "Tell Cai how I feel . . . *felt* about her, Lover Boy. You always were better at finding the right words to say to women."

"Good Lord," Tucker muttered grumpily. "Just climb over that damned horse and let's get this over with. You can rehearse what you're going to say to Cairo when it's done. Woody isn't going to speak for you, and neither am I. You'll have to tell her yourself."

Lawton slid his belly over the saddle and wrapped the rope around his hips. "But in case I'm not around to tell her, I want you to—"

"Damn it, would the three of you clam up!" Al blurted as he squirmed in the saddle. "All this talk is giving me the jitters."

"You better get yourself in hand, Kid," Tucker warned, flashing Al a stern glance. "You can't go trotting into town shaking like a leaf. There's too much at stake."

Al took the reins to Lawton's steed and led the supposedly dead marshal down the path to Canadian Station. "I just hope the whole lot of us don't wind up plugged with holes—"

"For God sake, Law, will you keep your damn head down," Tucker interrupted Al irritably. "There's no such thing as a talking corpse. If the Gardiners have somebody standing lookout like they usually do, they'll spot you in a second."

Lawton dropped his head against his steed's ribs and hung there like a slab of bacon. Suddenly, his thoughts turned to Cairo. An anguished expression settled on his chiseled features. He couldn't help but wonder what hideous torture she was enduring at the hands of the renegades who had taken her captive. Rape? Beatings? Or was she being carved with Idaho Joe's knife?

Lawton stared at the dirt beneath his horse's hooves. If those filthy bastards had laid a hand on Cai, he'd blow them to hell in pieces, even if it was the last thing he ever did. And as risky as this scheme was, it could very well be the last, thought Lawton. Al was as jumpy as a kangaroo. The poor kid was being put to the test long before he had sharpened his skills. If he had any flaws of character they would come floating to the surface like cream rising on fresh milk.

The time of reckoning had come. Lawton hoped he hadn't misjudged Al Fontain. To save his own hide, the kid could easily betray Lawton. There was a great deal riding on Al's ability to handle himself in the face of adversity and temptation. If Al buckled under the pressure, mayhem could break loose!

Lawton groaned. Maybe Tucker and Woody were right. Maybe this *was* his craziest idea ever. Maybe? Lawton almost laughed out loud. There was no doubt about it!

Chapter Twenty-Three

Cairo blinked as she awakened with a throbbing headache. She didn't know how long she had been unconscious, only that she had been carried inside the farmhouse and strapped to a bed. She could hear voices in the other room, but they were too muffled to make out the words.

For what seemed forever, Cairo lay there attempting to wrest her arms from the straps that held her immobile. When she heard footsteps approaching, she tensed in apprehension. As the door creaked open, Cairo focused on the bandit who had clubbed her over the head with his pistol to prevent her from breaking free earlier that morning.

"Get up," Nate growled unsympathetically after he cut the straps and stepped back to allow Cairo to right herself. "It's time you met the rest of the family."

While Cairo had been sleeping off the blow to the back of her head, Nate and Idaho Joe had searched the rest of the hotel to ensure Cairo had been alone. Then they had investigated the area in hopes of stumbling onto the gold Cairo had dug from the ground and stashed away. To Nate's fury, he had been unable to determine where the sly blonde had hidden the booty. He and Joe had searched every nook and cranny in the hotel and come up empty-handed.

Clamping his fingers into Cairo's forearm, Nate propelled her into the parlor. Cairo froze in her tracks when she came face-to-face with the female bandit who cavorted with the band of renegades who had overrun the ghost town.

There before Cairo, attired in the similar garb of a shirt, breeches, and boots, stood Jarita Gardiner. The woman had the same peaches-and-cream complexion, the same oval face, and matched Cairo's size and stature. Although Jarita's hair was a slightly darker shade of blond and her eyes were a lighter shade of green, Cairo was amazed at the similarities of their appearance.

I thought you were somebody else . . .

Lawton's words roared through Cairo's brain like a steam engine plunging through a dark tunnel. With startling clarity, Cairo suddenly understood the wariness that had constantly plagued Lawton. He had suspected her of being this female bandit! That's why he'd delivered those sermons about crime not paying, about how Belle Starr and Cattle Kate met with bad ends. And that's why he'd shot her when he thought she was taking aim at him instead of his unseen assailant. That was also why he had used her as his shield in the gun battle in the Creek Nation. He thought the bandits would recognize her and they wouldn't try to shoot *through* her to get *to* him!

For the first time in her confusing relationship with

Lawton, Cairo understood his insinuations and his peculiar behavior. But she was puzzled that he would consent to travel with her . . . unless he thought she would lead him to this band of outlaws. That must have been it, she decided. He had courted what he assumed to be perilous danger to apprehend these fugitives.

Jarita crossed her arms beneath her ample bosom and tossed her mane of blond hair over her shoulder. With scornful mockery, she regarded their hostage. "Well, well, if it isn't Lawton Stone's whore," she declared. "Finding you here will save me a trip to Elreno. And when that murdering marshal discovers we have taken his paramour captive, we'll have our revenge on him for killing Billy."

Cairo strained against Nate's arms, but he held her fast. She hated what she was hearing! From the sound of things, she was about to become the bait for a deadly trap that Lawton must have anticipated all along. Lawton had been mistrusting and suspicious, and with excellent reason! He had obviously disturbed this hive of hornets when he killed one of their members. Now these outlaws were out for blood—Lawton's!

"I never heard of Lawson Strohm," Cairo lied to save Lawton's life.

"Lawton Stone," Vance corrected as he rose from the sofa. "Of course you have, bitch," he smirked. "That loose-tongued doctor in Elreno told Sissy all about the two of you while she was leading him to the dugout to patch me up."

It was with tremendous effort that Cairo maintained her carefully blank stare. Damn that Frederick Pullman and his big mouth! What was he doing giving medical attention to this pack of murderers and thieves anyway?

A wave of jealousy swept over Jarita when she surveyed Cairo's well-sculptured figure and white-gold hair. Jarita was aware of her own attractive assets and she prided herself on her keen wit and good looks. But all the attention she'd received from the brigand had shifted to Cairo.

Jarita had always relished the power she held over men because of her comely features and shapely figure. It annoyed her to no end that the men were silently comparing her to Cairo. Even Jarita knew she couldn't match this chit's exquisite beauty and that galled her to the extreme!

"Maybe this witch won't be quite so sassy if Joe takes his knife to her," Jarita sneered.

Cairo flinched when her attention shifted to the scraggly bandit who wore a long-bladed dagger on his belt. She had the sickening feeling she had just encountered the man who had murdered her father.

If Cairo thought she had something to fear from Idaho Joe, she was mistaken, at least when it came to being stabbed. Idaho Joe had instantly transferred his fascination for Jarita to the more available and beautiful Cairo.

"Nobody's gonna carve on this feisty bitch until Lawton gets a look at her," Nate growled as he shoved Cairo into a chair and tied her arms behind her. "Joe, you ride into Elreno and leave a message for Lawton. Tell him we have his whore and he'll have to come get her if he wants her back."

Vance suddenly frowned. "Where are Miguel and Ricardo?"

"Dead," Hank Forbes reported as he sank down to massage his bandaged leg. "This vixen shot her way out of the closet. Unfortunately, Miguel and Ricardo were in the line of fire."

"She also saw the men burying the money." Nate, glared menacingly at Cairo. "She stole the loot, and after we end our feud with Stone, she's going to tell us where she hid it."

Disgusted that he had been the one appointed to thunder off to Elreno, leaving the other men to ogle Cairo, Idaho Joe snatched up the fake mustache, beard, and wig the gang employed as a disguise. After casting a lusty glance at the voluptuous beauty, Joe strode out the door to fetch his horse. The sight of Kid Fontain trotting toward town, leading another steed, caused Joe to stop dead in his tracks.

"Nate, Vance, get out here quick," he bellowed, and they poured out the door as Jarita peered cautiously around the corner to make sure she wouldn't be spotted by unwelcome intruders before she went outside.

The brigand squinted into the sunlight to see the clean-shaven young man they had met in the Cherokee Nation four months earlier. Panhandle Dick was nowhere to be seen—unless he was the unidentified body that dangled over the horse.

Left to her own devices, Cairo wormed and squirmed to free herself from the rope. She had to escape and warn Lawton! That panicky thought compelled her to channel every ounce of energy into wriggling her wrists loose.

Cairo scooted her chair toward the cabinet to retrieve a knife so she could cut herself free. It was difficult to rise with the chair strapped to her, but she managed to inch across the room to fish into the drawer, despite the fact that her hands were tied behind her. She groped for a knife, defying the muscles that screamed from being contorted in a most uncomfortable position. Finally, Cairo latched onto a knife and then sank back in the chair to saw at the ropes. It wasn't easy to slice on the rope without slashing her wrists, but Cairo grimaced and concentrated on her task. The knife she had randomly selected was dull and it seemed to take forever to whittle through the twisted braids.

"Curse it," Cairo hissed as she peered over her shoulder to monitor her task. "A sharper knife would have been nice!"

Cairo scolded herself for being so particular. She should have thanked her lucky stars for whatever interruption had drawn the bandits' attention outside. She had to free herself and take flight before they returned.

Al Fontain nearly suffered heart seizure when the gang of desperadoes, all of whom were armed to the teeth, flooded out of the farmhouse. He was scared stiff! For over an hour, he had mentally rehearsed his story, but suddenly his mind had gone blank.

He felt as if he were wearing a hangman's noose and hooked his forefinger in the collar of his shirt to relieve the pressure in his throat. He darted a glance toward the underbrush in which Tucker and Woody had taken cover in preparation for the attack.

Al's apprehensive gaze lanced off Jarita and bounced across the stony faces of the men who were staring at him with wary curiosity. There were supposed to be seven men, Al thought to himself. Where the hell were the other two? With Cairo?

Vance Gardiner assessed the young man's clean-cut appearance and then peered at the body that was strapped over the black stallion. Recognition registered in Vance's pale-blue eyes. Thoughtfully, he studied the bloody bullet hole in Lawton Stone's jacket. Dead . . . Good. It was about time that bastard met his end.

Al drew his plodding steed to a halt a few yards away from the congregation of criminals. He didn't dare risk letting them examine Lawton's supposedly dead body at close range.

"I came to collect the ten-thousand-dollar reward for killing Stone," Al announced, his voice shaky. Cursing his nervousness, Al inhaled a deep breath and battled for composure.

"Where's Panhandle Dick?" Nate demanded.

"Stone gunned him down in the Creek Nation when we tried to bushwhack him," Al replied, his voice still a mite wobbly. He wished he was anywhere but here, fielding this barrage of questions!

"When did you get Stone?" Vance queried as he ambled toward the limp corpse. "We heard he was headquartering in Elreno while he was sniffing at our heels." A suspicious frown knitted Vance's blond brows. "And how'd you find us anyway, Kid?"

Al inwardly grimaced, but he forced himself to shrug nonchalantly. "I got away after Panhandle Dick got all shot up," he elaborated. "I tracked Stone, but he met up with three other marshal friends of his. The four of them split up to follow your tracks after you robbed the pay wagon at Darlington. When Stone was alone last night, I finally got my chance to bushwhack him." With commendable acting ability, Al grinned. "I didn't know where the hell you were so I just started riding, hoping you'd find me. Looks like we found each other."

While Al was responding to the rapid-fire questions, Lawton was counting feet. He came up four feet short. Where the hell were the other two desperadoes who were reported to be riding with the gang? The last thing he needed right now was any surprise that could botch up his plans of rescuing Cairo.

"Where the hell are the other two hombres?" Tucker muttered to Woody while they crouched in the underbrush.

"How the devil would I know?" Woody scowled. "You take the Gardiners and I'll take the other two hooligans on the right. We'll leave the last one for Law."

"I'm more concerned about the invisible ones who might appear out of nowhere when we least expect them," Tuck grumbled uneasily. He drew his Winchester to his shoulder to take careful aim. "The ones we can't see are bound to give us trouble. If they're guarding Cairo, they could kill her before we get a shot at them."

While Cairo was whittling rope and Lawton was counting feet and Woody and Tucker were preparing to fire, Al was battling for control and failing miserably. He'd fumbled over the last two probing questions and his heart was about to beat him to death.

"I'd like to have my money," he declared, wishing Vance Gardiner would back away from the not-so-dead body that was draped over the stallion.

Vance smiled menacingly as he swaggered over to peer up at Al. "How do we know you didn't alert the posse to our whereabouts and sell us out for more money?" He glanced at his brother and the other members of the gang. "Altogether, we're worth thirty-five thousand, dead or alive."

"Hell, I came back to join up with you!" Al protested, and then gulped when Nate whipped out a pistol and pointed it at his palpitating chest. "I'm not trying to double cross you, I swear it!"

A deadly smile thinned Idaho Joe's lips as he regarded the nervous youngster. "If I were you, Kid, I'd be more concerned about how you were gonna ride out of here alive instead of how you're gonna collect the reward for Stone."

Lawton swore silently when Cairo's shaggy hound trotted over to him. The mutt reared up on its hind legs and began licking Lawton's face, hands, and shoulders to savor the taste of raw steak. That was all he needed while he was playing dead and wondering if Al was going to back down when his life was on the line. Although Lawton willed the mutt away, it insisted on slurping its rough tongue over his hands and cheeks.

Al trembled beneath the accusing stares that were directed at him. "I thought there was a code among men like us," he countered, wishing he had a firm grip on at least one of his pistols.

"There is," Vance grunted. "Trust don't come easy. You have to earn it, Kid."

"I proved myself when I ambushed Stone," Al contested, his voice rising with each syllable. "All I want is the bounty money and the chance to rejoin you."

"Well, we can't give you the money, even if we wanted to," Nate muttered. "Lawton's whore was hiding out in this ghost town and she dug up the cash and stashed it away. And until she talks, nobody's got spending money."

Lawton's jaw clenched. Hearing the insulting reference to Cairo tempted him to rear up and blast Nate to smithereens, but learning Cairo had swiped the booty pleased him to no end. Good for her! That would teach these bastards to call her his whore!

"I say we should let Joe carve on that slut," Jarita inserted. "She might not be so bold and stubborn if she risks having her face slashed to shreds."

Vicious bitch, thought Lawton. And jealous, no doubt. Even though he couldn't raise his head to appraise Jarita at close range, he knew for a fact that the chit couldn't match Cairo's spunk and beauty. No woman could. Jarita must dislike the competition. Her vanity was smarting.

When the conversation turned back to Al, leaving him to defend and explain himself as best he could, Lawton tried to decide when to make his move.

While Lawton was preparing to strike, Cairo was inside the farmhouse cursing a blue streak. She had hacked her way out of the rope and inched toward the window to determine what had drawn the outlaws' attention. The shock of seeing Lawton strapped over his stallion with a bullet hole in his back very nearly knocked Cairo to her knees. Bitter sorrow swamped her, putting instant tears in her eyes.

Lawton had been betrayed by Al Fontain who had vowed that he had seen the error of his ways. That miserable scoundrel had lied to save himself from a hitch in prison and then he had lied about the incident that had left Panhandle Dick dead.

Knowing she would never peer into Lawton's silver eyes again or view his crooked smile caused Cairo's heart to twist in her chest, wringing every ounce of emotion from it. She had suffered so much disappointment and grief, had lost everyone who truly mattered to her. What was the use of surviving in a world without Lawton? She would never have the chance to tell him that she understood why he was leery of her, that she had loved him with every ounce of her being.

Even though tears misted her eyes and her body quivered with fury and sorrow, Cairo scurried toward the window at the back of the cabin and slipped outside. She never broke stride as she raced toward the corral of horses. If nothing else, she was determined to alert the posse to the Gardiners whereabouts!

Nate caught sight of Cairo's escape attempt out of the corner of his eye. Cursing, he wheeled to fire a shot to discourage her. His barking pistol set off a chain reaction that caused all hell to break loose in the ghost town. The hound erupted in a howl and darted beneath Lawton's horse, causing the stallion to prance sideways. Lawton flung the ropes aside and grabbed for both Peacemakers, but his horse had turned a half-circle, leaving Lawton facing the wrong direction.

In the meantime, Al dived from his steed before he

was shot out of the saddle. Tucker and Woody opened fire and bodies scattered for cover like ants scurrying away from a contaminated den.

"Get that bitch!" Vance yelled to his brother.

When Nate charged after Cairo, Vance grabbed Jarita's arm and propelled her toward the cabin. Bullets ricocheted off the sides of the house, splintering wood. Men scrambled about, pumping lead to provide cover for each other.

Lawton slid to the ground, using his flightly steed as his shield. His gaze flew to Cairo, who had been tackled by Nate Gardiner before she could bound onto a nearby horse and thunder off to safety.

The fact that Lawton had sprung to life had escaped no one's notice. Suddenly he became everyone's target. He found himself dodging bullets right and left as he crawled toward the post office building to take cover. Before he could aim at Nate Gardiner, the bandit snatched Cairo up by her hair, employing her as his coat of armor. Roughly, he shoved Cairo onto a horse and swung up behind her. His pistol lay against her throat and his menacing glare riveted on Lawton.

"You want this feisty bitch, Stone? Then come and get her," Nate bellowed. "She'll be at the river, treading quicksand!"

When Nate galloped toward the cliff overlooking the South Canadian River, Lawton expelled a string of curses that hung over the town like a black cloud. He couldn't get a clear shot at Cairo's captor or the other men who had taken the cue and circled the buildings of the main street to make a mad dash to the river.

Lawton could predict what the bandits planned for him. Nate would hurl Cairo into the quicksand and then he and his men would position themselves in the brush to await Lawton's arrival. As soon as Lawton left himself vulnerable in his effort to rescue Cairo from drowning in quicksand, he would be riddled with bullets. Damn . . .

Woody and Tucker swore in unison while they watched the violence and heard Nate Gardiner's venomous threat. The desperadoes had fled toward the river and out of rifle range. Only Jarita and Vance Gardiner were tucked in the farmhouse, blasting away at Lawton and Al. Frantic, Woody and Tucker bolted to their feet and charged forward, but Lawton didn't bother to wait for his partners to provide cover for him.

Al couldn't provide protection for anyone but himself. He had been pinned down by the gunfire that blazed through the window of the house. Vance Gardiner was unloading his repeating rifle as fast as he could squeeze the trigger and Jarita was displaying her expertise with pistols. Al couldn't move without drawing deadly fire and all Lawton had for protection was his horse—that had wandered over beside the abandoned dry goods store to avoid the flying bullets.

Cursing the animal, Lawton braced his back against the rough-hewn walls of the post office and calculated the distance between him and his horse. Gritting his teeth, he made a frantic dash between the two buildings to grab its reins. A shower of bullets sprayed around the spooked animal, causing it to slam against the wall and wheel in a frantic circle.

Lawton jerked down on the reins and bounded into the saddle. While the frightened horse screamed in protest of the barrage of bullets, Lawton plastered himself against its back and spurred the steed, forcing him to plunge through the volley of bullets that came at him.

"What the blazes is Law doing?" Woody croaked as he dropped into the tall grass beside the corral fence.

Tucker's wild-eyed gaze was still fixed on Nate Gardiner who had just reached the river and skidded his winded steed to a halt. In the distance, Tucker could hear Cairo's screeches. She had been yanked from the saddle and was being dragged, kicking and screaming, toward the cliff that overlooked the river. Below her was a bed of quicksand that lay beside the swirling channel. Tucker could well imagine the terror Cairo was experiencing as she faced the prospect of being hurtled through the air to flounder in quicksand.

And Tucker was right. Cairo was scared to death! She'd had no time to breathe a sigh of relief that Lawton was still alive, not when Nate Gardiner was determined to see her dead. The man was a mass of quivering fury. He had been hoodwinked and he was hell-bent on vengeance, even if he never found the missing money. Nate no longer cared if Cairo took the secret to her watery grave, so long as he had his revenge on Lawton Stone.

While Nate dragged Cairo ever closer to the bluff, the other bandits squatted in the brush to wait for Lawton. Determined to foil Nate's deadly plans, Cairo dug in her heels and clutched at the bushes, refusing to budge when Nate tried to pull her to the edge of the cliff.

Cairo wished Nate Gardiner's thirst for revenge hadn't been considerably stronger than his greed. He wanted Lawton dead at all costs, and Cairo was the cost. Nate had to end his family's feud with Lawton Stone and only the lives of his brother and sister mattered to him. He was determined to hurl Cairo into the river as bait for Lawton.

For what seemed eternity, Nate struggled to pry Cairo's hands loose from every limb she latched onto. But as soon as he loosened her from one branch she grasped another and clung to it as if it were a matter of life and death, which it most certainly was!

Scowling at Cairo's plight, Tucker refocused on Lawton, who was guiding his steed toward the front door of the farmhouse. Tucker had ridden with Lawton for enough years to predict the younger man's actions on a few occasions. Suddenly he was sure of Lawton's plans. He was seeking bargaining power. The only thing he could do, if he had any chance of living long enough to rescue Cairo, was to take his own hostage.

"Head for the back door," Tucker growled to Woody as he bounded onto his feet and sprinted forward. "I'll wager Law is going to come through the front door to get Jarita. That daredevil will have her as his hostage or he'll die trying!"

Both men dashed toward the back door, blasting away at the rough timber and lock as they went. They intended to provide a distraction while Lawton made his life-threatening entrance, defying the barking pistols and rifle that would soon be trained on him.

Vance shoved his sister protectively behind him as Lawton clomped through the front door atop his wild-eyed steed. Although Vance had heard the whine of bullets against the back door, his menacing snarl was focused on the relentless marshal who had taken Billy's life. Vance wasn't sure he'd walk out of this encounter alive, but he damned well intended to take Lawton Stone with him when he was launched into eternity.

Murderous blue eyes clashed with glittering silver as Lawton's stallion clattered into the room, upending furniture as he went. Jarita's piercing scream mingled with the creak of the saddle and the thrashing of hooves as the two men focused murderously on each other and prepared to fire.

As quick as Vance Gardiner was, he was no match for Lawton's unerring aim and lightning speed. Two pistols blazed, but Lawton found his target first, causing Vance to jerk back and misfire. His bullet whistled over Lawton's head, just as Woody and Tucker burst through the back door.

Jarita stared at her fallen brother and then raised her pistol to seek her revenge, but Lawton nudged his steed forward to kick the weapon from her hand. When she wheeled to flee, Lawton leaned out to snatch her off the floor. Sputtering curses, Jarita tried to hurl herself away from her hated enemy. To her dismay, Lawton's arm tightened around her like a steel clamp.

"Sit still or you'll follow your brother to his grave," he growled as he stuffed the writhing blonde in the saddle in front of him.

Only when Lawton emphasized his threat by ramming his Colt into her ribs did Jarita cease her struggles. She had seen her brother fall beneath Lawton's smoking pistol and she doubted the man would grant her the slightest consideration just because she was a woman. This was one man who would never fall beneath her charms, she knew that for certain.

In hasty jerks, Lawton yanked on the cuffs of Jarita's jacket and pulled her arms around her midsection to fasten her sleeves in a knot behind her back. With Jarita bound in her own coat, Lawton clamped his left arm around her and wheeled the steed toward the door. Shoving Jarita forward, Lawton ducked beneath the doorjamb and clomped off the porch to race toward the river.

Tucker and Woody spared Vance Gardiner only a brief glance before they reversed direction to fetch two horses from the corral.

"I'll be waiting for that bastard in hell," Vance choked out on his last ounce of breath.

Tucker pivoted to stare unsympathetically into Vance's glassy blue eyes. "You've got a long wait ahead of you," he muttered in disgust. "Lawton's Stone's got space reserved in paradise. You're not likely to meet up with him again in this lifetime or the next."

Woody wasn't sure Vance heard Tucker's words. An eerie stillness settled over the renegade who had died as he lived—in a whirlwind of violence.

Chapter Twenty-Four

Nate was furious. He had tried unsuccessfully to drag Cairo to the edge of the bluff. He'd had a full-fledged battle on his hands, trying to pry her loose from every tree limb and scrub brush she passed. Cairo had set her feet and he had finally been forced to uproot her from the spot by scooping her wriggling body into his arms. And then the she-cat had practically clawed out his eyes in her effort to prevent being catapulted through the air and into the quicksand. The threat of his pistol no longer fazed her. She had practically dared him to shoot her a half-dozen times, but Nate refused to do it. She would be of no use to him in his attempt to lure Lawton to the river for an ambush if she were already dead.

Nate snarled when Cairo kicked him in the private part of his anatomy and doubled over to protect himself from another painful blow. Lightheaded though he was, Nate managed to snake out a hand to clutch at Cairo's long mane of silver-blond hair when she squirted out of his arms. And even though he yanked hard enough to pull her hair out by the roots, Cairo gritted her teeth and plunged forward, whirling to dart back in the direction she'd come. With lips clenched in fury, Nate scrambled after his fleeing hostage. He lunged at her, clamping his arms around her knees.

Cairo shrieked when the ground flew up at her with incredible speed. She barely had time to brace her hands in front of her before her face smashed into the grass. And she had no time to recover before Nate hooked his arm around her neck and hoisted her back to her feet, then wrenched her right arm up her back and herded her toward the river. Although Cairo wiggled and squirmed and bit at him, she couldn't stop him. Nate was determined to fling her into the bar of quicksand. By sheer strength alone Nate dragged Cairo to the perilous edge of the bluff, forcing her to peer down at impending doom.

"You can meet up with your lover in hell," Nate sneered before he shoved Cairo forward.

Her piercing scream broke the brittle silence. Wild-eyed, Cairo stared at the death trap beneath her. A helpless victim of the pull of gravity, Cairo, her heart thundering frantically, plunged through the expanse of nothingness.

As the sand and water swallowed her alive, Cairo clawed to return to the surface. Her life flashed before her in disjointed fragments, but one picture found its way to the center of her agonized mind. She could see Lawton's laughing silver eyes above her, glistening like the stars in heaven. She lost herself in that disarming smile of his and reached up to trace his ruggedly handsome features just one last time before she went to meet her Maker.

She regretted that she wouldn't have the chance to retract all her bitter remarks after she had become aware of why Lawton had done the things he'd done. How she lamented never having the chance to declare she had loved him above all else, even if stubborn pride had kept the words locked in her heart.

She would tell him one day, Cairo promised herself determinedly. When they met again in eternity . . .

Even above the drumroll of his stallion's hooves, Lawton could hear Cairo screaming for all she was worth. He stared murderously into the distance, watching Nate force Cairo off the ledge into the treacherous quicksand of the South Canadian River. A part of him died when Cairo's screech evaporated into deafening silence.

With eyes like molten steel, Lawton watched Nate scuttle toward the underbrush to wait with the rest of his band of murderers. He spurred his stallion and clamped a firm hold on Jarita. He refused to let the animal break stride as he galloped toward the cliff over which Cairo had just disappeared.

His body taut, his senses springing to life, Lawton snatched up the rope that lay over the pommel of his saddle. As he galloped toward the bluff, he sought out a prime target—a tree stump. He knew he had only one chance to secure the lariat to the stump and provide a lifeline to deliver him from the quicksand. If he missed his mark, he would be of no use to Cairo—if he wasn't too late to save her already.

Jarita's eyes widened in terror as the muscular steed

thrashed through the brush that clung to the steep incline of the hill. She had expected Lawton to rein his horse to a screeching halt, but the daredevil marshal seemed to have no intention of taking time to barter one life for another. He meant to plunge over the cliff on horseback and he was taking Jarita with him!

The color seeped from Nate Gardiner's face when he saw his sister sitting in front of Lawton. He was furious that he was unable to take aim on the marshal without hitting his sister first.

"That son-of-a-bitch," Nate sneered as he watched Lawton blaze a path toward the spot over which Cairo had toppled.

The other desperadoes who waited with pistols trained on the approaching steed couldn't believe their eyes, either. Lawton Stone had devised a way to protect himself during his rescue attempt. Jarita Gardiner shielded him from oncoming bullets and it was impossible to drop the marshal while he thundered toward them.

Nate didn't dare open fire on the stallion for fear his sister would catch a stray bullet or be catapulted into the quicksand. He had been outsmarted and left to watch in furious frustration as Lawton hurled the loop of the lariat over his head. Nate swore he was watching the approach of the devil himself on his demon stallion. The raven hair that capped Lawton's head glinted in the sunlight, matching the dark coat of the wild-eyed steed. The flash of silver in Lawton's eyes was like a lightning bolt. The snarl on his lips would have sent a grizzly bear into early hibernation.

Although Nate Gardiner prided himself on being afraid of nothing and no one, he felt a shiver of dread trickle down his spine. He listened with sickening anticipation to the thunder of hooves, the creak of leather, and to Jarita's frightened scream.

Nate had faced deadly opponents in his time, but he couldn't name another man who struck fear in him, like Lawton Stone did. Stone could be as ruthless and bloodthirsty as any desperado when he was furious. And he looked positively furious now! Jarita was at this vengeful devil's mercy and the menacing expression that was chiseled on Lawton's rugged face assured Nate that he had no compassion to spare.

Nate's heart hung in his chest like an anchor when Lawton spurred his stallion up the bluff. A flood of curses, all with Lawton's name attached to them, tumbled from Nate's lips. It struck him there and then that Lawton intended to repay him, an eye for an eye!

"Goddamn him!" Nate snarled as he flung his pistol aside and sprang from his hiding place in the underbrush.

Nate dashed after the horse and its two riders. Jarita's scream trailed off in the wind as she wrestled to free herself from her improvised straitjacket. Her frantic gaze bounced from the ground that whizzed beneath the stallion's pounding hooves to the swirling channel and the quicksand that rimmed the riverbed.

Lawton was oblivious to the astonished growls of the desperadoes who had monitored his daring approach. He was deaf to Jarita's scream. His gaze was fixed on the tree stump as he swerved his laboring steed toward his target on the rim of the cliff.

With lightning-quick accuracy, Lawton flung the

loop over the stump as they sailed past. When he felt his stallion break stride at the top of the cliff, Lawton gouged him in the flanks and bellowed at him to plunge ahead.

The stallion, his eyes wide with fear, his nostrils flared in apprehension, stretched out as if he were about to fly over the wide channel that swirled below him. Feeling the steed lunge into space, Lawton shoved Jarita from the saddle and clutched the rope he had secured to the tree stump.

Jarita's scream of terror followed her as she plunged off the cliff. The stallion's shrill whinny mingled with her screech as he splashed in the river, and Lawton's ferocious growl overshadowed them all. As he plummeted downward, he scanned the quicksand in search of Cairo but there was nothing to guide him to her location.

Although the stallion had leaped far enough out from the cliff to avoid the pit of quicksand that lined the channel, Lawton had purposely tossed Jarita and himself into the swirling death trap. A breath of hope swelled in Lawton's chest as he dragged himself to the surface via the rope. He spied Cairo's fingertips floating on the sandy bog. Holding tightly to the rope, Lawton pulled himself hand over hand through the sand, battling the suction of the undercurrent that tugged at him. His gaze momentarily darted to Jarita who had surfaced to expel another bloodcurdling scream for assistance.

The four men who had scampered to the bluff to attempt to retrieve Jarita found themselves surrounded by Woody and Tucker and Al. While Lawton dragged himself forward to clamp onto Cairo's hand before she disappeared forever, Nate clutched the rope that hung on Tucker's saddle. Frantic, Nate secured the lifeline and repelled his way down the face of the cliff to save his sister from the hideous fate he had planned for Cairo.

Lawton stretched forward just as Cairo's fingertips sank from view. Desperate, he groped to clutch at her, feeling as if he were moving in slow motion. Lawton swore he was fighting a losing battle. He had been to hell and back a half-dozen times in the course of an hour and still he was unable to rescue Cairo. After all he'd been through, he was still going to lose her!

It just wasn't fair! Lawton scowled as he groped in the sand to locate Cairo's limp arm. She had been an innocent victim, unjustly persecuted and caught in the middle of a deadly feud that didn't even concern her!

Lawton thought of all the unfortunate people who had perished because of the Gardiners. He had mourned each one of them, but not the way he was going to grieve if he lost Cairo.

His resentful thoughts scattered when his hand collided with cold flesh beneath the surface of quicksand. Lawton arched backward, sliding his hand along the rope. Gritting his teeth, he pulled with every ounce of strength he could muster. Ever so slowly, Cairo's limp body emerged. She was as lifeless as . . .

"Cai!" Lawton's bellowing voice trembled with turbulent emotion. He hadn't allowed himself to feel much of anything since the moment Nate Gardiner galloped toward the river with Cairo clasped in front of him. He had only reacted with cold instinct and calculated intellect, but his composure cracked as he drew Cairo's body against his to press a kiss to her blue-tinged lips.

It wasn't the sand in his eyes that provoked the tears. It was stark fear mingled with indescribable grief. He had retrieved Cairo from her sandy grave but he wasn't sure he had managed to snatch her from the arms of death. She was so still, so limp, so cold . . .

"Tucker!" Lawton's tormented howl almost sounded inhuman as it billowed up from the quicksand.

Tucker's bushy red head appeared above the ledge. Within seconds, Woody, Tucker, and Al had clutched the rope to drag Lawton and his lifeless bundle to safety. Like a spider walking up a perpendicular wall, Lawton planted his feet on the slope and ascended the cliff with Cairo clutched protectively against him. Although he tried to squeeze the water from her lungs, he could barely detect her heartbeat or feel her breath against his cheek. She was like a corpse . . .

Death had a frightening fragrance and a chilling silence all its own and Lawton was getting a telltale whiff of both as he clutched Cairo to him.

He scolded himself for allowing the thought to seep into his mind. He wasn't going to believe the worst until he was faced with no other alternative! She was going to live! She *had* to live!

While Lawton was struggling up the face of the cliff, Nate was dragging his sister from the quicksand. He had managed to lasso her by the shoulders, but she could offer no assistance at all with her arms wound around herself, her jacket sleeves tied behind her back.

"You bastard!" Nate hissed, thinking how Lawton had thrust Jarita into perilous danger. It didn't occur to him that he had been just as ruthless with Cairo.

Wailing like a banshee, Jarita skidded through the quicksand and bumped along the wall of dirt and rock that jutted from the cliff. When Nate finally clutched her in his arms, she collapsed in hysterics.

Seeing his sister so terrified sent Nate into a demented fury. The instant Lawton appeared above the edge of the cliff with Cairo draped over his arm, Nate charged like an angry rhinoceros.

With a malicious growl Nate rammed Tucker broadside and leaped on Lawton. Lawton was as vicious in his attack as Nate was in his. Nate vowed to repay Lawton for the torture he'd put Jarita through and Lawton swore revenge on Nate for cruelly abandoning Cairo in the quicksand. Flesh collided with flesh as both men released their pent-up emotions on each other.

When Al rushed forward to pry the men apart, Tucker grabbed his arm. "This is Law's fight," he told him. "Let him have his revenge for the hell he's been through." Tucker gestured his head toward Cairo. "We better see what we can do for the lady." His expression didn't offer much hope as he peered at Cairo's still body.

Although the three men crowded around Cairo to press the heels of their hands to her back, forcing her to breathe, they monitored the battle between Lawton and Nate Gardiner. Fury had given Nate twice his normal amount of strength, but still he was no match for Lawton, who was all swinging fists and striking feet. He answered every blow with devastating force, taking every ounce of his anger out on his mortal enemy.

The two men growled and snarled as they rolled and

tumbled down the slope. When Lawton sprawled on top of Nate, he delivered a right cross that sent stars spinning in front of the bandit's eyes. Blindly, Nate fought back, leveling a blow that knocked Lawton off balance.

Jarita took advantage of the fisticuffs that had distracted all the men. After worming the jacket from her shoulders, Jarita freed her hands and scrambled to her feet. Hastily, she glanced around to see Lawton's black stallion swimming downriver to locate a safe place to emerge from the water. While the steed shook himself off like a duck, Jarita darted into the bushes and scuttled along the slope to retrieve the horse.

Pulling into the saddle, Jarita reined the mount along the bank until she could scale the ridge. She disliked the idea of leaving her brother behind, but she could be of no use to him if she were handcuffed and led to jail beside him.

Revenge burgeoned in Jarita's mind as she sailed across the countryside to find refuge. Someday, somehow, she would find a way to get back at Lawton Stone for destroying her family! This feud wasn't over yet, Jarita vowed vengefully. She wouldn't rest until Lawton was dead and roasting in hell!

Woody clamped onto Lawton's broad shoulder to misdirect the blow that was aimed at Nate's puffy face. "Nate's unconscious. He and his friends will have their day in Judge Parker's court . . . and on the gallows. You can bank on it."

Woody's firm voice penetrated Lawton's tormented thoughts. He sank back on his haunches to peer at

Nate's limp form. When reality returned, he glanced up to see Tucker cradling Cairo's body in his arms, saw the grim expression that was stamped on the older man's features.

"We've got to get her to a doctor quickly," Tucker declared in a bleak voice. "She's just barely alive. If I ride to Elreno and bring the physician back here it may be too la—" His words trailed off as his gaze dropped to Cairo's waxen features.

A cold chill snaked down Lawton's spine. He was on his feet in less than a heartbeat to snatch Cairo from Tucker's arms. "Get my horse," he ordered, his eyes never leaving Cairo's face.

Tucker glanced around and cursed himself. Lawton's black stallion was nowhere to be seen and neither was Jarita Gardiner. He had been so preoccupied with Lawton's battle with Nate and Cairo's condition that he had forgotten to shackle her to a tree beside the other desperadoes.

Tucker grabbed the reins to the closest steed and tugged Cairo into his arms while Lawton mounted. "Keep you eyes open," Tucker cautioned. "It looks as if Jarita made her escape on your stallion. If she sees you, she'll be out for blood."

Lawton pressed his knees to the steed's ribs and veered north. That was when he spied the freshly dug grave and the wooden marker that stood over it.

"Oh God, no!" Lawton groaned when he read the epitaph. His shoulders slumped, realizing the full extent of Cairo's suffering the past few days. She had traveled across the Twin Territories, enduring Lawton's cruelty, only to find that her father's dream had become a ghost town. Rylan Calhoun had perished before Cairo could be reunited with him. One look at the freshly dug grave was proof of who had been forced to see to the burial. Lawton had left her alone to face more disaster than he'd realized.

His eyes dropped to the hauntingly lovely face that rested against his shoulder. He wondered, in spite of Cairo's incredible determination, if she still had the will to live. She had suffered so many heartaches in such a short span of time, had suffered ten times over for sins she had never committed.

"I'm so sorry, Cai . . ." Lawton murmured as he reined the steed toward Elreno. "Don't leave me. I swear I'll make it all up to you."

With heavy heart, Lawton trotted north. The time it took to cover the distance between Canadian Station and Elreno seemed to span eternity. Lawton couldn't get there fast enough to suit himself with Cairo seeming to hover between life and death.

Chapter Twenty-Five

Frederick Pullman was just sitting down to a quiet evening meal when the front door burst open and Lawton sailed inside with Cairo clutched in his arms. They were both covered with a layer of sand. The bluish tinge on Cairo's face brought Frederick straight out of his chair.

"Put her in my room," he insisted as he opened the door.

Bleakly, Lawton strode inside and eased Cairo onto the sheet Frederick had placed on the bedspread.

"Quicksand," Lawton murmured, his agonized gaze riveted on Cairo's expressionless face. "I don't know how long she was under before I got to her. The Gardiners used her as bait to get to me."

The news filled Frederick with guilt. His blundering remarks to Jarita Gardiner had brought Cairo disaster. "I'll fetch my bag," he mumbled in a humble tone before he pivoted on his heels.

"I'll get her undressed," Lawton volunteered.

One look at Lawton's chiseled face and his grim

expression prompted him to swallow his protest.

When Frederick left, Lawton peeled away Cairo's shirt and breeches before brushing the clinging sand from her hair and face. His gaze dropped to the wad of money that tumbled from her pocket and onto the floor. He recalled hearing the Gardiners report that Cairo had stolen their loot and Lawton wondered bleakly if she would live to reveal the location of the rest of it. The thought of losing Cairo was tearing him to pieces.

Lovingly, his eyes flooded over her shapely form, wishing he could touch her and bring her to life. He silently willed her to open her eyes, but she showed no signs of rousing while Lawton cleansed off the sand and tucked her in bed.

"Why don't you help yourself to the food on the table while I examine Cairo," Frederick suggested as he plunked down on the opposite side of the bed.

Lawton glared at him. "No thanks, I'd rather—"

"I'm the doctor, Marshal Stone," Frederick snapped as he leaned over to check Cairo's pulse.

If that was supposed to reassure Lawton, it didn't. "I'm staying because I love her," he blurted out, surprising himself and the physician.

Frederick tilted his head to return the unblinking stare. "You aren't the only one," he tossed back.

Lawton gnashed his teeth until he very nearly ground off the enamel. "But *I* want to be the only one who has the right to love her, to touch her, to look at her—"

"*You?* A tumbleweed marshal who never stays in one place long enough to collect dust?" Frederick scoffed insultingly. "I hardly think you're the kind of man a woman like Cairo needs." He stared down into Cairo's peaked face and his expression softened. "I believe the choice is still up to the lady . . . if she lives to make a choice, which she might not if you don't stop badgering me while I'm trying to examine her."

Lawton got up and left, though he would have preferred to remain by Cairo's side. Even as gravely ill as she was, Lawton could barely abide the thought of another man staring at her exquisite body. He was being ridiculously possessive, he knew. And he was tormented by the speculations of how many violations Cairo had suffered while she had been held captive. Had all the men taken their turns?

Lawton scowled. He didn't want to think about that. He wanted a drink . . . or six . . .

He sailed out the door to retrieve a bottle of whiskey from one of the twenty-three saloons that lined the streets of town. Having made his purchase, Lawton returned to make himself at home in Frederick's parlor. It was a half-hour later before the physician emerged from the bedroom.

"Well?" Lawton wanted immediate answers.

"I'm not God," Frederick muttered in exasperation. "I can't work miracles. We'll just have to wait and see if she rouses to consciousness." He snatched up the bottle and helped himself to a stiff drink of Lawton's rotgut. "Go ahead and say it. I know you're thinking it. I can *see* you thinking it. You hold me personally responsible for Cairo's ordeal because I revealed too much to those desperadoes."

He had unloaded the tormenting guilt from his conscience. Now Frederick only had to deal with the anxiety of wondering if Cairo would survive.

Lawton stared at the contents of his glass. "I'm as guilty as you are," he muttered. "So don't think you get to shoulder all the blame. Half of it belongs to me. I'm the one who abandoned her in that ghost town to begin with."

"It doesn't make me feel a damned bit better," Frederick grumbled before taking another gulp of whiskey.

"Me, either," Lawton murmured as he swirled the liquor around in his half-empty glass and chugged it. *Half-full* glass, he silently corrected himself. Every thought that crossed his mind was going to be optimistic until Cairo had regained consciousness, he vowed firmly.

Darkness spread over the countryside like a black velvet cloak while the two men kept their vigil and drowned their sorrows in the bottle of whiskey. If he could have made it so, Lawton would have seen Cairo breezing out of the bedroom to cuddle up in his lap, but she didn't come and she never called to him. Each time he stared at the bedroom door he was met with haunting silence.

It was the front door rather than the bedroom door, that creaked open two hours later. Al, Tucker, and Woody had delivered their prisoners to Sheriff Jubal Newton and had come to check on Cairo. To their chagrin, Dr. Pullman offered no encouraging news.

"We'll have to wait and see" was all Frederick had to say.

At midnight, Frederick shuffled his guests out of his house, insisting that he would notify them if there was any change in Cairo's condition. Lawton was most reluctant to leave. What he really wanted was to slide into bed beside Cairo, to hold her all through the night.

"Come on," Tucker urged Lawton as he steered his friend out the door. "Cairo's in good hands."

"That's what worries me. Frederick has proposed to her at least twice already," Lawton grumbled resentfully.

Lawton Stone was hooked. He hadn't been the same since Cairo Calhoun barged into his life. Woody prayed Cairo would survive to grant Lawton the chance to prove himself worthy of her affection . . .

His thoughts trailed off when he remembered he had information to convey to Lawton. "We found the two men we couldn't account for. They were sprawled in the hotel at Canadian Station. According to one of the bandits, Cairo shot them when they discovered her hiding place in the closet. It seems that shaggy mutt gave her away and the outlaws went looking for her."

"We found your stallion at a farm south of town," Al piped up. "The owners said one of their horses had disappeared and your steed was left behind. There've been no other reports as to Jarita Gardiner's whereabouts."

Lawton mulled over the disturbing thoughts as he rode back to the hotel. He knew that Jarita would be plotting her revenge. He only hoped she was too busy hating him to think of gathering reinforcements from the area. At this rate, he'd never be free of the price on his head. There would always be some greedy renegade who hungered to collect the bounty. And until Jarita was in custody, Lawton could enjoy not one moment's peace.

Lawton sighed as he sank onto his bed. Not knowing about Cairo's condition was killing him, bit by agonizing bit! He wanted Cairo in his arms, not the pillow he was clutching so fiercely that he feared he'd split the seams and feathers would flutter around the room.

An hour later Lawton was still twisting and turning and getting no sleep whatsoever. After changing into fresh clothing, Lawton walked into the darkened hall. His troubled thoughts meandered and his footsteps took him where they would. He was a tormented man with too many regrets, too many unfulfilled dreams, too many nightmares . . .

Through the dome of cold stillness that covered her, Cairo felt a comforting warmth settle beside her. As much as she yearned to sidle toward that compelling heat, her chest felt as if it had been anchored at the bottom of this strange icy abyss.

The unexplainable warmth speared through the frigid darkness, rekindling the flame that had been doused in the very depths of her soul. Although Cairo hadn't the strength to move and her mind was floundering through a tangled jungle of thoughts, she felt herself being eased onto her side.

She couldn't be certain because she had no idea where she really was, but she thought she felt the moist whisper of breath against her throat. A strength that had escaped her in this state of limbo seemed to glide over her icy flesh, massaging away the stiffness in her muscles. She absorbed the comforting warmth, reveled in the flicker of life that blossomed in the shriveled space that had once been her heart. There were words, too, although Cairo was too dazed to comprehend them—tender words that pulsated through her.

Cairo wanted to reach out to this strange radiating heat and energy that enveloped her, but her arms and legs refused to respond to the feeble, incoherent messages that rippled through her brain. She wanted to grasp that glowing feeling that called to her in the distance, but she was too weary and weak. It was the *wanting to* that provided the precious lifeline between her foggy world of chilling silence to the warmth of life.

Lawton gently draped Cairo's limp arm over his waist and drew her head against his shoulder. Gently, he eased her leg over his hip, stroking and massaging her. His hand drifted over her thigh and swirled down her back. With an aching that twisted his heart, he sought out Cairo's cold, unresponsive lips, wishing he could revive her with his kiss, rouse her with his caress.

Since the moment he rolled out of his bed at the hotel, Lawton had been stung by the overwhelming need to hold Cairo in his arms. Although Frederick had shuffled Lawton out of the house, he had slipped into the bedroom window. Cradling Cairo's limp body to his, molding her against his muscular contours was the soothing balm that healed his troubled soul. He needed to be with Cairo no matter what happened, even if she . . .

Lawton pushed that thought aside and cuddled Cairo all the closer. "Don't leave me, sweet angel," he pleaded, his voice wavering with tormented emotion. "If you go away, you'll take the sunshine from my days and the moonlight from my nights." He combed his fingers through the gleaming tendrils of silver-blond hair. "You are the Oklahoma moonlight," he whispered against her cheek. "You're the reason God made the moon and stars. You've given my life deeper meaning. Don't take it away from me so soon after I've discovered how much I love you . . ." His lips feathered over her in the slightest breath of a kiss. "I can no longer remember what my life was like without you, Cairo, but I know I don't want to go back to the way it was before you came along . . ."

Only now, only when Lawton held Cairo's limp body in his arms and whispered his desire for her to live, did the tension that had plagued him for the past forty-eight hours drain away. Finally, he slept, holding Cairo in the possessive circle of his arms, daring death to steal her away from him. He would provide her with the strength to fight for her life, the energy to stir from her trancelike state. His spirit was her own—strong, unyielding, defiant.

Frederick was shocked when he eased open the bedroom door the following morning to check on his patient. He expected to find Cairo in bed, but he certainly hadn't anticipated seeing Lawton there with her!

"What do you think you're doing?" Frederick hissed furiously.

Lawton pried one eye open to regard the flush-faced physician. While he was contemplating whether to dignify the question with an answer, Frederick stamped to the foot of the bed.

"I swear you are the strangest marshal I've ever met!" he fumed. "You disregard rules as if you were above them. Correct me if I'm wrong, Mr. Stone, but breaking and entering is still considered an unlawful offense, is it not?"

Unaffected by the doctor's sarcastic tirade, Lawton flashed him a devilish grin. "I didn't break anything when I entered, Freddie. The window wasn't locked."

"You are twisting the facts to suit your own purposes! And the name is *Frederick!*" he spluttered. "I'm getting very tired of watching you bend the laws to accommodate you. This is *my* house and *my* patient, *I* make the rules around here and *you* are going to follow them. Now get out of *my* bed!"

Frederick's indignant voice had risen to a roar. Cairo roused from the groggy depths of unconsciousness to snuggle closer to the warm strength that cradled her.

Both men stared goggle-eyed at Cairo's unexpected movement. Delighted beyond words, Lawton dropped a kiss to her lips and felt the slightest hint of a response. He wanted to shout to high heaven!

The kiss roused Cairo to another plateau of consciousness and her arm glided up Lawton's shoulder. Lawton elevated a dark brow when her fingertips drifted over his face. With a triumphant grin that was as wide as Oklahoma Territory, Lawton glanced at the fuming physician.

"Don't you dare say it, damn you," Frederick muttered acrimoniously.

"Don't say what?" A mock-innocent smile quirked Lawton's lips. He was so relieved he swore he could have walked on air. "That my presence and my kiss brought her back to life?"

"Blast it, I asked you not to say it!" Frederick scowled.

The exchange prompted Cairo's eyes to flutter open. Through the fuzzy blur that clouded her vision, she saw the same image that had followed her into the cold, suffocating depths of the quicksand. Silver eyes sparkled down on her like mystical starlight. An irresistible smile bracketed Lawton's sensuous mouth.

"Lawton? Is that really you?" Cairo swore her voice had rusted and granules of sand lined her throat.

His chuckle reverberated against her breasts, causing her to inch closer to his hard length. "Yes, it's me, little nymph," he murmured before pressing his lips to hers.

"Are we both dead?" she questioned, staring solemnly into his ruggedly handsome features, battling her way through the cobwebs that cluttered her mind.

Beneath the quilt, his masterful hands explored her pliant flesh. "Not hardly, love. Not hardly . . ."

Frederick snapped his medical bag shut, spun around, and stalked out. He had harbored the hope that Cairo would come to her senses and accept his marriage proposal, but the look on her pale features told Frederick what he hadn't wanted to know. No matter what Frederick thought of this bold, unconventional marshal, Cairo was hopelessly in love with him. It was in her eyes, in the way she rimmed her fingers over his bronzed features.

When Frederick retreated, Lawton focused his full attention on Cairo, devouring her with his eyes. His hands, as if they possessed a will of their own, roamed over her silken flesh, providing the fire to inflame her soul.

The feel of his skillful caresses fueled Cairo's sagging spirits until they burgeoned with new life. She blocked out the terrifying nightmare that had left her wavering between life and death. She concentrated solely upon the hot, electrifying sensations that Lawton's arousing touch instilled in her. Weak though she was, she responded to the pleasure he offered, to the intimate promises of his kisses.

Although Lawton was on fire for her, he restrained the passion that raged inside him. He wanted nothing more than to make wild sweet love to this bewitching goddess, but Cairo had just returned from the dead. He wouldn't risk causing a relapse just because he wanted her in the worst possible way. He had waited all through the night. He could wait a little longer . . . for Cairo's sake.

Cairo sighed in disappointment when Lawton eased off the bed to don his breeches and shirt. "You gave so little for such a short span of time . . ." she pouted groggily.

Lawton leaned over the bed to brace his sinewy arms on either side of her shoulders. "I would give you so much more," he assured her before his lips fluttered over hers like a butterfly's wings skimming the earth. "But you are in no condition to accept it, little minx. You need your rest."

Cairo mustered the energy to loop her arms over his broad shoulders and toy with his midnight hair. "At last I understand," she sighed tiredly. "And I forgive you . . ."

There was a wealth of meaning in her words and in the depths of her emerald eyes. Lawton hadn't asked forgiveness when he apologized for hurting her, but he could tell by her tender expression that she no longer condemned him for his unpardonable behavior.

"But Lawton . . . ?" She stared straight into his eyes. The faintest hint of a smile quirked her soft mouth. "You did face life-threatening situations a few times when you were with me," she confessed. "It was when I wanted you so badly that I tried to kiss you to death . . ."

A quiet chuckle rumbled in his chest as he traced her cupid's-bow lips and the delicate bones of her jaw and cheeks. "I'll be back after you've had the chance to recuperate and we'll see who can kiss the breath out of who."

Lawton's gaze lanced off hers, feeling awkward with the topic of conversation he felt compelled to broach. "And it doesn't matter about those . . . other men. I still . . ."

Lawton unfolded himself to tower over her, still unable to meet her befuddled gaze. "Just make sure you get all the rest you need, Cai. I'll be back when I've completed my task. Jarita Gardiner is still on the loose. She poses too great a threat to ignore." Lawton crammed the hem of his shirt into his breeches and strapped on his holsters.

What other men? Cairo wondered as Lawton moved across the room. Did he think she had been molested? Was that what he was trying not to say for fear of upsetting her? Thanks to his daring rescue, there had been no time for her to be violated by those renegades. And she would tell him so . . . just as soon as she mustered the energy to keep her eyes open when they were about to slam shut . . .

But despite the bright sunlight that sprayed into the room, Cairo sank into the depths of darkness. She was so very tired that she wondered if even a century-long nap would revive her.

While Cairo was drifting in hazy dreams, Frederick tiptoed back into the room to examine his patient. He sighed in relief when he pressed the palm of his hand to her forehead to check for fever. Cairo was made of sturdy stuff, he speculated. She had been through a most terrifying ordeal, which Lawton and the other marshals had described in detail the previous night. And she had survived because of her fierce inner strength, her stubborn will and resilience, Frederick convinced himself. It was *not* because Lawton had sneaked in the window and into her bed to hold her all through the long night! The legendary Lawton Stone did *not* work miracles!

Assured that Cairo would recover, given time and plenty of rest, Frederick returned to the parlor before setting out to make his rounds. To his chagrin, Lawton had propped himself negligently against the door and was staring at him.

"Barring any complications, she should be up and around in a few days," Frederick predicted as he shrugged on his coat. "I'll have Miss Gibson bring some food over from the restaurant this afternoon." His eyes riveted on Lawton. "If you want to pay Cairo a visit, use the front door next time."

Lawton nodded in compliance. "I may be gone a couple of days, but I will honor your request when I return."

"I'd appreciate that," Frederick grunted as he shouldered past the marshal.

When Frederick clambered into his carriage, Lawton ambled down the street to the hotel, humming the chorus to "Skip to My Lou."

"Just coming in? Or are you already up and out for the day?" Tucker mocked dryly when he spied Lawton. Since he knew the answer, he didn't wait for Lawton to respond before he fired another inquiry. "How's Cairo?"

"Better," Lawton reported. "She's conscious now. Freddie says she'll need a few days to recuperate."

"And in the meantime?" Woody prodded.

"We track Jarita down," Lawton replied, his expression sobering in the span of a second. "She still holds a grudge against me. I intend to get to Jarita before she finds some fiendish way to avenge me and gathers reinforcements to break Nate out of jail."

"So where do we start?" Al Fontain asked.

"At the farmhouse where Jarita left Lawton's horse," Tucker grumbled. "Good Lord, Kid, I'm not sure we'll ever be able to make a marshal out of such raw material. And it's no wonder you didn't have much success at a life of crime. You have a lot to learn!"

"Ease up on him," Lawton scolded as he ambled down the street to retrieve his horse. "Al proved his worth yesterday while he was staring down the barrels of five loaded pistols. The kid deserves a medal, if you ask me."

Al blessed Lawton with a grateful smile. "Thanks, Law. I was afraid I'd botch up the rescue attempt when they started pelting me with questions."

"You did fine," Lawton assured Al as he swung into the saddle. "After Tuck teaches you all you need to know about tracking, you'll be as good as he is at marshaling."

"He will not!" Tucker protested, his thick chest swelling with indignation. "I've got twenty years' experience on this green kid!"

"Not all of it good, though," Lawton taunted before he burst out in another booming chorus of "Skip to My Lou."

Al hung back beside Woody, staring pensively at Lawton's back. "He doesn't sing very well, does he? Have you ever told him that?"

Woody chuckled as he settled himself comfortably in the saddle. "Nope, not yet, and you won't, either, if you know what's good for you. Law doesn't take kindly to remarks about his crooning. When the prisoners complain about it, he cuts their rations in half. And by the time the jail wagon reaches Fort Smith, the convicts usually beg him to sing so they can eat their fill. Most of them do anyway," Woody amended. "There are always a few hardened criminals who hold such a grudge against Lawton that they'd prefer to die before they buckle to his iron will."

"Like the Gardiners," Al murmured.

"Exactly like the Gardiners," Woody grumbled. He couldn't help but wonder how the clever Jarita Gardiner planned to wreak her vengeance, especially now that she had lost a second brother to Lawton's blazing pistol and the third brother was locked up, awaiting his date with a hangman's noose.

Lawton was wondering the same thing. He figured Jarita had contacts in the area, men who were bedeviled by her beauty, men who would do anything she asked of them. He wanted to take her captive before she could make plans, gather reinforcements, and rekindle the bloody feud. Curse it, where was that minx? She surely hadn't gone far, not with her brother in the Elreno jail.

* * *

Cairo sighed in pure boredom. Frederick had kept her cooped up for three days. A flood of well-meaning women, bearing piles of food, had come and gone from the room. And each one, as she left, urged Cairo to rest. "Doctor's orders," they all said.

Cairo had the feeling every one of the women who had come to play nursemaid was aspiring to gain the position as Frederick's wife, and that each one of them would have preferred for Cairo to be up and gone, to lessen the competition. All of them had come to visit Cairo, singing praises to Frederick's name. She wondered if the handsome physician knew how popular he was with the female population.

Although Cairo appreciated all the concern, she diagnosed her own condition and was certain that she was simply suffering from exhaustion and sniffles caused by her dowsing in the quicksand. Despite "doctor's orders," Cairo had crawled from bed and paced around the house to ease her restlessness. Lying flat on her back was boring unless Lawton was nearby, which he hadn't been since she'd roused to consciousness. Even though she knew how relentless Lawton Stone could be when he was trailing outlaws, she still missed having him around.

There was so much she wanted to say to him, things she couldn't write in a letter before she returned to Missouri to resume her previous life. Oklahoma held too many unpleasant memories, too many heartaches and broken dreams.

As much as Cairo loved that raven-haired rake with the dancing silver eyes, she knew it would never work between them. Lord, he'd been away for only three days and she was already on the verge of climbing walls! She couldn't tolerate waiting three months while he conducted his dangerous forays in the Twin Territories. Cairo cringed at the thought of never knowing if some brigand had placed a price on his head to dispose of him, if a well-aimed bullet had found its fatal mark.

Lawton should go on doing what he did best—apprehending dangerous criminals. And Cairo should return to St. Louis to do what she did best—instructing students in the classroom. Her experiences and adventures with the Gardiners would last her a lifetime! She had been forced to shoot two men to save her own life, forced to bury the dead. She had risen to meet the challenges she had faced, but she was not about to make a habit of it!

Even if Lawton could endure the constant threat to his life, the violence, the uncertainty of the future, Cairo couldn't. She had to get away, to bury the love that had no place in her life or Lawton's. She couldn't change him. She had the feeling Lawton had only confessed his love when he learned the truth about her. Because he felt guilty about all the things he'd done to her, he offered compassion that had been misinterpreted as love.

Cairo had no right to make demands on him, even if she loved him the way she did. She couldn't prey on his guilt and regret when she knew he had mistaken those tormenting emotions for affection. Holding onto Lawton would be like trying to catch a sunbeam in her hand. The sparkling beams would only turn to shadows if she tried to capture him.

Heaving a frustrated sigh, Cairo sank back on her bed to sleep. Tonight there would be no one to help her wile away the hours. Frederick had taken Sarah Gibson to the party that was being held at a newly constructed home on the opposite side of town. Cairo didn't expect Frederick back until late and she expected no other company at all.

She didn't bother to remove her garments or fetch her nightgown from the luggage Sheriff Jubal Newton had returned to her at Lawton's request.

Lawton . . . Cairo closed her eyes and let her mind wander through all the sweet dreams they had made amid the turmoil of battles, feuds, and misconceptions. She could see him hovering over her, his eyes full of hungry desire that matched her own. She could almost feel the scorching heat of his touch, the inner fire that blazed within her when she was in the magic circle of his arms.

Ah, I'm going to miss that silver-eyed devil, she thought to herself. Yet, she knew she couldn't have him and expect to share a peaceful life with him. Besides, a man like Lawton Stone needed no one. He was self-sufficient—a pillar of strength. Their love had been a wild, star-crossed affair. It was a time that had come and gone like the ever-changing wind . . .

Cairo sank into a deep sleep. She knew that while there were some kinds of love that had no beginning nor end, she and Lawton would never enjoy one of them. Their affection for each other had a time and a season, and that, Cairo bleakly reminded herself, was all. She would only torment herself by wanting more than she knew she could have without chaining Lawton to a normal life he couldn't endure.

It didn't matter what either of them felt, Cairo convinced herself as she flounced onto her back. Whatever was between them, it wasn't meant to last. She would do herself a great favor if she didn't allow herself to forget that when sentimental emotion tried to convince her otherwise!

Chapter Twenty-Six

For three days Lawton had been tracking the elusive Snowbird, moving in figure eights and then in circles. He had interrogated two farmhands who had reportedly been seen with the shapely blonde, but both men vehemently denied knowing her. Even when Lawton pressed them, they refused to offer information about her.

According to the hopscotch trails Jarita left behind, she had returned to the ghost town to search for the money Cairo had taken. From the look of things, she had been unsuccessful.

Lawton and his partners had come upon one of Jarita's campsites and the abandoned dugout where she had lingered for a short time, but she was still running loose. Jarita was cunning, he'd give her that. Her brothers had taught her well. She had been milling around the area, never staying in one place long enough to be apprehended.

If only he had begun the hunt immediately after he'd taken Cairo to Doc Pullman's, Lawton chastised himself. But he'd been worried sick and unable to stay away from Cairo while she battled for her life. The time he'd spent with Cairo left Jarita's trail cold. He was two days behind her.

Maybe that female bandit was planning a jail break to free her brother so they could continue this feud? Mulling over that thought, Lawton swung to the ground to survey the hoofprints that disappeared into the shallow creek.

"If you were bitter and grieving, where would you go?" Woody pondered aloud.

"Considering the extremes to which the Gardiners went when Lawton shot Billy and wounded the two remaining brothers, I'd say the Snowbird would want to get back at Lawton. Hell, she may even be following us, waiting her chance to ambush him," Al speculated.

Tucker shook his head to contradict the theory. "She's smart enough to know she couldn't succeed at that without risking her own life," he contended. "The odds are too great, with the four of us riding together."

Al scratched his head and stared into the distance. "Then how could she enjoy the most revenge without actually killing Lawton as she'd like to do?" he asked himself. "What could possibly hurt him worse than simply gunning him down?"

The words were no sooner out of Al's mouth before all four men stared apprehensively at each other.

"Good Lord!" Tucker croaked. "We should have been taking turns standing guard over Cairo instead of tramping off on this wild-goose chase."

Lawton suffered the same anguish he'd endured when he saw Nate Gardiner shove Cairo over the bluff into the quicksand. The thought of Jarita leading them astray and then doubling back to dispose of Cairo turned Lawton's blood to ice. The Snowbird was vengeful and desperate. She had wanted to blow Lawton to smithereens, but there were other lawmen around and she hadn't had the chance. So she had probably resorted to her second alternative—Cairo, who also knew where the money was stashed. If Jarita could recover the money and dispose of Cairo, she would feel some degree of satisfaction. With the money, Jarita could hire herself a mercenary army of desperadoes to launch an attack against the jail and against Lawton.

Damn, why hadn't he thought of it sooner? Some U.S. marshal he'd turned out to be! He'd been so preoccupied with thoughts of Cairo that he'd merely been following the Snowbird's tracks without carefully analyzing his quarry.

As if all four men had read each other's minds, they bounded onto their horses and thundered toward Elreno. Lawton swore he would hate himself until his dying day if he arrived too late. Cairo was still on the mend and unable to defend herself. What chance would she have against the vengeful Jarita Gardiner? The Snowbird thrived on greed and revenge and she was angry and desperate.

Lawton thundered across the prairie at breakneck speed. God, he hoped he and his partners were mistaken about the Snowbird's intentions. If Cairo was safe and sound, he would post guards around the clock.

Lawton wasn't sure he could take another showdown like the one at Canadian Station. He'd had one helluva time corraling his emotions long enough to think straight. And he'd suffered all the tortures of hell while he waited for Cairo to rouse from what had come dangerously close to eternal sleep. Lawton wasn't sure he could cope with those same tormenting emotions again so soon.

The nudge of a cold pistol barrel brought Cairo awake with a start. Her eyes popped open to see Jarita Gardiner glaring murderously at her from behind the gleaming weapon.

"Get up!" Jarita hissed, giving Cairo another jab with the pistol.

If Cairo hadn't seen Jarita at close range she might not have recognized the woman who had tucked her hair beneath a wide-brimmed hat and concealed her feminine figure beneath padded men's clothes. But there was no mistaking Jarita's voice or the flashing green eyes beneath the shadowy veil of her hat.

"I want that stolen money and Lawton Stone's head on a platter, and you're going to help me," Jarita sneered, her voice threaded with contempt.

Even considering the hell Cairo had been through, she was still as determined as she'd always been. She was also stubborn to the core. Her near brushes with disaster had served to make her much stronger, not weaker.

Cairo met Jarita's disdainful glare without batting an eyelash. This may well be Cario's night to die, but there was no way in hell that Jarita Gardiner would enjoy the ultimate victory. Cairo would take the secret to her grave and she would not be used as a pawn to lure Lawton to another death trap, either!

"I'll get up," Cairo informed her. "But that is all I'm

going to do."

"We'll just see about that," Jarita jeered. She cocked the trigger of her Colt. The deadly sound dropped in the silence, but it didn't crack Cairo's firm resolve.

Having been at gunpoint several times before, Cairo was numb to the threat. She had certainly endured worse, at the hands of Jarita's brothers. Cairo wasn't frightened; she was downright angry!

"If you're smart, you'll sneak out the same way you came in, Jarita," Cairo advised as she gathered her legs beneath her and stood up. "Shooting me will accomplish nothing, except adding another crime to your dossier. I'm never going to tell you what you want to know."

"You're a fool," Jarita scoffed, annoyed by Cairo's daring defiance. "All martyrs ever get are marble headstones for their valor. You'll still be just as dead."

"And you'll be without your stolen booty to support you. And Lawton Stone will track you all the way to the ends of the earth."

"But he will suffer to the extreme, knowing I've taken his whore's life," Jarita countered.

"Then you are the fool if you believe I matter to him," Cairo parried. "I'm just one of the many women Lawton has known. He was aptly named. Surely you've realized that by now. He was born without a heart, without sentimental emotion." Her taunting gaze slid over Jarita's concealing garments, noting her rigid stance and gritted teeth. "Nothing cracks Stone . . ."

Jarita despised Cairo's calm defiance. "Where's the money, bitch?"

In response, Cairo tilted her chin a notch higher.

With a burst of fury and impatience, Jarita backhanded Cairo. Even though Cairo was knocked off balance and the back of her knees collided with the edge of the bed, she lifted her leg to kick the pistol from her challenger's hand. The Colt discharged, causing the bullet to ricochet off the metal headboard and lodge in the wall.

Jarita pounced. Her fingers clamped into Cairo's neck. All the suppressed grief and frustration that had been bottled up inside her for the past few days came gushing out and a string of curses leaped from her curled lips. Although she often portrayed the dignified lady to gain information for her bandit brothers, her repertoire of obscenities was extensive. Her anger revealed the sinister side of her personality. The bitter revenge that Jarita had directed toward Lawton was suddenly transferred to Cairo. Jarita could almost see Lawton laughing at her in the depths of Cairo's eyes and she swore another blue streak.

In demented fury, she attempted to choke the life out of her victim. To her credit, Cairo was as much the tigress as Jarita was. She fought back with every ounce of strength she could muster. She shoved Jarita away before the female bandit could do her worst.

Jarita stumbled over the chair and crashed into the wall. Wildly, she glanced around her, searching for her discarded weapon. If this daring bitch wanted to die, Jarita would grant her wish! Then she would seek Lawton out and riddle him with bullets, no matter who else got caught in the crossfire. These two menaces had destroyed Jarita's family and Nate was headed for the gallows. No matter what, the Gardiners would have their revenge!

Cairo sprang at Jarita the instant she saw her outstretched hand clamp around the pistol. Her fingers closed over Jarita's, directing the Colt toward the wall before it barked and smoked for the second time.

Jarita yanked on Cairo's hair and tried to claw her face. Cairo, having seen Lawton double his fist and level a devastating blow, employed the same tactic on Jarita. Unfortunately, it only served to make Jarita more furious than she already was. Jarita struck in blind rage, catching Cairo on the side of the head.

Again Jarita pounced at the fallen pistol, determined to cut this vixen down. This would be her first act of revenge on Lawton. He would return to find his whore stone-cold dead and he would know the agony Jarita had suffered at his hands! Damn that bastard to hell!

The color drained from Lawton's face when he heard the crack of a pistol in the distance. He spurred his steed into a thundering gallop, racing frantically toward the whitewashed cottage on the edge of town.

The second shot may as well have plowed through Lawton's heart. The terror of not knowing whether Cairo was dead or alive was killing him anyway. His imagination was running wild and he cursed the dismal visions that kept leaping into his mind's eye.

Lawton was off his steed in a single bound, charging toward the front door of Frederick's cottage. Each time he collided with a stick of furniture, he flung it out of his way and lunged through the darkness. His eyes were fixed on the dim glow of golden light that seeped from beneath Cairo's bedroom door. But it seemed to take forever to dash through the parlor and into the hall. He could hear the crash of furniture, the screeches, and he endured nine kinds of hell before he barged through the door.

The racket in the hall drew Jarita's attention. She had just retrieved her pistol a third time when Lawton burst into the room. Here at last was the true source of her frustration! Here was the man who had brought death and destruction down on her family.

Soundly cursing Lawton's name, Jarita rolled onto her back to take aim.

"No!" Cairo railed.

She lunged forward to misdirect the bullet. Lawton swore vehemently when Cairo flung herself in the path of the pistol, as well as the Peacemaker he had aimed at Jarita. His body trembled, realizing how close he'd come to squeezing the trigger. If he *had* fired, he would have shot Cairo in the back.

Suddenly, there arose such a clatter of upended furniture and roaring curses in the hall that Lawton swore a stampede of elephants had tromped into the house. The commotion momentarily distracted him, but he reacted to the sound of Jarita's discharging pistol. Instinctively, he dived sideways. When he rolled to his knees, he saw Cairo's fists clenched around Jarita's wrist.

Scrambling across the room on all fours, Lawton snaked out a hand to force Jarita's arm to the floor and smash the pistol beneath his bootheel.

Jarita's eyes spewed venom when she found herself restrained. "I hate you," she seethed. "Hate you . . . !"

Her screeching voice trailed off into hysterical sobs. She offered no regrets for what she'd tried to do, only another round of salty curses that consigned Lawton to the fiery pits of hell.

Al, Woody, and Tucker wedged inside the door to view the three bodies that were sprawled atop each other.

"Al, put the cuffs on the Snowbird," Tucker ordered brusquely. His concerned gaze strayed to Cairo, who was pale and trembling. "You okay, honey?"

Cairo rolled sideways to sink down on the floor before nodding affirmatively to Tucker. Her eyes drifted to Lawton, cherishing the sight of him, wanting to throw her arms around him and hold him for all the times she'd longed to be in his arms the past few days and couldn't.

"Traitor!" Jarita screamed as Al snapped the shackles on her wrists. "Worthless bastard," she spat into his face.

"Take her to jail," Lawton muttered. "She and Nate can enjoy their family reunion behind bars before she's carted off to the penitentiary."

While Jarita directed a few more vicious curses to all lawmen everywhere and to Lawton Stone in particular, Lawton stared somberly at Cairo. When everyone had filed out, Lawton took Cairo's hand and drew her to her feet and into his arms.

"If you're up to physical battles, does that mean you've recovered enough to make love to me?" he teased gently.

Maybe Lawton could quickly switch moods after such a harrowing experience, but Cairo certainly couldn't! She had been mulling over his unflappable composure in her mind before Jarita had attacked her. Cairo knew she would never be more than a lusty interlude between Lawton's dangerous manhunting expeditions. She'd never be able to come to terms with knowing exactly what kind of life-threatening showdowns he faced each day. She could barely cope with it now, even when she wanted him so badly she could almost taste him!

Cairo flung herself away and snatched up her satchels. "I'm taking the first stage out of Elreno." She surprised herself when she said the words without her voice cracking in two.

Lawton blinked in disbelief as Cairo sailed toward the door. "You can't leave. I love you!"

"Not enough, you don't," Cairo battled the urge to toss her luggage aside and dart into his arms. He sounded so surprised, so hurt . . . Lawton hurt? The man *never* buckled to any emotion!

"How much do I have to love you to get you to stay?" he growled as he stalked after her.

"More than you can possibly imagine, I can tell you that! If anything, you've confused regret and compassion for love." Cairo kept right on walking, certain she was doing the best thing for both of them. "The stolen money is buried inside the south foundation of the hotel in Canadian Station," she informed him. "There's a scrawny hound in town that needs a home. Please find him one. He was the only friend I had for a time."

"For chrissake, woman, will you slow down!" Lawton exploded as he sidestepped the upturned furniture. "I said I love you and I do! And I think you love me, even if you won't admit it. We have to talk!"

"There's nothing left to say," Cairo grumbled as she tossed her satchels over Lawton's stallion.

"The hell there isn't!" he bellowed at the stubborn beauty in frustration. "I want you to marry me." His voice softened considerably. "I want you to love me back, from now until forever . . ."

A mist of tears clouded Cairo's eyes as she stared down at the muscular hulk of man from atop the saddle. "I *do* love you, Lawton," she assured him with a tremulous sigh. "I guess I always have and I probably always will. But you live on the edge and I want a normal life. You don't even know what that is. And you wouldn't be content with it, even if you did. Danger is your middle name and hunting criminals is the only game you know how to play. There isn't room for me in your life."

Well, didn't that beat all! For the first time in his life, he was really and truly in love. But the object of his affection, the firebrand who'd just admitted she loved him, too, was riding out of his life, just as she'd come in—like a veritable whirlwind. What kind of justice was that?

"I'm planning to make room for you . . . for us . . ." Lawton declared.

Cairo wiped at the tears and scoffed down at him. "How much room? A month here and there between forays?" She nudged the steed down the street. "No thank you. You would become resentful when I demanded more than a few stolen moments between battles."

"I would not!" Lawton scowled as he loped along behind the stubborn minx who had stolen his horse and left him afoot. "I plan to be around a helluva lot more than that! You get into too much trouble when you're left alone too long."

"Me?" she hooted. Swiveling in the saddle, she gaped at him. "I'm a simple schoolteacher from Missouri. I never found myself in the middle of so many perilous

adventures until I met you. *You're* the one who attracts trouble, not *me!*"

"And *you're* the one who attracts people who attract trouble," he hurled at her.

The loud voices in the street had attracted Al, Tucker, and Woody's attention as they filed out of Sheriff Newton's office. Tucker grinned as he watched Lawton trotting alongside his own stallion, which the sassy blonde had confiscated without being charged with horse thieving.

"Well, well, it looks like the little lady has the legendary Lawton Stone down to begging," Tucker snickered. "I never thought I'd live to see this day."

"And *you* keep calling *me* Lover Boy," Woody smirked. "*I've* never created such a scene."

Al propped himself against the outer wall of the jail and sighed appreciatively. "She sure is pretty, isn't she? All fire and spirit. You may have called Jarita Gardiner the Snowbird, but Cairo Calhoun is definitely a *Fire*bird. And boy, is she giving Lawton hell!"

"Cairo has indeed lit a fire under Lawton," Tucker agreed with a hearty chuckle. "Now who said Stone doesn't burn?"

Tucker was right! Stone did burn and Lawton was ablaze with frustration. Cairo was letting loose with both barrels and Lawton was in the direct line of fire.

"All I asked of you was safe passage through the Twin Territories. And all I got was shot up, shot down, and buried in quicksand," Cairo raged on. "That is not what I call a peaceful existence. I want children and a dependable husband and a home and—"

"—How many?" Lawton interrupted.

Cairo clamped her mouth shut and stared bemusedly at him. "How many what? Homes? I should think one would be enough."

"No, children," he clarified.

"More babies than you'd be around to make," she snapped crossly.

"A home where?" he fired at her.

"How the blazes do I know?" Cairo exploded in exasperation.

"And who'll be your husband? Freddie the physician?"

Cairo glared at him. "I don't know, but I'm sure I'll find a suitable match as soon as I get over you."

A roguish grin bracketed his sensuous lips. "How soon do you expect to be over me?"

Her breath came out like air rushing from a deflating balloon. "How should I know? I only know that it won't work . . ." Her voice trailed off when Lawton abruptly reached up to pluck her out of the saddle and into his arms.

Lawton carried Cairo, worming and squirming, toward the hotel. "Damn, Cairo Calhoun, you are one stubborn woman," he declared despite her outraged protests as he stepped with her in his arms onto the boardwalk and into the lobby.

"Put me down!" Cairo spluttered.

"Not until we find a private place to talk this out," Lawton marched up the steps to his rented room.

When Lawton disappeared into the hotel, toting his wriggling bundle, Al frowned curiously. "What do you suppose Law plans to do with her?"

Tucker burst out laughing. "Damn, Kid, if you can't

figure that out all by yourself, you've got more to learn than I ever dreamed possible!" He gestured his bushy red head toward the abandoned steed. "Go fetch Law's black stallion, Kid. I've got the feeling that if Law does any riding tonight, it won't be the kind that requires a horse and saddle."

Woody reprimanded Tucker as Al ambled down the street to do as he'd been ordered. "Don't say things like that, Tuck. It get my glands in an uproar."

"You were born with your glands in an uproar, Lover Boy," Tucker teased.

Woody sighed. "I could do with a little female companionship right about now . . . Make that a lot," he quickly amended as arousing visions danced in his head.

Tucker pushed away from the wall and ambled across the street toward the saloon. "I need a drink. Old as I am, I know better than to tangle with women. But watching Lawton's got me thinking things that will only get a crusty old man like me into trouble."

"Hey! What am I supposed to do with Lawton's horse?" Al called to the marshals who had swaggerd toward the saloon.

Woody glanced at Tucker and grinned. "You're right. That boy has a lot to learn. If he had any sense he'd know Lawton isn't going to need his horse until morning . . . if even that soon."

Tucker scowled. "Damn it, Woody, now you're getting *my* glands all stirred up!"

Chapter Twenty-Seven

The instant Lawton set Cairo to her feet she sought out the farthest corner and stuffed herself in it. Her chin tilted to a belligerent angle and she crossed her arms beneath her heaving breasts in a gesture of stubborn defiance. Cairo knew how vulnerable she was to this mountain of a man and she didn't dare let him within ten feet of her. She had to be sensible and realistic. She had to consider what was best for both of them. Oh certainly, Lawton could promise all sorts of things now to discourage her from leaving, but she knew she was only a temporary fascination. Within a month, he would seek out the adventure that was so much a part of his life with some lame excuse that he was duty-bound to trot off to be with his partners.

The firm set of Cairo's delicate jaw and the spark in her emerald eyes assured Lawton that he would need a silver-tongued lawyer to plead his case for him. Lawton knew his limitations when it came to his feelings, so instead of stumbling through an explanation, he merely heaved a sigh. "Tell me what you want, Cai."

"I want you to leave this room, this town, this territory," she declared in rapid staccato.

"I was referring to your long-term future," he clarified.

Her arms dropped to her side and her chin elevated another stubborn notch when he took a step toward her. "I already told you that I wanted to lead a normal life. *Normal,* Lawton. You are *not* normal!"

He took a second step in Cairo's direction, prompting her to take a defensive step backward. "Since you hardly qualify as normal yourself, I don't see how that's possible, minx."

Green eyes flashed. "If you intend to mock everything I say, there is no point in continuing this conversation," she retaliated.

He took another step forward, backing her as far into the corner as she could possibly go. "I think the real point here is whether you truly love me," he said. "I'm willing to compromise . . . Are you?"

"I seriously doubt that your idea of compromise will coincide with mine," she countered, watching him like a wary doe.

She knew how quickly this lion of a man could pounce. And if he did, she would find herself captured in those strong, sinewy arms. She never had been able to think straight when her body was molded to his. She had to keep a safe distance!

Lawton was getting nowhere fast. His tactic of countering all her arguments was failing miserably. Although he was not adept at explanations, it seemed he was going to have to fumble his way through one. The whole story of his painful past spilled out. "I've spent my whole life condemning women because of my own miserable excuse of a mother. She was a whore who found herself with an unwanted child," Lawton begrudgingly admitted without glancing at Cairo. "I wouldn't know my own father if he ran head-on into me."

Pacing back and forth to gather steam, Lawton continued. "The man I called Father took my mother in and tried to make a respectable life for her. He gave me a name. But when I was five years old, my mother decided she'd had all the respectability she could tolerate and she ran off with the first man who caught her fancy."

Torment flooded his face before he managed to conceal his emotions. "For years, I bore the agony of thinking I was such a despicable child that my mother had abandoned me. My stepfather's own bitterness rubbed off on me. He swore off women forever and I watched him wither away because I think he'd actually fallen in love with my mother. But she didn't care who she hurt because she never knew the meaning of love and devotion. She wanted excitement and adventure, not a family and lasting ties."

Cairo's eyes followed Lawton as he paced the room like a caged tiger. "I'm sorry," she murmured sympathetically.

Lawton didn't seem to hear her. At long last he had allowed himself to voice the torments of his childhood, his innermost feelings. And once he started, the emotions came tumbling out. "My stepfather took to drinking until it became his addiction, his crutch. Our small farm fell into ruin and the bills piled up. When I was twelve he decided to end it all and I was left without a home or a family. As far as I could tell, love and women were things that destroyed men. With a chip on my shoulder and a grudge against any sentimental emotions, I took odd jobs at neighboring ranches to support myself. When I was old enough and competent enough to handle weapons, I joined the Army to help clear the area of the Indian problem since I couldn't seem to battle my own problems. It seemed easier to fight a battle I could see rather than the invisible ones that were tangled inside me."

A mist of tears clouded Cairo's eyes as she watched Lawton wear a path on the rug. Her heart went out to him. His childhood was so unlike the warm and loving atmosphere she had enjoyed with her parents. Lawton had never learned the meaning of caring and sharing within a family. He'd been on his own, forced to deal with his unpleasant past and cynical concepts.

Cairo well remembered how devastated she had been when her mother had died in a futile attempt to give birth to a second child after two miscarriages. The infant only outlived her mother by a day. Cairo had endured that heartache eight years ago and the pain was still there. But being abandoned had been much worse on Lawton who hadn't been old enough to understand. He had no one to explain the disappointments of life to him.

"I'm no saint," Lawton admitted abruptly. "I admit I've had my share of women, because I'm a man with a man's need. But I refused to become so involved with a woman that it devastated me the way it did my stepfather. It was safer not to care, not to feel more than temporary pleasure."

Still he didn't venture a glance in Cairo's direction. He just rattled on, talking more than he had in all his thirty-one years. "I thought life was cut and dried. If a man was lucky he'd get by without having his heart torn out by the taproot by some scheming female who used him for her own selfish purposes."

Finally Lawton paused from his pacing and fixed his somber gaze on the bewitching blonde. "And then you came along to shatter every rule I'd written about life and love and women. The first time I saw you, I thought you were Jarita Gardiner, come to lure me into an ambush for killing her youngest brother and wounding the other two. I was positively certain you wanted me dead. And even knowing that, I was still obsessed with you. I still wanted you."

He gave a hollow laugh. "You'll never know the hell I went through. I knew I was the world's biggest fool because of my fascination for you. I kept waiting for you to attempt to kill me. And when I shot you in what I thought was self-defense, it nearly killed me."

The expression on his face testified to that mental anguish and Cairo was deeply moved by his words and his display of emotions. She was seeing a human side of Lawton Stone that she never knew existed.

"Lawton, I—"

He held up his hand to stop her. If he was going to bare his heart and soul, he wanted no interruption for fear he'd become derailed from his train of thought. "I decided to try a different tactic by confessing I loved you, hoping to earn your loyalty before you and your brothers satisfied your vendetta. But I think I knew, even then, that I had truly fallen in love with you. I was not only risking my life, but also my heart."

"Lawton, I—"

"And then, all of a sudden, there was danger at every

turn and unforeseen complications," he plowed on without allowing Cairo to squeeze a word in edgewise. "I wanted you out of my life before you completely destroyed me the way my mother destroyed my stepfather. And when you *were* out of my life, Al Fontain confessed that he had falsely identified you and that you weren't Jarita Gardiner after all. But by then, you thought I was a raving lunatic."

"If you would only let me say—"

He wouldn't. He was still plowing ahead like a steam-powered freight train. "I swore dying would have been easier than finding you captured by the Gardiners. And when I feared you wouldn't survive that tormenting ordeal, I felt myself dying on the inside."

"It seems to me—"

Again Cairo was cut off by his deep, persistent voice. "If you leave me now, I'll go back to the way I was, only I'll be worse. I'll be an empty shell of a man who fights everybody's battles for them because I can't wage war on my own troubled emotions."

Lawton wheeled to face her. His expression so genuine that Cairo was thunderstruck. "I want a real life, Cai . . . with you and nobody else. I want to know what it's like to love and be loved in return. I want children who know their father, little ones who bask in the warmth of their father's love for their mother. I want all the things I never had! I want you because you're the only woman I've ever loved. You're the one who can make my life worth living. I'm willing to compromise by giving up my badge and settling down to build the home and the ranch I've always wanted and never had. All the adventure I want is winning your love and keeping it until we turn old and gray together. Will you stay, Cai? Will you love me as long and well as I want to love you?"

Cairo was dumbstruck. She had expected a one-sided compromise in which she did all the giving and he did all the taking. But he was offering the supreme sacrifice. And the most startling part of all was that Lawton Stone actually looked as if he meant every word he said!

Lawton never thought he'd see the day that Cairo Calhoun stood speechless. She'd always had an answer for everything and had been quick to counter any remark or insult he'd ever flung at her.

"You've tried to interrupt me for the past fifteen minutes. Here's your chance to say something . . . Anything!" he prompted her.

Cairo tried to speak, but her tongue was glued to her palate. Her lips opened and shut like the damper on a chimney but no words came out. Her heart had swelled with so much pleasure it very nearly suffocated her. Lawton Stone really did love her! She wasn't the time he was killing between gun battles. He wanted a future, a home and her . . . for all the right reasons!

When Cairo continued to stand there gaping at him as if he were a creature from another planet, Lawton rushed on, hoping to assure her that he'd given the matter plenty of serious consideration.

"I've decided to buy the abandoned land that Canadian Station sets on and build a ranch with the reward money and salary I've been saving all these years. It seems to me that the hotel could be refurbished to make a grand home. The blacksmith barn would stable horses and cattle, all of which could be sold to the army posts at Fort Sill, Fort Reno, and to the Indian agencies to supply mounts and beef. The other buildings in town would serve as sheds and tackrooms. A few head of sheep would ensure the grass is clipped and—"

He paused to peer into Cairo's wide green eyes, then he continued. "I know what became of your father and I'm sorry we didn't arrive in time. But I think he would be pleased if you claimed the land he'd chosen when he made the run into Oklahoma. We can enjoy the dream he wasn't allowed to fulfill in this new territory. And when our time comes, we'll join him on the hill that overlooks the river . . . side by side throughout eternity." His silver eyes probed deeply into hers "I mean it, Cai. I want you by my side now and forever because you're the only woman I'll ever love."

Cairo abandoned her corner of the room to fly into his arms. Tears streamed down her cheeks as her pent-up emotions came flooding out. She clung to Lawton, holding on to him as if he were the most precious treasure life had to offer . . . because he was! She wanted to share his dreams, to transform the ghost town into a ranch that was teeming with love and laughter and new life. Her father would have been delighted by Lawton's thoughtfulness.

Lawton closed his eyes and savored the feel of Cairo's body molded tightly to his. His arms encircled her trim waist and he bent his head to nuzzle his chin against her cheek.

"Does this mean you'll stay with me, Cai?" Am I forgiven for all my unjustified suspicions?" he murmured.

Cairo tilted her head back, allowing the mane of

silver-gold to stream down her back. She saw the love shining in the depths of his glittering silver eyes. He was offering a love to last eternity.

How could she have possibly thought she could leave Lawton Stone behind when he had taken possession of her heart, soul, and body? She would have withered away for the want of his love if she had tried to leave him. Now his love was hers for the taking—her dream come true.

"For a woman who usually speaks volumes, you haven't said much of anything," Lawton teased as he dropped a kiss to her petal-soft lips.

She smiled as she reached up to rearrange his raven hair. "What I have to say defies words," she murmured provocatively as her hand glided over his shoulders to nimbly loosen the buttons on his shirt.

When her fingers slid against the carpet of thick hair that matted his chest, Lawton's breath lodged in his throat. It still mystified him that the mere touch of her hand could ignite such wildfires inside him. He was like a torch that had been saturated with oil, awaiting the flame of her caress, the breath of her kiss.

"I think perhaps I should show you how I feel about you and your plans for our future," she whispered against his thudding chest. "Sometimes vocal confessions seem frightfully inadequate . . ."

Lawton swore he'd melted down into the consistency of marmalade when Cairo pushed his shirt from his shoulders to grant herself the freedom to explore his bare flesh. Her lips whispered over his chest in the slightest breath of a kiss. Her fingertips swirled over his belly and hips with such maddening skill that he feared he would drip onto the floor in a pool of bubbling desire. For a man who had been hailed as a pillar of strength, who possessed a core of solid rock and a will of iron, he suddenly wasn't living up to his reputation!

And what a devastating temptress she had become! *His* temptress, he thought with tremendous pride. He had taught her all she knew about passion . . . until that ruthless band of outlaws had . . .

Lawton stiffened at the revolting thought of what Cairo had endured. He feared she intended to seduce him to prove her affection. But was it too soon for her to face those haunting nightmares? Would he touch her and remind her of the humiliating ordeal she had endured? As much as he longed to make wild sweet love to her, he could wait . . . if he had to.

Cairo frowned when Lawton took her hands from him and retreated a step. And what was more surprising was that he suddenly refused to meet her quizzical gaze.

"Maybe we should simply say the words to each other." Lawton's voice was ragged from his unappeased desire. "Maybe we should wait until you've had the chance to put your . . . er . . . experiences . . . with . . ." He hem-hawed and sighed awkwardly. "Uh . . . until you've . . . well, you know . . . with those desperadoes."

Cairo's mind groped to fill in all the blanks he'd left in his jumbled explanation of his standoffish behavior. It finally dawned on her what he was trying to avoid saying. Cairo suddenly recalled the comment he'd made while she was recovering from her ordeal in the quicksand. At the time, she hadn't had the chance to clear up his misconceptions.

As she sashayed toward him, her hand slid along the

waistband of his breeches and Lawton gasped for breath.

"Curse it, I'm trying to show noble restraint and consideration!" he blurted out, battling the ravenous hunger that was gnawing at him.

"Admirable, to be sure, but hardly necessary," Cairo chortled lightheartedly. "Because of your daring rescue, I was spared any . . . er . . . uh . . . experiences with . . . well, you know," she explained, poking fun at his fumbling attempt to explain himself.

"You were?" Relief washed over his craggy features. With a roguish grin, he snaked out an arm to tow Cairo toward him. "Well, in that case . . ." His voice dropped to a seductive growl that sent a fleet of goose bumps cruising over her skin.

Lawton kissed her with fierce possessiveness as he molded her body into his. Cairo instantly melted in his arms, reveling in the sweet magic of his embrace. She displayed not one iota of reserve when she returned his fervent kiss and bold caress. Her hands roamed everywhere at once, making him her cherished possession, assuring him that she was as hungry for him as he was for her.

"Lord, it seems a lifetime since I've made love to you," Lawton breathed as his lips skimmed over her throat. "Years, in fact. I've wanted—"

Cairo touched her forefinger to his sensuous lips to shush him. "For a man who has always had an aversion to idle chatter, you're suddenly babbling like a magpie." Intent on enticing him into silence, Cairo retreated to tug at her gaping shirt. Buttons flew and the garment fluttered to the floor in a crumpled heap. Having received his undivided attention and most appreciative stare, Cairo hooked her thumbs in the band of her breeches and slowly pushed them off her hips. When she was wearing nothing but a provocative smile, she sashayed across the room, flinging him a seductive glance over her shoulder.

Lawton swore his heart would burst while he watched Cairo peel off her clothes in the most tantalizing manner imaginable. He took one look at her well-sculptured figure and he went hot all over. Even his eyebrows ached with the want of this gorgeous nymph!

Mesmerized, he watched Cairo stretch out on the bed, striking a most sensuous pose. Lawton swallowed the entire roomful of air and unleashed passion roared in his ears like an approaching thunderstorm. When Cairo crooked her finger in silent invitation, Lawton feared his boneless legs would fail him before he joined her in bed.

Where he found the strength to move, Lawton didn't know. Desire alone must have swept him across the room and to Cairo's side. He moaned when Cairo's adventurous hands trailed over the dark furring of hair that trickled down his belly. He had allowed her to remove his breeches, permitted her to have her way with him. Her fingertips and lips seared his flesh as she discarded the last of his clothing. With deliberate concentration, she showered him with passionate kisses and tantalizing caresses that drove him mad with wanting.

His body reacted instinctively to the feel of her skillful touch. He reveled in the pleasure of being loved to ultimate distraction. Cairo touched him everywhere, tenderly at first and then with fervent possessiveness.

She stroked him, teased him, pleased him, left him discovering things he'd never known about passion that was embroidered with love.

Finally Lawton could endure no more of the sweet, maddening torment. He had to return the pleasure she'd bestowed on him. She was the light of his life, his reason for being, and he'd never get enough of her.

"Lord, Cai, do you have any idea how much I love you?" he asked before his lips sought hers in a devouring kiss.

When he raised his raven head, a challenging sparkle glinted in her emerald eyes. "So you keep saying," she purred as her index finger trailed over his shoulder to sketch designs on his belly. "But I keep wondering how long it's going to be before you get around to showing me how deep this supposed affection runs."

He grinned rakishly as his hand scaled her hip to encircle each breast. When Cairo instinctively arched toward his caress, his eyes twinkled with masculine pride. He exulted in the power he held over her. He could touch her and she surrendered completely to him.

"I'm going to show you just how deep my love runs," he vowed. "I hope you don't have anything else planned for the rest of the night. It may take me a good long while . . ."

As his lips followed in the wake of his masterful hands, Cairo couldn't think of anything she wanted to do for the rest of her life except love this magnificent man. Never in her wildest dreams had she expected to earn the legendary Lawton Stone's love and devotion, but she had indeed won her place in his heart and soul. He had made love to her several times before, but never quite like this! He worshipped her with tender caresses and reverent kisses. Each display of passion was entwined with genuine affection.

His skillful hands and lips claimed possession of her body. He whispered his need for her, his love for her, with each bone-melting kiss and nerve-shattering caress. He savored her; he devoured her; he pleasured her until she was writhing helplessly in his arms.

Cairo begged shamelessly, urging him to fulfill the monstrous cravings he'd aroused in her. Her body quivered with needs that burgeoned in the core of her being and blossomed on each nerve ending.

When Lawton braced himself above her, Cairo's tangled lashes fluttered up to meet his silvery gaze. The expression in his eyes held her hypnotized. She was so stirred by the sentimental emotion mirrored there that she feared she would burst with pride and pleasure.

"Make no mistake, my wild sweet love," Lawton whispered as his muscular body uncoiled upon hers. "You're every breath I take. I don't want you because I need you to satisfy these raging passions." He glided upon her, becoming the living flame within her. "I want you because I love you . . . even more tomorrow than today . . . until the end of time."

As his body enveloped her, holding her to him as if she were a vital part of him, Cairo offered herself to him in total abandon. Her senses were filled with the taste, scent, and feel of him. Her hands slid down the whipcord muscles of his shoulders to his hips, absorbing him, reveling in the ecstasy that loving him aroused in her.

Her breath caught in her throat when his taut body drove into hers. She met each hard thrust, giving all within her power to give, sharing a splendor that defied description.

Pulsating tremors riveted her when she was swept away by the most remarkable sensations she'd ever experienced. A startled gasp escaped her lips when fierce, intense pleasure engulfed her. Cairo dug her nails into Lawton's muscled back as the world careened crazily around her. She was holding on for dear life while she flew through a dizzying whirlpool of darkness, sensation upon sensation encompassing her as Lawton shuddered above her.

"I love you so much it hurts," Cairo gasped as she nuzzled her cheek against his chest. "It almost frightens me to think of ever losing you."

Lawton smiled down into her flushed features. "I'm not going anywhere, sweetheart," he assured her, his voice thick with the aftereffects of sublime passion. "Each time you tried to escape me, I followed like your shadow." He bent to savor her petal-soft lips. "Just try to escape me for more than a few hours at a time and see where it gets you."

Cairo's emerald eyes twinkled not only with pleasure but also with a flare of mischief. "I warned you that I would be very demanding of your time," she reminded him. "You may find yourself wishing you had a few hours alone."

He grinned as he slid down her silken body to flick his tongue at the ripe buds of her breasts. "Somehow I can't imagine that being alone would compare to this. And when you want me, you have but to send a message and I'll . . ."

His voice trailed off when a fleeting thought skipped across his mind. "And speaking of that . . ." He stared quizzically at her. "Who sent you those two messages while we were in Fort Smith? I could have sworn the Gardiners were making contact with you to plan my Waterloo."

Cairo glanced at the wall, but his hand cupped her chin, forcing her to meet his inquisitive gaze. "Answer me, Cai," he demanded. "There will be no more secrets between us—ever."

"In light of your marriage proposal, those messages no longer matter," she hedged.

His eyes narrowed. "Cairo . . ." His voice held a subtle warning that he was going to pester her until she told him what he wanted to know.

She sighed in resignation. "The first one, accompanied by the flowers, was a marriage proposal from a man I knew in St. Louis. And if you hadn't made such a to-do about it I wouldn't have carried that business with the flowers to such extremes," she added with an impish grin. "The second note was from Daniel Siler, the lawyer. He offered legal advice if I found myself in need of it. His other offer was a bit more personal—"

Lawton's burst of laughter interrupted her. "I'll just bet it was." He went back to stroking and caressing her curvaceous body. "A pity neither man knew what they were going to be missing," he whispered against her quivering flesh. "Now you belong to me and there will be no other men in your life."

Cairo drew his head back to hers, aching to have her lips beneath his, hungry for the taste of his kiss. "No other man could satisfy me," she assured him. "Once I've had the best, no one else would do."

He smiled rakishly "Lord, what you do to my male pride, woman, not to mention the effect you have on my male anatomy . . ."

Her forefinger drifted over the bunched muscles of his back to caress his lean hips. "I feel like loving you again . . ." she whispered as she moved provocatively beneath him.

"And I feel like letting you," he whispered as he lowered his head to offer her a kiss that held intimate promises of the ecstasy to come.

"I do love you so," Cairo murmured back to him.

"Keep reminding me," Lawton replied between breathless kisses. "I'll never tire of hearing it."

They set sail on the most intimate of journeys, proving the strength of their love for each other. And when the loving was over, they nestled in each other's arms and drifted into blissful dreams.

A little while later, they roused to the gnawing of hungry needs that constantly demanded feeding while they were cuddled in each other's arms. They basked in a love that had been tested and tried, time and time again, until neither of them could deny its right to blossom and grow. It was a love for all times and all seasons—a love that burned as bright as Oklahoma moonlight.

Epilogue

Oklahoma Territory
April 1892

Tucker McGuire halted his steed on the rise of ground that overlooked the sprawling ranch that had once been known as Canadian Station. An amused chuckle rattled in his chest each time he spied the sign that greeted travelers who passed by. The marker that had once indicated the town of Canadian Station now declared this panoramic ranch to be:

Cairo, Oklahoma—closest place to paradise, this side of heaven

"Every time we pass this way, the ranch looks better and better," Woody commented. His gaze drifted over the refurbished hotel, barn, and outbuildings that had received a fresh coat of white paint and boasted an ever-growing herd of livestock.

Al Fontain sighed appreciatively at the landscape.

Although he had learned the ropes of marshaling, thanks to Woody and Tuck, he had to admit he would have delighted in exchanging places with Lawton. The ex-marshal had become a most respected citizen in these parts. He had been selling livestock to army posts and Indian agencies, as well as to the hopeful land seekers who were lining up to make the run into the area that had once belonged to the Cheyenne and Arapaho in western Oklahoma, on the nineteenth of April.

On the twenty-second of September, 1891, the surplus lands belonging to the Iowa, Sac and Fox, and the Shawnee-Pottawatomie tribes had been opened to white settlement by run. According to reports, twenty thousand people had made the run for the seven-thousand quarter sections of available land. The value of horses had skyrocketed before the run of '91, and in anticipation of the run of '92, Lawton had supplied a great number of horses and other livestock to the would-be settlers and he had turned a handsome profit the past two years.

"Sure looks as if Law has made a name and a place for himself in Oklahoma," Al commented.

Before Tucker could voice a remark, strange noises blared out the open windows of the converted hotel.

"What the hell is that?" Tucker cringed at the annoying racket.

Woody nudged his steed past the sign that welcomed them to Cairo, Oklahoma. "My God, I think Law is teaching the twins to sing," he groaned. "And here I thought I'd heard my last chorus of 'Skip to My Lou!"

"Good Lord, a trio!" Tucker grumbled in dismay.

Al sighed heavily. "Of all the things Lawton Stone can do exceptionally well, he never could carry a tune.

It sounds as if his two sons are carrying on the family tradition."

As the threesome neared the house, they noticed the farm hands cupping their ears for relief. But nothing helped. All that could be said for the crooning was that it was loud! Even the mongrel hound that had taken such a liking to Lawton at first licking was howling at the annoying noise.

"Law! You have guests out here!" Tucker bellowed over the eardrum-shattering sound.

The scuffling of feet heralded the arrival of Lawton, bookended by two miniature copies of their father. At two years of age, Rylan and Derrick Stone were pint-size versions, except for their bright green eyes, of the giant who filled the doorway to overflowing.

"Uncle Tuck! Uncle Woody! Uncle Al!" the twins bugled as they plunged forward in greeting.

"I was just teaching the boys to sing," Lawton announced as he ambled off the step.

"So we heard," Tucker grunted. He swung from the saddle to scoop up one of the rambunctious twins.

"You're sure doing a bang-up job with those singing lessons," Woody smirked before he whisked the other toddler up in his arms and tickled him until he giggled and cried uncle. He glanced curiously around him. "Where's Cai? I would have thought she would have refused to let you give the boys singing lessons."

Lawton grinned as he took the reins and tethered the horses. "Cai doesn't complain about my singing anymore. In fact, she rarely complains about anything I do."

"Wrapped her around your little finger, did you?" Tucker's voice indicated he suspected it was the other way around.

His thoughts trailed off when Cairo sailed out the front door, and he sighed appreciatively. Cairo had always been breathtaking with her lustrous mane of silver-blond hair, dancing green eyes, and curvaceous figure. Now she was absolutely radiant! The sun caught in the silky tendrils and lifted the waist-length strands like an unseen hand. She had matured into a full-fledged woman the past three years. In all his travels, Tucker had never met another woman to match Cairo's exceptional beauty and spirit. She was, he thought, one of a kind, just like her husband.

The instant Cairo appeared to greet their unexpected guests, Lawton's gaze fell on his bewitching wife. Tucker knew right then and there that Lawton *was* in fact the one who was wrapped around Cairo's finger. There was so much love and pride in Lawton's expression that it put a sentimental lump in Tucker's throat.

When Cairo invited them inside, Tucker hung back beside Lawton. A teasing grin settled on his weather-beaten features. "Admit it, Law. You're so henpecked you molt twice a year."

Lawton shrugged off the taunt. "I'm so damned happy, Tuck, you can't even rile me with your jibes. I feel like singing all the time."

"Don't yield to the temptation," Tucker advised. "All your farmhands will quit and you'll be managing this place by yourself."

With a chuckle, Law followed Tucker inside. While Cairo and the housekeeper set food on the table, Lawton quizzed his ex-partners about their activities. Tucker, Woody, and Al had recently accepted positions as marshals in Oklahoma because Judge Parker's jurisdiction had been divided among the new regions of the expanding territory. The lawlessness that plagued the far reaches of the area had become the concern of these three competent marshals.

Although Tucker, Woody, and Al talked of their forays in No Man's Land, which now fell under the jurisdiction of Oklahoma Territory, Lawton felt no restless urge to rejoin the ranks of the marshals. He knew exactly where he wanted to be—offering his sons the childhood he'd never had. He never believed it possible to be so content. Cairo had enriched his life so thoroughly that it was filled beyond capacity.

An uneasiness settled over Cairo as she observed Lawton chuckle at one of Tucker's many anecdotes of misadventure during their campaigns. When Woody mentioned some of their mutual acquaintances, Lawton listened intently. And when Al announced there was another position open in the area, Cairo cringed. She couldn't help but wonder if Lawton pined for the adventure of traveling with his former partners. She felt guilty about confining him.

While the foursome chatted, Cairo cleared the table and ambled out the back door. Impulsively, she strolled toward the section of the river that was skirted by a gentle slope of sand that Lawton had marked off as a safe area for bathing and wading. Tucking the hem of her skirt between her legs and into the buckle of her belt, Cairo waded out to the sand bar that lay only six inches beneath the meandering bend of river.

She sighed as she grappled with her thoughts. Each time the marshals passed through or stayed the night, Cairo went through agony. She knew all he had to do was announce that he was ready to rejoin the ranks and a badge would be pinned on his chest. It had been almost three years since Lawton had resigned. Was he becoming restless with this new life of his? Was he having second thoughts that he refused to admit to her because of the promises he'd made that night when he'd proposed?

"Is something troubling you, Cai?"

Cairo jerked up her head to see Lawton, arms folded over his chest and feet askance, standing on the riverbank.

"No," she lied with a cheery smile. "I thought you might like some time alone with your friends."

Silence stretched between them and Cairo glanced away.

"Tucker asked me to rejoin them to patrol the land which will be open for settlers," Lawton said quietly.

"I rather thought he would." Cairo braced herself for disappointment. Biting her trembling lips, she raised her eyes to peer into those entrancing pools of mercury. "Are you?"

"*Are* I what?

Cairo glared at him, unable to control her mounting concern and frustration. "You know perfectly well what!" she flared, stamping her foot and splattering water on herself.

His dark brows lifted in taunt. "Do I see signs of that legendary Calhoun temper surfacing?" He clucked his tongue in disapproval. "I thought we had passed that stage a long time ago, love."

"Curse it! Answer me!" Cairo demanded impatiently as she splashed through the water to confront him face to face. "Are you going with them or aren't you?"

"And leave you to every hot-blooded horse trader, homesteader, and soldier who happens by under the pretense of buying our prize stock when I know damned good and well they simply want to see if I'm still around so they can carry you off?" Lawton snorted explosively. "I'd spend all my time wondering if you'd still be here when I got back."

He still hadn't answered the question to her satisfaction. "You know I can take care of myself," Cairo reminded him. "Now, are you going or not?"

"Not." His arm slid around her waist, drawing her full length against him. His smiling lips skitted over her sweet mouth like a bee courting nectar. "Do you remember when I told you I'd love you more tomorrow than today?"

Cairo nodded mutely, distracted by the flood of warmth that surged through her when Lawton cradled her in his arms. It had been almost three years and still she was so enthralled with his dynamic man that she couldn't think straight when he touched her.

Lawton tipped her head back, forcing her to meet his unblinking stare. "Nothing has changed, except that my feelings for you grow deeper and stronger with every tomorrow we share." His forefinger traced her features with adoration. "This is where my heart is, Cai. My days of marshaling are a closed chapter. I never really started living until I met you and I don't plan to give you up to go chasing criminals."

Effortlessly, he scooped her into his arms and waded over to the sandbar. The suggestive gleam in his eyes caused Cairo to glance apprehensively toward the house. "We have guests and the twins—"

"Are being doted over by their adopted uncles,"

Lawton murmured as he made short work of divesting Cairo of her clothes, as well as his own.

"But—"

When he plied her with a few dozen soul-shattering caresses and kisses, Cairo forgot what she'd intended to say, but a new thought sprang to mind and then to tongue. "Are you sure you aren't sorry you married me? The truth, Lawton," she demanded, cupping her hands around his handsome face. "If you honestly want to ride with your ex-partners, then say so. I won't like it, but I'll understand and I won't try to stop you. I want you to be happy."

A disarming smile drifted across his lips. "Do you truly?"

Cairo voiced no protest as he bent her backward and followed her to the sandbar. "I truly do," she murmured as she traced his craggy features.

"Loving you makes me immensely happy," he whispered as his hands set out on an arousing journey over her silken flesh. "I couldn't leave you even if I tried. You have my heart, my soul, and my sons. You are my life."

Relief and desire were reflected in her shimmering green eyes. A smile that rivaled the midday sun lighted her face as she drew his lips to hers. "Then you should indeed be a happy man, Mr. Stone, because I love loving you. And I delight in having my way with you . . . every chance I get."

Lawton's lighthearted laughter echoed in the breeze that skimmed the river. "And you, Mrs. Stone, can have your way with me any time you want."

While Tucker, Woody, and Al attempted to undo the damage done by Lawton's singing lessons with the twins, Cairo and Lawton set sail on a river of rapture. He fully intended to reassure his feisty wife that he wanted to remain by her side, to explore the boundless love that had been bottled up inside him until she had come along to set him free from his troubled past. She had made it easy for him to express the emotions that had been deeply buried.

In the aftermath of love, Lawton gazed down into Cairo's face. His smile said it all. Cairo needed no other reassurance, in light of the way he had seduced her and sent her soaring past reality. She could see the love and devotion glowing in his silver eyes. She could feel the aura of affection emanating from him. They belonged together and nothing would ever tear them apart again. They had been through hell together and this was their heaven—a love that expanded, year after wondrous year.

"I don't have to say it, do I, Cai?" Lawton murmured adoringly. "You know how I feel about you."

Cairo burst into an impish grin as she looped her arms around his neck. "Mmm. Yes, I know, but let's pretend I forgot so you can refresh my memory."

His carefree laughter died beneath her steamy kiss as the eternal fire blazed anew. As the sun marched across the sky, they reaffirmed their love in ways that words could never accurately express.

Lawton had become a most devoted husband and father. Cairo wouldn't have changed one thing about this silver-eyed rake with glistening midnight hair. Her hopes and dreams were centered around him and she loved him with all her heart.

Well actually, Cairo thought as they strolled hand in hand to the house, she would like to change one thing about him: his singing. But she allowed him that one minor flaw since he was close to perfect in every other way. When he made wild sweet love to her, it more than compensated for the fact that he couldn't carry a tune better than a bullfrog.

"What are you thinking?" Lawton murmured as they stopped beside the back door.

Cairo set aside her thoughts of songs and bullfrogs and looped her arms around Lawton's sturdy neck. "I was just thinking how much I love you," she whispered back to him.

"Are you sure that's what you were thinking?" Lawton eyed her suspiciously.

"Close enough," Cairo tittered before she blessed him with a steamy kiss and then sashayed inside to visit with their guests.

Lawton smiled. What a wonderful way to spend the afternoon. And ah . . . what a splendid way to spend a life! He was as happy as one man could get! Cairo, Oklahoma, was indeed the closest place to paradise, this side of heaven, and he had laid claim to the whole puffy cloud and the resident angel who'd just made love to him. Cairo had Lawton swearing he could hear harps strumming in the distance. It made a man want to burst out in song.

And Lawton did just that, much to his friends' dismay and his wife's loving amusement.